PENGUIN  CLASSICS

THE GARDEN OF THE FINZI-CONTINIS

GIORGIO BASSANI was born in Bologna in 1916 to a Jewish family who returned to their home town Ferrara soon after the end of the First World War. He attended school in Ferrara and the Faculty of Arts in the University of Bologna. After graduating he became involved in anti-Fascist activities which resulted in his imprisonment in 1943. Released after the fall of Mussolini, he married and moved to Florence, with his wife Valeria, where they lived under assumed names. At this time, during the Salò Republic, a number of his relatives were transported to the Buchenwald death camps. Bassani settled in Rome, where his daughter Paola was born in 1945 and his son Enrico in 1949. Bassani worked as a teacher, a translator of Hemingway and Voltaire among others, and as a scriptwriter on films by Michelangelo Antonioni and Mario Soldati. He became editor of the international literary magazine *Botteghe Oscure* and later a fiction editor at Feltrinelli, where he was responsible for 'discovering' and publishing Giuseppe di Lampedusa's *The Leopard* (1956). Despite this unrivalled success, he was to leave Feltrinelli in a dispute when in 1963 he refused to publish Alberto Arbasino's novel *Fratelli d'Italia*. Concerned throughout his life with civic and political as well as cultural issues, he was vice president of RAI television network and in 1965 became president of 'Italia Nostra', a national heritage organization.

An extraordinarily versatile author, Bassani has won numerous prizes as poet, novelist, short-story writer and essayist. His *Cinque storie ferrarese* won the 1956 Strega Prize. In 1974 his fiction was collected together and published under the title *Il romanzo di Ferrara*. The four main collections of his poems have been widely acclaimed and were gathered together in 1982 as *In rima e senza*. *The Garden of the Finzi-Continis* won the Viareggio Prize and has sold more than a million copies in Italy alone. Three films have been made of his work, most notably Vittorio de Sica's adaptation of the present novel in 1970. In his last years Bassani suffered from Alzheimer's and died in 2000. He is buried in the Jewish cemetery at Ferrara.

JAMIE MCKENDRICK, born in Liverpool, 1955, has published four collections of poetry, the most recent being *Ink Stone* (2003). He has translated a number of Italian poets, including Valerio Magrelli, and has edited *The Faber Book of Italian 20th-Century Poems* (2004).

GIORGIO BASSANI

The Garden of the Finzi-Continis

Translated by JAMIE MCKENDRICK

PENGUIN BOOKS

PENGUIN BOOKS

Published by the Penguin Group
Penguin Books Ltd, 80 Strand, London wc2r orl, England
Penguin Group (USA) Inc., 375 Hudson Street, New York, New York 10014, USA
Penguin Group (Canada), 90 Eglinton Avenue East, Suite 700, Toronto, Ontario, Canada m4p 2y3
(a division of Pearson Penguin Canada Inc.)
Penguin Ireland, 25 St Stephen's Green, Dublin 2, Ireland
(a division of Penguin Books Ltd)
Penguin Group (Australia), 250 Camberwell Road, Camberwell, Victoria 3124, Australia
(a division of Pearson Australia Group Pty Ltd)
Penguin Books India Pvt Ltd, 11 Community Centre, Panchsheel Park, New Delhi – 110 017, India
Penguin Group (NZ), 67 Apollo Drive, Mairangi Bay, Auckland 1310, New Zealand
(a division of Pearson New Zealand Ltd)
Penguin Books (South Africa) (Pty) Ltd, 24 Sturdee Avenue, Rosebank, Johannesburg 2196, South Africa

Penguin Books Ltd, Registered Offices: 80 Strand, London wc2r orl, England

www.penguin.com

First published as *Il giardino dei Finzi-Contini* in Turin 1962
Published in Penguin Classics with an Introduction 2007

4

Introduction copyright © Jamie McKendrick, 2007
All rights reserved

The moral right of the author has been asserted

Set in 10.5/13 pt Monotype Dante
Typeset by Rowland Phototypesetting Ltd, Bury St Edmunds, Suffolk
Printed in England by Clays Ltd, St Ives plc

ISBN: 978-0-141-18836-2

www.greenpenguin.co.uk

Penguin Books is committed to a sustainable future
for our business, our readers and our planet.
The book in your hands is made from paper
certified by the Forest Stewardship Council.

Contents

Introduction

If you were to tell someone who had never read *The Garden of the Finzi-Continis* that it's an extraordinary study of first love, you might just be taken on trust. If you claimed Giorgio Bassani combines such a story with a subtle portrait of the artist in his youth, a kind of *Künstlerroman*, you might be straining credibility. – Another Proust perhaps? But it doesn't end there. The book is also one of the great novels of witness to the dark years of the mid-twentieth century. For informing both of these interwoven stories, shadowing them, is the fate of a small community of Jews in Ferrara, to which the narrator and his beloved Micòl belong, leading up to and following the 1938 Racial Laws in Italy. The book does indeed find a way to represent this double maelstrom, the personal and the public, the individual and the historical, from which the narrator emerges as a grief-stricken survivor, but a survivor committed to memorializing, in the most durable form he can, the exact features of his experience.

Memory is at the heart of the novel, and the heart's own memory is put to the fore in the epigraph from Alessandro Manzoni: '. . . what does the heart know? Just the least bit about what has happened already.' We are told in the Prologue that the main events of the novel are recounted by a narrator looking back some twenty years and impelled by his sense of loss. Within the story itself, after a mere few weeks of absence from the Finzi-Continis' house, the narrator already suffers anxiety concerning 'those sites that belonged to a past which, though it seemed remote, was still recuperable, was not yet lost'. Throughout we sense the inexorable need of the narrator, and through him of Bassani himself, to recover the full import of what he has lived through. Ever further away, and harder of access, the past continues to exist in all its vividness. That the novel is (at least in part) fiction does not for Bassani represent an obstacle to truth-telling, rather it enforces a deeper obligation to accuracy. He speaks tellingly in an interview of having 'written and rewritten every page [of his work] . . . with the intention to tell the truth, the whole truth', and this remark seems especially apt for *The Garden of the Finzi-Continis*.

Writing did not come easily to Bassani. It was, by his own account, an arduous process, alternately urged on and put off by long bicycle rides. In this novel the narrator's bike is rarely absent, and yet no trace of the struggle of composition remains. Effectively Bassani began, as he continued, a poet; and though prose became his essential medium he kept faith with that beginning. Never 'poetic' – by which we usually understand vague and decorative – his prose was always poetry by other means. There is a constant tact and luminous exactitude in all his writing. And especially in *The Garden of the Finzi-Continis* the reader encounters that rare thing in the novel: a shaped conception that lyrically heightens every element of the story. Bassani himself tells how several stories were resolved by comprehending the images that underpinned them: in one, for example, he saw two spheres moving on conflicting axes, in another parallel lines receding into the distance. This discloses something distinctive about his imagination, a kind of geometric faculty. *The Garden of the Finzi-Continis* itself may be seen as a series of circular forms, circles within circles, and circles which overlap.

Most of his novels and stories were written in Rome but were almost exclusively set in, or rather centred on, Ferrara. Although he was born – he claims 'accidentally' – in Bologna in 1916, it was Ferrara, a small, ancient city in the Po Valley, that was his imaginative heartland, his *patria* and matrix. Bassani's first foray into fiction refers to the unnamed Ferrara ominously as 'A City of the Plain'. (To evade the Racial Laws, this was published in 1940 under the pseudonym of Giacomo Marchi.) Another early story merely calls Ferrara 'F'. It seems as though his image of the city needed gradually to mature both as actual location and as imaginative entity, almost as a character, before he allowed it to assume its proper name in his fiction. In 1973, more than a decade after the publication of *The Garden of the Finzi-Continis*, he began to see that his short stories, two collections of them, and his four novels all formed parts of a (hexagonal) composite whole, and with this in mind they were adjusted and assembled into a single inclusive work: *Il romanzo di Ferrara*, The Novel of Ferrara.

Although as free-standing as the other novels, *The Garden of the Finzi-Continis* (*Il giardino dei Finzi-Contini*, 1962) is a central work within this sequence of interconnected narratives. Leaving aside the short stories, the other novels include *The Gold-Rimmed Spectacles* (*Gli occhiali d'oro*, 1958), a short masterpiece which charts the friendship between Bassani's young Jewish narrator and a homosexual doctor, both of whom are pushed to the margins of an increasingly intolerant Fascist Ferrara; *Behind the Doors* (*Dietro la porta*, 1964), a dark, uneasy tale of schoolboy friendship and betrayal; and *The Heron* (*L'airone*, 1968), a chilling study of post-war bitterness and malaise. None of these stories, written in this (for Bassani) astonishingly productive decade, needs the buttressing or support of the others, and yet they share a restricted historical period (essentially that of Italian Fascism and its post-war submergence), a civic setting and a number of central characters. Among these characters, the first three novels, including the present one, also share an unnamed first-person narrator, who is, I think we are meant to assume, a version, but an earlier version – with all the fictive latitude that word implies – of Bassani himself.

The Prologue to *The Garden of the Finzi-Continis* begins with a visit to an Etruscan cemetery at Cerveteri, and the novel proper in Ferrara's Jewish cemetery at the Finzi-Continis' lavish and histrionic tomb. Cemeteries and gardens alternate through the narrative, the former almost spectrally superimposed on the latter. Only in the Prologue and Epilogue (and once in the middle) does the narrator allude to the fact that nearly all of its protagonists will be murdered in German death camps, without a gravestone to recall their existence. Yet the story continually broods on what passes away and what remains, on time itself, and builds a memorial out of ruination.

Within the novel Bassani makes a number of references to the remarkable history of the Jews in Ferrara. Their presence there is first documented in 1227. In the 1490s, under the powerful d'Este family which ruled Ferrara for three hundred years, the city welcomed and benefited from the influx of Spanish Jews and, early in the next century, of persecuted German Jews. The latter group especially, as Bassani mentions, retained something of their distinct identity. This period of tolerance came to an end when in 1598 the city fell under the control of the Papal Legations and the community was forced within the Ghetto, a triangle of streets – Via Mazzini, Via Vignatagliata and Via Vittoria – which are central to the novel. Apart from a brief respite under Napoleon (1797–9) and again in 1848, the Ghetto remained as such until the Unification of Italy in 1859. The emancipation of the Jews at that date marked a new era of hope and optimism for the community which would come to a sinister and largely unforeseen close in 1938 with the introduction of the Racial Laws.

According to Bassani, before the war there were about seven hundred and fifty Jews living in Ferrara, of whom one hundred and eighty-three were deported to German death camps, mostly under the puppet Salò Republic in 1943. Bassani elsewhere recounts an event which foreshadowed this disaster. On 28 October 1941, after a rally commemorating the March on Rome, a Fascist mob, largely composed of students, broke into the Temple in Via Mazzini at Ferrara, the oldest synagogue still in use in Italy. They attacked the rabbi and his family in their apartment and then broke into the two synagogues or 'Schools' housed on separate floors. They destroyed the furnishings and ritual objects, the chandeliers, the marble banisters, the paving stones, the big cupboards holding the scrolls of the Torah, even the cases with the prayer shawls, or *tallitot*. Although this event is not mentioned in *The Garden of the Finzi-Continis*, it nevertheless reverberates throughout, and may account for the extraordinarily vivid and moving evocation of the Italian synagogue early in the novel and for the focal recurrence of the Temple throughout.

The description of the Temple reveals another aspect of Bassani's unique gift: his architectural sense of space and his visual acuteness.

(A formative friendship for the young Bassani was with his tutor at Bologna University, the great art critic Roberto Longhi.) This too is related to his 'geometric' imagination. But in Bassani space is always faceted by time, and description is never uncoupled from the narrative movement, slowed down as it may be, towards what will occur. Even stylistically, in his prolonged sentences, often interrupted by parentheses, we sense a counter-impulse to slow time down, to savour as much as is humanly possible of its fullness, before it pushes on towards a vanishing point of loss and destruction. Here his instinct as a novelist is very like the tennis games he describes in the Finzi-Continis' garden, which continue on past dusk into the darkness with a stubborn refusal to abandon the joy of playing.

Throughout the novel the Jewish community is presented as both united and divided. In addition to the shadowy group that attend the Fanese synagogue, there is the already mentioned distinction between the two synagogues within the Temple: the German 'School' with its stolid, Homburg-hatted congregation and the more operatic and volatile Italian 'School'. There are also linguistic differences which can be seen even within the Finzi-Contini family itself: in the uncles and grandmother who speak a peculiar Hispanic-Veneto dialect, the Professor with his courtly scholastic Italian and Micol who, on matters close to her heart, abandons Italian for Ferrarese dialect. And there are also the social divisions which keep the very wealthy Finzi-Continis, perhaps against their will, aloof from the congregation. The narrator despairs of explaining these complexities to his Gentile friends and yet the novel achieves this feat with spectacular success.

Politically, too, this community is seen as divided. Bassani is unsparing in his account of these divisions which cut across it in unpredictable ways. The narrator's father, like many of his Ferrarese co-religionists, and for that matter like so many fellow Italians, is an enthusiastic Fascist, and unjustly finds Professor Ermanno's anti-Fascism yet another snobbish taint. Bassani's refusal to portray a folkish and homogeneous community is an important part of his contract with memory. He insists on their 'normality' in the light of a brutal reality that would have them abnormal, or even sub-normal.

They have a categorical specialness forced upon them. A figure like the narrator's father, for example, is certainly flawed but no less lovable for his quirks and failings – despite his deluded views, we can sympathize with him when the narrator self-righteously takes him to task on that account. Though Bassani himself was a militant anti-Fascist, and was jailed in 1943 for his activities – an experience he refers to, only once and laconically, in the novel – his morality never submits to a black-and-white historical overview. Such a view stands accused in the person of Giampi Malnate, even if the accusation is tempered with affection. (It is one of the story's crueller ironies that the Communist Malnate should in the end die fighting for Fascism on the Russian Front.) Yet nothing that these complexities introduce alleviates the novel's grief at the loss of this community.

Just as the Jews of Ferrara are far from unified, so also other social divisions beyond that community mark the narrator's consciousness. He is aware of his exclusion, not on grounds of race but of class, from other groups within the city and the country. In the Prologue, he notes the camaraderie of the working-class girls who, arms linked, block the road in a small Lazian town, singing. They have a carefree, erotic presence that challenges the older narrator, and leaves him as an outsider, a bystander, an admirer. Something of the same thing can be found in the digression on vertigo, as he prepares to scale the garden's wall. Here, he remembers his childhood admiration for the fearless workers – farm-workers, builders, labourers, 'frog-catchers and catfish anglers' who venture up and down the steep climb of the Montagnone fortifications. As a child, he feels threatened by them, by their rough hands and wine-dark breath, and both repelled and attracted. Among several deftly drawn portraits, the foul-mouthed Tuscan girl, who queens it over her coconut shy in the travelling circus and is so taken by the manly Malnate, exerts a magnetic attraction for the narrator. The comic and grotesque figure of Perotti, doorman, coachman and chauffeur of the Finzi-Continis, is another signal presence. He is the employee who seems to have acquired a sinister control over the family, and casts a shadow over the idyllic house and grounds. Only when the narrator begins to fathom Perotti's tense, vicarious pride in the Finzi-Continis' possessions is he accorded a flicker of appeal. Though the novel's milieu is mainly upper middle class, Bassani brings a psychological definition and credibility to every character he portrays.

In keeping with the ethnic variety within Ferrara's small Jewish community, *The Garden of the Finzi-Continis* is dizzyingly multilingual. Apart from its original Italian, the uncles' curious dialect and the frequent phrases in Ferrarese, we encounter Malnate's Milanese, words and phrases in Hebrew, Yiddish, Latin, German, as well as English and French. Bassani's use of these background languages never serves as linguistic display, but rather as an exact record of a uniquely complex community which, at one point, he describes by the Latin phrase *'intra muros'* (literally 'between walls' or cloistered, but here with the sense of being within a ghetto). This phrase is picked up in *Inside the Walls (Dentro le mura)*, the first book of his Novel of Ferrara, a collection of short stories. Also within *The Garden of the Finzi-Contini* walls are ever-present and more than structural. They, the walls of the city, its towers, bastions and its underground, tomb-like arsenals begin to gather an increasing symbolic freight. There is a very real sense in which for this community the Racial Laws of 1938 meant the walls were closing in.

To present a novel so sustainingly full of life as something walled-in and sepulchral would be very misleading. The imagery that Bassani has found to capture states of enchantment is most powerfully centred on the Finzi-Continis' garden, the Barchetto del Duca itself. Unspoilt, Edenic, spacious, with all its botanical profusion, the garden seems to hold out against this sense of constriction. The city itself is a mixture of open vistas and cramped enclosures, but there is nothing forced about the symbolism that suffuses Bassani's Ferrara, from the dizzy parapets of Montagnone to the curious earthworks that undermine the city walls.

In the novel we can see how the walls themselves inscribe circles within circles. The smaller walled circle of the garden of the Finzi-Continis meets the outer circle of the city walls at the Mura degli Angeli (the Wall of Angels). It is here, where the circumferences of these two walls almost touch, that the charged childhood meeting between the narrator and Micòl takes place. Instead of entering the garden, he becomes distracted by the underground world of the chamber where he hides his bike. This mound was the former repository for the Renaissance city's arms, and is now a gloomy echo-chamber which wraps the narrator in a state of childish erotic reverie in which he imagines all kinds of intricate and absurd complications in his future. It is at exactly the same point that he arrives at the end of the novel: uninvited and furtive, he enters by night and then pursues a train of desecrating imaginings that seal his separation from Micòl. (As readers, we never know whether these suspicions on her account have any foundation, another example of the author's – as opposed to the narrator's – tact.) But the novel explores a whole series of intersecting and enclosing circles. The Commercial Club, as I've translated *Il Circolo dei Negozianti*, is literally a 'Circle' which his father belonged to and is expelled from in the wake of the Racial Laws. Based on the actual 'Marfisa' club, from which Bassani (an excellent tennis player and tournament winner) was himself excluded, the Eleonora d'Este Tennis Club is, in the original, another *Circolo* from which the narrator is expelled along with all other Jewish players. They are then invited to play on the Finzi-Continis' court, and it is at this point that the narrator, ten years after his failed attempt, finally enters the garden for the first time. But the walls of the city enclose other walls, including the huddle of streets that constituted the old Ghetto. The Jewish community itself comprises not just one but several circles that have some overlap yet remain distinct.

One source of the present novel's extraordinary resonance is a series of almost subliminal interior echoes and parallels which testify to Bassani's poetic imagination at work. The narrator who will finally, in writing this story, give an account of his community has two examples before him, neither of whom adequately fulfils the role he seeks and yet both of whom supply him with the necessary nourishment to undertake the task. First there is his father, a kind of oral historian of the community, who mixes extempore stories from the past with riffs of sparkling and malicious gossip. Then there is Professor Ermanno Finzi-Contini, a kind of elective father, more bowed and solemn and antiquarian, who modestly alludes to his own researches into Italian Jewry, and offers the use of his library to the narrator for his thesis, hoping the latter might take up where he left off. Although the narrator follows neither of these offered paths or precedents, his own procedure somehow includes and honours both.

As with the parallel play of cemeteries and gardens, we find similar though less conspicuous structurings throughout. Towards the end of the novel, for example, the narrator conducts two crucial bedside conversations. The first is with Micòl, ill with flu, propped up in her bed, half outside the blankets. During this talk, he finally confronts the hopelessness of his desires. The second, some chapters later, is with his now insomniac father, tormented with worry and self-reproach, also sitting up in bed with his chest outside the sheet. For the narrator, this conversation effects an emotional reconciliation with his father (and also, in a way, with himself). These parallel scenes dealing with loss and restoration have an uncanny resonance and an indelible emotional impact.

As a remarkable account of first love, the novel manages to be both idyllic and psychologically convincing; and at the same time harrowingly aware of separation and loss. It is also a study of a developing consciousness. We intimately observe his time at school and university, and his first literary and artistic enthusiasms both for the past and the present age, notably Ungaretti, Montale, Saba and Morandi. The novel traces the narrator's aesthetic and political formation – the two aspects, however uncomfortably, are always wedded. And yet, though the 'I' of the narrator is continually to the fore, Bassani's alter ego is anything but triumphant. He can be priggish, petulant and self-abasing, defeated by trivialities and by his own timidity. The narrator, and by implication the artist, is never lifted above his milieu. One of the most remarkable features of this novel is how his own failures are made so apparent. It is finally Micòl, artistically a dilettante and politically all but indifferent, who is seen to have a prescience about life, a precocious knowingness about erotic love – for which tennis, once again, supplies the most memorable image – and an unobstructed view of the past, the present and the future that is denied to the other characters, the narrator included.

Translator's Note

The text I have used for this translation is Giorgio Bassani's *Opere* (I Meridiani, Mondadori, 3rd edition, 2004) which incorporates the author's final 1980 revisions and so differs from the texts used for the other two extant translations by Isobel Quigley and William Weaver. My only departure from the final text is to restore the epigraph from Alessandro Manzoni to its place at the start of this novel where, for reasons which should become clear to the reader, it rightfully belongs. (In turning his six books into one inclusive work, *Il romanzo di Ferrara*, Bassani decided to set the epigraph at the head of the entire work, thus giving it even more prominence.) In note 2 to Part II, Chapter 5, I have included the one paragraph cut by Bassani of which I regret the omission.

To preserve the linguistic variety of the novel I have retained most of the words and phrases and all of the verses in other languages as they are in the original. I have limited myself to translating, in the form of footnotes, those which belong to Hebrew or various Italian dialects. An Italian reader of Bassani would have a fair chance of guessing the meaning of the latter, whereas an English reader is likely to be more at sea. The endnotes translate and source lines of poetry in Italian and other languages, provide brief notes on some lesser known historical or cultural figures and also gloss some specific terms from Italian history.

I have also retained most of the descriptive titles – Signora, Signorina, etc. – as they are in the original. It should be noted, though, in the case of Ermanno Finzi-Contini, that the term 'professór' in Italian is somewhat more vague and honorific than the English term 'Professor'.

*

I am deeply indebted to Stella Tillyard and Elizabeth Stratford for the multitude of improvements they have suggested. I would also like to thank Valerie Lipman, Giorgia Sensi, Luca Guerneri, Antonella Anedda, Peter Hainsworth, Vicky Franzinetti, Simon Carnell, Erica Segre and David Kessler for their help with particular difficulties.

J.McK.

The Garden of the
Finzi-Continis

Certo, il cuore, chi gli dà retta, ha sempre qualche cosa da dire su quello che sarà. Ma che sa il cuore? Appena un poco di quello che è già accaduto.

Of course, for whoever pays heed to it, the heart always has something to say about what's to come. But what does the heart know? Just the least bit about what has happened already.

Alessandro Manzoni, *I promessi sposi*, chapter VIII

Prologue

For many years I have wanted to write about the Finzi-Continis –
about Micòl and Alberto, Professor Ermanno and Signora Olga –
and about the many others who lived at, or like me frequented, the
house in Corso Ercole I d'Este, Ferrara, just before the last war
broke out. But the impulse, the prompt, really to do so only occurred
for me a year ago, one April Sunday in 1957.

It was during one of our usual weekend outings. Ten or so friends
piled into a couple of cars, and we set out along the Aurelia soon
after lunch without any clear destination. A few kilometres from
Santa Marinella, intrigued by the towers of a medieval castle which
suddenly appeared on our left, we had turned into a narrow unpaved
track, and ended up walking in single file, stretched out along the
desolate sandy plain at the foot of the fortress – this last, when
considered close up, was far less medieval than it had promised to
be from the distance, when from the motorway we had made out
its profile against the light and against the blue, blazing desert of the
Tyrrhenian sea. Battered by the head-on wind, and deafened by the
noise of the withdrawing tide, and without even being able to visit
the castle's interior, as we had come without the written permit
granted by some Roman bank or other, we felt deeply discontented
and annoyed with ourselves for having wanted to leave Rome on
such a day, which now on the seashore proved little less than wintry
in its inclemency.

We walked up and down for some twenty minutes, following the
curve of the bay. The only person of the group who seemed at all
joyful was a little nine-year-old girl, daughter of the young couple
in whose car I'd been driven. Electrified by the wind, the sea, the

crazy swirls of sand, Giannina was giving vent to her happy expansive nature. Although her mother had tried to forbid it, she had rid herself of shoes and socks. She rushed into the waves that beat on the shore, and let them splash her legs above the knee. In short, she seemed to be having a great time – so much so that, a bit later, back in the car, I saw a shadow of pure regret pass over her vivid black eyes that shone above her tender, heated little cheeks.

Having reached the Aurelia again, after a short while we caught sight of the fork in the road that led to the Cerveteri. Since it had been decided we should return immediately to Rome, I had no doubt that we would keep straight on. But instead of doing so, our car slowed down more than was required, and Giannina's father stuck his hand out of the window, signalling to the second car, about twenty-five metres behind, that he intended to turn left. He had changed his mind.

So we found ourselves taking the smooth narrow asphalted street which in no time leads to a small huddle of mainly recent houses, and from there winds on further towards the hills of the hinterland up to the famous Etruscan necropolis. No one asked for any explanations, and I too remained silent.

Beyond the village the street, in gentle ascent, forced the car to slow down. We then passed close by the so-called *montarozzi* which have been scattered across that whole stretch of Lazian territory north of Rome, but more those parts towards the hills than towards the sea, a stretch which is, therefore, nothing but an immense, almost uninterrupted cemetery. Here the grass is greener, thicker and darker coloured than that of the plain below, between the Aurelia and the Tyrrhenian sea – as proof that the eternal sirocco, which blows from across the sea, arrives up here having shed en route a great part of its salty freight, and that the damp air of the not too far-off mountains begins to exercise its beneficent influence on the vegetation.

'Where are we going?' asked Giannina.

Husband and wife were sitting in the front seat with the child in between them. Her father took his hand off the wheel and let it rest on his daughter's dark brown curls.

'We're going to have a look at some tombs which are more than four or five thousand years old,' he replied, with the tone of someone who is about to tell a fairy tale, and so doesn't mind exaggerating as far as numbers go. 'The Etruscan tombs.'

'How sad,' Giannina sighed, leaning her neck on the back of the seat.

'Why sad? Haven't they taught you who the Etruscans were at school?'

'In the history book, the Etruscans are at the beginning, next to the Egyptians and the Jews. But, Papa, who d'you think were the oldest, the Etruscans or the Jews?'

Her father burst out laughing.

'Try asking that gentleman,' he said, signalling towards me with his thumb.

Giannina turned round. With her mouth hidden behind the back of the seat, severe and full of diffidence, she cast a quick glance at me. I waited for her to repeat the question. But no word escaped her. She quickly turned round again and stared in front of her.

Descending the street, always at a slight gradient and flanked by a double row of cypresses, we came upon a group of country folk, lads and lasses. It was the Sunday *passeggiata*. With linked arms, some of the girls at times made exclusively female chains of five or six. How strange they look, I said to myself. At the moment we passed them, they peered through the windows with their laughing eyes, in which curiosity was mingled with a bizarre pride, a barely concealed disdain. How strange they looked, how beautiful and free.

'Papa,' Giannina asked once again, 'why are old tombs less sad than new ones?'

A yet more numerous brigade than those that had passed us earlier, which took up almost the whole thoroughfare, and sang in chorus without thinking of giving way, had almost brought the car to a halt. Her father put the car into second gear as he thought about this.

'Well,' he replied, 'the recent dead are closer to us, and so it makes sense that we care more about them. The Etruscans, they've been dead such a long time' – once again he lapsed into the fairy-tale voice – 'it's as though they'd never lived, as though they were always dead.'

Another pause, this time a longer one. At the end of which – we were already very close to the widened space in front of the necropolis's entrance packed with cars and mopeds – it was Giannina's turn to become the teacher.

'But now that you say that,' she gently put it, 'it makes me think the opposite, that the Etruscans really did live, and that I care about them just as much as about the others.'

The whole visit to the necropolis that followed was infused by the extraordinary tenderness of this remark. It had been Giannina who had helped us understand. It was she, the youngest, who in some way led us all by the hand.

We went down into the most important tomb, the one reserved for the noble Matuta family: a low underground living room which accommodated a score of funeral beds disposed within the same number of niches carved in the tufa walls, and densely adorned with painted murals that portrayed the dear departed, everyday objects from their lives, hoes, rakes, axes, scissors, spades, knives, bows, arrows, even hunting dogs and marsh birds. And in the meantime, having willingly discarded any vestige of historical scruple, I was trying to figure out exactly what the assiduous visits to their suburban cemetery might have meant to the late Etruscans of Cerveteri, the Etruscans of the era after the Roman conquest.

Just as, still today, in small Italian provincial towns, the cemetery gate is the obligatory terminus of every evening *passeggiata*, they came from the inhabited vicinity almost always on foot – I imagined – gathered in groups of relatives and blood kindred, or just of friends, perhaps in brigades of youths similar to those we had met head-on in the street before, or else in pairs, lovers, or even alone, to wander among the conical tombs, hulking and solid as the bunkers German soldiers vainly scattered about Europe during the last war, tombs which certainly resembled, from outside as much as from within, the fortress dwellings of the living. Yes, everything was changing – they must have told themselves as they walked along the paved way which crossed the cemetery from one end to the other, the centre of which, over centuries of wear, had been gradually incised by the iron wheel-rims of their vehicles, leaving two deep parallel grooves. The world was not as it once was, when Etruria, with its confederation of free, aristocratic city-states, dominated almost the entire Italic peninsula. New civilizations, cruder and less aristocratic, but also stronger and more warlike, by this stage held the field. But in the end, what did it matter?

Once across the cemetery's threshold, where each of them owned a second home, and inside it the already prepared bed-like structure on which, soon enough, they would be laid alongside their forefathers, eternity did not perhaps appear to be such an illusion, a fable, an hieratic promise. The future could overturn the world as it pleased. There, all the same, in the narrow haven devoted to the family dead, in the heart of those tombs where, together with the dead, great care had also been taken to furnish many of the things that made life beautiful and desirable; in that corner of the world, so well defended, adorned, privileged, at least there (and one could still sense their idea, their madness, after twenty-five centuries, among the conical tombs covered with wild grass), there at least nothing could ever change.

When we left it was dark.

From Cerveteri to Rome is not that far, normally an hour by car would be enough. That evening, however, the journey was not so short. Halfway, the Aurelia began to be jammed with cars coming from Ladispoli and from Fregene. We had to proceed almost at a walking pace.

But once again, in the quiet and torpor (even Giannina had fallen asleep), I went over in my memory the years of my early youth, both in Ferrara and in the Jewish cemetery at the end of Via Montebello. I saw once more the large fields scattered with trees, the gravestones and trunks of columns bunched up more densely along the surrounding and dividing walls, and as if again before my eyes, the monumental tomb of the Finzi-Continis. True, it was an ugly tomb – as I'd always heard it described from my earliest childhood – but never less than imposing, and full of significance if for no other reason than the prestige of the family itself.

And my heartstrings tightened as never before at the thought that in that tomb, established, it seemed, to guarantee the perpetual repose of its first occupant – of him, and his descendants – only one, of all the Finzi-Continis I had known and loved, had actually achieved this repose. Only Alberto had been buried there, the oldest, who died in 1942 of a lymphogranuloma, whilst Micòl, the daughter, born second, and their father Ermanno, and their mother Signora Olga, and Signora Regina, her ancient paralytic mother, were all deported to Germany in the autumn of 1943, and no one knows whether they have any grave at all.

I

The tomb was huge, solid and truly imposing, a kind of temple, something of a cross between the antique and the oriental, such as might be encountered in those stage-sets of *Aida* or *Nabucco* very much in vogue at our theatres only a few years back. In any other cemetery, including the neighbouring municipal cemetery, a grave of such pretensions would not have provoked the slightest wonder, might even, mixed in among the rest, have gone unheeded. But in ours it stood out alone. And so, although it loomed some way from the entrance gate, at the end of an abandoned field where for more than half a century no one had been buried, it made an eye-catching show of itself.

It seems that a distinguished professor of architecture — respon sible for many other eyesores in the city – had been commissioned to construct it by Moisè Finzi-Contini, Alberto and Micòl's paternal great-grandfather, who died in 1863, shortly after the annexation of the Papal States' territories to the Kingdom of Italy, and the resulting final abolition, in Ferrara as well, of the Jewish ghettos. A big landowner, 'Reformer of Ferrarese Agriculture' – as could be read on the plaque, eternalizing his merits as 'an Italian and a Jew', that the Community had had set above the third landing on the staircase of the Temple in Via Mazzini – but clearly a man of dubious artistic taste: once he'd decided to establish a tomb *sibi et suis* he'd have let the architect do as he liked. Those were fine and flourishing years – everything seemed to favour hope, liberality and daring. Over-whelmed by the euphoria of civic equality that had been granted, the same that in his youth, at the time of the Cisalpine Republic,[1] had made it possible for him to acquire his first thousand hectares of reclaimed land, it was easy to understand how this rigid patriarch had been induced, in such solemn circumstances, to spare no expense. It is likely that the distinguished professor of architecture was given a completely free hand. And with all that marble at his disposal – white Carrara, flesh-pink marble from Verona, black-speckled grey marble, yellow marble, blue marble, pale green marble – the man had, in his turn, obviously lost his head.

What resulted was an extraordinary mishmash into which flowed the architectonic echoes of Theodoric's mausoleum at Ravenna, of the Egyptian temples at Luxor, of Roman baroque, and even, as the thickset columns of the peristyle proclaimed, of the ancient Greek constructions of Cnossos. But there it stood. Little by little, year after year, time, which in its way always adjusts everything, had managed to make even that unlikely hotchpotch of clashing styles somehow in keeping. Moisè Finzi-Contini, here declared 'the very model of the austere and tireless worker', passed away in 1863. His wife, Allegrina Camaioli, 'angel of the hearth', in 1875. Then in 1877, still youthful, their only son, Doctor of Engineering Menotti, followed more than twenty years later in 1898, by his consort Josette, from the Treviso branch of the baronial family of the Artoms. Thereafter the upkeep of the chapel, which gathered to itself in 1914 only one other family member, Guido, a six-year-old boy, had clearly fallen to those less and less inclined to tidy, maintain and repair any damage whenever that was required, and above all to fight off the persistent inroads made by the surrounding weeds that were besieging it. Tufts of swarthy, almost black grass of a near-metallic consistency, and ferns, nettles, thistles, poppies were allowed to advance and invade with ever greater licence. So much so that in 1924, in 1925, some sixty years from its founding, when as a baby I happened to see the Finzi-Continis' tomb for the first time – 'a total monstrosity', as my mother, holding my hand, never failed to call it – it already looked more or less as it does today, when for many years there has been no one left directly responsible for its upkeep. Half drowned in wild green, with its many-hued marble surfaces, originally polished and shining, dulled with drifts of grey dust, the roof and outer steps cracked by baking sunlight and frosts, even then it seemed changed, as every long-submerged object is, into something rich and strange.

Who knows from what, and why, a vocation for solitude is born. The fact remains that the same isolation, the very separateness with which the Finzi-Continis surrounded their deceased, also surrounded the *other* house they owned, the one at the end of Corso Ercole I d'Este. Immortalized by Giosue Carducci and Gabriele D'Annunzio, this Ferrara street is so well known to lovers of art and poetry the world over that any description of it would only be superfluous. As is well known, it is in the very heart of that northern zone of the city which the Renaissance added to the cramped medieval quarters, and which for that reason is called the *Addizione Erculea*.[2] Broad, straight as a sword from the Castello to the Mura degli Angeli, flanked its whole length by the sepia bulk of upper-class residences, with its distant, sublime backdrop of red bricks, green vegetation and sky, which really seems to lead you on towards the infinite: Corso Ercole I d'Este is so handsome, such is its touristic renown, that the joint Socialist-Communist administration, responsible to the Ferrara Council for more than fifteen years, has recognized the obligation to leave it be, to defend it against any and every possible disruption by speculative building or commercial interests, in short to conserve the whole original aristocratic character of the place.

It is a famous street: and what is more, it remains effectively undisturbed.

All the same, with particular reference to the Finzi-Contini house, although one can reach it even today from Corso Ercole I – unless you want to add on more than half a kilometre across a huge clearing, barely or not at all cultivated; and although this still incorporates the historic ruins of a sixteenth-century building, once a residence or extensive 'pleasure dome', which were acquired, as usual, by the same Moisè in 1850, and later transformed by his heirs, through a series of adaptations and restorations, into an English manor-house in a neo-Gothic style: despite so many interesting features which still survive, who knows anything about it, I wonder, and who even remembers it? The Touring Club Guide does not mention it, and this lets any passing tourists off the hook. But even in Ferrara itself, the few Jews left that make up the dwindling Jewish community have the air of having forgotten it.

Although the early twentieth-century Touring Club Guides never failed to recognize it, in a curious tone poised between the lyrical and the worldly, the current edition does not mention it, and this is certainly unfortunate. Still, to be fair: the garden or, to be more precise, the vast parkland, which before the war encircled the Finzi-Contini house and stretched for almost ten hectares up to the Mura degli Angeli on one side and the Barriera di Porta San Benedetto on the other, and representing in itself something rare and exceptional, no longer exists, literally speaking. All the broad-canopied trees, limes, elms, beeches, poplars, plane trees, horse chestnuts, pines, firs, larches, cedars of Lebanon, cypresses, oaks, holm oaks, and even the palm trees and eucalyptuses, planted in their hundreds by Josette Artom during the last two years of the First World War, were cut down for firewood, and for some time the land had returned to the state it was in when Moisè Finzi-Contini acquired it from the Marchesi of Avogli: one of the many great gardens ringed within the city walls.

Which leaves the house itself. Except that the huge, singular edifice, badly damaged by a bombardment in 1944, is still today occupied by fifty or so families of evacuees, belonging to the city's wretched sub-proletariat, not unlike the plebs of the Roman slums, who continue to cluster especially in the entrance of the Palazzone of Via Mortara: an embittered, wild, aggrieved tribe (some months back, I heard, they received with a hail of stones the Council's Inspector of Hygiene, who had come on his bicycle to survey the place). And so as to discourage any future eviction on the part of the Overseers of the Local Monuments of Emilia and Romagna, it seems they had the bright idea of scraping the last remnants of antique murals from the walls.

So why, now, send unsuspecting tourists into such a trap? – I figure the compilers of the last Touring Club Guide must have asked themselves. And in the end what exactly would there be left to see?

2

If the tomb of the Finzi-Contini family could be mocked as 'a monstrosity', then their house, islanded down there among the mosquitoes and frogs of the Panfilio canal and the drainage ditches, and enviously nicknamed the *magna domus*, no, that – not even after fifty years – quite qualified for mockery. Oh, little enough was required to get all het up about it. All you needed to do, I suppose, was to find yourself walking along the interminable outer wall which separated the garden from Corso Ercole I d'Este, a wall interrupted, almost halfway, by a solemn, darkened oak gate, lacking, as it happens, any door handles; or else, from the other side, from atop the Mura degli Angeli girding the park, to gaze deep into the wild intricacy of trunks, branches and foliage, as far as a glimpse of the strange sharpened profile of the manor-house, with, far behind it, the edge of a clearing, the grey stain of the tennis court – and then the ancient injury of their aloofness and seclusion would once again return to torment, to burn inside almost exactly as it had before.

What a typically nouveau-riche notion, what presumptuousness! – my father liked to repeat, with a kind of impassioned rancour, every time he felt called on to confront this question.

Yes, yes, I know – he'd admit – the former owners of the place, the family of the Marchesi Avogli, had the 'bluest' blood running in their veins, the garden and the ruins flaunted *ab antiquo* the highly decorative title of Barchetto del Duca – all very well and good, I wouldn't argue with that, and all the better that Moisè Finzi-Contini, who should take the undeniable credit of having 'spotted' the bargain, set himself back no more than the proverbial few coppers in clinching it. But so what? – he added immediately – just for this was it really necessary that Menotti, Moisè's son, aptly named in dialect, from the colour of his eccentric fur-lined overcoat, *al matt mugnaga*, the apricot nutcase, was it really necessary for him to move himself and his wife Josette to such a far-off inconvenient part of the city, unhealthy even in those days not to mention now, and on top of everything else to such a deserted, melancholy, utterly inappropriate place?

It was no great hardship for them, the parents, who belonged to a different age, and who could, after all, easily bear the luxury of spending all the coppers they cared to on those old stones. Especially not for her, Josette Artom, of the Treviso branch of the Artom barons (in her day a magnificent woman, blond, big-breasted, blue-eyed, and in fact her mother was from Berlin, an Olschky). Besides being so crazy about the House of Savoy that in May 1898, a little before she died, she took the step of sending a congratulatory telegram to General Bava Beccaris, who fired on those poor devils, the socialists and anarchists in Milan, and besides being a fanatical admirer of Bismarck's Germany, the land of the spiked helmet, from the time her husband Menotti, forever prostrate before her, installed her in his Valhalla she'd never bothered to hide her aversion to Jewish social life in Ferrara (for her it was always too claustrophobic, as she'd say) nor to hide, which is the truth however bizarre it may sound, *her fundamental anti-Semitism*.

But as for Professor Ermanno and Signora Olga, all the same (he a studious man and she a Herrera of Venice, and thus born into a *very good* Western Sephardic family, without doubt most respectable but rather fallen in the world, and besides which highly orthodox), what kind of people did they mean to become? Real aristocrats? Certainly, one can understand that the loss of their son Guido, the first-born who died in 1914, only six years old, following a very sudden attack of infantile paralysis, American variety, against which even Corcos could do nothing, must have been a terrible blow for them – most of all for her, Signora Olga, who from then on never stopped wearing mourning. But setting that aside, wasn't it the case that, due to living in such a cut-off way, they too had started acting like grandees and had fallen into the same deluded and inflated

notions of Menotti Finzi-Contini and his worthy consort? Aristocracy
– tell us another! Instead of giving themselves such airs, they'd have
done much better, the both of them, not to forget who they were,
and where they came from, if we're to believe that the Jews –
Sephardic and Ashkenazi, Western and Levantine, Tunisian, Berber,
Yemenite and even Ethiopian – in whatever part of the world, under
whatever skies history has scattered them, are and will always be
Jews, which is to say close relatives. Old Moisè wasn't one to give
himself airs, not him! He didn't have aristocratic mists befuddling
his brain! When he was living in the ghetto, at no. 24, Via Vignatagliata, at the house where he'd have been quite content to end his
days, withstanding the pressures brought to bear by his snooty
Treviso-born mother-in-law, impatient to transfer the family with
all haste to the Barchetto del Duca, it was he who went shopping
every morning in Piazza delle Erbe with his shopping-basket under
his arm; he who brought his family up from nothing and for this
very reason was nicknamed *al gatt*, the cat. Because yes – if it was
true that 'La' Josette had come down to Ferrara accompanied by a
considerable dowry, which consisted of a villa in the Treviso province with frescos by Tiepolo, of a fat cheque and jewels, make that
a heap of jewels, which on opening nights, against the red velvet
backdrop of their private box, drew the gaze of the entire theatre to
her swelling décolletage, then it was no less certain that it had been
al gatt, and he alone, who had assembled in the Ferrara plain,
between Codigoro, Massa Fiscaglia and Jolanda di Savoia, the thousands of hectares on which even today the main part of the family
patrimony depends. The monumental tomb at the cemetery – that
was the only mistake, the only failing (above all of taste) of which
one could accuse Moisè Finzi-Contini. That and nothing else.

This was how my father would go on – particularly at Passover,
during the lengthy dinners that continued to be given at our house
even after the death of grandpa Raffaello, attended by a score of
friends and relatives, but also at Yom Kippur, when those same
friends and relatives come back round to our house to end their fast.

But I remember one Passover supper during which my father
added something new and surprising to his usual grumblings –

bitter, generic, always the same, made above all for the pleasure of recollecting the time-worn tales of the Jewish community.

It was in 1933, the year of the so-called *infornata del Decennale*.[1] Thanks to the 'clemency' of il Duce, who had suddenly had the inspired idea of opening his forgiving arms wide to every 'agnostic or enemy of yesterday', even in the circles of our Community the number of those enrolled within the Fascist Party had managed to rise at a stroke to ninety per cent. And my father, who sat down there, at his usual place at the head of the table, the same place from which for long decades grandpa Raffaello had been wont to hold forth with a completely different authority and severity, had not failed to congratulate himself on this turn of events. The rabbi Dr Levi had done very well to refer to it in the speech he recently gave at the Italian School synagogue when, in the presence of the major civic dignitaries – the Prefect, the Fascist Party's Federal Secretary, the Podestà,[2] the Brigadier-General of the local garrison – he had commemorated the Albertine Statute![3]

Yet he wasn't entirely happy, Papa. In his boyish blue eyes, full of patriotic ardour, I could detect a shadow of disappointment. He must have perceived a small hitch, a little unforeseen and displeasing hindrance.

And in fact, having begun at a certain point to count on his fingers how many of us, of us Ferrarese *Judim*, still remained 'outside', and having at last arrived at Ermanno Finzi-Contini – who had never taken up party membership, that's true, but considering the very sizeable agricultural estates he'd inherited it was hard to figure out why he hadn't – all of a sudden, as though fed up with himself and his own discretion, my father decided to disclose two curious bits of news: between them there was perhaps no direct relationship – he began by saying – but they were no less significant for that.

First: that the lawyer Geremia Tabet, when, in his role as *Sansepolcrista*[4] and intimate friend of the Federal Secretary, he presented himself at the Barchetto del Duca to offer the Professor a membership card with his name already on it, it was not only returned to him, but, shortly after, of course most politely but equally firmly, he was shown the door.

'And with what excuse?' someone asked faintly. 'No one ever dreamt that Ermanno Finzi-Contini was such a lion.'

'With what excuse did he refuse it?' my father burst out laughing. 'Oh, with one of the usual ones: that he was a scholar (I'd love to know of what!), that he was too old, that he'd never in his life been involved with politics, etc., etc. But the good fellow was canny about it. He must have noticed that Tabet had gone black in the face, and so, just like that, he slipped into his pocket five thousand in notes.'

'Five thousand lire?'

'Absolutely. To be spent on the Seaside and Mountain Summer Camps for the *Opera Nazionale Ballila*.[5] He'd thought it through perfectly, no? But listen now to the second piece of news.'

He then went on to inform the whole table exactly how, a few days earlier, with a letter he'd sent to the Community's Council by way of the lawyer Renzo Galassi-Tarabini (in the whole world could he have found anyone more grovelling, arse-licking and *halto*** than that?) the Professor had officially asked permission to restore at his own expense, 'for the use of his family and anyone else who should be interested', the small, old Spanish synagogue in Via Mazzini, which for at least three centuries had had no religious function and now served as a storeroom.

* Ferrara Jewish dialect: bigoted; plural *halti*.

3

In 1914, when little Guido died, Professor Ermanno was forty-nine years old, and Signora Olga twenty-four. The child felt ill, was put to bed with a very high fever, and quickly fell into a profound torpor.

Dr Corcos was called out urgently. After a silent, interminable examination conducted with furrowed brow, Corcos brusquely lifted his head and solemnly stared first at the father then at the mother. The looks that he gave them were long, severe and strangely disdainful. At the same time, beneath his thick Umberto-style, down-curved moustache that was already completely grey, his lips shaped themselves into a bitter, almost vituperative grimace, for use in desperate cases.

'There's nothing to be done,' the doctor meant by those looks and that grimace. But also perhaps something else. And this was that he also, ten years earlier (and maybe he spoke of it that same day before taking his leave or only did so five days later, as without doubt happened, turning to grandpa Raffaello, as the two of them slowly walked together at the imposing funeral), he also had lost a young boy, his Reuben.

'I've been through this torture myself, I too know what it means to watch a five-year-old child die,' Elia Corcos suddenly declared.

With lowered head and hands resting on his bicycle handlebars, grandpa Raffaello walked alongside him. He seemed to be counting one by one the cobblestones of Corso Ercole I d'Este. At those truly unexpected words coming from the lips of his sceptical friend, he turned round, astonished, to look at him.

But what did Elia Corcos himself really know? He had given the child's motionless body a lengthy examination, reached his own baleful prognosis, and then, lifting his eyes had fixed them on the petrified ones of the two parents: the father an old man, the mother still just a girl. Down what roads would he have to journey to read those hearts of theirs? And who else would ever do so in the future? The epitaph dedicated to the little dead child in the tomb-monument at the Jewish cemetery (seven lines blandly enough carved and inked in on a humble upright rectangle of white marble) would say nothing but:

HERE LIES

GUIDO FINZI-CONTINI
(1908–1914)

CHOICE SPIRIT AND FORM

YOUR PARENTS WERE READY

TO LOVE YOU EVER MORE

NOT TO GRIEVE FOR YOU SO SOON

Ever more. A suppressed sob, that was all. A weight on the heart to be shared with no other person in the world.

Alberto was born in 1915, Micòl in 1916: more or less my contemporaries. They were neither sent to the Jewish elementary school of Via Vignatagliata, which Guido had attended without completing the first grade, nor later to the *Liceo Ginnasio*[1] G. B. Guarini, precocious crucible for the city's finest, Jewish and not, and therefore a choice that was at least pragmatic. Instead, both Alberto and Micòl were educated privately; Professor Ermanno every now and then breaking off his own solitary studies of agriculture, physics and the history of Italy's Jewish community, in order to supervise their progress himself. These were the mad, but in their way generous, early years of Emilian Fascism. Each and every action, everyone's behaviour, had to be judged – even by those who, like my father, willingly quoted Horace and his *aurea mediocritas* – by the crude markers of patriotism or defeatism. To send one's children to the state schools was in general considered patriotic, not to send them, defeatist, and therefore to all those who did send their kids there, in some way offensive.

Notwithstanding this, although utterly cut off, Alberto and Micòl Finzi-Contini had always kept up a tenuous rapport with the outside world, with children like us who went to the 'public' schools.

There were two teachers from the Guarini who acted as go-betweens.

Professor Meldolesi, for example, who in the fourth year taught us Italian, Latin, Greek, history and geography, on alternate afternoons would take his bicycle and, from the suburb of little villas that had sprung up in those years beyond Porta San Benedetto, about whose views and prospects he would frequently boast to us, and where he lived alone in a furnished room, would ride it as far as the Barchetto del Duca, to remain there sometimes for as long as three hours. And Signora Fabiani, the maths teacher, would do likewise.

From Fabiani, to tell the truth, we never got to know anything. Of Bolognese origins, a childless widow in her fifties, with a churchy air, she always seemed rapt to the point of ecstasy whenever she questioned us. She would continuously roll her light-blue, Flemish eyes and whisper to herself. She was praying. Praying, no doubt, for us poor things, almost all of us utterly incompetent at algebra, but also perhaps to expedite the conversion to Catholicism of those genteel Israelites to whose house she repaired twice every week. The conversion of Professor Ermanno and of Signora Olga, but above all of the two children, Alberto, so very clever, and Micòl, so vivacious and pretty, must have seemed to her a happening too significant, too urgent, for the probability of its success to be jeopardized by some silly lapse of discretion at school.

Professor Meldolesi, by contrast, was not in the least discreet. He was born at Comacchio of a farming family, and for his whole school career educated in a seminary (he had very much the typical characteristics of a priest, of a small, sharp-eyed, almost feminine country priest). He then went to study Arts at Bologna in time to be present at the final lectures of Giosuè Carducci,[2] of whom he boasted to be the 'humble scholar'. The afternoons spent at the

Barchetto del Duca, in an atmosphere saturated with the Renaissance, with tea served at five among the whole gathered family –
and Signora Olga would very often return from the park at that
hour, her arms weighed down with flowers – not to mention later,
perhaps, upstairs in the library, sometimes after darkness had fallen,
enjoying the erudite conversation of Professor Ermanno, those
extraordinary afternoons evidently represented for him something
too precious to deprive himself of the chance to turn them into a
series of little speeches and digressions for our benefit.

From the evening in which Professor Ermanno had revealed to
him how Carducci, in 1875, had been the guest of his parents for
some ten days, then had shown him the room he had occupied, let
him touch the bed he had slept in, and gone as far as to give him,
to take home, so that he could scrutinize it at his leisure, a 'sheaf'
of letters in his own hand sent to the Professor's mother by the
poet, his agitation, his enthusiasm knew no limits. He went so far
as to convince himself, and to try to convince us, that that famous
verse from the *Canzone di Legnano*:

O bionda, o bella imperatrice, o fida

which clearly prefigures the still more famous lines:

Onde venisti? Quali a noi secoli
sì mite e bella ti tramandarono . . .[3]

and at the same time, the great Maremman poet's clamorous conversion to the Savoyard 'eternal, regal feminine', were inspired precisely
by the paternal grandmother of his two private pupils, Alberto and
Micòl Finzi-Contini. Oh, what a magnificent topic this would have
been – Professor Meldolesi had once sighed in class – for an article
to send to that same *Nuova antologia* where Alfredo Grilli, his friend
and colleague Grilli, had for some time been publishing his subtle
glosses on Serra! Sooner or later, employing, it hardly needs to be
said, all the tact such a situation demanded, he might even signal
this possibility to the owner of the letters. And, heaven permitting,

given the years that had passed since, and given the importance and, it goes without saying, the perfect decorousness of a correspondence in which Carducci addressed the lady only as 'adorable Baroness', or 'most genteel host', and suchlike, one could only hope that this latter gentleman would not withhold his permission. In the happy prospect of a yes, he, Guido Meldolesi, would take care of the whole thing and, should he be given an explicit agreement by the one who had every right to bestow or withhold it, he would copy the letters out, one by one, accompanying those blessed shards, those venerated sparks of the great wordsmith with a minimal commentary. And what did it need, in fact, the text of this correspondence? Little else but a general introduction, glossed if at all with some sober historical and philological footnotes . . .

Apart from the teachers we had in common, there were also the exams held for private students – exams that took place in June at the same time as the other exams, those of the state schools – which brought us at least once a year into direct contact with Alberto and Micòl.

For us at school, especially if by passing we would be going up a year, these were perhaps the most enjoyable days. As though suddenly regretting the lessons and homework we'd just been rid of, we seemed unable to find a better place to meet up in than the school vestibule. We would hang about this vast entrance hall, cool and twilit as a crypt, crowding around the great white sheets which recorded our final results, fascinated by our own names and those of our companions, and to read them like that, transcribed in lovely calligraphy and exposed behind glass on the other side of a fine metalwork grating, induced in us a state of wonder. It was great to have nothing more to dread from school, great to be able to go out soon after into the bright blue light of ten in the morning that lured us through the entry postern, great to have in front of us long hours of laziness and liberty to spend however we pleased. Everything was utterly delightful, those first days of the holidays. And what happiness at the constant thought of our imminent departure for the sea or the mountains, where all notion of study, which still hung over and harassed others, would for us be all but wiped away!

And so it was, among these others (mainly big rough country lads, sons of peasants, prepared for the exams by local village priests, who, before crossing the threshold of the Guarini would look around bewildered like calves being led to the slaughterhouse), there would be Alberto and Micòl Finzi-Contini: not in the least bewildered, accustomed for years, as they were, to presenting themselves and acquitting themselves triumphantly. Perhaps they were a shade ironic, particularly towards me, when, crossing the entrance hall, they discerned me among my school friends and greeted me with a wave and a smile. But always polite, perhaps fractionally too polite, and good-natured. Exactly like guests.

They would never come on foot, much less by bicycle, but in a carriage, a dark-blue brougham that had huge wheels with tyres, red axles, and was all shiny with varnish, glass and nickel-plating.

The carriage would wait in front of the big entrance gate of the Guarini for hours and hours, only moving to seek out shade. Moreover, it should be said that to look closely at all the details of the equipage, from the big powerful horse, with its clipped tail and cropped and combed mane, which every now and then gave a majestic back-heel, to the miniature coat of arms that stood out in silver against the blue field of the doors, even at times to be given permission by the indulgent coachman in his informal livery, yet perched on the box-seat as on a throne, to climb up onto one of the steps of the footboard, and thus to contemplate at our leisure, our noses pressed against the glass, the entirely grey interior, sumptu-ously padded and in semi-darkness (it seemed like a drawing room: in one corner there were even some flowers threaded into a thin-necked oblong vase shaped like a calyx . . .), this too could be a real pleasure, and indeed it was: one of the many adventurous pleasures which abounded in those marvellous late spring mornings of our adolescence.

4

So far as I was personally concerned, in my relationship with Alberto and Micòl there was always something more intimate. The knowing looks, the confidential nods that brother and sister both directed towards me whenever we met in the grounds of the Guarini, were signs, I fully realized, of just this private understanding between us.

Something more intimate. But what exactly?

Certainly, to start off with, we were Jews, and this on its own would be more than enough. Nothing at all need ever have actually transpired between us, not even what little came from having exchanged the odd word. But because we were who we were, at least twice a year, at Passover and Yom Kippur, we came with our respective parents and close relatives to a particular doorway in Via Mazzini – and it often happened that having crossed its threshold together, the hallway we entered next, severe and dimly lit, would unleash a rite of hat-lifting, hand-shaking, obsequious bowing among grown-ups who, for the rest of the year, had no other occasions to practise such things; to us children this alone would be enough for us, meeting elsewhere, and above all in the presence of the uninitiated, to prompt the shadowy look or the smile of special complicity or connivance.

That we were all Jewish, however, and enrolled in the registers of the same Jewish community, in our case counted for little. What, after all, did that word 'Jewish' mean? What sense could expressions such as 'The Jewish community' or 'The Jewish Faith' possibly have, *for us*, seeing that they entirely left aside the existence of a far greater intimacy, a secret one, to be valued only by those who shared it, which derived from the fact that our two families, not by choice, but by virtue of a tradition more ancient than any possible memory, belonged to the same religious observance, or more accurately to the same 'School'? When we met each other at the Temple's entrance, generally at dusk, after the proper, dutiful exchange of civilities in the dim entrance hall it was almost always as a group that we climbed the steep stairs which led to the second floor. Commodious, crowded with all kinds of people, reverberant as a church with organ notes and singing – and so high, up among the rooftops, that some May evenings, with its great windows flung open west towards the setting sun, we would find ourselves at a certain point basking in a kind of golden mist . . . – that was the Italian synagogue. So Jews certainly, but Jews who had grown up observing the same particular rite, we alone could truly realize what it meant to have your own family bench in the Italian synagogue, up there on the second floor, rather than down on the first floor, in the German one, so severe and contrasting in its almost Lutheran gathering of prosperous, burgherly Homburg hats. Nor was that the whole story: since it might well be understood even outside Jewish society that an Italian synagogue is distinct from a German one, with all the social and psychological details such a distinction implies, who else could begin to precisely delineate – to give just one example – 'the Via Vittoria bunch'? This phrase usually referred to the members of four or five families who had the right to attend the small, separate Levantine synagogue, also known as the 'Fanese', situated on the third floor of an old Via Vittoria house, and so to the family Da Fano of Via Scienze, to the Cohens of Via Gioco del Pallone, to the Levis of Piazza Ariostea, to the Levi-Minzis of Viale Cavour, and to who knows which other isolated family group: all of them anyway people who were slightly odd, types always a shade ambiguous and evasive, whose religion, which in the Italian School had taken a more working-class and theatrical, almost Catholic turn, that was clearly reflected even in the character of the people themselves, largely extrovert and optimistic, typical of the Po valley, had in their case remained essentially a cult to be practised by the few, in semi-secret oratories at which it was opportune to arrive by night, in small numbers, slinking down the darkest and least known alleys of the Ghetto. No, no, it was only we, born and brought up *intra muros*, only we who could know and fully understand these things – things that were so elusive and irrelevant, but not for that any less real. As for the others, all the others, and first among them my much loved daily companions from both school and play, it was futile to think they might be instructed in such an occult zone of knowledge. Poor things! On this subject, they could only be considered crude simpletons, irretrievably condemned to live out their whole lives in the deepest pits of ignorance, or to being, as even my father would say, benignly grinning, *negri goìm*.*

So, on these occasions we climbed the stairs together, and together we made our entrance into the synagogue.

And since our benches were close by, down there at the bottom of the semicircular enclosure entirely bounded by a marbled balustrade at the centre of which loomed the *tevah*, or lectern, the rabbi would read from, and both of them in plain view of the monumental cupboard of carved black wood which guarded the scrolls of the Law, the so-called *sefarim*, together we would cross the great hall's sonorous floor paved with white and pink lozenges. Mothers, wives, grandmothers, aunts, sisters, etc. had separated from us men in the vestibule. They disappeared in single file inside a little opening in the wall that gave onto a small dark room, whence, with the help of a spiral staircase, they climbed even higher into the women's gallery, and in a short while we could see them again peeping down from between the openings of their hen-coop's grille, right up under the ceiling. But even like this, dwindled in our company to only males – which meant myself, my brother Ernesto, my father, Professor Ermanno, Alberto, and occasionally Signora Olga's two bachelor brothers, the engineer and Dr Herrera, down from Venice for the occasion – even like this we made a large enough group. And an imposing one at that. So much so that whenever we arrived during the ceremony we would awaken the most intense curiosity before we'd got halfway across the floor.

---

* Ferrarese dialect: literally, 'black (or benighted) Gentiles'.

As I said, our benches were neighbouring, one behind the other. We had the foremost one, in the first row, and the Finzi-Continis sat immediately behind us. Even if we'd wanted to, it would have been hard to ignore each other.

Attracted by the difference between us, as much as my father was repelled by it, I was always on the alert for the slightest gesture or whisper coming from the bench behind. My vigilance was unfaltering. I picked up the chatty asides of Alberto, who, although he was two years older than me, had still to enter the *Minyan*,* and who nevertheless hurried, as soon as he arrived, to wrap himself in the large black-striped and white wool *tallit*† which once belonged to 'grandpa Moisè'; but I was equally attentive to Professor Ermanno, affectionately smiling at me through his thick lenses, who would beckon to me with a sign of his finger to look at the copper etchings that illustrated an old Bible he had brought out especially for me from the small drawer. Likewise I would listen open-mouthed to Signora Olga's brothers, the railway engineer and the phthisiologist, chirruping away to each other half in Venetian dialect, half in Spanish ('*Cossa xé che stas meldando? Su, Giulio, alevantete, ajde! E procura de far star in pie anca il chico . . .*'‡), and then they'd suddenly stop, to intone together in an extraordinarily high-pitched voice the Hebrew replies to the rabbi's litany. My head was nearly always turned to one side or the other. In a line on their bench, the two Finzi-Continis and the two Herreras were there, little more than a metre away, and yet remote, unreachable, as though all round them was a protective wall of glass. There was little resemblance between the two pairs. Tall, thin, bald, their long pale faces shadowed with beards, always dressed in blue or black, and besides habitually imparting to their devotions an intensity, a fanatical ardour of which their brother-in-law and nephew, one could tell at a glance, would never be capable, those Venetian relatives seemed to belong to a world that was utterly removed

* Congregation of a minimum of ten adult males.
† Prayer shawl; plural: *tallitot*.
‡ Mixture of Spanish and Venetian dialect: 'What are you up to? Come on, Giulio, get up, will you! And make the boy stand up as well.'

from Alberto, with his tobacco-coloured jersey and long socks, and from Professor Ermanno's English knitwear and ochre linen, his air of a scholar and a country gentleman. All the same, however different they were, I sensed a deep kinship between them. What did they have in common, all four of them seemed to say, with the distracted, whispering, *Italian* congregation, who even in the Temple, before the wide open doors of the Ark of the Lord, remained trapped in all the pettiness of their daily lives, of business, politics, even sport, but never concerned with the soul and with God. I was a small boy then, between ten and twelve years old. A confused impression, admittedly, but still essentially true, joined in me with a feeling of scorn and humiliation, equally confused but which stung nevertheless, that I belonged with the others, the congregation, the rabble to be kept at bay. And my father? Facing the glass wall behind which the Finzi-Continis and the Herreras, always courteous but distant, effectively kept on ignoring him, his behaviour was the opposite of mine. Instead of trying to approach them, I saw him (medical graduate and free-thinker, army volunteer, since 1919 card-holder of the Fascist Party, and sports enthusiast, in short the modern Jew) deliberately exaggerate his own healthy intolerance of any fawning or saccharine profession of faith.

When the serene procession of the *sefarim* began to pass along the aisle (wrapped in rich copes of embroidered silk, their silver crown askew and sporting little tinkling bells, the sacred scrolls of the Torah seemed like a display of royal infants exhibited to the people so as to prop up a tottering monarchy) the doctor and the engineer Herrera were ready to duck forward from their bench, kissing whatever corner of the cope came within reach, eagerly, with an almost indecent greed. What did it matter that Professor Ermanno, copied by his son, confined himself to covering his eyes with a border of the *tallit*, and to whispering a prayer, barely moving his lips?

'What a mawkish fuss, what *haltud!*'* my father would comment later, with disgust, at the dinner table, without this in the least

---

* Ferrara Jewish dialect: bigotry.

impeding him, immediately afterwards, from once again returning to the theme of the Finzi-Continis' hereditary pride, the absurd isolation in which they lived, or even to pronounce on their aristocratic, subterranean, persistent anti-Semitism. But at that moment, without having anyone else to hand on whom he could vent his spleen, he took it out on me.

As usual, I had turned round to stare.

'Would you kindly keep still for just one moment?' he hissed between his clenched teeth, exasperated and fixing me with his blue, choleric eyes. 'You don't know how to behave properly even in the Temple. Just look at your brother – he's four years younger than you, and could teach you manners!'

But I took no notice. Soon after, I would be doing the same thing again, turning my back on the psalm-chanting Dr Levi, oblivious of the warning.

Now, if he wanted to regain control of me – physically, I mean, only physically – all my father could do was wait for the solemn blessing, when all the sons were gathered under the paternal *tallitot* in a series of tents. And there, finally (the synagogue verger Carpanetti had already begun his rounds with his long taper lighting one by one the thirty silver and gilded bronze candelabras – the whole room ablaze with lights), awaited in awe, Dr Levi's voice, usually so colourless, suddenly assumed the prophetic tone in keeping with the consummate, final moment of the *berachah*.*

'*Jevareheha Adonai veishmereha* . . .'† slowly began the Rabbi, bent down almost prostrate over the *tevah*, after having once more covered his towering white biretta with the *tallit*.

'Come on then, boys,' my father would say, brisk and joyful, snapping his fingers, 'Come on in under here!'

True, even at that moment, escape was still a possibility. Papa had his work cut out, for all his strong grip – his hard sportsman's hands on the scruff of our necks, of mine in particular. Although vast as a tablecloth, grandpa Raffaello's *tallit*, which we used, was

---

* Hebrew: Blessing.

† Hebrew: God bless and keep you . . .

altogether too worn smooth and full of holes to guarantee the kind of hermetic seal my father would have liked. And so, through the holes and tears which the years had wreaked on the fabric, frail as could be and pungent with must and antiquity, it was not difficult, at least for me, whilst there beside him, to observe Professor Ermanno, his hand resting on Alberto's brown hair and the fine light-blond hair of Micòl, who had just rushed down from the women's gallery, as he pronounced, one by one, following behind Dr Levi, the words of the *berachah*. Above our heads, our father, who knew no more than twenty words in Hebrew, the usual ones of family conversation – and besides he would never have bowed down – kept silent. I could guess the suddenly embarrassed expression on his face, his eyes, half-sardonic, half-intimidated, raised towards the ceiling's modest stucco work or the women's gallery. But meanwhile, from where I was, I could peer up with ever replenished awe and envy, at the lined and sharp visage of Professor Ermanno, who at that moment seemed transfigured. I watched his eyes, which I could have sworn were full of tears behind his glasses. His voice was thin and sing-song, but utterly tuneless, his Hebrew pronunciation, often doubling up the consonants, and with the 'z's, 's's and 'h's far more Tuscan than Ferrarese, seemed to have been filtered through the dual distinction of culture and class.

I watched him. For the entire duration of the blessing, Alberto and Micòl – they too – never stopped exploring among the breaches in their tent. And they smiled and winked at me, both of them strangely inviting, especially Micòl.

5

Once, however, in June 1929, the very day on which the marks for the yearly exams were posted up on the Guarini vestibule noticeboards, something special, something far more direct, took place.

In the oral exams I hadn't done that well.

Despite the fact that Professor Meldolesi had bent over backwards to help me, going so far as to ensure, against all the rules, that it was he who would examine me, I hardly ever reached the heights of the many sevens and eights which adorned my school report in the literary subjects. Questioned in Latin on the *consecutio temporum*, I made a whole series of gaffes. In Greek, too, I had answered with some difficulty, particularly when a page of the Teubner edition of the *Anabasis* was put under my nose and I was asked to translate a few unprepared lines. Later I redeemed myself a bit. In Italian, for example, besides having been able to give a résumé, with some nonchalance, of the contents of both *I promessi sposi* and *Le ricordanze*, I had recited by heart the first three octaves of *Orlando furioso* without once tripping up. And Meldolesi, at the ready, rewarded me at the end with a 'Bravo!' loud enough to cause the whole examining board, even myself, to smile. Overall, though, I repeat, my performance, even in the Arts, fell way short of the reputation I enjoyed.

But the real fiasco was in maths. Since the year before, I just couldn't get any grip on algebra. And worse still, having banked on Meldolesi's unfailing support for the final grades, I had always treated Professor Fabiani rather shoddily: I studied the minimum to scrape a six, and often enough not even to that minimum level. Of

what earthly use could maths be for someone who'd be applying to
study literature? – I continually told myself, even on that morning,
as I cycled up Corso Giovecca towards the Guarini. Alas, for the
orals in algebra, as in geometry, I'd hardly bothered to open my
mouth. Which meant . . . ? Poor Signora Fabiani, who during the
last two years had never dared give me less than a six, and in the
examiners' meeting she surely wouldn't have dared to . . . here I
avoided even mentally pronouncing the word 'fail', so much did the
idea of failing, with all its consequences of crushingly tedious private
lessons during which I'd have to subject myself all summer long to
Riccione, so much did it seem an alien and absurd concept when
referred to myself. To me, of all people, who had never suffered the
humiliation of being forced to retake in October, and who had even
been awarded in first-, second- and third-year *Ginnasio* 'for hard
work and good conduct' the position of 'Guard of Honour to the
Monument of the Fallen and at the Parks of Remembrance' – *me*,
failed, reduced to mediocrity, forcibly demoted amongst the most
anonymous masses! And as for my father? Just supposing Signora
Fabiani had forced me to resit in October (she taught maths at the
Liceo too, for which reason she had examined me herself, it being her
right!), where would I muster the courage, going from there in a few
hours, to return home, sit down in front of my father and start
eating dinner? Perhaps he would smack me. That, all considered,
would have been the best solution. Any punishment at all would
have been preferable to that look of reproach which would have
frozen me to the spot from his mute, terrible, clear blue eyes . . .

I entered the Guarini's main hall. A group of boys, among whom
I immediately recognized several friends, were quietly milling round
the intermediate years' noticeboard. Having leant my bike against
the main entrance's wall, I approached with trepidation. No one
had noticed my arrival.

I looked from behind a fence of shoulders stubbornly turned
towards me. My sight misted over. I looked again: and the red five,
the only number in red ink in a long row of black numerals, seared
itself on my soul with the violence of a branding iron.

'So what's the big deal?' Sergio Pavani asked, giving me a gentle thump on the back. 'It's not worth making a tragedy out of a five in maths! Have a look at mine –' he laughed – 'Latin and Greek.'

'Don't take it so badly,' Otello Forti added. 'I have to resit one as well – English.' I stared at him, utterly stunned. We had been class mates and had shared a desk from elementary school, and had been used to studying together from that time on, one day at his house, one day at mine, and both of us were convinced of my superiority. Never would a year pass without my going up a year in June, whilst he, Otello, always had to redo some subject or other.

And now, suddenly, to find myself compared to an Otello Forti, and to make it worse, compared *by him*! To find myself cast down to *his* level!

What I did or thought in the four or five hours that followed, starting, as soon as I left the Guarini, with the effect wrought upon me by meeting Professor Meldolesi (he smiled, the good fellow, hatless and tieless, with striped shirt collar turned out over his jacket lapels, and was quick to confirm for me Fabiani's 'unbudgingness' towards me, her categoric refusal to 'close her eyes yet one more time') – followed by a description of the long, desperate, aimless wanderings to which I abandoned myself, having received a gentle cuff on the cheek in the name of friendship and encouragement from the same Meldolesi, is not worth recounting. It's enough to say that around two o'clock in the afternoon, I was still cycling around along the Mura degli Angeli, in the vicinity of Corso Ercole I d'Este. I hadn't even telephoned home. With my face streaked with tears, my heart overflowing with enormous self-pity, I pedalled away almost unaware of where I was, and entertained vague thoughts of suicide.

I stopped beneath a tree – one of those old trees, lindens, elms, plane trees, horse chestnuts which, a dozen years later, in the frozen winter of Stalingrad, would be sacrificed for firewood, but which in 1929 still raised their great umbrellas of greenery high above the city's ramparts.

All around, a complete desert. The little beaten-earth track that like a sleepwalker I'd taken there from Porta San Giovanni snaked on between the century-old trunks towards Porta San Benedetto and the railway station. I stretched out beside my bicycle, face down in the grass, with my burning face hidden in my arms. The warm air wafted round my extended body: my only desire was to remain like that as long as could be, with my eyes closed. Against the narcotic background choir of the cicadas, the odd isolated sound stood out sharply: a cock crowing, the noise of beaten cloth most likely made by a woman out late washing clothes in the khaki waters of the Panfilio canal, and finally, very close, only inches from my ear, the ever-slowing ticking of the bike's back wheel, still in search of stasis.

I was thinking that, at home, by this time, they will surely have known – thanks perhaps to Otello Forti. Were they sitting around the table? Probably; even if, soon enough, they will have finished eating. Perhaps they were looking for me. Perhaps they had already collared that very Otello, the good, the inseparable friend, and given him the task of scouring the whole city on his bicycle, plus Montagnone and its walls as well, so it was not in the least improbable that, out of the blue, I'd find him in front of me, his face schooled to sadness by the circumstances, but in truth happy as a lark – I'd be able to see at a glance – that he hadn't to resit anything but English. No, perhaps, overcome by anxiety, at a certain point, my parents would have had recourse to the police station. My father would have gone in person to speak to the police chief in Castello. I could almost see him: stammering, having grown suddenly, frighteningly old, a mere shadow of his former self. He was weeping. Ah, but if only, around one o'clock, at Pontelagoscuro, he could have seen me as I stared at the Po's currents from the height of the iron bridge (I stayed there a good while looking down. How long? At the very least twenty minutes!), yes, then he'd definitely have been scared and yes, then at last he'd have understood, yes then he . . .

'Psst!'

I woke up with a start.

'Psst!'

I slowly raised my head, turning it left towards the sun. I blinked. Who was calling me? It couldn't be Otello. Who was it then?

I was about halfway along the city walls, which in their entirety stretched for three kilometres, starting from the end of Corso Ercole I d'Este and finishing at Porto San Benedetto in front of the station. It had always been a particularly lonely place. So it was, thirty years ago, and it still is today, despite the fact that to the right especially, facing the industrial zone, from 1945 on, scores of variously coloured workers' cottages have sprouted, in comparison with which, and with the factory chimneys and warehouses that compose their background, the brown, scrubby, half-rocky spur of fifteenth-century fortifications looks day by day ever more absurd.

I looked and looked, half closing my eyes against the glare. At my feet – only then did I notice – the crowns of its noble trees swollen with midday light like those of a tropical forest, stretched out the domain of the Barchetto del Duca: immense, truly heart-stopping with the little towers and pinnacles of the *magna domus* at its centre, half-hidden in green, and its whole perimeter bounded by a wall which was interrupted a quarter of a kilometre further on to allow for the flow of the Panfilio canal.

'Hey! But you must be blind as well!' came the happy voice of a girl.

Because of those blond tresses, the distinctive blond streaked with Nordic flax in the style of the *fille aux cheveux de lin*,[1] which could only have belonged to her, I instantly recognized Micòl Finzi-Contini. She peered over the wall as if over a window sill, leaning over with her shoulders forward and her crossed arms flat. She could not have been more than twenty-five metres away (near enough then for me to see her eyes, which were large and clear, perhaps too large at that time for the little, thin, child's face) and she was looking at me up from under.

'What are you doing up there? I've been here watching you for ten minutes. I'm sorry if you were sleeping and I woke you. And . . . my condolences!'

'Condolences? Whatever for?' I stammered, feeling my face go red all over. I had got up in the meantime.

'What time is it?' I asked, raising my voice.

'I make it three,' she said, with an appealing twist of her mouth. And then: 'I suppose you'll be hungry.'

I was dumbfounded. So even they knew! For a moment I even believed the news of my disappearance had been broadcast to them on the phone by my father or mother, to them and to an endless host of people. But it was Micòl who promptly put me right.

'This morning I went into the Guarini with Alberto to see the results. So are you very upset?'

'And you? Did you get put up a year?'

'We still don't know. Perhaps they're waiting for all the other private students to finish before posting the marks. But why not come down? At least come a bit closer so I don't have to get hoarse shouting.'

It was the first time she had spoken to me, the first time I had ever heard her speak. And I immediately noticed how similar her pronunciation was to Alberto's. They both spoke in the same way: stressing the syllables of certain words of which only they seemed to know the true sense, the real weight, but then sliding bizarrely over other syllables which one might have thought had more importance. They made a point of expressing themselves this way. They even gave it a name: Finzi-Continish.

Letting myself slip down the grassy slope, I drew near to the base of the wall. Although there was shade – a shade that reeked of dung and nettles – down there it was warmer. And now she looked at me from up above, her blond head in the sun, relaxed as though our meeting had not been in the least a casual, utterly fortuitous one, but as though from early infancy we had met in that exact spot on innumerable occasions.

'But you're making such a big fuss about it all,' she said. 'Why's it so bad to have to do another subject in October?'

She was making fun of me, it was clear. After all, it was not so unheard of for such a misfortune to befall someone of my type, from such a common background, so 'assimilated' as to be almost, in fact, a *goy*. What right did I have to make such a fuss?

'I think your head's full of strange ideas,' I replied.

'Oh yes?' she sniggered, 'Then be so good as to tell me why you haven't gone home to eat?'

'Who told you that?' The words escaped me.

'We know what we know. Even we have our informers.'

It was Meldolesi, I thought; it couldn't have been anyone else (and as it happens I was right). But what did it matter? All of a sudden I was aware that the question of my being failed was secondary, a babyish matter that would sort itself out.

'How', I asked, 'do you get up there? You look as though you're standing at a window.'

'I'm standing on my trusty ladder,' she replied, overstressing the syllables of 'trusty' in her usual disdainful way.

From over the wall, just then, came a deep, short, slightly raucous volley of barks. Micòl turned her head and cast over her shoulders a bored look, though tinged with affection. She made a face at the dog, then turned back to where I was.

'Uffa!' she calmly sighed. 'It's Jor.'

'What kind of dog is it?'

'He's a Great Dane. Only a year old, but he already weighs a ton. He follows me everywhere. I often try to cover over my tracks, but in a little while there he is again – quite sure of finding me. He's *awful*.'

She smiled.

'D'you want me to let you in?' she asked, becoming serious again. 'If you'd like I'll show you how right now.'

6

How many years have passed since that far-off June afternoon? More than thirty. And yet, if I close my eyes, Micòl Finzi-Contini is still there, leaning over her garden wall, looking at me and talking to me. In 1929 Micòl was little more than a child, a thin, blond thirteen-year-old with large, clear, magnetic eyes. And I was a boy in short trousers, very bourgeois and very vain, whom a small academic setback was sufficient to cast down into the most childish desperation. We both fixed our eyes on each other. Above her head the sky was a compact blue, a warm already summer sky without the slightest cloud. Nothing, it seemed, would be able to alter it, and nothing indeed has altered it, at least in memory.

'Well, do you want to, or don't you?' Micòl pressed me, becoming angry.

'I don't really know . . .' I began, nodding at the wall. 'It looks very high to me.'

'That's because you haven't looked properly,' she replied impatiently. 'See over there . . . and there . . . and there,' pointing her finger to make me look. 'There's lots of notches, and even a nail, up there on top. I put it in myself.'

'I see . . . there must be some footholds,' I murmured uncertainly, 'but . . .'

'Footholds?' she interrupted, bursting out laughing. 'Me, I'd call them "notches".'

'That's too bad, because they're called "footholds",' I insisted stubbornly and tartly. 'You can tell you've never been mountaineering.'

Since childhood I have always suffered from vertigo and though it was a modest climb it had me worried. As a child, when my mother with Ernesto in her arms (Fanny had not yet been born) took me out on Montagnone, and sat down on the grass on the vast square in front of Via Scandiniana, from the top of which one could just barely make out our house's roof from among the sea of roofs around the big jetty of the church of Santa Maria in Vado, it was with considerable fear, I remember, that I went to lean on the parapet that skirted the square on the side nearest the country, and looked down over a drop of some thirty metres. Someone was always climbing up or down that dizzyingly steep wall: farmers, manual workers, young bricklayers, each of them with a bicycle on his shoulders. Amongst them were old men too, mustachioed frog-catchers and catfish anglers, laden with rods and baskets, all of them inhabitants of Quacchio, of Ponte della Gradella, of Coccomaro, of Coccomarino, of Focomorto, all of them in a hurry, and rather than go the long way by Porta San Giorgio or Porta San Giovanni (because at that time, on that side, the ramparts were still intact, without any penetrable breaches for at least five kilometres) they preferred to take, as they called it, 'the wall route'. They left the city, in that case, by crossing the great square, passing me by without even noticing me, stepping over the parapet and letting themselves drop until the tips of their toes rested on the first outcrop or crevice in the decrepit wall, and then, in no time at all, they would reach the meadow below. They came from the country; and then they would come up with those narrowed eyes that seemed to me to be boring into my own as I peeped timidly over the parapet – but I was quite wrong about that as they were understandably only focusing on the next handhold. Always, in any case, all the time they were thus occupied, suspended over the abyss – a pair of them, usually, one following the other – I would hear them chattering away in dialect, no more or less perturbed than if they had been trudging along a footpath in the middle of some fields. How calm, strong and brave they were! – I'd tell myself. After they had come up to within a few inches of my face, mirroring it in their own sclerotic ones, more often than not I was enveloped in the wine-reek of their breath, as they grasped with their thick callused fingers the inner edge of the parapet, as their whole bodies emerged out of the void and – lo and behold! – there they were safe and sound. I'd never be able to do such a thing, I told myself every time, watching them move away, full of admiration but also a kind of recoil. Never ever.

It was the same type of feeling I was once more experiencing just then in front of the outer wall on top of which Micòl was inviting me to climb. The wall certainly did not look as high as the ramparts of Montagnone. But all the same it was smoother, a good deal less corroded with the years and the inclement weather. And what if, scrambling up there, I thought to myself, my eyes fixed on those 'notches' Micòl had pointed out to me, what if faintness overcame me and I was to fall? I might easily be killed.

However it was not so much for that reason that I still hesitated. Holding me back was a different repugnance than the purely physical one of vertigo, analogous but different, and stronger at that. For a moment I began to repent of my so recent desperation, my stupid puerile laments of a 'failed' boy.

'And besides, I don't see why here of all places I should force myself to become an Alpine mountaineer. If I'm being invited into *your* house, I'm very grateful but, frankly, it seems to me a whole lot easier to enter over there,' and saying this I lifted my arm in the direction of Corso Ercoli I d'Este, 'through the main entrance. It would hardly take a moment. I'll get the bike and be there in no time.'

I immediately understood that this proposal was not to her liking.

'No . . . no . . .' she said, contorting her face in an expression of intense distaste, 'if you go that way Perotti's bound to see you, and then that will be it, there'll be no more fun in the whole thing.'

'Perotti? Who's he?'

'The doorkeeper . . . you know. Perhaps you've already seen him. He's the one who's also the coachman, and accompanies us as a *chauffeur*. If he sees you, and there's no way he *won't* see you, since, apart from the times he goes out with the carriage or the car, he's always there on guard, damn him! And after that, it absolutely means I'll have to take you into the house as well, and you tell me if that's . . . what d'you think?'

She was looking straight into my eyes, serious now, even though as calm as could be.

'All right,' I replied, turning my head and nodding towards the embankment, 'but what should I do with my bike? It's not like I can just leave it there, untended. It's brand new, a Wolsit: with dynamo lights, a saddlebag with a repair kit and a pump – do you think I'd let them steal my bike – on top of everything else . . .'

I didn't finish my sentence, struck down once more with anxiety about my inevitable confrontation with my father. That very evening, as late as possible, I'd have to return home. What other choice did I have?

I'd turned my eyes towards Micòl whilst I was speaking: she had seated herself on the wall, with her back turned towards me. Now she confidently lifted her leg and sat astride it.

'What are you up to?' I asked, surprised.

'I've just had an idea about your bike, and in the meantime I'll show you the best places to put your feet. Pay attention to where I'm putting mine. Look!'

She vaulted nonchalantly over onto the top of the wall, and thence, grabbing hold of the big rusty nail she had shown me before, began to climb down. She came down slowly but surely, searching out the footrests with the tips of her little tennis shoes, now with one, now with the other, and always finding them without apparent effort. She climbed down gracefully. All the same, before touching the ground, she missed one foothold, and slid the rest of the way. She fell on her feet but had hurt the fingers of one hand, and also, grazing the wall, her little pink dress – for the seaside – had been torn slightly under the arm.

'What a fool I am,' she grumbled, bringing her hand to her mouth and blowing on it. 'It's the first time that's happened to me.'

She had cut her knee as well. She drew up a fold of her dress far enough to uncover her strangely white and strong-looking thigh, already a woman's, and she leant over to examine the scratch. Two long blond locks, the fairer ones, escaped from the clip she used to keep them bound together, fell down over her face, hiding her forehead and eyes.

'What a fool,' she repeated.

'You'll need some disinfectant,' I said mechanically, without approaching her, in that slightly plaintive tone that, in our family, we all used for this kind of thing.

'Disinfectant? You must be joking!'

She quickly licked the wound, a sort of affectionate kiss, and immediately sat up straight.

'Come on then,' she said, all red and ruffled.

She turned, and began to climb up sideways along the bank's sunlit edge. She used her right hand to steady herself, grasping tufts of grass; meanwhile, her left hand, raised to her head, was undoing and refitting her circular hairclip. She repeated the manoeuvre several times as fluently as though she were combing her hair.

'Do you see that hole there?' she asked me, as soon as we'd arrived at the top. 'You can hide your bike in there. No problem.'

She pointed out to me, about fifty metres away, one of those grassy, cone-shaped hillocks, not more than two metres high, with an opening that is nearly always buried, which you come across quite frequently going round the walls of Ferrara. At first sight, they look a bit like the Etruscan *montarozzi* of the Roman countryside, though obviously on a much smaller scale. Except that the often huge underground chambers which some of them lead to have never housed any of the dead. The ancient defenders of the walls used them to store their arms: culverins, arquebuses, gunpowder and so on. And perhaps also those odd cannon balls of much-prized marble which in the fifteenth and sixteenth centuries had made the Ferrarese artillery so feared across Europe, and some examples of which you can still see in the castle, lying there like ornaments in the central courtyard and on the terraces.

'Who would dream that there could be a new Wolsit hidden down there? You'd have to have been told. Have you ever been inside?'

I shook my head.

'No? I have. Hundreds of times. It's *stunning*.'

She moved on decisively, and having picked the Wolsit off the ground, I followed her in silence.

I drew level with her at the threshold of the opening. It was a kind of vertical crack, cut directly into the mantle of grass with which the mound was thickly clad, and too narrow to permit the entry of more than one person at a time. Immediately beyond the threshold began the descent, and one could only see down into it eight, maybe ten metres, but no more than that. Beyond there was nothing but darkness. As though the underground passage came up against a black curtain.

She leant in to look, then suddenly turned round to me.

'You go on down,' she whispered, smiling weakly, embarrassed. 'I'd prefer to wait up here.'

She drew back, linking her hands behind her back, and leaning her back against the grassy wall beside the entry.

'It's not like you're scared?' she asked, still in lowered tones.

'No, no,' I lied, and bent down to lift the bike onto my shoulders.

Without saying another word I went past her, heading on into the tunnel.

I had to move carefully, also because the bicycle pedal kept knocking against the wall; and to begin with, for at least two or three metres, it was as though I'd been blinded: I could see absolutely nothing. But ten or so metres from the entrance hole ('Be careful,' I heard Micòl's already distant shout behind me, then: 'Mind the steps there!') I began to make out something. The tunnel came to an end a short space ahead: it only continued for a few more metres in descent. And it was just there, beyond a kind of landing which I sensed, even before arriving, was surrounded by a completely different kind of space, that the stairs which Micòl had warned me of began.

When I reached the landing, I stopped for a moment.

The infantile fear of the dark and the unknown which I'd felt the moment I'd moved away from Micòl as I ventured slowly further and further into the bowels of the earth gradually gave way to a no less infantile sense of relief. As though, having left Micòl's company, I had just in time escaped some great danger, the greatest danger a boy of my age ('a boy of your age' was one of my father's favourite expressions) might ever meet. Oh yes, I thought, this evening when I get home my Papa may well beat me. But at this point I could easily face his blows with equanimity. A subject to retake in October, Micòl was right, was just a joke. What was a subject in October compared to, I trembled, all those things that might have taken place between us, down here, in the dark? Perhaps I would have had the courage to give her, Micòl, a kiss: a kiss on the lips. But then what? What would have happened next? In the films I'd seen, and in novels, kisses had to be long and passionate! Actually, compared to 'all those things', kisses were merely a not-too-worrying detail, if after lips met, and the two mouths were joined, each seeming almost to enter the other, mostly the thread of the story would not be picked up again until the next morning, or even not until several days later. If Micòl and I had managed to kiss each other in that way – and the darkness might certainly have helped things along – after that kiss time would have continued to move at its usual stately pace without any strange or providential interruption arriving to transport us safely to the morning after. In that case, what would I have had to do to fill up the minutes and hours that lay between? Oh, but that hadn't happened, luckily. It was just as well I'd been saved.

I began to descend the steps. I now realized that some faint rays of light from behind were filtering down through the tunnel. So a little by sight and a little by hearing (the bike had only to knock against the wall, or my heel to slip on a step, and immediately an echo increased and multiplied the sound, measuring out the spaces and distances), I quite quickly came to sense the sheer vastness of the place. It must have been a chamber some forty metres in diameter, round, with a vaulted dome of at least the same height. Who knows, perhaps it communicated by way of a system of secret corridors with other underground chambers of the same type, dozens of them, nestled under the body of the ramparts. Nothing could have been easier to imagine.

The chamber floor was of beaten earth, smooth, compact and dank. As I groped along the curve of the walls, I stumbled on a brick, and trod down on some straw. At last I sat down, resting with one hand gripping the wheel of the bike I'd leant against the wall, and the other arm around my knees. The silence was only broken by the occasional rustle and squeak: rats probably, or bats . . .

And if the other things had happened, if they had, would that really have been so terrible?

It was almost a certainty I wouldn't have gone back home, and my parents, and Otello Forti, and Sergio Pavani, and all the others, the police station included, would have then had a real hunt to find me! For the first few days they'd have worn themselves out looking everywhere. Even the newspapers would have reported it, bringing up the usual hypotheses: kidnap, mishap, suicide, clandestine flight abroad, and so on. Little by little, however, things would have calmed down. My parents would have finally been reconciled to the loss (after all, they still had Ernesto and Fanny), and the search would have been called off. And, in the end, the person who'd be held responsible would have been that stupid sanctimonious Signora Fabiani, who'd have been sent off to 'some other placement' as punishment. Where? To Sicily or Sardinia, naturally. It would have served her right, and taught her not to be so sneaky and spiteful.

As for me, seeing everyone else had become so reconciled to my absence, I would get used to it as well. I could rely on Micòl outside: she would have been able to provide me with food and everything else I needed. And she would have come every day, climbing over her garden wall, summer and winter. And every day we would have kissed, in the dark, because I was her man, and she was my woman.

And anyway, who was to say I wouldn't go outside ever again? During the day, obviously, I'd sleep, only interrupting my slumbers when I felt Micòl's lips brushing my own, and later I'd fall asleep again with her in my arms. By night, however, I could easily make prolonged sorties, especially if I choose the hours after one or two o'clock, when everyone else would be asleep, and almost no one left on the city streets. It would be odd and scary, but in the end good fun, to pass by Via Scandiana, see our house again, and the window of my bedroom, by this stage converted into a kind of sitting room, and then to make out in the distance, hidden in shadow, my father just then returning from the Commercial Club, and it wouldn't even cross his mind I was alive and watching him. In fact, there he was taking the keys out of his pocket – opening the door, entering, and then calmly, just as though I, his eldest child, had never existed, shutting the door with a single hefty push.

And Mamma? Would it not be possible, one day or another, for me to try to let her know, perhaps by way of Micòl, that I wasn't really dead? And even to see her, before, fed up of my life underground, I finally left Ferrara and disappeared for ever? Why not? What was to stop me!

I don't know how long I remained there. Perhaps ten minutes, perhaps less. I remember precisely that as I climbed up the stairs and threaded the tunnel again (without the weight of the bicycle I moved far more nimbly) I kept on embellishing these fantasies. And Mamma? – I asked myself. Would she also have forgotten me, like the rest of them?

Finally I found myself in the open air again, and Micòl was no longer waiting for me where I'd left her a little before, but rather, as I saw almost at once, screening my eyes against the sun with my hand, was once more sitting astride the garden wall of the Barchetto del Duca.

She seemed busy arguing and reasoning with someone on the other side of the wall: probably the coachman Perotti, or even Professor Ermanno in person. It was clear what had happened: seeing the ladder leaning against the wall, they must have immediately been aware of her little escape. Now they were asking her to come down. And she wasn't sure whether she wanted to obey.

At a certain point, she turned round, and clocked me on top of the bank. Then she blew out her cheeks as if to say:

'Phew! About time!'

And the last look she gave before disappearing behind the wall – a look accompanied with a smile and a wink, just as when, at the synagogue, she spied me from under the paternal *tallit* – had been for me.

II

I

The time when I actually managed to pass beyond, beyond the wall surrounding the Barchetto del Duca, and make my way between the trees and clearings of the great private wood as far as the *magna domus* itself and the tennis court, was something like ten years later.

It was in 1938, about two months after the Racial Laws had been passed. I remember it well. One afternoon towards the end of October, a few minutes after having left the table, I'd received a telephone call from Alberto Finzi-Contini. Was it or wasn't it true, he immediately wanted to know, dispensing with any preamble (it is worth noting that for more than five years we had had no occasion to exchange a single word) – was it or wasn't it true that I 'and all the others', with a letter signed by the vice-president and secretary of the Eleonora d'Este Tennis Club, had all been banned from the club: 'thrown out' as it were?

I denied this firmly: it wasn't true. At least, as far as I was concerned; I'd received no such letter.

As though he considered my denial of no consequence, or wasn't even willing to listen to it, he immediately proposed that I should come round to play at their house. If I could put up with a white clay court, he went on, with not much in the way of surrounds; and if, above all, given that I was sure to be a far better player than them, I could 'be kind enough' to give him and Micòl a knock-up, both of them would be very glad and 'honoured'. Any afternoon at all would be fine, he added, if the idea appealed to me. Today, tomorrow, the day after – I could come when I wanted, bringing with me whoever I wanted, even on Saturday, if that was better. He had to stay in Ferrara for at least another month, since the Milan

Polytechnic courses wouldn't be starting until 20 November (as for Micòl, she was taking things easier and easier – being this year *fuori corso*[1] for History, and having no need to go around begging official signatures, who knows if she'd even set foot in the department at Ca' Foscari) and didn't I see what lovely weather we were having? Whilst there was still time, it would be a real waste not to make the most of it.

He sounded these last words with less conviction. It seemed as though he had felt the chill of some less pleasant thought, or a sudden, unmotivated feeling of boredom had descended to make him wish that I wouldn't come round or take any notice of his invitation.

I thanked him, without clearly committing myself to anything. What was the call about? – I asked myself in some consternation, putting down the phone. All considered, since the time he and his sister had been sent to study outside Ferrara (Alberto in 1933, Micòl in 1934, more or less the same years that Professor Ermanno had been given permission by the Community to restore for 'the use of the family and others concerned' the former Spanish synagogue which was incorporated in the Via Mazzini Temple, and from then on the bench behind ours in the Italian School synagogue had remained empty) we hadn't seen each other except on rare occasions, and those only briefly and at a distance. During this whole time we had become so remote from each other that one morning in 1935, at Bologna station (I was already in the second year of my Arts course and I went back and forth almost every day by train), having been brusquely shouldered aside on platform one by a dark-haired, pale-faced young man, with a tartan blanket under his arm, and with a porter laden with baggage at his heels, who was propelling himself with big strides towards the fast train to Milan about to leave, for a moment I completely failed to recognize this figure as Alberto Finzi-Contini. And that time – I continued thinking – he had not even felt the least need to greet me. When I had turned round to protest at being knocked over, he merely gave me a distracted glance. And now, by contrast, what was all this effusive and slippery courtesy about?

'Who was it?' my father asked, as soon as I had entered the dining room.

There was no one else in the room. He was sitting in an armchair next to the sideboard with the radio, as usual anxiously awaiting the two o'clock news.

'Alberto Finzi-Contini.'

'Who? The boy? Such an honour! And what did he want?'

He scrutinized me with his blue, bewildered eyes, which a long time ago had lost hope of my obedience, trying to guess what was going on in my mind. He well knew – his eyes were telling me – that his questions got on my nerves, that his continual attempts to meddle in my life were without discretion or justification. But good God, wasn't he my father? And hadn't I noticed how he'd grown old this last year? It wasn't possible for him to confide in Mamma and in Fanny: they were women. Nor could he do so in Ernesto – too *putìn*.* So who then could he talk to? Was it possible I didn't understand it was me he needed?

Through clenched teeth I told him what the call had been about.

'And will you be going, then?'

He didn't give me a chance to answer him. Regardless, with all the animation I saw in him at the slightest chance offered him to drag me into any kind of conversation, especially of a political nature, he'd already rushed headlong into a résumé of what he called 'the real point of the situation'.

It was unfortunately true – he had begun to recapitulate in his tireless way – last September, on the 22nd, after the first official announcement on the 9th, all the newspapers had published that additional circular from the Party Secretary which spoke of various 'practical measures' of immediate application for which the provincial Federations would be responsible with regard to us. In future, 'the prohibition of mixed marriages remaining statutory, the exclusion of all youths, recognized as belonging to the Jewish race, from all state schools of whatever kind and level', as well as the exemption, for the same, from the 'highly honorific' duty of military

* Venetian dialect: small, young.

service, we 'Israelites' would then not even be able to place our death announcements in the newspapers, let alone be listed in telephone directories, or keep domestic help of the Aryan race, or frequent 'recreational clubs' of any kind whatsoever. And yet, despite all this . . .

'I hope you won't want to start on the usual story,' I interrupted him, shaking my head.

'What story?'

'That Mussolini is more *good* than Hitler.'

'I know, I know,' he said. 'But you have to admit it's true. Hitler's a bloodthirsty maniac, whereas Mussolini is what he is, as much of a Machiavellian and turncoat as you want, but . . .'

Again I interrupted him. Did he or did he not agree, I asked, looking him straight in the face, with the idea of Leon Trotsky's essay I'd 'passed' to him a few days earlier?

I was referring to an article published in an old number of the *Nouvelle Revue Française*, a magazine several entire years of which I jealously guarded in my bedroom. What had happened was that, I can't remember why, I had treated my father disrespectfully. He was offended, had gone into such a sulk that, at a certain point, hoping to re-establish normal relations, I could think of no other strategy than to make him privy to my most recent reading. Flattered by this sign of respect, my father did not need to be persuaded. He read the article straight away, rather he devoured it, underlining with a pencil a great many lines, and filling the margins with pages of dense notes. Basically, and this he declared openly, the writings of 'that scapegrace and ancient best mate of Lenin' had been for him, too, a real revelation.

'But of course I agree with it!' he exclaimed, happy, and at the same time disconcerted, to see me inclined to have a discussion. 'There's no doubt about it – Trotsky's a magnificient polemicist. What vividness and powers of expression! Quite capable of composing the article straight in French. Sure,' here he smiled with pride, 'those Russian and Polish Jews may not be very likeable, but they've always had an indisputable genius for languages. They have it in their blood.'

'Let's drop the question of language and get down to the arguments,' I cut him short with a sour professorial tone which I immediately regretted.

The article spoke clearly – I continued, more placidly. In its phases of imperialist expansion capitalism is bound to manifest its intolerance regarding all national minorities, and the Jews in particular, who are *the* minority par excellence. And now, in the light of this general theory (Trotsky's essay was written in 1931, which shouldn't be forgotten: that is, the year in which Hitler's real ascent to power began) what did it matter whether Mussolini was a better person than Hitler? And anyway, was it really true that he was better, even in terms of character?

'I see. I see . . .' my father kept on meekly repeating as I spoke.

His eyelids were lowered, his face screwed up into a grimace of pained forbearance. At last, when he was quite sure I had nothing further to add, he placed his hand on my knee.

He could see – he repeated once again, slowly raising his eyelids. If I'd just let him speak: according to him I took everything too grimly, I was too extreme.

How come I didn't realize that after the communiqué of 9 September, and more particularly after the additional circular of the 22nd, things at least in Ferrara had gone ahead almost as before? It was quite true, he admitted, smiling melancholically, that during that month, among the seven hundred and fifty members of the Community there had been no deaths considered worthy of record in the *Padano* (if he wasn't wrong, only two old ladies from the Via Vittorio Hospice had died: a certain Saralvo and a Rietti, and the latter wasn't even from Ferrara but from a Mantuan village – Sabbioneta, Viadana, Pomponesco, or something like that). But we should be fair: the telephone directory had not been withdrawn to be replaced by a newly purged edition. There had not yet been any *havertà*,* maid, cook, nanny, or old governess, in service to any of our families, who, all of a sudden discovering in themselves 'a racial awareness' had felt it imperative to pack their bags. The Commercial

* Hebrew: handmaid.

Club which for more than ten years had had as its vice-president the lawyer Lattes, and which he had frequented constantly on an almost daily basis, had recorded no such walk-outs up until that date. And Bruno Lattes, son of Leone Lattes, had he by any chance been expelled from the Eleonora d'Este Tennis Club? Without giving the least thought to my brother Ernesto, who, poor thing, had been all this time watching me with his mouth ajar, imitating me as though I was who knows what great *haham*,* I had given up playing tennis, and I had done wrong, if I'd let him say so, very wrong to close myself off, to segregate myself, not go out to see anyone any more, and then, with the excuse of university and a seasonal railcard, to continually sneak off to Bologna (and I wasn't even willing to spend time with Nino Bottecchiari, Sergio Pavani and Otello Forti, up until last year my inseparable friends, here in Ferrara, yes, first one and then the other, they hadn't stopped phoning me, poor boys! I should consider, in contrast, young Lattes. If the *Padano* was to be credited, he had not only taken part in the open tournament but also in the mixed doubles, playing with his partner, the lovely Adriana Trentini, daughter of the province's chief engineer. He was doing exceptionally well – they'd already got through the first three rounds and were now getting ready for the semi-finals. No, you can say what you want about good old Barbicinti, such as that he sets too much store by his own petty nobility's coat of arms and too little store by the grammar of the tennis propaganda articles which the Federal Secretary gets him to write every now and then for the *Padano*. But that he was a gentleman, not at all hostile to Jews, a harmless enough Fascist – and in saying 'harmless enough Fascist' my father's voice trembled, a little tremor of timidity – as far as that's concerned there's no doubt or cause for dispute.

As regards Alberto's invitation, and the behaviour of the Finzi-Continis in general, what was it for, out of the blue, all their fussing, all their almost frantic neediness to make contact?

What had happened the week before for Rosh Hashanah at the Temple had already been strange enough (as usual, I hadn't wished

---

* Hebrew: sage or teacher.

to go, and once again had put myself in the wrong). Yes, it was already strange enough, at the climax of the service and with the seats almost all taken, to see Ermanno Finzi-Contini, his wife, and even his sister-in-law, followed by the two children and the inevitable uncles, the Herreras from Venice – in short, the whole tribe, without distinctions of gender, make their solemn return to the Italian School after a *good* five years of scornful isolation in the Spanish synagogue. They had a look about them too, benign and satisfied, no more or less than if they had meant, by their presence, to reward and *pardon* not only the assembled company but the entire Community. And this alone was apparently not sufficient. For now they'd reached the point of inviting people to their home, to the Barchetto del Duca, just imagine, where since the days of Josette Artom, no fellow citizen or outsider had ever set foot, except perhaps in situations of dire emergency. And did I care to know why? Of course, because they were pleased with what was happening! Because to them, *halti* as they'd always been (anti-Fascist, sure, but above all *halti*) *deep down the Racial Laws gratified them!* Had they been good Zionists one could have understood! Given that here in Italy, and in Ferrara, they always found themselves so ill at ease, so out of place, they could at least have benefited from this situation and taken themselves off, once and for all, to Eretz! But not at all. Apart from fumbling every now and then for a wee bit of cash to send to Eretz (which was nothing to boast of, anyway) the thought of going had never even crossed their minds. They had always reserved their serious bits of spending for aristocratic baubles: as when, in 1933, to find an *ehal* and a *parochet** worthy of a place in their private synagogue (authentic Sephardic furnishings, I ask you – not Portuguese, or Catalan, or Provençal, but real Spanish and to the exact measurement!), they rushed off in a motor car, dragging a Carnera lorry behind them to no less a place than Cherasco, in the province of Cuneo, a village which up until 1910 or earlier had been the dwelling of a small Jewish community now extinct, and where the cemetery was only still functioning because some Turin families who'd originated there,

* Hebrew: *ehal*: Ark; *parochet*: curtain before the Ark.

Debenedetti, Momigliano, Terracini and so on, kept on burying their dead there. Likewise Josette Artom, Alberto and Micòl's grandmother, in her time, unceasingly imported palms and eucalyptuses from the Botanical Gardens of Rome, the one at the foot of the Janiculum – and because of this and needless to say for reasons of prestige, had forced her husband, poor Menotti, to at least double the width of the already exaggerated gateway that gave onto Corso Ercole I d'Este. The truth is that their mania for collections, of things, of plants, of whatever, little by little ends up with them wanting to do the same with people. Huh! And if they, the Finzi-Continis, so missed being stuck in a ghetto (and the Ghetto – that's where they clearly want to have everyone locked away, even if it meant making a sacrifice for this wonderful ideal and parcelling out bits of the Barchetto del Duca to make a kind of kibbutz of it, of course under their noble patronage), they should feel perfectly free to go ahead and do so. Speaking for himself, and quite sincerely, he'd much prefer to go to Palestine. Or better still Alaska, Tierra del Fuego or Madagascar . . .

That was a Tuesday. I can't explain how, a few days later, on the Saturday, I decided to do exactly the opposite of what my father wanted. I'd deny that it had to do with the typical filial mechanism of contradiction and disobedience. What suddenly prompted me to drag out my racket and tennis gear from the drawer they had lain in for more than a year had been nothing other than a luminous day, the light and caressing air of an early autumnal afternoon, unusually sunny.

But in the meantime certain things had happened.

First of all, two days after Alberto's call, I think, and so it must have been Thursday, the letter that 'welcomed' my resignation as a member of the Eleonora d'Este Tennis Club had actually arrived. Typed, but with the signature, in full spread, of NH[2] Marchese Barbicinti at the foot of the page, the express delivery did not descend to personal or particular details. In the driest tone, and a mere few lines, clumsily mimicking a bureaucratic style, it went straight to the point, declaring it without doubt 'inadmisible' (*sic*) any further attendance of my 'esteemed person' at the Club. (Could the Marchese Barbicinti ever rid himself of the habit of peppering his prose with certain spelling mistakes? It seems not. But taking note of and laughing about them was a bit more difficult this time than it had been in the past.)

And secondly, the next day, there had been another phone call for me from the *magna domus*, and not from Alberto, this time, but from Micòl.

The outcome was a long, no, an extremely long conversation, the tone of which was maintained, thanks mainly to Micòl, along the lines of a normal, ironic, rambling chat between two seasoned university students who, as children, might even have had a bit of a crush on one another, but who now, after something in the region of ten years, have nothing else in mind than to bring about an innocent get-together.

'How long is it since we've seen each other?'

'At the very least five years.'

'And so, what are you like now?'

'Ugly. A spinster with a red nose. And you? On the subject, I read, I read . . .'

'Read what?'

'That's it. Two or so years ago, in the *Padano*, must have been the culture page, that you'd participated in the Venice Littoriali[3] of Culture and Art . . . Making a bit of a splash, eh? My compliments! But then you always did very well in Italian, even at *Ginnasio*. Meldolesi was truly *spellbound* by some of your class essays. I seem to recall he even brought us one to read.'

'No need to make fun of me. And you, what are you up to?'

'Nothing. I should have graduated in English at Ca' Foscari last June. But instead – fat chance. Let's hope I can get through this year, idleness permitting. D'you think they'll let the *fuori corso* finish *anyway*?'

'I haven't the least doubt about that, though my saying so won't cheer you up. Have you chosen the subject for your thesis yet?'

'I've chosen, so far no more than chosen, to do it on Emily Dickinson – you know, the nineteenth-century American poet, that archetypally *awful woman* . . . but what can you do? I'll have to be tied to the Professor's apron strings, waste a whole fortnight in Venice, the Pearl of the Lagoon – but a short while there's enough for me . . . All these years I've stayed there as little as possible. Besides, to be honest, studying's never been my forte.'

'Liar. Liar and snob.'

'No. I swear it's true. And this autumn, trying hard to be as good as gold, I feel even less cut out for it. D'you know what I'd rather do, dear boy, instead of burying myself in the library?'

'Why not tell me.'

'Play tennis, go out dancing and flirting, you can imagine.'

'All of them healthy recreations, including tennis and dancing, which if you cared to you could just as easily pursue in Venice.'

'Sure I could – with that pair of governesses Uncle Giulio and Uncle Federico always snapping at my heels!'

'Well, you can't claim anyone's going to stop you playing tennis. As for me, whenever I can, I take the train and make off to Bologna . . .'

'Go on, tell the truth, you make off to *make out*, round at your true love's.'

'No. Not at all. I have to graduate myself next year, I'm still not sure whether in Art History or Italian – but now I think it'll be Italian – and whenever I feel like it I permit myself an hour of tennis. I hire an excellent paying court in Via del Castello or at the Littoriale, and no one can stop me. Why don't you do the same at Venice?'

'The question is that to play tennis or go dancing you need a *partner*,[4] but at Venice I don't have anyone remotely *suitable*. And I tell you, Venice may well be beautiful, I wouldn't deny it, but I don't feel at ease there. I feel provisional, displaced . . . a bit as though I'm abroad.'

'Do you stay at your uncles'?'

'Yeah. Just to sleep and eat there.'

'I see. All the same, two years ago, when the Littoriali were held at Ca' Foscari, I'm grateful you didn't come along. I mean it. It was the ghastliest day of my life.'

'How come? After all . . . I should tell you that at one moment, finding out you were performing, I did think of rushing off to be a bit of a *claque* for . . . the local flag. But listen, changing the subject: d'you remember that time on the Mura degli Angeli, out here, the year you were made to retake your maths exams in October? You must have sobbed your eyes out, *poor little fellow*: you had such eyes! I wanted to console you. It even crossed my mind to get you to climb over the wall and come into the garden. And what reason did you have for not coming in? I know you didn't, but I can't remember why.'

'Because someone disturbed us at the crucial moment.'

'Oh yes, Perotti, the gardener, that dog of a Perotti.'

'Gardener? Coachman, I seem to recall.'

'Gardener, coachman, *chauffeur*, doorman, everything.'

'Is he still alive?'

'Are you kidding?!'

'And the dog, the actual dog, the one that barked?'

'Who? Jor?'

'Yes, the Great Dane.'

'Yes he's also alive and vegetating.'

She had repeated her brother's invitation ('I don't know if Alberto has called you, but why not come round for a bit of a knock-up at our house?'), but without insisting, and without the slightest mention, in contrast to him, of the Marchese Barbicinti's letter. She mentioned nothing but the real pleasure of seeing each other again after such a long time, and of enjoying together, in the teeth of so many things that might prevent it, whatever good times were still possible while the season lasted.

2

I wasn't the only one to be invited.

When, that Saturday afternoon, I emerged at the end of Corso Ercole I (I'd avoided the Giovecca and the town centre, and come round by way of the near-ish Piazza della Certosa), I immediately noted in the shade in front of the Finzi-Continis' gateway a small group of tennis players. There were five of them, four boys and a girl, who'd also come by bike. My lips drew back in a grimace of disappointment. Who were these people? Apart from one whom I didn't even know by sight, older, around twenty-five, with a pipe between his teeth, long white linen trousers and a brown corduroy jacket, the others, all of them in coloured pullovers and shorts, had the look of regular players at the Eleonora d'Este. They had just arrived and were waiting to be let in. But since the gate had still not been opened, every now and then they would leave off their loud chatter and laughter and, as a sign of light-hearted protest, rhythmically ring their bicycle bells.

I was tempted to slope off. Too late. They'd already stopped ringing their bells and begun to stare at me with interest. One of them whom, as I approached, I recognized with a glance to be Bruno Lattes, was even greeting me by waving his racket at the end of his long and extremely skinny arm. He wanted to be recognized, though we had never been great friends – he was two years younger than me, and we hadn't seen much of each other even at Bologna, in the Literature Department – and at the same time to usher me forwards.

By this stage I'd come to a halt, face to face with Bruno, my left hand leaning on the smooth oak of the gate.

'Good afternoon,' I said and grinned. 'What brings this gathering here today? Has the open tournament ended by any chance? Or have you all been knocked out?'

My tone and words had been carefully chosen. In the meantime I was observing them one by one. I looked at Adriana Trentini, her lovely, very blond hair, her long tapering legs – magnificent legs, admittedly, but their skin was too white and speckled with strange red patches that always surfaced when she was hot. I looked at the taciturn young man in the linen trousers and brown jacket (certainly not from Ferrara, I told myself). I looked at the other two boys, much younger than him and even than Adriana, the two of them still at school perhaps or at the Technical College, and so, having 'moved up' during the last year when, bit by bit, I'd removed myself from every circle of the city, they were pretty well unknown to me. And I looked at last at Bruno, there in front of me, ever taller and drier, and because of his ever swarthier skin like a vibrant, nervous, young black. And that day, too, he was prey to such nervous agitation he was able to transmit the force of it through the light contact of the two front tyres of our bikes.

Between the two of us passed the inevitable quick glance of Jewish complicity which, partly in anxiety and partly in distaste, I had already foreseen. Still looking at him, I then added:

'I trust that before venturing out to play on foreign soil you have asked *Signor* Barbicinti's permission.'

The unknown young man, the one not from Ferrara, astonished at my sarcastic tone or because he felt uneasy, moved a little to the side of me. Instead of holding me back, this only spurred me on.

'Please, put my mind at rest', I insisted, 'that this is an absence with proper leave and not a great escape.'

'What are you saying!' Adriana interrupted with her usual recklessness – quite innocent, but no less irritating for that. 'Don't you know what happened last Wednesday, during the mixed doubles' finals? Don't tell me you weren't there, and why not give your eternal Vittorio Alfieri[1] pose a rest. While we were playing, I saw you among the spectators. I saw you clearly.'

'I wasn't there at all,' I replied drily. 'I haven't hung around the place for at least a year.'

'And why not?'

'Because I was sure one day or another I'd be chucked out anyway. And in fact I wasn't wrong. Here's the little document of expulsion.'

I took the envelope out of my jacket pocket.

'I assume you'll have received one too,' I added, turning to Bruno.

It was only then that Adriana seemed to remember. She twisted her lips. But the chance of breaking important news to me, which I was evidently uninformed about, quickly banished any other thought of hers.

'He needs to be told,' she said.

She sighed, lifting her eyes towards the sky.

Something very unpleasant had happened – she then began to tell me in a schoolmistressy voice, whilst one of the younger boys turned to press the gate's sharp little buzzer made of black horn. All right, I didn't know but, in the open tournament which started halfway through last week and was now over, she and Bruno had reached the finals – no less – a thing of which no one had ever dreamt they might be capable. And then? The final was under way when things took the strangest of turns (honestly, it would make your eyes pop out: Désirée Baggioli and Claudio Montemezzo, two great hopes of the game put in difficulty by a non-classified pair, so much so that they'd lost the first set ten–eight, and were finding the going very tough in the second) when suddenly, by an unprecedented decision of the Marchese Barbicinti, acting on his own behalf, as ever the arbitrating judge of the tournament, and once more, in short, the Big Chief, the game was brought to a sudden halt. It was six o'clock, and admittedly the visibility wasn't good. But not so bad that they couldn't have gone on for at least another couple of games. Good Lord, was this the way things should be done? At four games to two in the second set of an important match, he had no right, in the absence of proof to the contrary, to suddenly shout 'Stop play!', to rush onto the court with his arms spread wide, proclaiming the match suspended because of 'the impending darkness' and postponing the continuance of play and the conclusion of the match to the afternoon of the day after. And besides, the Marchese was hardly acting in good faith. Even if she hadn't already noticed at the end of the first set that he was in cahoots with that 'black soul' Gino Cariani, the GUF[2] secretary – they had drawn slightly apart from the crowd alongside the small pavilion for the changing rooms – and that same Cariani, perhaps to be less conspicuous, had been standing with his back completely turned to the court – if this wasn't enough to tell you, the expression on the Marchese's face when he bent to open the little entry gate, so pale and shocked she'd never seen anything like it, 'he looked a right little wimp', it would have been clear as day to her that the 'impending darkness' was nothing but the feeblest excuse, 'utter bullshit'. Was there really any doubt about it? Nothing further was said of the interrupted match, although Bruno, the morning after, had also received the same registered delivery letter that I'd had; 'the one I wanted to show her'. And she, Adriana, had been left so disgusted and indignant with the whole thing that she'd sworn never again to set foot in the Eleonora d'Este, at least for a good while. Did they have something against Bruno? If they did, they could easily have stopped him entering the tournament in the first place. They could have been straight with him and said: 'Because of the way things are, we're sorry but we can't let you take part.' But with the tournament already begun, and nearly finished, and not only that: him a mere hair's breadth away from winning one of the titles, they should never have behaved the way they did. Four–two. What daylight robbery! The kind of filthy trick you'd expect from complete Zulus, not civilized, well-brought-up people.

Adriana Trentini talked on, ever more fervently, and now and then Bruno would put in a word and add some details.

In his view the match was stopped thanks mainly to Cariani, from whom, as anyone who knew him could tell, one could hardly expect anything else. It was only too obvious: a half-pint nobody like him, with his bird-boned look and consumptive's chest, whose only thought, from the first moment he'd got into the GUF, had been to carve out a career for himself, and so he'd never missed an opportunity, in public or in private, of licking the Federal Secretary's boots. (Hadn't I seen him at the Caffè della Borsa on the rare occasions he managed to sit at the small table of the 'old heavies of the *Bombamano*'?[3] He'd puff himself up, curse, unleash swear words bigger than himself, but as soon as the consul Bolognesi, or Sciagura,[4] or some other bigshot of the group contradicted him, you could see him quickly put his tail between his legs and, just to be forgiven and return to favour, he'd be ready to fawn and take on the most servile tasks, like scurrying off to the tobacconist to buy a packet of Giubek for the Federal Secretary, or telephoning the 'Sciagura household' to warn his 'ex-washerwoman wifey' of the great man's imminent return . . .). A 'worm of that ilk' would certainly not pass up a chance, you could bet your life on it, to ingratiate himself with the Party once again! The Marchese Barbicinti was what you'd expect – a venerable sort, agreed, but rather lacking in 'grey matter', and anything but a hero. If they kept him on to run the Eleonora d'Este they did so because he looked the part, and above all for his name, which to them must have represented some glorious lure for the unwary. So it must have been a great laugh for Cariani to put the wind up the doddery old gent. Perhaps he'll have said to him 'And tomorrow? Has it crossed your mind, Marchese, what will happen tomorrow evening when the Federal Secretary'll be here for the dance party, and will have to give a . . . Lattes that splendid silver cup and the customary Roman salute? For my part, I can foresee a terrible scandal. And big trouble, endless trouble. If I was in your place, given that it's starting to get dark, I wouldn't hesitate to stop the match.' It wouldn't have needed any more than that, 'it's a dead cert', to have prompted him to bring the tournament to that grotesque and abrupt end.

Before Adriana and Bruno had finished bringing me up to date with these events (and whilst doing so Adriana even managed to introduce me to the burly stranger: Malnate he was called, Giampiero Malnate, a recently qualified chemist working at one of the new synthetic rubber factories in the industrial zone), the big gate finally opened. A man of about sixty appeared on the threshold, big, stocky, with grey hair cut short, from which the half-past-two sun, gushing in a bright stream through the vertical gap behind him, extracted luminous metallic reflections. He had a moustache equally short and grey under a fleshy, violet nose – a bit like Hitler's, it struck me, both the nose and the little moustache. It was him in person, old Perotti – gardener, coachman, *chauffeur*, doorman, the whole lot and more, just as Micòl had described him. He had not changed in the least since my time at the Guarini when, enthroned on the box-seat, he waited impassively till the school's dark and menacing cave mouth, which had swallowed up his little, fearless, smiling 'charges', finally decided to restore them, no less serene and self-confident, to the vehicle made of glass, varnish, nickel-plating, padded material, fine planished hardwoods – exactly like a precious casket – whose conservation and conveyance were entirely his responsibility. His little eyes, sharp and grey as his hair, sparkling with a Venetian peasant's canny hardness, still seemed to be laughing good-naturedly beneath his thick, almost black, eyebrows, exactly as they had been. But at what, this time? Because we had been left there waiting for at least ten minutes? Or at himself, kitted out in a striped jacket and white gloves – all brand new and perhaps donned especially for the occasion?

And so we entered, and were welcomed on the other side of the gate, which was shut with a sudden massive bang at the hands of the assiduous Perotti, by the heavy barking of Jor, the black-and-white Great Dane. He came down along the driveway, the huge dog, then trotted alongside us with an air that wasn't in the least intimidating. But nevertheless Bruno and Adriana fell silent.

'He doesn't bite, does he?' asked Adriana fearfully.

'Don't worry yourself, Signorina,' Perotti replied. 'With the three or four teeth he still has left, it's not like he's fit to bite anything, not even polenta some days . . .'

Whilst the decrepit Jor, halted in the middle of the drive in a sculptural pose, fixed us with his frosty, expressionless eyes, one dark the other light-blue, Perotti began to offer excuses. He was sorry to have made us wait – he said. It wasn't his fault, but the fault of the electric current, which didn't always work (but luckily Signorina Micòl had suspected as much and had sent him to check whether by chance we'd arrived), apart from the distance, which regrettably was more than half a kilometre. He couldn't ride a bicycle, but once Signorina Micòl got something into her head . . .

He sighed, rolled his eyes, and once more smiled, who knows why, disclosing from between his thin lips a toothscape as compact and strong as the Great Dane's was feeble. Meanwhile, with his raised arm, he pointed out the driveway which, after a hundred metres, advanced into a thicket of rattan palms. Even for those who could use a bicycle, he warned, it would take three or four minutes just to arrive at the 'Palazzo'.

3

We were really very lucky with the season. For ten or twelve days the weather remained perfect, held in that state of magical suspension, of glassy, luminous, soft immobility which is the special gift of some of our autumns. In the garden it was hot, just slightly less than if it was summer. Whoever wanted to could go on playing tennis until half past five or later, without fear that the evening damp, so marked towards November, would damage the gut strings of the racket. At that hour, naturally, you could hardly see a thing. And yet the light that continued to shed a golden hue down at the foot of the grassy inclines of the Mura degli Angeli, which were overrun, especially on Sundays, with a quiet, many-coloured crowd (kids chasing a ball, maids knitting away beside prams, soldiers on leave, lovers in search of places where they could kiss), that last light tempted you to keep on playing, regardless of whether you were all but blind. The day was still not over; surely it was worth playing on just a little longer.

We came back every afternoon, announcing our visits by a phone call at first, then not even that; and always the same group, with the occasional exception of Giampiero Malnate, who had known Alberto since 1933, in Milan, and contrary to what I'd thought that first day, meeting him in front of the Finzi-Continis' gate, not only had he never before set eyes on the four youngsters who accompanied him, but neither had he anything at all to do with the Eleonora d'Este, or with its vice-president and secretary, the Marchese Ippolito Barbicinti.

The days seemed excessively beautiful and yet at the same time undermined by the approaching winter. To lose even one of them would be a real crime. Without making an appointment with each other, we always arrived around two, immediately after lunch. Often, in the first days, it so happened that we all once again found each other in a group in front of the gate, waiting for Perotti to come and open it. But the introduction, after something like a week, of an intercom and a remote-controlled unlocking device meant that, the entry into the garden no longer being problematic, we would arrive in ones or twos, as chance would have it. As for me, I didn't miss a single afternoon; not even to follow one of my usual courses in Bologna. The same went for the others, as far as I can recall. Neither Bruno Lattes, nor Adriana Trentini, nor Carletto Sani, nor Tonino Collevatti, whose number was increased, as well as by my brother Ernesto, by another three or four boys and girls. The only one, as I've said, who came less regularly was *the* Giampiero Malnate (as Micòl began to call him, and soon enough the rest of us followed suit). He had to keep to the factory's hours, he explained on one occasion: it wasn't that strict, admittedly, considering that the Montecatini plant where he worked had not, to date, produced a single kilo of synthetic rubber, but all the same it was a schedule. Whatever the cause, his absences never lasted for more than two days in succession. Besides, he was the only one, myself excepted, who did not seem that bothered about playing tennis (and to be honest he was not much of a player), and was often quite content, when he appeared on his bike after work, to umpire a match or to sit apart with Alberto, smoking a pipe and talking.

Our hosts were even more assiduous than we were. We might sometimes arrive before the Piazza's distant clock struck two: however soon we got there, we were sure to find them already on court, not playing each other, as they had been doing that Saturday when we came out into the clearing behind the house where the court was, but busy checking that everything was in order, the net at the right height, the clay well rolled and the lines swept, the balls in good condition, or else stretched out on two deckchairs with wide straw hats on their heads, motionlessly sunbathing. They could not have behaved better if they had been the owners of the house, although it was clear that tennis, as physical exercise, as a sport, interested them only up to a certain point. Despite this, they stayed on till the final match (always at least one of them, but sometimes both) without ever taking their leave earlier on the pretext of an engagement, or because of some duty, or feeling unwell. Some evenings it was actually they, in almost total darkness, who would insist on playing 'another couple of points, the last ones!' and would shepherd back on court whoever was on the point of deserting it.

As Carletto Sani and Tonino Collevatti had immediately declared, without bothering to lower their voices, it wasn't as if the court itself was anything special.

Being fifteen-year-olds, too young to have had any experience of tennis courts other than those which deservedly filled the Marchese Barbicinti with pride, they immediately began to expatiate on the many shortcomings of this kind of 'potato patch' (as one of them had called it, curling his upper lip with distaste). These were: practically no backcourt area, especially behind the far service line; a bumpy surface and, to make things worse, poor drainage, so even a little rain would turn it into a quagmire; no evergreen hedge to reinforce the surrounding wire fence.

Despite all this, no sooner had they finished their 'duel to the death' (Micòl hadn't managed to stop her brother reaching five-all, and at this point they stopped play) than they leapt in to denounce these same defects, not just without a shadow of reserve but with a sort of bizarre self-lacerating enthusiasm, as though the two of them were in competition.

Oh yes, Micòl had remarked, while she was still drying her hot face with a thick towel, for people like us, 'spoilt' by the red-clay courts of the Eleonora d'Este, it must be very hard to feel at ease on their dusty potato patch! And the backcourt space? How could we play with so little room behind us? What an abyss of decadence we poor folk had fallen into! But she had no reason to reproach herself. She had told her father innumerable times that the wire netting all round needed to be set back at least another three metres. But would he listen? He, her father, had always hedged, falling back each time on a typical farmer's perspective, which thinks that earth not used for planting things in is merely thrown away (also predictably bringing up the fact that she and Alberto had played on this sorry excuse for a court since they were children and so they could perfectly well continue to play on it as grown-ups). All that effort for nothing! But now things had changed. Now they had guests, 'illustrious guests'. A good reason for her to take up the cause again with renewed vigour, wearing down and tormenting her 'grey-haired progenitor' so much that by next spring she felt confident she could guarantee that she and Alberto would be able to offer us 'something more worthy'.

She spoke more than ever in her characteristic mode, and grinned. We had no other option but to deny it, and reassure her in unison that on the contrary everything, the court included, was absolutely fine, better than fine, also praising to the skies this green corner of the grounds, beside which the remaining private parks, Duke Massari's included (it was Bruno who remarked on it, just at the moment when Micòl and Alberto were leaving the court, holding hands), faded into so many neatly tended, bourgeois gardens.

If the truth must be told, the tennis court was far from 'worthy', and besides, being just one, it forced us all to take overlong breaks off-court. Thus, at four o'clock on the dot every afternoon, perhaps above all so that the two fifteen-year-olds of our very mixed company should not miss the hours of much more intense sporting activity that they might otherwise have passed under the wing of the Marchese Barbicinti, Perotti would invariably appear, his bullish neck tense and flushed from the effort of holding upright in his gloved hands a huge silver tray.

That tray was overflowing: rolls of anchovy spread, smoked salmon, caviare, paté de foie gras, pork prosciutto; with little vol-au-vents filled with a sauce of chicken and béchamel; with tiny *buricchi* which must have come from the prestigious little kosher pastry-shop which Signora Betsabea, the famous Signora Betsabea (Da Fano) had run for decades in Via Mazzini to the pride and delight of the entire citizenry. And that wasn't the end of it. The good Perotti had still to lay out the contents of the tray on the wickerwork table already prepared for this, in front of the court's side entrance, beneath a broad parasol in red and blue segments, which was attended to by one of his daughters, either Dirce or Gina, both about the same age as Micòl, and both in service 'at home', Dirce as a maid, Gina as cook. (The two male children, Titta and Bepi, the first about thirty, the second eighteen, took care of the park in the dual role of park and kitchen gardeners, and the most we ever saw of them was their bending figures, working in the distance, when they would turn the beam of their blue ironic eyes in our direction as we passed by on bikes – we never managed any contact beyond that.) She, the daughter, in her turn, had brought along with her, down the path which led from the *magna domus* to the tennis court, a trolley with rubber wheels, also laden with decanters, jugs, beakers and glasses. Within the porcelain and pewter jugs were tea, milk and coffee, and within the Bohemian cut-glass decanters, beaded with pearls of moisture, was lemonade, fruit juice and *Skiwasser* – this last a thirst-quenching drink made of water and raspberry syrup in equal measures, with the addition of a slice of lemon and a few grapes, which Micòl preferred to all other drinks and on which she particularly prided herself.

Oh, that *Skiwasser*! In the breaks between games, besides guzzling the odd roll which always, and not without a show of religious nonconformism, she chose from among those filled with pork prosciutto, Micòl would often throw back a whole glass of her favourite 'drinkette', continually prompting us to do the same, 'in homage', as she would say laughing, 'to the deceased Austro-Hungarian Empire'. The recipe, she told us, had been given to her in Austria itself, at Offgastein, in the winter of 1934: the only winter that she and Alberto 'in coalition' had been allowed to go on their own for a fortnight to ski. And though *Skiwasser*, as the name testified, was a winter drink, for which reason it should have been served boiling hot, still, even in Austria there were some people who in summer, so as not to stop drinking it, drank it this way, in icy 'draughts' but without the slice of lemon, and then they called it *Himbeerwasser*.

However that was, we should take note, she added and raised a finger with comic emphasis, it was by her own initiative that the grapes – 'indispensable!' – had been added to the classic Tyrolean recipe. It was her idea, and she stood by it – it was no laughing matter. The grapes stood for Italy's special contribution to the holy noble cause of *Skiwasser*, or rather of this, to put it more precisely, special 'Italian variant, not to mention Ferrarese, not to mention . . . etc., etc.'

4

It took some time before the other denizens of the house let themselves be seen.

Speaking of which, something strange occurred even that first day, which I only remembered halfway through the week after, when the fact that neither Professor Ermanno nor Signora Olga had turned up made me suspect that all those whom Adriana Trentini called, en masse, 'the old guard', had reached a unanimous decision to keep their distance from the tennis playing – perhaps so as not to embarrass us, or, who knows, so as not to disturb by their presence parties which in the end were not really parties but simply gatherings of the youngsters in the garden.

The curious event occurred right at the start, a short while after we had taken our leave of Perotti and Jor, who remained there watching us cycle into the distance along the driveway. Having crossed the Panfilio canal by way of a strange, stocky bridge of black girders, our two-wheeled patrol had then come within two hundred metres of the lonely Neo-Gothic hulk of the *magna domus*, or, to be more precise, of the sad, gravel-covered forecourt which, completely in the shade, extended before it, when all our attention was drawn to two motionless figures right in the middle of the forecourt: an old woman seated in an armchair, with a heap of cushions supporting her back and a young woman, blond and buxom, who looked like a maid, standing behind her. As soon as she saw us advancing, the old woman was shaken by a kind of start. After this, she immediately began a series of sweeping gestures with her arms to signal no, we shouldn't keep going ahead towards the forecourt where she was, given that there, behind her, there was nothing but the house itself, but rather we should take a left turn down the path covered by a trellis of small climbing roses which she pointed out to us, at the end of which (Micòl and Alberto were already playing: couldn't we hear from where we were the regular thunks their rackets made as they knocked the ball back and forth?) we should automatically arrive at the tennis court. She was Signora Regina Herrera, Signora Olga's mother. I had already recognized her from the singularly brilliant whiteness of the thick hair gathered up at the nape of her neck, hair which I'd admired every time I'd seen it at the Temple since I'd first glimpsed it through the grating of the women's gallery as a young child. She waved her arms and her hands with hectic energy, at the same time signing to the girl, who it turned out was Dirce, to help her up. She was tired of being there: she wanted to go back in. And the maid obeyed her order with unhesitating solicitude.

One evening, however, contrary to all expectations, it was Professor Ermanno and Signora Olga who appeared. They gave the impression of having passed the tennis court by sheer chance, returning after a long stroll in the grounds. They were arm in arm. Smaller than his wife, and much more stooped than he had been ten years earlier, at the time of our whispered conversation from one bench to another in the Italian School synagogue, the Professor was wearing one of his usual light linen suits with a black-banded panama hat tilted down over the thick lenses of his pince-nez, and leaning, as he walked, on a bamboo cane. Dressed in mourning, the Signora was carrying in her arms a thick bunch of chrysanthemums gathered in some remote part of the garden during their walk. She pressed them against and across her breast, wreathing them with her right arm in a tenderly possessive, almost maternal manner. Although still straight, and a whole head taller than her husband, she too had aged considerably. Her hair had grown uniformly grey – an ugly, dismal grey. Beneath her bony projecting brow her coal-black eyes shone as ever with a stricken, fanatical ardour.

Those of us who were sitting around the sunshade rose to our feet, and those who were playing stopped.

'Please don't put yourselves out,' the Professor began in his kind and musical tones. 'Do please sit down, and don't let us disturb the game.'

He was not obeyed. Micòl and Alberto, but especially Micòl, saw to introducing us. Besides announcing our names and surnames, she lingered over whatever details concerning each of us might rouse her father's interest: most of all our occupations and studies. She had begun with me and Bruno Lattes, speaking about both of us in an exterior, remarkably objective manner, as though to stop her father, in this particular circumstance, from showing any possible sign of special recognition or favour. We were 'the two literary figures of the gang', 'salt of the earth'. She then moved on to Malnate. Here before us was a great example of devotion to science! – she exclaimed with ironic emphasis. Only chemistry, for which he nursed an evidently irresistible passion, could have induced him to leave a metropolis as full of opportunities as Milan (*'Milàn l'è on grand Milàn!'**) to bury himself in a 'mini-city' like our own.

'He works in the industrial zone,' Alberto explained, straightforward and serious. 'For a Montecatini plant.'

'They're meant to be producing synthetic rubber,' Micòl sniggered, 'but up till now it seems they haven't managed it.'

Professor Ermanno coughed. He pointed his finger at Malnate.

'You were a university friend of Alberto's, isn't that right?' he asked gently.

'Well, in a way,' he replied, agreeing with a nod. 'Though we were in different faculties, and I was three years ahead, but all the same we became great friends.'

'Of that I'm sure. My son has spoken of you very often. He's also told us of having been at your house many times, and of the great kindness and hospitality of your parents. Would you thank them on our behalf when you see them next? In the meantime we are delighted to have you here at our house. And do please come back . . . come here any time you'd like.'

He turned towards Micòl, and asked her, pointing to Adriana:

* Milanese dialect: 'What a big place Milan is!'

'And who is this young woman? If I'm not wrong she must be a Zanardi . . .'

The conversation proceeded in this manner until all the introductions had been made, including those of Carletto Sani and Tonino Collevatti, characterized by Micòl as 'the two great promises' of Ferrara's tennis circles. Finally Professor Ermanno and Signora Olga, who had stayed at her husband's side the whole time without saying a word, limiting herself to the occasional benevolent smile, made their way, still arm in arm, towards the house.

Although the Professor had taken his leave with a more than cordial 'See you soon!' it would not have crossed any of our minds to hold on too literally to that promise.

But the following Sunday, whilst Adriana Trentini and Bruno Lattes on one side of the net and Désirée Baggioli and Claudio Montemezzo on the other were most keenly contesting a match whose outcome, according to the declarations of Adriana, who had promoted and organized it, should 'at least morally' recompense her and Bruno for the dirty trick played on them by the Marchese Barbicinti (but the event was not turning out the same as before: Adriana and Bruno were losing, and rather badly): towards the end of the match, the entire 'old guard' emerged from out of the path of the climbing roses. They seemed like a small cortège. Leading them were Professor Ermanno and Signora Olga. They were followed, a little after, by the Herrera uncles from Venice: the first, with a cigarette between his thick protruding lips and his hands clasped behind his back, looking around him with the slightly embarrassed air of a town dweller who, against his will, has found himself in the countryside; and the second, a few yards further back, supporting Signora Regina on his arm and adjusting his stride to the snail-like pace of his mother. If the phthisiologist and the engineer were in Ferrara, I said to myself, it must be to attend some religious ceremony. But what? After Rosh Hashanah, which fell in October, I couldn't remember what rite there was in autumn. Succoth maybe? Probably. Unless the equally probable firing of the engineer Federico from the state railways had prompted the calling of a most unusual family reunion . . .

They sat down in a dignified manner, hardly making any noise. The only exception being Signora Regina. As soon as she had been settled down in a deckchair, she boomed out in a deaf person's voice a few words in their household jargon. She bewailed the *mucha* humidity of the garden at that time of day. But beside her, her son Federico was in attendance, and in an equally loud voice was ready to hush her up (though his had a neutral timbre: a tone of voice that my father also paraded on occasion when, in 'mixed' surroundings, he wanted to communicate exclusively with some member of the family). She should keep *callada*, that is, quiet. There were the *musafir*.

I moved close to Micòl's ear.

'I can manage to make out *"callada"*. But what on earth does *"musafir"* mean?'

'Guests,' she whispered in reply. 'But *goyische* ones.'

Then she smiled, childishly covering her mouth with her hand and winking: style Micòl 1929.

Later, at the end of the match, and after the 'new acquisitions' Désirée Baggioli and Claudio Montemezzo had been introduced in their turn, I happened to find myself apart with Professor Ermanno. The day was dying away across the park in its usual milky diffused shadows. I had moved some yards away from the court's little entrance gate. My eyes fixed on the distant Mura degli Angeli, I heard behind my back Micòl's sharp voice prevailing over all the others. Who knows who she was angry with or why.

'*Era già l'ora che volge il disìo . . .*'[1] an ironic quiet voice recited, very close by.

I turned round astonished. It was Professor Ermanno himself, seemingly happy to have startled me, and smiling good-naturedly. He gently took me by the arm, and thence, very slowly, keeping some way away from the wire-netting surround and every now and then coming to a halt, we began to walk round the tennis court. Having almost effected a complete tour, we retraced our steps. Back and forth, the darkness gradually deepening round us, we went through this same manoeuvre a number of times. Meanwhile we talked, or rather, for the most part, he, the Professor, talked.

He began by asking my opinion of the tennis court, if I really found it execrable. Micòl had no doubts on this subject: if he were to follow her advice, they'd have to give it a complete overhaul, utterly modernize it. For his part, he remained unsure. Maybe, as usual, his 'dear little whirlwind' was making too much of it. Maybe it wasn't absolutely necessary to turn everything upside down, as she seemed to want.

'In any case,' he added, 'in a few days it'll start to rain, no use pretending otherwise. Don't you think it might be better to put off whatever needs to be done until next year?'

This said, he went on to ask me what I was doing, and what my plans were for the immediate future. And how my parents were.

Whilst he was asking me about my 'Papa', I noticed two things. First of all that he was having difficulty in addressing me with 'tu', in fact a little while after, coming to an abrupt halt, he explicitly asked me if this was all right, and straight away, with some warmth and sincerity, I begged him not to use the 'lei' form with me, or I'd be upset. Secondly, that the interest and respect which showed in his voice and face whilst he was asking how my father was (especially in his eyes – the lenses of his glasses, magnifying them, emphasized the gravity and meekness of their expression) didn't seem at all forced, or the least bit hypocritical. He reminded me to pass on his best wishes. And his 'congratulations' as well – for the many trees that had been planted in our cemetery since my father had taken over responsibility for it. Regarding this, would some pine trees be of any use? Some cedars of Lebanon? Some fir trees? Or weeping willows? I should put it to my father. If by any chance they would be useful (these days, with the methods of modern agriculture, transplanting broad-trunked trees had become a simple matter), he would be only too pleased to provide whatever number were required. It was a wonderful idea, I had to admit! Thickly planted with lovely tall trees, even our cemetery would be able, in the course of time, to rival that of San Niccolò del Lido in Venice.

'Don't you know it?'

I replied that I didn't.

'Oh, but you must, you really must try to go there as soon as you can!' he insisted with much animation. 'It's a national monument! Besides, as a literary man, you'll most certainly remember the start of Giovanni Prati's *Edmenegarda*.'[2]

I was forced once again to confess my ignorance.

'Well,' the Professor continued, 'it's precisely there that Prati begins his *Edmenegarda*, in the Lido's Jewish cemetery, which in the nineteenth century was considered one of the most romantic sites in Italy. But make sure, if and when you do go, that you don't forget to tell the cemetery caretaker straight away (he's the one with the entrance keys) that you want to visit the *old* one, this is important, the old cemetery, where no one's been buried since the eighteenth century, and not the other, the modern one, next to it but quite separate. I discovered it in 1905, just imagine. Even though I was almost twice your present age, I was still unmarried. I was living at Venice (I'd been living there for two years), and I would go and visit the place, even in winter sometimes, whenever I wasn't at the State Archives burrowing through manuscripts concerning the various so-called 'Nations' into which the sixteenth- and seventeenth-century Venetian Jewish Community were divided – the Levantine Nation, the Northern, the German and the Italian. It's true I hardly ever went there on my own,' here he smiled, 'and that, in a certain sense, deciphering the gravestones one by one, many of which date back to the early sixteenth century, and are written in Spanish or Portuguese, I was continuing with my archival researches in the open air. Oh, they were delightful afternoons I spent there . . . what peace and serenity . . . with the small entrance, facing the Laguna, which opened only for us. We became engaged right there within the cemetery, Olga and myself.'

He remained silent for a short while. I took the opportunity to ask him what exactly was the subject of his archival research.

'At the outset I began with an idea of writing a history of the Venetian Jewry,' he replied, 'a subject which Olga herself had suggested to me, and which Roth, the English Jew Cecil Roth,[3] had treated so brilliantly some ten years later. But then, as often happens with historians who become too . . . passionately involved, some particular seventeenth-century documents which I came across began to engross all my attention, and ended up taking me off course. I'll tell you, I'll tell you all about it if you come back . . . It has the makings of a real novel, however you look at it . . . but, anyway, instead of the fat historical tome which I aspired to write, at the end of two years' work I hadn't managed to put together (apart from marrying, that is) anything but two pamphlets: one, that I still believe may be of use, in which I've gathered together all the cemetery's inscriptions, and the other in which I've made public the existence of those seventeenth-century papers I was telling you about, but only that, narrating the facts, without venturing on any interpretation with respect to them. Would you be interested in looking at them? Yes? One of these days you must let me present you with copies. But besides all this, please do go, I really recommend it, to the Jewish cemetery at the Lido (the *old* section, I repeat!). It's worth the trouble, you'll see. You'll find it just as it was thirty-five years ago, exactly the same.'

We turned back slowly towards the tennis court. At first sight, it seemed as though no one was left there. And yet, in the almost total darkness, Micòl and Carletto Sani were still playing. Micòl was complaining: apparently 'Cochet' was hitting the ball too hard, hardly the behaviour of a 'gentleman', and in that darkness it was 'frankly too much'.

'I heard from Micòl that you weren't sure whether to graduate in Art History or in Italian,' Professor Ermanno was saying to me in the meantime. 'So have you decided yet?'

I told him that I had, that I'd made up my mind to do my thesis in Italian. My uncertainty – I explained – had been due to the fact that up until a few days ago I'd still been hoping to be supervised by Professor Longhi, who had the chair in Art History, but that, at the last moment, he had put in for a two-year study leave away from teaching duties. The thesis I would have wanted to write under his supervision would have looked at a group of Ferrara painters in the second half of the fifteenth and the early sixteenth centuries: Scarsellino, Bastianino, Bastarolo, Bonone, Caletti, Calzolaretto and some others. Only with Longhi's guidance, writing on material like this, would I have had a chance to produce something of quality.

And so, since he, Longhi, had obtained two years of leave from the Ministry, it had seemed to me a better idea to fall back on some other thesis, but in the Italian department.

He had stood there listening to me, deep in thought.

'Longhi?' he asked finally, twisting his lips in doubt. 'What does this mean? Have they already appointed the new chair in Art History?

I didn't understand.

'But surely,' he insisted, 'the Professor of Art History at Bologna, I've always heard that it was Igino Benvenuto Supino, one of the most illustrious figures of Italian Jewry. So then . . .'

He had been – I interrupted – had been, until 1933. But after 1934, in place of Supino, put out to grass having passed his retirement age, they had called in Roberto Longhi. Didn't he know, I proceeded – happy this time to find *him* lacking in information – the crucial essays of Roberto Longhi on Piero della Francesca and on Caravaggio and his school? Didn't he know the *Officina ferrarese*, a work that had created such an uproar in 1933, at the time of the Ferrara Renaissance Exhibition held the same year in the Palazzo dei Diamanti? My thesis would have been based upon the last pages of the *Officina*, where the theme had been touched, albeit magisterially, but without full development.

I talked on, and Professor Ermanno, more hunched than ever, stood and listened to me in silence. What was he thinking about? About the number of 'illustrious' university figures which Italian Jewry had supplied from the Unification to the present time? Probably.

Suddenly I saw him grow animated.

Looking around, and lowering his voice to a stifled whisper, as if he were letting me into something no less than a state secret, he divulged the big news: that he possessed a batch of Carducci's unpublished letters, written by the poet to Professor Ermanno's mother in 1875. If I would be interested in seeing them, and if I considered them a fitting subject for a graduation thesis in Italian, he would be only to pleased to let me have them.

Thinking of Meldolesi, I couldn't help smiling. What had become of that essay he'd meant to send to the *Nuova antologia*? So after talking so much about it, had he actually managed to do nothing? Poor Meldolesi. Some years back he'd been transferred to the Minghetti in Bologna – to his great satisfaction, as can be imagined! One day I really would have to track him down . . .

Despite the darkness, Professor Ermanno realized I was smiling.

'Oh, I know, I know,' he said 'for some time you youngsters have had a low opinion of Giosuè Carducci! I know that you prefer figures such as Pascoli or D'Annunzio to him.'

It was easy for me to convince him that I'd been smiling for quite a different reason, that being disappointment. If I'd only known that some of Carducci's unpublished letters were to be found in Ferrara! Instead of proposing to Professor Calcaterra, as unfortunately I had already done, a thesis on Panzacchi, I could easily have suggested a 'Carducci in Ferrara' theme which would undoubtedly have been of more interest. But who knows: perhaps if I was to speak frankly to Professor Calcaterra, who was a very decent person, he might still let me switch from Panzacchi to Carducci without making too much of a fuss about it.

'When are you hoping to graduate?' Professor Ermanno finally asked me.

'I'm not sure. I'd like it to be next year in June. Don't forget that I, too, am *fuori corso*.'

He nodded several times in silence.

'*Fuori corso*?' he then sighed. 'Well, that's not so bad.'

He made a vague gesture with his hand, as if to say that, with all that was happening, both I and his children would have plenty of time on our hands, if not too much.

My father had been right. He didn't finally seem all that distressed by this fact. Quite the reverse.

5

It was Micòl who wanted to show me the garden. She was very keen on the idea. 'I'd say I had a certain right to do so,' she'd sniggered, looking at me.

It was not on that first day. I'd played tennis until late, and it was Alberto, when he had finished competing with his sister, who accompanied me as far as a kind of Alpine hut in miniature, half hidden in a thicket of fir trees and about a hundred metres away from the court – the *Hütte* as he and Micòl called it – and in this hut or *Hütte*, used as a changing-room, I'd been able to change, and later, as darkness fell, to take a hot shower and get dressed again.

But the next day, things fell out differently. A doubles match with Adriana Trentini and Bruno Lattes playing against the two fifteen-year-olds (with Malnate perched atop the umpire's chair playing the role of patient scorer) had quickly assumed the guise of one of those games that never end.

'What should we do?' Micòl had asked me at a certain point, rising to her feet. 'I've the impression that it'll be a good hour before you, me, Alberto and our friend the Milanese will get a chance to swap places on court. Listen: what if during the wait us two were to slope off for a brief tour of the plants?' As soon as the court's free – she had added – Alberto will be sure to call us. He'd stick three fingers in his mouth, and honour us all with his famous whistle!

Smiling, she had already turned towards Alberto, who was stretched out nearby on a third deckchair with his face hidden beneath a straw hat and dozing off in the sun.

'Isn't that so, Sir Pasha?'

From under his hat Sir Pasha had agreed with a nod of his head, and we went off together. Yes, her brother was remarkable – Micòl meanwhile continued explaining. When circumstances required, the whistles he could come up with were so ear-shattering that beside them those of shepherds were merely laughable. It was odd though, wasn't it, that someone like him could do that? Just looking, you wouldn't think much of him. And yet . . . who knows where he fetched up all that breath from!

And so it was, nearly always whiling away the wait between one match and the next, that we began our long forays together. The first times we took our bikes with us. The garden being 'some' ten hectares in size, and the driveways, large and small, extending over a dozen or so kilometres, a bicycle was, to say the least, indispensable, my fellow traveller had promptly declared. True, today – she admitted – we'll limit ourselves to a 'survey' down there, towards the sunset, where she and Alberto, as children, often used to go to watch the trains being shunted in the station. But if we went on foot, how, even today, would we manage to get back? We'd risk being caught out by Alberto's 'oliphant', without the chance of getting ourselves back with the required dispatch.

So that first day we went to watch the trains manoeuvring in the station. And then? Then we turned back, round by the tennis court, across the forecourt of the *magna domus* (deserted as always and sadder than ever) and, doubling back, we went beyond the dark wooden bridge over the Panfilio canal, took the entrance driveway back till we reached the tunnel of rattan palms and the gate on Corso Ercole I. Having arrived here, Micòl insisted that we thread our way down the winding path that followed right round the surrounding wall: first to the left, alongside the Mura degli Angeli, so far that in a quarter of an hour we had again reached that zone of the park from which the station was visible, and from there we explored the opposite side, far more wild and rather dark and melancholy, which flanked the deserted Via Arianuova. We were there, making our way with some difficulty through the ferns, nettles and thorny bushes, when suddenly in the distance behind the thick mesh of tree trunks Alberto's sheep-herding whistle was heard calling us back with all haste to our 'hard labours'.

With a few variations in the route, we repeated these far-flung expeditions a number of times in the afternoons that followed. When space permitted it, we pedalled alongside each other. And meanwhile we talked – mostly about trees, at least to begin with.

This was a subject I knew nothing, or almost nothing, about – which caused Micòl no end of astonishment. She looked at me as though I was some kind of monster.

'Is it possible you can be so uninformed?' she exclaimed. 'Surely you must have studied a little botany at school!'

'Let's see now,' she pursued the point, her eyebrows ready to rise at some further, shocking lapse. 'May I enquire, please, what kind of tree milord thinks that one down there is?'

She might just as well have been singling out an honest elm or a native lime tree as some exceptionally rare African, Asiatic or American plant which only a specialist would be able to identify, since they had everything there, at the Barchetto del Duca, absolutely everything. As for me, I always replied at random: partly because I seriously couldn't distinguish an elm from a lime tree, and partly because I realized that nothing gave her more pleasure than seeing me make a mistake.

It seemed absurd to her that such a person as myself existed in the world without sharing her own feelings of passionate admiration for trees, 'those huge, quiet, strong, profound beings'. How could I not *understand*, good Lord, how come I didn't *feel* it? At the end of the tennis clearing, for example, to the west of the court, there was a group of seven slender, extremely tall *Washingtoniae graciles*, or desert palms, separated from the rest of the greenery behind (the usual thick-trunked trees of the European forest: oaks, ilexes, plane trees, horse chestnuts, etc.), surrounded by a good stretch of lawn. Every time we passed nearby, Micòl always had some new words of tenderness for the isolated group of *Washingtoniae*.

'There they are, my seven dear old men,' she might say. 'Look what venerable beards they have!'

But seriously – she would insist – didn't they seem even to me like the seven hermits of the Thebaid,[1] dried up by the sun and by fasting? What elegance, what *saintliness* they had in their brown, dry, curved, scaly trunks! Truly they seemed like so many John the Baptists, dieting on nothing but locusts.

But her sympathies, as I've already said, were not limited to exotic trees.[2]

For one enormous plane tree, with a whitish, warty trunk thicker than any other in the garden, and I believe than any in the entire province, her admiration overflowed into reverence. Naturally it hadn't been her 'grandma Josette' who'd planted it, but Ercole I d'Este in person, or maybe even Lucrezia Borgia.

'It's almost five hundred years old, can you imagine that?' she sighed, narrowing her eyes. 'Just think for a moment all it must have witnessed since it first saw the light!'

Then it seemed as though the gigantic plane tree also had eyes and ears: eyes to see us with, and ears to hear us.

For the fruit trees, for which a large tract of ground had been reserved, protected from the north winds and exposed to the sun in the immediate shelter of the Mura degli Angeli, Micòl nursed an affection very like – I'd noticed – that which she showed towards Perotti and all the members of his family. She spoke to me of them, of those humble domestic plants, with the same good nature, the same patience, and often having recourse to local dialect, which she adopted only in her relations to Perotti, or to Titta and Bepi, whenever we should happen to meet them, and stop to exchange a few words. We ritually stopped every time before a large plum tree with a mighty trunk like an oak's – her favourite. *'Il brogn sèrbi'*, the sour plums, which grew on that plum tree over there, she told me, had always seemed extraordinary to her, since her childhood. She preferred them to any Lindt chocolate. Then, when she was sixteen, she lost all desire for them, they no longer gave her any pleasure, and today she'd rather have Lindt chocolates or for that matter non-Lindt chocolates (but bitter ones, only bitter ones) to *'brogne'*. In the same fashion, apples were *'i pum'*, figs *'i figh'*, apricots *'il mugnàgh'*, peaches *'il pèrsagh'*. Only dialect could do justice to these things. Only the dialect word would allow her, in naming trees and fruits, to bunch up her lips in a heartfelt grimace somewhere between tenderness and mockery.

Later, when tree-spotting was exhausted, 'the pious pilgrimages' began. And since all pilgrimages, according to Micòl, had to be undertaken on foot (otherwise what kind of pilgrimages would they be, for heaven's sake?), we stopped using our bikes. And so we would walk, nearly always accompanied every step of the way by Jor.

To start with I was taken to see a small, lone landing-stage on the Panfilio canal, hidden amongst a thick growth of willows, white poplars and arum lilies. From that tiny dock, completely embayed with a mossy terracotta bench, it was likely that in the old days they might have set sail for the River Po as well as for the Castello's Moat. And she and Alberto themselves had even set sail from there when they were children, Micòl told me, for long excursions in a two-paddle canoe. By boat, they had never got as far as the foot of the Castello's towers (I was quite aware that nowadays the Panfilio only reached the Castello's Moat by way of underwater channels). But that hadn't stopped them getting as far as the Po, right up to Isola Bianca. Now, *ça va sans dire*, there was no point in thinking of using the canoe any more: it was partly stove-in, covered in dust, reduced to being 'the ghost of a canoe'. Some time I'd be able to see it in the coach-house when she remembered to take me there. However the landing-stage bench she'd always, always, kept going back to. Perhaps because she was still using it to prepare for her exams, utterly undisturbed, when it was hot, or perhaps because . . . The fact was that this spot had always remained in some way *hers*, and hers only – her own secret refuge.

Another time we ended up at the Perottis, who lived in a real farmhouse between the big house and the fruit groves.

We were received by old Perotti's wife, Vittorina, a sad, wan-looking *arzdòra*,* thin as a rake and of an indefinable age, and by Italia, the wife of Titta, the elder son. She was a plump, robust thirty-year-old from Codigoro, with light-blue, watery eyes and red hair. Seated on the threshold in a wicker chair, and surrounded by a crowd of chickens, she was breast-feeding, and Micòl leant down to caress the baby.

---

* Ferrarese dialect: roughly speaking, matriarch.

As she did so, she asked Vittorina in dialect: 'And so, when are you going to ask me back to eat some more of that bean soup?'

'Whenever you'd like, *sgnurina*. Long as you're happy with . . .'

'We should really arrange it one of these days,' Micòl replied seriously. 'You ought to know', she added turning to me, 'that Vittorina makes these *monster* bean soups. With braised pork crackling of course . . .'

She laughed and said:

'D'you want to have a look at the cowshed. We have a *good* half-dozen cows.'

Preceded by Vittorina we made our way towards the cowshed. The *arzdòra* opened the door with a huge key she kept in the pocket of her black apron, then stepped aside to let us pass. As we crossed the threshold I was aware of a furtive look she gave the two of us – a look that seemed troubled but at the same time secretly pleased.

A third pilgrimage was devoted to the sacred places of the *'vert paradis des amours enfantines'*.[3]

In the previous days we had passed by those parts several times, but always on bikes, and never stopping there. There it is – Micòl then told me, pointing with her finger – the very spot on the outer wall where she used to lean the ladder, and there were the 'notches' ('Yes sir, the notches') she'd use when, as it fell out, the ladder wasn't available.

'Don't you think we should have a commemorative plaque placed here?' she asked me.

'I suppose you'll have already worked out the wording.'

'It's almost there. "Here in this place, avoiding the vigilance of two enormous hounds . . ."'

'Stop. You were mentioning a plaque, but from the way it's going I reckon you'll need a big inscription stone like the Bollettino della Vittoria. The second line's far too long.'

A quarrel sprang from this. I took the part of the stubborn interrupter, and she, raising her voice and behaving like a spoilt child, went on to accuse me of the 'usual pedantry'. It was clear – she cried out – that I'd *sniffed out* her intention to leave my name off the plaque, and so, out of pure jealousy, I wasn't even willing to hear her out.

Then we calmed down. She began once more to talk of when she and Alberto were children. If I really wanted to know the truth, both she and Alberto had always felt equally envious of those, like me, who had the good fortune to study in a state school. Didn't I believe her? It had come to such a point with them that every year they anxiously awaited exam time just for the pleasure of being able to go to school like other children.

'Then how come if you both so wanted to go to school that you went on studying at home?' I asked.

'Papa and Mamma, particularly Mamma, were dead set against it. Mamma has always had an obsession with germs. She claimed that schools were specially made to disseminate the most frightful diseases, and it never helped at all that Uncle Giulio, whenever he came here, tried to persuade her that this wasn't so. Uncle Giulio would tease her, even though he's a doctor, and doesn't have much faith in medicine, but rather believes in the inevitability and usefulness of diseases. There was no way that he could convince Mamma, after the great misfortune of Guido, our little older brother who died before Alberto and I were born, in 1914. After that he didn't dare touch on the subject! Later, as you can guess, we rebelled a bit: we managed to go to university, the two of us, and even to Austria to ski, one winter, as I think I've already told you. But as children, what could we do? I often used to escape (but not Alberto – he's always been a good deal more placid than me, and much more obedient). Besides, one day I stayed out a bit too long, on a trip round the walls, getting a lift from a group of boys on their bicycle crossbars. When I got home, and saw how desperate they were, Mamma and Papa, from that time on (as Micòl was such a good sort, with a heart of gold!) from that time on, I decided to be well behaved and have never skived off again. The only relapse was that June of 1929 in *your* honour, my dear sir!'

'And I thought I was the only one,' I sighed.

'Well, if not the only one, certainly the last. And besides, as far as entering the garden goes, I've never invited anyone else in.'

'Is that the truth?'

'I swear it is. I was always looking in your direction, at the Temple
... when you turned round to talk to Papa and Alberto you had
such blue eyes! In my heart of hearts I'd even given you a nickname.'

'A nickname? And what would that be?'

'Celestino.'

' *"Che fece per viltade il gran rifiuto . . ."*,'[4] I stammered.

'Exactly!' she exclaimed, laughing. 'All the same, I think for some
time I had a little crush on you.'

'And then what happened?'

'Then life separated us.'

'What an idea though – to put up a synagogue just for yourselves.
Was that still all because of a fear of germs?'

She signalled agreement with her hand.

'Well . . . more or less . . .' she said.

'D'you mean more?'

Yet there was no way to make her confess the truth. I was well
aware that the reason Professor Ermanno, in 1933, had asked to
restore the Spanish synagogue for his and his family's use had been
the shameful *'infornata del Decennale'*. It was this that made him do
it. She, however, maintained that once more the crucial factor was
her mother's will. The Herreras, in Venice, belonged to the Spanish
School. And since her mother, grandma Regina, and her uncles
Giulio and Federico had always been most attached to family tra-
ditions, her father to keep her mother happy . . .

'But now, how come you've returned to the Italian School?' I
objected. 'I wasn't there at the Temple on the evening of Rosh
Hashanah – I haven't set foot in there for at least three years.
Though my father, who was there, has described the event to me
in the smallest detail.'

'Oh, have no fear, your absence has been greatly noticed, Sir
Free-Thinker!' she replied. 'By me as well.'

She became serious again and said:

'What d'you expect? . . . now we're all in the same boat. At this
point even I'd find it rather ridiculous to keep on trying to preserve
so many distinctions.'

On another day, the last, it began to rain, and whilst the others took refuge in the *Hütte* playing rummy or ping-pong, the two of us, unconcerned about getting soaked, ran halfway across the park to shelter in the coach-house. The coach-house served now only as a storeroom – Micòl had told me. At one time, however, a good half of the inner chamber had been kitted out as a gym, with climbing poles, ropes, symmetrical bars, rings, wall bars and so on – all this with the sole intent that she and Alberto might present themselves well prepared also for the annual exam in physical education. They weren't exactly serious lessons, the ones Professor Anacleto Zaccarini, who had been pensioned off years before and was more than eighty (just imagine it!) came to give them every week. But they were certainly amusing, perhaps more so than all the others. She never forgot to bring along to the gym a bottle of Bosco wine. And old Zaccarini, gradually turning from his usual ruddy-nosed and red-cheeked self to a peacock-purple, would slowly drain it to the last drop. Some winter evenings when he left, he looked as though he was actually emitting his own light . . .

It was a long, low construction of brown bricks, with two side windows defended by sturdy grilles, a leaking tile roof and its external walls almost entirely covered by ivy. Not far from Perotti's hayloft and the glassy parallelepiped of a greenhouse, its approach was through a broad, green-painted gate which looked out towards the opposite part of the Mura degli Angeli in the direction of the main house.

We stopped for a while on the threshold with our backs to the big door. The rain was pelting down in long diagonal streaks, on the lawns, on the huge black masses of the trees, on everything. It was cold. Our teeth chattering, we both looked around us. The enchantment which had till then held the season in suspense had been irreparably broken.

'Should we go in?' I finally proposed. 'It'll be warmer inside.'

Within the vast chamber, at the end of which, in shadow, shone the tops of two polished, blond climbing poles that stretched to the ceiling, a strange smell diffused itself, a mixture of petrol, lubricating oil, old dust and citrus fruits. It's such a good smell, Micòl suddenly said, aware that I was inhaling it deeply. She also liked it very much. And she pointed out to me, leaning against a side wall, a kind of high scaffolding of dark wood, groaning under the weight of big, round, yellow fruit, bigger than oranges and lemons, which I hadn't noticed before. They were grapefruit, hung there to season, she explained, produced in the greenhouse. Had I never tried them? – she then asked, taking one and offering it me to sniff. It was a shame she didn't have a knife with her to cut it into two 'hemispheres'. The taste of the juice was a hybrid: it was both like orange and lemon, with an additional bitterness all its own.

The centre of the coach-house was taken up by two vehicles: one long grey Dilambda and a blue carriage whose uplifted shafts were only just lower than the climbing-poles behind.

'Now we don't use the carriage any more,' Micòl remarked. 'On the few occasions Papa has to go into the country he goes by car. And the same for me and Alberto when we have to go – he to Milan, me to Venice. It's the unflagging Perotti who takes us to the station. At home the only ones who can drive are him (and he's a terrible driver) and Alberto. I can't – I haven't got my licence yet, and I'll really have to decide next spring . . . because . . . the problem is also this huge beast of an engine drinks *like a fish!*'

She drew close to the carriage. Its appearance was just as shiny and efficient as the car's.

'D'you recognize it?'

She opened one of the doors, got in and sat down. Then, patting the material of the seat next to her, she invited me to do likewise.

I accordingly entered and sat on her left. No sooner had I made myself comfortable than, slowly turning on its hinges with the sheer force of inertia, the carriage door shut on its own with the dry, precise click of a trap.

Now the beating of the rain on the coach-house roof became inaudible. It truly seemed as though we were in a small drawing room, a cramped and suffocating one.

'How well you've kept it,' I said, unable to suppress the sudden emotion which registered in my voice as a slight tremor. 'It still seems new. The only thing missing is a vase of flowers.'

'Oh, as for flowers, Perotti sees that they're in place when he takes Grandma out.'

'So you still use it then!'

'Not more than two or three times a year, and only for a tour of the garden.'

'And the horse? Is it still the same one?'

'Still the same old Star. He's twenty-two. Didn't you see him, the other day, at the back of the stall? By now he's half-blind, but harnessed to the carriage, he still cuts a . . . *lamentable figure.*'

She burst out laughing, shaking her head.

'Perotti has a real mania about this carriage,' she continued bitterly. 'And it's mainly to please him (he hates and despises motor cars – you've no idea how much!) that every now and then we let him take Grandma out for a ride up and down the driveways. Every fortnight or so he's in here with buckets of water, sponges, doeskins and rug-beaters – and that explains the miracle, that's why the carriage, especially when seen at dusk, still manages more or less to hoodwink everyone.'

'More or less?' I protested. 'But it looks brand new.'

She snorted with boredom.

'Do me a favour, and don't talk drivel.'

Spurred by some unpredictable impulse, she brusquely moved away, and huddled up in her corner. Her brow furrowed, her features sharpened with the same rancorous look with which, sometimes when playing tennis, and utterly focused on winning, she would stare straight ahead. Suddenly she seemed to have grown ten years older.

We stayed for a few moments like this, in silence. Then, without changing position, her arms hugging her sun-tanned knees as though she was frozen (she was in short stockings, a light cotton T-shirt and a pullover tied by its sleeves round her neck), Micòl started to speak again.

'Perotti would like to waste vast quantities of time and elbow grease on this ghastly old wreck!' she said. 'No, listen to what I'm saying – here where it's so gloomy you can make a great fuss about the wonder of it, but outside, by natural light, there's nothing to be done about it, thousands of little defects glare at you, the paintwork stripped in many places, the spokes and hubs of the wheels are all eaten away, the material of this seat (now you can't see it but I can assure you it's so) is worn away practically to a cobweb. And so I ask myself: what's Perotti bursting his blood vessels for? Is it worth it? The poor creature wants to have Papa's permission to repaint the whole thing, to restore and beaver away at it to his heart's content. But Papa's havering about it as usual and can't decide.'

She fell silent; and moved very slightly.

'Consider, in contrast, that canoe,' she went on, at the same time pointing out to me through the carriage-door window, which our breath had begun to mist over, a greyish, oblong, skeletal shape leaning against the wall opposite the grapefruit frame. 'Consider the canoe, and admire how honestly, with what dignity and moral courage, it's faced up to the full consequences of its utter uselessness, as it needed to. Even things, even they have to die, my friend. And so, if even they have to die, it's just as well to let them go. Above all, there's far more style in that, wouldn't you say?'

III

I

Countless times during the following winter, spring and summer, I kept thinking back to what had happened (or rather hadn't happened) between Micòl and me, inside that carriage so beloved of old Perotti. If on that rainy afternoon, in which the luminous Indian summer of 1938 had suddenly come to an end, I had at the very least managed to say what I was feeling – I thought with bitterness – perhaps things between us would have gone differently from the way they did. To have spoken to her, to have kissed her: it was then – I couldn't stop telling myself – then, when everything was still possible, that I should have done it! But I was forgetting to ask myself the crucial question: whether in that supreme, unique, irrevocable moment – a moment that, perhaps, had shaped both my life and hers – I was really ready to risk any act or word at all. Did I already know then, for example, that I was *truly* in love? The truth is: I didn't know it. I didn't know it then, and I wouldn't know it for another two full weeks, when bad weather, having set in, had irremediably dispersed us and the occasions for which we'd gathered.

I remember how the insistent rain, falling uninterruptedly for days and days, as a prelude to winter, the rigid, gloomy winter of the Po valley, had made any further visits to the garden out of the question. And yet, despite the change of season, everything proceeded in such a way as to deceive me that nothing had substantially changed.

At half past two on the day after our last visit to the Finzi-Continis' – more or less the time when, one after the other, we would have emerged from the tunnel of little climbing roses, shouting out 'Hi!' or 'Hello!' or 'Greetings!' – the telephone at my house rang and put me in contact, as though with the real thing, with the voice of Micòl. That same evening it was I who telephoned her, and the next afternoon it was again she who took the initiative. We might have kept our conversations going just as we had on those latter occasions, when grateful now as we were before that Bruno Lattes, Adriana Trentini, Giampiero Malnate and all the others had left us alone and shown no sign of remembering us. And besides, when had we, Micòl and I, ever given a thought to them during our long excursions in the park – so long that often when we returned we found no trace of them, either on the court or in the *Hütte*.

Pursued by the worried looks of my parents, I closed myself up in the cupboard that housed the telephone. I dialled the number. It was almost always she who answered – with such alacrity that I suspected she must be forever carrying the phone around with her.

'Where are you speaking from?' I once tried to ask her.

She started to laugh.

'Well . . . from home, I guess.'

'Thanks for that information. I just wanted to know how come you always manage to answer in a flash, so quickly, I mean. Do you have the phone on your desk like a businessman? Or from morning till night do you pace around the apparatus like the caged tiger in Machatý's *Nocturne*?'[1]

I seemed to detect a slight hesitation from the other end of the line. If she got to the phone before the others did, she then replied, that was, apart from the famous speed of her reflexes, because of her gift of intuition – an intuition which, every time the thought of phoning her passed through my mind, ensured that she was in the vicinity of the telephone. She then changed the subject. How was my thesis on Panzacchi going? And Bologna – when would I be resuming my usual journeys back and forth, if only for a change of air?

Sometimes, however, someone else answered – either Alberto, or Professor Ermanno, or one of the two maids and even, on one occasion, Signora Regina, who displayed a surprising acuity of hearing when it came to the telephone. In such cases, of course, I was forced to announce my name and to state that it was 'Signorina'

Micòl I'd like to speak to. After some days, though – at first this would embarrass me even more, but I gradually got used to it – after some days it was enough for me to drop my 'Hello' into the receiver for the person on the other end hurriedly to pass me on to the one I was seeking. Even Alberto, when it was he who picked up the phone, did not behave any differently. Micòl was always there, ready to snatch the receiver from whoever's hand it was in, as though they were always gathered together in a single room, a *living room*, drawing room or library, each of them sunk into a vast leather armchair within a few steps of the telephone. I really began to suspect that. To inform Micòl, who, at the trilling of the phone (I could almost see her) would suddenly look up, they perhaps confined themselves to offering her the receiver from a distance, Alberto, when it was he, no doubt doing so with a wink poised between the affectionate and the sardonic.

One morning I decided to ask her to verify my guesswork, and she heard me out in silence.

'Isn't it true?' I pressed her.

Apparently it wasn't. Since I was so keen to know the truth – she said – here it was, then. Each of them had a telephone line in their own room (after she'd got one for herself, the rest of the family had also ended up having them installed). They were the most useful mechanisms, she wholeheartedly recommended them: they let you phone out at whatever time of the day or night without disturbing anyone or being disturbed, and they were especially convenient at night-time. Saved you even putting a foot out of bed. What a weird idea! – she added, laughing – whatever made me think that they'd all be gathered together as though in a hotel lobby? Why on earth would they be doing that? It was strange though that when it wasn't she who answered directly, I never heard the click of the phone being lifted.

'No,' she categorically reiterated. 'To safeguard personal liberty, there's nothing like a private phone line. Honestly – you should get one yourself, in your own room. Just think how we'd be able to talk, especially at night!'

'And so you're phoning me now from your bedroom?'

'I certainly am. And from my bed as well.'

It was eleven in the morning.

'You're not exactly an early bird.'

'Oh, not you as well!' she complained. 'It's one thing for my father, who's worn down with worries and seventy years old, to keep getting up at six-thirty to set us a good example, as he puts it, and to stop us loafing around in feather beds, but it's honestly a bit much when our best friends start preaching at us. Do you know what time yours truly got up, my dear boy? At seven. And you dare to wonder that I'm back in bed again at eleven! Besides, it's not as though I was sleeping – I've been reading, scribbling some notes for my thesis, and looking out of the window. I always do a whole lot of things when I'm in bed. The warmth of the blankets undoubtedly spurs me into activity.'

'Describe your room for me.'

She clicked her tongue three times as a sign of refusal.

'No way. That's *verboten. Privat.* Though, if you insist, I could tell you what I can see from the window.'

She could see through the glass, in the foreground, the bearded tips of her *Washingtoniae graciles* which the wind and the rain were beating at so 'vilely'. Who knows if the solicitude of Titta and Bepi, who had already begun to wrap the usual straw coats around their trunks as they did every winter, would be enough to protect them in the succeeding months from a frostbitten death which threatened every year the grim weather returned, and which till then they'd always luckily avoided. Then, further off, partly hidden by strips of wandering mist, she could see the four towers of the Castello which the heavy rainshowers had turned black as clinker. And behind the towers, with a bruised look that would make you shudder, and that too hidden every now and then by the mist, the distant marble stonework of the Duomo's façade and bell-tower . . . Oh, that mist! She couldn't bear it when it was like this – it made her think of dirty rags. But sooner or later the rain would cease, and then the mist, in the morning, pierced by weak rays of sunshine, would be turned into something precious, something delicately opalescent, which in its changing reflections of tone was exactly like those *làttimi* which her room was full of. Winter was a pain, it's true, not least because it put an end to tennis, but it had its compensations. 'Since every situation, however sad and annoying it is,' she concluded, 'in the end offers certain compensations, and often significant ones.'

'*Làttimi*?' I asked. 'What are they? Something to eat?'

'No. Not at all,' she protested petulantly, appalled as usual by my ignorance. 'They're things made with milky glass. Normal glasses, champagne glasses, ampoules, dainty vases, little boxes, stuff you might find among the junk in antique dealers' shops. In Venice they call them *làttimi*, and elsewhere *opalines* or even *flûtes*. You've no idea how much I *adore* these things. There's nothing at all I don't know about the subject. Try testing me and see.'

It was in Venice, she went on, perhaps prompted by the local mists, so different from our big gloomy Paduan fogs, mists which are infinitely more lovely and luminous and which only one painter in the world had managed to do justice to – and that wasn't late Monet but 'our' De Pisis – it was in Venice that she'd first got so interested in *làttimi*. She had spent hours going round antique shops. There were some, especially in the San Samuele district, around Campo Santo Stefano, or in the Ghetto, at the far end towards the station, that practically sold nothing but. Her uncles Giulio and Federico lived in the Calle del Cristo, near San Moisè. Late afternoons, not knowing what else to do, and naturally with the housekeeper Signorina Blumenfeld glued to her side – a prim *jodé** sixty-year-old from Frankfurt am Main, who'd been in Italy for more than thirty years, a real bore! – she would go out into Calle XXII Marzo in search of *làttimi*. From San Moisè, Campo Santo Stefano is a short walk. Unlike San Geremia, which is in the Ghetto – if you go by San Bartolomìo and the Lista di Spagna it takes at least half an hour to get there, and yet it's very close indeed. You just have to take a *traghetto* along the Grand Canal as far as Palazzo Grassi and then leap off at the Frari . . . But returning to the *làttimi*, what a thrill, the thrill of a dowser, she got every time she managed

---

* Ferraresa Jewish dialect: a Jewish woman.

to unearth a new and especially rare one! Did I want to know how many pieces she'd collected? Almost two hundred.

I carefully avoided telling her that what she was saying hardly seemed consistent with her declared aversion to any, even the briefest, attempt to keep things, objects, from the inevitable death which – even for them – lay in wait, and to the mania for preserving them that Perotti in particular had. I wanted her to go on describing her room, and to forget her earlier proscriptions of '*verboten*' and '*privat*'.

I succeeded. She kept on talking about her *làttimi* (she had arranged them neatly on three high, dark mahogany shelves which stretched almost the whole length of the wall which faced the one alongside which her bed had been placed) and in doing so her room, I'm not sure how conscious she was of this, was gradually taking shape, and all its details were being delineated.

Thus: of windows, there were two. Both of them faced south, and were so high off the floor that to look out from them, with the park stretching out beneath and the roofs which beyond the park's edge extended out of sight, it seemed as though one were looking out from the deck of a transatlantic liner. Between the two windows was a fourth shelf – the shelf for English and French books. Against the left-hand window was an office-type desk, flanked by a small table for the portable typewriter on one side, and on the other by a fifth bookshelf, this one for Italian literature, classic and modern, and for translations: mainly from Russian – Pushkin, Gogol, Tolstoy, Dostoevsky, Chekhov. On the floor, a large Persian carpet, and at the centre of the room, which was long but rather narrow, three armchairs and a chaise longue to stretch out on while reading. Two doors: one for the entrance, at the end, by the left-hand window, which directly communicated with the staircase and lift, and another a few inches from the opposite corner of the room which led to the bathroom. At night she slept without ever fully closing the shutters, keeping a little lamp at the bedside table always on, and the trolley with a thermos of *Skiwasser* (as well, of course, as the telephone!) so they could be reached merely by stretching out an arm. If she woke up in the night, all she needed to do was take a sip of *Skiwasser* (it was so comfy always having it ready nice and hot – why didn't I too get myself one, a thermos?). After which, she would slump back down, and let her eyes rove over those misty, luminescent, treasured *làttimi*. That way, sleep would creep up on her as stealthily as a Venetian 'high tide', and quickly submerge and 'prostrate' her.

But these were not our only topics of conversation.

As though she too wanted to deceive me into thinking that nothing had changed, that everything was continuing between us the same as 'before' when, that is, we had been able to see each other every afternoon, Micòl never lost the chance to remind me of that series of 'incredible', wonderful days we had spent together.

We'd always spoken of a whole range of things, then, whilst walking around in the park: of trees, plants, our childhoods, our relatives. In the meantime Bruno Lattes, Adriana Trentini, *the* Malnate, Carletto Sani, Tonino Collevatti and, with them, those who visited later, hardly merited more than the odd reference or sign, the whole lot of them designated in the cursory and rather disdainful phrase 'those others over there'.

Now, however, on the telephone, our talks continually harked back to them, and especially to Bruno Lattes and Adriana Trentini, who, according to Micòl, had a 'thing' going on. Was I serious? – she kept saying to me. How could I not have noticed that they were going out together? It was so blatant! His eyes never left her for a moment, and she too, though she treated him like a slave, whilst she played the flirt a bit with everyone, with me, with that bear of a Malnate, and even with Alberto, she too was obviously smitten. *Dear* Bruno! With his temperament (let's be honest, a bit impressionable, or how else explain the way he reveres two well-meaning blockheads of the calibre of little Sani and that youth Collevatti!), with his temperament these last months can hardly have been easy on him, given the situation. No question about it, Adriana was up for it (one evening, in the *Hütte*, she had happened to see them half stretched out on the sofa kissing like there was no tomorrow) though whether she was the type of person to be able to keep *something* so demanding alive, in defiance of the Racial Laws, and of both his and her relatives, that was another question. Bruno truly can't have been having an easy time of it, this winter. And it's not as though Adriana was a bad catch, far from it! Almost as tall as Bruno, blond, with that lovely skin like Carole Lombard's – at another time she might have been exactly what Bruno dreamt of, given how much he clearly went for the 'decidedly Aryan' type. That she was also a bit of an empty-headed flirt, and unconsciously cruel, couldn't be denied. Didn't I recall the look she'd given poor Bruno that time when, as a pair, they lost the famous return match against the duo Désirée Baggioli and Claudio Montemezzo? It was mainly her, and not Bruno at all, who lost the match for them, with that endless series of double-faults she contrived – at least three every service game! And yet, completely unaware, for the whole match she did nothing but berate him with foul mutterings as if he, the poor creature, wasn't done in and depressed enough on his own account. Seriously, it would have been a total joke if it wasn't for the fact that, all considered, the whole event had ended up as rather a bitter one! But so it goes. Without doing it deliberately, moralists like Bruno always fall for little types like Adriana, and from this springs a whole raft of jealous scenes, furtive tailings, unpleasant surprises, tearful episodes, sworn denials, even comings-to-blows, and infidelities, I'm telling you, endless infidelities. No, in the end, Bruno ought to have lit a candle in gratitude to the Racial Laws. He would have to face up to a difficult winter, it was true. But the Racial Laws, not always without some consolations then, would have saved him from committing the most blatant stupidity – of getting engaged.

'Don't you agree?' she once added. 'And also because he, like yourself, has literary ambitions, he's someone who's drawn to writing. I seem to remember having seen, two or three years ago, some of his verses published in the literary pages of the *Padano* all under the title "Poems of an Avant-gardist".'[2]

'Alas!' I sighed. 'But what are you trying to say. I don't understand.'

She silently laughed – I could clearly hear her.

'Yes indeed, at a final reckoning,' she went on, 'a bit of *gall and wormwood* won't do him much harm. '*Non mi lasciare ancora, sofferenza*'[3] as Ungaretti says. He wants to write? Let him take what's

coming to him, and then let's see. Besides, you just have to look at
him to tell – it's as clear as day that pain is what he fervently desires.'

'You're disgustingly cynical. You and Adriana make quite a pair.'

'You're wrong about that. And actually you've offended me.
Compared to me, Adriana's blameless as an angel. Capricious perhaps, but unconscious, innocent like *"tutti / le femmine di tutti / i
sereni animali / che avvicinano a Dio"*.[4] Whereas Micòl's good, I've
told you already and I'll tell you again, and she knows what she
does – remember that well.'

Although far less often, she did also mention Giampiero Malnate,
towards whom she'd always behaved curiously, basically in a critical
and sarcastic way, as though she were jealous of the friendship that
bound him and Alberto (a bit exclusive, to tell the truth), but at the
same time was reluctant to admit it, and for that reason was driven
to 'smash the idol'.

In her view, even physically Malnate wasn't that impressive. Too
big, too bulky, too much like a 'father' to be taken seriously in this
respect. He was one of those excessively hairy men who, however
many times a day they shave, still always look dirty, a bit unwashed
– and this, let's be honest, wouldn't do. Perhaps, as far as one could
see through the thick lenses of his glasses, his camouflage (it seemed
that they made him sweat, and that made you want to take them
off him), his eyes weren't really that bad: grey, 'steely', the eyes of
a strong, silent type. But too serious and severe. Too constitutionally
marriageable. Belying their effect of scornful misogyny, they were
full of the threat of feelings so eternal that they'd scare off any girl,
even the quietest and meekest.

He was always so sulky, that's it; and not nearly as original as he
seemed to think himself. Did I want to bet that, with the right line
of questioning, he'd not come out and claim that he felt ill at
ease in city clothes, and much more at home anywhere in the
windjammer, plus-fours and ski-boots that he'd be kitted out in for
his unmissable weekends on Mottarone or Monte Rosa? His trusty
pipe, when seen in this light, was fairly revealing – it stood for a
whole system of sub-Alpine, masculine austerity, like a flag.

He was great friends with Alberto, but as for Alberto, with his temperament passive as a punchbag, he always befriends everyone and no one. They'd lived whole years together at Milan, and that certainly had to be given weight. Didn't I also find a bit too much, all the same, their endless confabulations? Pst! Pst! Woof! Woof! No sooner would they meet each other than they were at it again, drawing apart from everyone else and muttering away. And heaven knows what about! Girls? She somehow doubted it. Knowing Alberto, who had always been rather reticent – not to say mysterious – about such matters, honestly, she wouldn't place the smallest bet on it.

'Are you two still seeing him?' I got round to asking one day, throwing off the question in the most unconcerned tone I could muster.

'Oh yes . . . I think he comes round every so often to visit his Alberto . . .' she answered calmly. 'They shut themselves up in his room, take tea, smoke their pipes (even Alberto started puffing away at one a short while back), and talk and talk, happy as sandboys, doing nothing but talk.'

She was too intelligent, too sensitive not to have guessed what I was hiding under my indifference: and that being, all of a sudden, a sharp, and symptomatic, desire to see her again. Yet she behaved as though she had understood nothing, without signalling even indirectly the chance that, sooner or later, I too might be invited round.

2

That night I spent in turmoil. Fitfully, I slept, I woke up, I slept again, and every time I slept I kept on dreaming of Micòl.

I dreamt, for example, of finding myself, just like that very first day I set foot in the garden, watching her play tennis with Alberto. Even in the dream I never took my eyes off her for a second. I kept on telling myself how wonderful she was, flushed and covered with sweat, with that frown of almost fierce concentration that divided her forehead, all tensed up as she was with the effort to beat her smiling, slightly bored and sluggish older brother. Yet then I felt oppressed by an uneasiness, an embittered feeling, an almost unbearable ache. I asked myself in desperation – what was left of that young girl from ten years ago in the twenty-two-year-old Micòl, in her shorts and cotton T-shirt, this Micòl who had such an athletic, modern, free and easy air (above all free!) that she made you think she'd done nothing else for the last few years than swan around in the Meccas of international tennis – London, Paris, the Côte d'Azur, Forest Hills? But yes, I answered myself, they're still there from the child she was: the weightless blond hair, with streaks verging on white, the blue, almost Scandinavian irises, the honey-coloured skin, and on her breastbone, every now and then leaping out from her T-shirt collar, the little gold disc of the *shaddai*.[1] But what else?

Then we were closed inside the carriage, in that stale, grey penumbra: with Perotti sitting in the box-seat up front, looming, motionless, mute. I reasoned with myself that if Perotti was up there, with his back stubbornly turned towards us, he was obviously doing this so as not to have to see what was – or what might be – going on inside the carriage, no doubt out of a servile discretion.

Yet he was nevertheless aware of *everything*, of course he was, the sinister old bumpkin! His wife, the wan Vittoria, prying through the partly ajar double doors of the coach-house – every now and then I could make out the woman's little reptile head, lustrous with plastered-down, crow-black hair, as she peeped round the edge of the door – his wife stood as a sentry there, fixing him with her harassed, discontented eye, and making stealthy gestures and coded grimaces at him.

Next we were in her room, Micòl and I, but not even then were we alone, but rather '*plagued*' – as she herself had whispered to me – by the habitual third party, which this time was Jor, crouched in the centre of the room like a gigantic granite idol, who stared at us with his two frosty eyes, one black, the other blue. The room was long and narrow, full like the coach-house of things to eat: grapefruits, oranges, mandarins and above all *làttimi*, ranged in a row like books on the boards of vast black shelves, severe and ecclesiastic, reaching up to the ceiling. Only the *làttimi* were not at all the glass objects that Micòl had told me about, but, just as I'd supposed, cheeses – little round driplets of off-white cheeses shaped like bottles. Laughing, Micòl insisted that I try one of them, one of her cheeses. At this she stood on tiptoe, and was about to touch with the stretched-out index finger of her right hand one of those which had been set on the topmost shelf – those were the best ones, she explained to me, the freshest. But not at all, I wasn't going to have one – I felt anxious not only because of the dog's presence but also because I realized that outside, whilst we were arguing, the lake tide was rapidly rising. If I were to delay any further, the high water would have locked me in, would have stopped me being able to leave her room unnoticed. For it was secretly and by night that I had come into Micòl's bedroom. Secretly hidden from Alberto, Professor Ermanno, Signora Olga, grandma Regina, her uncles Giulio and Federico and the earnest Signorina Blumenfeld. And Jor, who was the only one to know, the sole witness of the *thing* that was *also* between us, couldn't tell anyone about it.

I also dreamt that we spoke openly together, at last without any dissimulation, with our cards on the table.

As usual we quarrelled a bit, Micòl arguing that the *thing* between us had begun from the first day, that is, from when she and I, still utterly surprised to meet again and recognize each other, had made off to see the park, and I, for my part, claiming instead that not at all, in my opinion, the *thing* had begun a good while earlier, on the telephone, from the moment she had announced that she'd become 'ugly', 'a spinster with a red nose'. Obviously I hadn't believed her. All the same she couldn't even have a glimmer, I added with a catch in my throat, of how much those words of hers had tormented me. In the days that followed, before I saw her again, I had gone over them again and again, and couldn't rid myself of the unease they caused.

'Well, perhaps it's true,' at this point Micòl seemed to agree, placing her hand on mine. 'If the idea that I'd become ugly and red-nosed caused you such distress, then I give in – it means that you're right. But now, what's to be done? That excuse of playing tennis isn't going to wash any more, and here at home, besides, with the risk of being stranded by the high water (d'you see how it's like Venice?) – it's neither right nor proper that I should let you come in.'

'Why should you need to?' I parried. 'You could go out yourself, after all.'

'*Me*, go out?' she exclaimed, widening her eyes. 'Just think for a moment, *dear boy*. Where would I go out to?'

'I . . . I'm not sure,' I stuttered in reply. 'To Montarone, for example, or Piazza d'Armi near the Aqueduct, or, if you're unhappy to be seen with me, the Via Borso side of the Piazza della Certosa. *Everyone* who's going out together has always gone there – I don't know about your parents, but mine, in their time, did. And to go out a bit together, honestly, what was the harm in that? It's not like we're making love! It's just the first rung, on the brink of the abyss. But from there to the bottom of the abyss, there's still a long way to go!'

I was on the point of suggesting that if, as it seemed, not even Piazza della Certosa suited her, we could always meet up in Bologna, having taken two separate trains. But I kept quiet, drained of courage, even in dreams. And besides, shaking her head and smiling, she immediately declared that it was useless, impossible, '*verboten*'. She would never have gone with me, outside her home and the garden. And what was all this about? – she winked at me, amused. After she'd let herself be dragged around all the usual 'open air' resorts beloved of 'the Eros of our wild native town', was I perhaps hoping to take her to Bologna now? Perhaps to some 'grand hotel' there, one of those favoured by her grandma Josette, like the *Brun* or the *Baglioni*, where we'd have to show at the reception – had I thought of that? – our fine documents complete with racial provenance.

The next evening, as soon as I'd returned from a quick, unexpected trip to Bologna, to the university there, I tried to telephone.

Alberto answered.

'How are things?' he crooned ironically, showing this once that he'd recognized my voice. 'It's ages since we saw each other. How are you? What are you up to?'

Disconcerted, with my heart racing, I began to blather away. I bundled up a whole bunch of things: news about my graduation thesis that loomed above me like an unscalable wall, and comments on the weather, which after the last bad fortnight, seemed to be offering some hope of improvement – but it wasn't worth trusting: the sharp air made it quite clear we were now in the middle of winter, and we might as well forget those fine days of October. Most of all, I dwelt on my brief trip to Bologna.

In the morning, I told him, I had passed by Via Zamboni, where, after having sorted out various things in the secretary's office, I'd been able to check out in the library a certain number of entries from the Panzacchi bibliography which I was preparing. Later, around one o'clock, I'd gone to eat at the Pappagallo – certainly not the so-called '*pasta asciutta*' restaurant at the foot of the Asinelli which, besides being extremely dear, as far as its cooking went seemed distinctly inferior to its reputation, but rather to the other Pappagallo '*in brodo*', in a little side street off Via Galliera, which, as its name suggests, was famous for its vegetable soups and boiled meats, as well as for its very modest prices. Then in the afternoon

I'd seen some friends, gone round the bookshops of the city centre, drunk tea at Zanarini's, the one in Piazza Galvani, at the end of the Pavaglione. It had been a reasonably good trip – I ended up saying – 'almost as good as it was when I used to attend regularly'.

'Just imagine,' I added at this point, inventing the whole thing – who knows what devil had suddenly prompted me to tell a story of this kind, 'before going to the station I even had time to have a quick look around the Via dell'Oca.'

'The Via dell'Oca?' Alberto asked, suddenly becoming animated, although at the same time a bit reserved.

That was all I needed to be spurred on by the same sour impulse which sometimes made my father appear, set beside the Finzi-Continis, far more boorish and 'assimilated' than he actually was.

'What?' I exclaimed. 'You mean to say that you didn't know that in Bologna's Via dell'Oca there's one of the most famous houses of ill repute in all Italy!'

He coughed.

'No. I didn't know it,' he replied.

He then mentioned, in a different tone of voice, that in a few days' time he too would have to leave for Milan, where he'd be staying for at least a week. June wasn't after all as far away as it seemed, and he still hadn't found nor, to tell the truth, had he even sought out, a professor who would let him cobble together 'any old bits for a thesis'.

After which, once again changing the subject, he asked if by chance, not long ago, I'd passed by along the Mura degli Angeli on my bicycle. He'd been out in the garden to see what damage the rain had done to the tennis court. But partly because of the distance and partly because of the already fading light, he hadn't been able to determine whether or not it was me, the guy who was up there, stock still, not having got off the saddle, and leaning a hand against a tree trunk to look. Oh, so it was me, then? he went on, after I'd admitted, not without some hesitation, having taken the Mura route back home from the station: that was because, I explained, of the inner disgust I always felt coming across certain 'ugly mugs' that would be gathered in front of the Caffè della Borsa, in Corso Roma, or strung out along the Giudecca. – Ah, so it *was* me, he repeated. He was sure it had been! Anyway, if it was me, why on earth hadn't I answered his shouts and whistles? Hadn't I heard them?

I hadn't, I once again lied. In fact I hadn't even been aware that he'd been in the garden. At this stage we really had nothing more to say to each other, nothing at all to bridge the sudden gulf of silence that had opened between us.

'But you . . . weren't you wanting to speak to Micòl?' he said at last, as though remembering.

'That's right,' I replied. 'Would you mind putting her on?'

He would gladly do so, he told me, if it wasn't for the fact that (and it was *truly* odd 'the little angel' hadn't even let me know) Micòl had left early in the afternoon for Venice, she too meaning to break the back of her thesis. She had come down for lunch all dressed up for the journey, with her bags and everything packed, to announce her intention to her 'astonished little family'. She had said how bored she was of being weighed down with this task hanging over her. Instead of taking her degree in June, she was aiming for February: which at Venice, with the Marciana and the Querini-Stampalia libraries at hand, she could easily manage, whereas at Ferrara, for a host of reasons, her thesis on Dickinson would never press on at anything like the required speed. This is what the girl said. But who knows whether she would be able to hold out against Venice's spirit-dampening atmosphere, and against a house, the uncles' house, which she didn't care for. It would be easy to imagine her back at base in a week or two with nothing to show for it. He'd think he was dreaming if ever Micòl managed to keep herself away from Ferrara uninterruptedly for twenty days . . .

'Oh, well!' he concluded. 'But what would you say (only this week's impossible, and so is next week, but the one after, yes, I really think that would work), what would you say to the idea of us all taking a motoring trip as far as Venice? It would be fun just to land on her unannounced – let's say, you, me and Giampi Malnate!'

'It's an idea,' I said. 'And why not? There's time to discuss it further.'

'In the meantime,' he went on, with an effort in which I sensed a desire to compensate me for what he'd revealed to me, 'in the meantime, sorry – that's if you've nothing better on – why not come round here, let's say tomorrow, around five in the afternoon? Malnate should be there too. We'll have some tea . . . listen to some records . . . have a chat . . . I'm not sure how you, as a literary man, will feel about spending time with an engineer (as I'll be) and an industrial chemist. But if you'd do us the *honour*, compliments aside, do come – it would be a pleasure for us.'

We carried on for a while longer, Alberto ever more keen and excited about this idea of his, which he seemed to have thought up on the spot, to have me round to his house, and I drawn but at the same time put off. It was quite true, I remembered, that a little before, from the Mura, I had stayed almost a half-hour staring at the garden and, especially, at the house, which from where I was, and through the almost bare boughs of the trees, I could see cut out against the evening sky with the fragile, shimmering air of an heraldic emblem. Two windows on the mezzanine floor, at the level of the terrace from which one went down into the park, were already lit up, and electric light also glowed further up, from the solitary, topmost little window which barely opened beneath the apex of the peaked roof. For a long while, my eyeballs aching in their sockets, I stood there staring at the little light from that high window (a small, tremulous glow, suspended in the ever-darkening air like starlight); and only the distant whistles and Tyrolean yodel-ling of Alberto, awakening in me, as well as the fear of being recognized, the anxiety once more to hear Micòl's voice on the phone without delay, had, at a certain point, been able to dislodge me from the spot.

But now, on the other hand – I disconsolately asked myself – what did it matter to me to go round to *their* house, now, when I would no longer find Micòl there?

Yet the news my mother gave me as I left the small telephone cupboard, which was that just before noon Micòl Finzi-Contini had asked for me ('She asked me to tell you that she had to leave for Venice, to say goodbye, and to say that she'll write,' my mother added, looking elsewhere), was enough to make me quickly change my mind. From that moment the time that separated me from five o'clock of the next day began to move with extraordinary slowness.

3

It was from then that I began, you could say on a daily basis, to visit Alberto's personal flat – he called it a studio – and it was a studio in fact, with the bedroom and bathroom adjoining it. It was from there, behind the door of that famous 'chamber', passing in the corridor alongside, that Micòl would hear resound the indistinct voices of her brother and his friend Malnate, and where, during the course of the whole winter, apart from the maids arriving with a tea trolley, I never caught sight of any other family member. Oh, that winter of 1938–9! I remember the long and motionless months which seemed to be suspended above time itself, and my feelings of desperation – in February it snowed, Micòl postponed her return from Venice – and even now, at a distance of more than twenty years, the four walls of Alberto Finzi-Contini's studio still represent for me a kind of vice, a drug as necessary as it was unconscious each day I went there . . .

It wasn't as though I was at all desperate that first December evening in which I once more rode by bike across the Barchetto del Duca. Micòl had left. And yet I pedalled along the entrance drive, in the mist and darkness, as if in a short while I was expecting once more to see her and only her. I was excited, light-hearted, almost happy. I looked ahead, with the front light planing over those sites that belonged to a past which, though it seemed remote, was still recuperable, was not yet lost. There was the grove of rattan palms, there, further on, on the right the hazy shape of Perotti's farmhouse, from one first-floor window of which leaked a faint yellowish glow, and there still further in the distance was the ghostly scaffolding of the Panfilio bridge, and there, finally, heralded a fraction before by the screak of tyres on gravel, was the enormous hulk of the *magna domus*, impervious as a solitary rock, utterly dark except for a vivid white light that streamed from a little door on the ground floor, apparently left open to welcome me.

I got off the bike, stopping to examine the deserted threshold. Within, part blacked out by the left-side door which was shut, I could see the steep staircase covered by a red carpet – a fiery, bloody, scarlet red. At every step there was a brass stair rod, glowing and glinting as though it was gold.

Having leant the bike against the wall, I bent down to secure the padlock. I was still bent there, in the dark, next to the door from which, besides the light, the hearty warmth from a radiator gushed forth – in the darkness I didn't seem able to close the lock, so I'd just thought of lighting a match – when the unmistakable voice of Professor Ermanno sounded from somewhere very near.

'What are you up to? Are you locking it?' asked the Professor as he stood on the threshold. 'Not a bad idea, that. One never knows. You can never be too careful.'

I immediately straightened up, as usual unsure whether behind his slightly querulous kindness he was making fun of me.

'Good evening,' I said, taking off my hat and stretching out my hand.

'Good evening, my dear boy,' he replied. 'But keep your hat on, please keep it on!'

I felt his small plump hand rest inertly in my own and then as quickly withdraw. He was not wearing a hat but an old sporting beret tilted down over his spectacles, and a woollen scarf wrapped round his neck.

He gave a diffident glance towards the bicycle.

'You have locked it, haven't you?'

I said that I hadn't. Then, upset, he insisted that I went back, and obliged him by locking it properly, since – he repeated – one never knows. A theft would be unlikely – he went on from the threshold as I once again attempted to hook the lock around the spokes of the back wheel. One couldn't entirely trust to the garden wall. Along its outer perimeter, especially on the side of the Mura degli Angeli, there were at least a dozen points where a moderately adept boy would have no difficulty in climbing over. Then making a getaway, even weighed down by the bicycle over his shoulders, would be almost as straightforward an operation for such a boy.

Finally I managed to click the lock shut. I raised my eyes but the threshold was once again deserted.

The Professor was waiting for me inside the little entrance lobby, at the foot of the stairs. I went in, shut the door, and only then realized that he was looking at me with a troubled, regretful air.

'I'm wondering', he said, 'if it wouldn't have been better for you to actually bring the bicycle in . . . Yes, take my advice. The next time you come, bring the bicycle in with you. If you put it there beneath the stairs it won't give the slightest trouble to anyone.'

He turned round and began to walk up the stairs. More hunched than ever, still with that beret on his head and scarf round his neck, he ascended slowly, holding on to the banister. All the while talking, or rather muttering, as though his words were directed to himself rather than to me.

It was Alberto who had told him I was coming round that day. For this reason, since Perotti was suspected of having a touch of fever (it was only a minor attack of bronchitis, but it needed looking after to avoid the spread of infection) and since Alberto – always so forgetful, distracted, with his head in the clouds – was really not to be relied on, he had had to assume the responsibility himself of 'standing at the ready'. Doubtless, if it had been Micòl, he would have had no cause for worry, since Micòl, who knows how, always found time to look after everything, taking care not only of her own studies but also of the general running of the whole household, even of the kitchen 'stoves'. She had a passion for that almost as strong as for novels and poetry – it was she who at the end of the week would do the accounts with Gina or Vittorina, she who would *schacht** the poultry with her bare hands, and this despite the fact that she really loved the creatures, poor thing! But unfortunately Micòl wasn't at home today (had Alberto warned me she wasn't

* Yiddish: ritually slaughter.

here?), having had to leave for Venice yesterday afternoon. His not being able to rely either on Alberto or on their 'angel of the hearth' nor even, as if that wasn't enough, on the indisposed Perotti, explained why this time he'd had to stand in as doorman.

He also spoke of other things I don't remember. I do recall, though, that in the end he came back to Micòl, but this time to complain about her 'restlessness of late', due of course to 'many factors', though . . . here he broke off suddenly. During all this time in which not only had we reached the top of the stairs, but had gone down two corridors, and crossed various rooms, Professor Ermanno had always preceded me, never letting me overtake except when he was turning off the lights in passing.

Rapt with all I was hearing about Micòl (that detail about her, with her bare hands, being the one who'd cut the throats of the chickens in the kitchen strangely intrigued me), I looked around but almost without seeing. Besides, what we were passing through was not so unlike other houses which belonged to Ferrara's high society, Jewish or not, laden like them with the usual furnishings, monumental wardrobes, heavy seventeenth-century chests of drawers with feet carved in the shape of lions' paws, refectory-type tables, old Tuscan leather chairs with bronze studs, *Frau* armchairs, intricate glass and ironwork chandeliers hanging from the centre of coffered ceilings, thick carpets the colour of tobacco, carrot and ox-blood stretched out everywhere over darkly lustrous parquet. Here, perhaps, there were a greater number of nineteenth-century paintings, landscapes and portraits, and of books, most of them rebound, in rows behind the glass doors of huge, dark mahogany bookcases. The mammoth radiators released heat on a scale which at home my father would have declared plain crazy (I could just hear him saying it!): a heat redolent of a luxury hotel rather than a private home, and of such intensity that, almost immediately, breaking out in a sweat, I'd had to take off my overcoat.

With him in front and me in tow, we crossed at least a dozen rooms of differing size, some vast as real halls, some small, even tiny, and linked to each other by corridors which were not always straight nor on the same level. At last, having reached halfway down one such corridor, Professor Ermanno came to a halt in front of a door.

'Here we are at last,' he said.

He flicked his thumb towards the door and winked.

He apologized for not being able to come in himself, as – he explained – he had to go over some accounts of their holdings in the country. He promised to have 'one of the girls bring up something hot', and then, having been assured that I'd come again – he had put aside for me the copies of his little studies on Venetian history, I wasn't to forget! – he shook me by the hand, and speedily disappeared at the end of the corridor.

I went in.

'Ah! You're here!' Alberto greeted me.

He was slumped in an armchair. He levered himself up with both hands on the armrests, got to his feet, put down the book he had been reading, leaving it open with its spine up on a little low table beside him, and came towards me.

He was wearing a pair of vicuña grey trousers, one of his fine pullovers the colour of dry leaves, brown English lace-ups (they were real Dawsons – he would later inform me – which he'd found in a little Milanese shop near San Babila), a flannel shirt, without a tie, open at the collar, and carrying a pipe between his teeth. He shook my hand without too much warmth, as he stared at a point behind my back. What was attracting his attention? I had no idea.

'Excuse me,' he murmured.

He let go of me, bending his long back sideways, and as he brushed past I realized that I'd left the double door half-open. Alberto was already there, however, to see to it personally. He grasped the handle of the outer door, but before drawing it towards him he stuck his head out into the corridor to look around.

'And Malnate,' I asked. 'Isn't he here yet?'

'No, not yet,' he replied as he came back.

He took my hat, scarf and coat from me, and disappeared into the small adjoining room. Through the communicating door I was thus able to see something of it: a part of the bed with a woollen coverlet in sporty red and blue squares, a pouffe at the foot of the bed, and, hanging on the wall beside the little doorway to the bathroom, this also half-open, there was a small male nude by De Pisis in a simple frame of light-coloured wood.

'Do sit down,' Alberto said meanwhile. 'I'll be back in a moment.'

He did indeed return immediately, and now, seated in front of me, in the armchair I'd seen him pull himself out of with the faintest show of fatigue, perhaps of boredom, he considered me with that strange expression of detached, objective sympathy which was a sign in him, I knew, of the liveliest interest in others of which he was capable. He was smiling at me, revealing the large incisors he'd inherited from his mother's family: too large and strong for his pale, long face, and for the gums they were set in, as bloodless as the face.

'Would you like to listen to a bit of music?' he proposed, turning on a radiogram placed in a corner of the studio at the side of the entrance. 'It's a Philips, really the best.'

He made as though to get up again from the armchair, but then abandoned the attempt.

'No, wait,' he said, 'perhaps later.'

I looked around.

'What records have you got?'

'Oh, a bit of everything: Monteverdi, Scarlatti, Bach, Mozart, Beethoven. I also have at my *disposal* a good deal of jazz, but don't be put off: Armstrong, Duke Ellington, Fats Waller, Benny Goodman, Charlie Kunz . . .'

He went on listing names and titles, cool and courteous as ever but without much interest, no more or less than if he'd been offering me a selection of dishes which he himself had made sure of tasting beforehand. He only became more animated, fractionally more, in demonstrating to me the virtues of *his* Philips. It was – he told me – a rather exceptional player, thanks to certain particular 'technical devices' he'd worked out himself and which a skilful Milanese technician had put into effect. These modifications principally concerned the quality of the sound, which now didn't merely come through a single loudspeaker, but from four separate sources of sound. There was, in fact, one speaker which only picked up bass notes, a second for the mid-range sounds, a third for the treble, and a fourth for the very high. So that from the chosen speaker, let's say, the highest notes, even whistles – here he sniggered – would 'come through' to perfection. And don't, for heaven's sake, think for a moment that the speakers can be placed close up to one another! In the radiogram unit there are only two of them: the speaker for the medium-range sounds, and the one for the treble notes. The one for the very highest range he'd had the idea of hiding there at the end of the room, near the window, whilst the fourth one, for the bass, he'd fitted in under the sofa on which I was sitting. All this with the design of producing a certain stereophonic effect.

Dirce entered at that moment, in a blue canvas blouse and white apron, tight at the waist, dragging behind her the tea trolley.

I saw an expression of slight quarrelsomeness cross Alberto's face. The girl must also have noticed it.

'It was the Professor who ordered that I bring it immediately,' she said.

'It doesn't matter. We might as well have a cup ourselves.'

Blond and curly-haired, with the flushed cheeks of the Veneto's Alpine foothills, Perotti's daughter, silently and with lowered eyes, prepared the tea cups, placed them on the small table and finally withdrew. A good scent of soap and talcum powder remained in the room. Even the tea, it seemed to me, was flavoured with it.

As I drank, I kept looking round me. I admired the room's furnishings, all so rational, functional, modern, in complete contrast with the rest of the house, and yet, all the same, I couldn't quite work out why I was afflicted by an ever-increasing sense of unease, of oppressiveness.

'D'you like the way I've arranged the studio?' asked Alberto.

He seemed suddenly anxious to have my approval: which, naturally, I didn't begrudge, praising the simplicity of the furniture – having got to my feet, I went to examine more closely a large draughtsman's table set alongside and near the window, and sporting a finely turned and jointed metal lamp – and especially the side-lighting which – I said – I not only found very relaxing but also excellent for working by.

He let me run on and seemed pleased.

'Did you design the furniture yourself?'

'Not exactly. I copied a bit from *Domus* and *Casabella*, and a bit from *Studio*, you know, that English magazine . . . and a carpenter from Via Coperta made them for me.'

Hearing me approve of the furniture – he added – couldn't fail to gratify him. For a place to work or just hang out in, what was the point of surrounding oneself with ugly stuff or even antique junk? As for Giampi Malnate (he coloured very faintly as he named him), he'd insinuated that, furnished in this manner, it resembled a *garçonnière* more than a studio, besides arguing, like the good Communist he was, that *things* can at the most only provide some palliative or surrogate, himself being opposed in principle to any kind of surrogate or palliative, and even to technical expertise, whenever it assumed that a drawer which closes perfectly, just to give an example, might offer a resolution to all the individual's problems, including those of morality and politics. He, however – touching his chest with a finger – had a different opinion. Whilst respecting Malnate's views (he was a Communist – absolutely, didn't I know that?), he found life already confused and tedious enough without the household goods and furniture, the silent, faithful companions of our domestic life, having to be so as well.

It was the first and last time that I would ever see him become heated, and take sides with one set of ideas rather than another. We drank a second cup of tea, but by then the conversation had languished, to such an extent it was necessary to have recourse to some music.

We listened to a couple of records. Dirce returned, carrying a tray of pastries. At length, towards seven o'clock, a telephone on a desk next to the draughtsmen's table began to ring.

'D'you want to bet it's Giampi?' Alberto murmured, rushing towards it.

Before lifting the receiver he hesitated for a second: like a gambler who, having been dealt his cards, puts off the moment of discovering his luck.

But it really was Malnate, as I quickly gathered.

'So what are you doing? You're not coming then?' Alberto said with disappointment, with an almost puerile whine in his voice.

The other spoke rather at length (stuck between Alberto's shoulder and neck, the receiver vibrated with the force of his calm Lombard voice). At the end I heard a 'Bye' and the conversation was over.

'He's not coming,' Alberto commented.

He slowly returned to the armchair. He let himself drop into it, stretched himself, and yawned.

'It seems he's been kept in at the factory,' he added, 'and will be there for another three or four hours. He says he's sorry. And asked me to send you his regards.'

4

Rather than the generic 'See you soon' I exchanged with Alberto, whilst taking my leave of him, it was a letter from Micòl, arriving a few days later, which convinced me to return.

This letter was witty, neither too short nor too long, written on the four sides of two sheets of blue paper which her impetuous fluent handwriting had rapidly filled, without hesitations or corrections. Micòl begged me to forgive her: she had left unexpectedly. She hadn't even said goodbye to me, and this had not been very stylish of her, she was only too willing to admit. She had tried to phone me, however – she added – before she'd left, and in the eventuality that I couldn't be contacted, she'd asked Alberto to track me down. Since this had happened, had Alberto kept his promise of finding me, 'at the cost of his life'? Famous as he was for his phlegmatism, he always ended up letting all of his contacts drop, and yet he had such a real need of them, poor thing! The letter went on for another two and a half pages, explaining about her thesis which was by then 'sailing on towards the finishing-line', referring to Venice – which in winter 'simply made one want to weep' – and coming to an unexpected conclusion with a verse translation of an Emily Dickinson poem.

This:

> Morii per la Bellezza; e da poco ero
> discesa nell'avello,
> che, caduto pel Vero, uno fu messo
> nell'attiguo sacello.

« Perché sei morta? », mi chiese sommesso.

Dissi: « Morii pel Bello ».

« Io per la Verità: dunque è lo stesso

– disse –, son tuo fratello. »

Da tomba a tomba, come due congiunti

incontratisi a notte,

parlavamo così; finché raggiunti

l'erba ebbe nomi e bocche.[1]

It was followed by a postscript which said, word for word: '*Alas, poor Emily*. Such are the kind of consolations one's forced to find in abject spinsterhood!'

I liked the translation, but was struck most of all by the postscript. Who was it referring to? To '*poor Emily*' or was it, rather, to a Micòl in self-pitying, depressive mode?

Replying, I took care, once again, to hide behind a thick smoke-screen. After having referred to my first visit to her house, and kept silent on how disappointing it had been for me, and after promising that I should very soon be returning there, I prudently confined myself to literature. Dickinson's poem was wonderful – I wrote – but her translation was also excellent, particularly in the way it showed a somewhat dated taste, a bit 'Carduccian'. Most of all I appreciated her faithfulness. With dictionary in hand, I had compared her version with the original text in English, finding nothing questionable except, perhaps, one detail, which was where she had translated 'moss' which actually meant *muschio, muffa, borraccina* with 'erba', grass. I continued by saying that all the same, even in its present state, her translation worked very well, and in such things a beautiful inaccuracy was always better than a ploddingly correct ugliness. The fact I'd pointed out was, however, easily remedied. All that was needed was a small change in the final stanza, such as:

Da tomba a tomba, come due congiunti

incontratisi a notte,

parlavamo; finché il muschio raggiunti
ebbe i nomi, le bocche.

Micòl replied two days later with a telegram in which she thanked me 'truly, with heartfelt gratitude!' for my literary advice, and then, the next day, with a letter containing two new typed versions of the translation. In turn, I sent a letter of some ten sides which quarrelled, word by word, with her postcard. All considered, by letter we were far more clumsy and lifeless than on the telephone, so much so that in a short while we stopped corresponding. In the meantime, however, I had taken up visiting Alberto's studio, regularly, more or less every day.

Assiduous and punctual, Giampiero Malnate would also come with almost the same regularity. Talking, disputing, often arguing (in short, hating and loving each other from the first moment), it was thus that we got to know each other deeply, and we very quickly adopted the 'tu' form of address.

I remembered how Micòl had expressed herself on the subject of his 'physique'. I too found him, Malnate, bulky and oppressive. Like her, I too very often felt a kind of acute intolerance for his sincerity, his loyalty, for the eternal plea he made for manly openness, for that calm faith of his in a Lombard and Communist future which shone from his grey, too-human eyes. Despite this, from the first time that I sat in front of him, in Alberto's studio, I was filled with a single desire: that he should respect me, that he should not consider me as an interloper between himself and Alberto, that, finally, he would not deem as utterly mismatched the daily trio which, certainly not from his own initiative, he found himself a part of. I think that the adoption also on my part of smoking a pipe goes back precisely to that period.

The two of us spoke of many things (Alberto preferred to listen), but, obviously, most of all about politics.

These were the months that immediately followed the Monaco Pact, and it was this, and its consequences, which was the most recurrent topic of our conversations. What would Hitler do now that the Sudetan lands had been incorporated within the Greater

Reich? In what direction would he strike next? For myself, I wasn't a pessimist, and every now and then Malnate would think I was right. In my opinion, the *entente* which France and England had been forced to subscribe to at the end of the crisis that had occurred last September wouldn't last for long. True. Hitler and Mussolini had induced Chamberlain and Daladier to abandon Beneš's Czecho-slovakia to its fate. But then what? With the change of Chamberlain and Daladier for younger, more decisive men (that's the advantage of the parliamentary system! – I exclaimed), within a short while France and England would be in a position to dig in their heels. Time would surely play in their favour.

Yet if the conversation turned to the war in Spain, now on its last legs, or if there was any reference to the Soviet Union, Malnate's behaviour towards the Western democracies and towards me, to all intents and purposes ironically considered their representative and paladin, would abruptly become less flexible. I can still see him thrusting his big brown head forwards, his forehead shining with sweat, to fix his gaze upon mine with his usual, unbearable attempt at emotional blackmail, caught between moralism and sentimental-ism, to which he willingly had recourse, whilst his voice took on a low, warm, persuasive, patient tone. Who were they, then – he'd ask – who were the people truly responsible for the Francoist rebellion? Weren't they by any chance the French and English right, who'd not only tolerated it, at the start, but then, later, even supported and applauded it? Just as the Anglo-French response, correct in its form but actually ambiguous, had allowed Mussolini in 1935 to swallow up Ethiopia in a single mouthful, so in Spain it had mostly been the blameworthy dithering of Baldwin, Halifax and Blum that had swung the balance of fortune in Franco's favour. It was pointless to blame the Soviet Union and the International Brigade, he insinuated ever more gently, pointless to make Russia the easy scapegoat for every idiot, responsible if events down there were now at the point of collapse. The truth was quite different: only Russia had understood, from the very beginning, exactly what il Duce and the Führer were. She alone had clearly foreseen the inevitable alliance between them, and had consequently acted in time. On the contrary, the French and English right wings, sub-verting the democratic order as did every right wing of every country in every period, had always looked on Fascist Italy and Nazi Germany with ill-concealed sympathy. Sure, to French and English reactionaries, il Duce and the Führer might seem slightly incon-venient types, a shade crude and exaggerated, but still in every way preferable to Stalin, because Stalin, as we all know, has always been the devil. Having attacked and invaded Austria and Czechoslovakia, Germany was already pressing on the borders of Poland. So, if France and England were reduced to the level of gawping and accepting everything, the blame for their present impotence fell squarely on the shoulders of those fine, worthy, eye-catching gentle-men in top hats and tail-coats (so well suited at least in their manner of dressing to the nineteenth-century nostalgia of *so many* decadent, literary types . . .) who were now in government.

But Malnate's polemics became even more heated every time the topic of Italian history over the last decades cropped up.

It was obvious – he said: for me, and for Alberto too, Fascism in the end represented nothing but the sudden, inexplicable illness which afflicts and betrays the healthy organism, or else, to use a phrase dear to Benedetto Croce, the guru you share (here Alberto never failed to shake his head desolately, as a sign of denial, but Malnate paid no attention to this), 'the Invasion of the Hyksos'.[2] For us two, in conclusion, the Liberal Italy of Giolitti, Nitti, Orlando and even that of Sonnino, Salandra and Facta, had all been fine and dandy, the miraculous product of a golden age to which, in every respect, if only that were possible, it would be desirable to return. And yet we were wrong, just see how wrong we were! The illness had not arrived in the least bit unannounced. It began a long way back, in fact, in the earliest years of the Risorgimento, which were characterized by – let's admit it – an almost total absence of the people's participation – the real people – in the cause of Liberty and Unity. Giolitti? If Mussolini had been able to get over the crisis caused by the murder of Matteotti, in 1924, when all around him seemed to be losing their heads and even the King started swithering, we had *our* Giolitti to thank for that, and Benedetto Croce too –

both of them quite willing to install in power whatever monstrous toad happened to be around – anything to make sure the progress of the working classes would be impeded and slowed down. It was actually them, the Liberals we worshipped, who gave Mussolini the time to get his second wind. Less than six months later, il Duce had repaid them for their services by crushing the freedom of the press and dissolving the other parties. Giovanni Giolitti retired from political life, withdrawing to his country estates in Piedmont. Benedetto Croce went back to his precious philosophic and literary studies. But there were others, far less responsible, in fact entirely guiltless, who had had to pay far more painfully for all this. Amendola and Gobetti were bludgeoned to death. Filippo Turati was snuffed out in exile, far from the Milan where but a few years earlier he had buried his poor wife Anna. Antonio Gramsci had been thrown into one of our illustrious jails (didn't we know that he'd died in prison last year?). Italy's urban proletariat and its agricultural labourers, together with their natural leaders, had lost every effective hope of social justice and human dignity, and now for almost twenty years had been vegetating and dying in silence.

It was not easy for me to oppose these ideas, for various reasons. In the first place because Malnate's political knowledge, the Socialism and anti-Fascism he'd taken in in his family with his mother's milk, quite overpowered my own. In the second place because the role he'd boxed me into – the role of literary decadent, as he said, whose political formation had been under the guidance of Benedetto Croce's writings – seemed to me inadequate and inaccurate, and therefore had to be refuted before any further disagreement between us could get under way. The truth was that I preferred to be silent, moulding my face into a vaguely ironic smile. I submitted to him, and kept quiet.

As for Alberto, he too said nothing; in part because as usual he had nothing to say, but mainly to facilitate his friend's attacks on me – this was the main advantage, I reckoned. When three people are shut up for days arguing in a room, it is almost always the case that two of them end up in alliance against the third. So as to be in agreement with Giampi, to show his solidarity, Alberto seemed ready to accept anything from him, including the fact that he, Giampi, would often tar us with the same brush. It was true: Mussolini and his ilk were gathering together all kinds of slurs and defamations against the Jews – Malnate would, for example, claim. Last July's infamous Race Manifesto, drawn up by ten so-called 'Fascist scholars' – it was hard to know whether it was more shameful or more ridiculous. But having admitted this – he added – could either of us tell him how many anti-Fascist 'Israelites' there had been in Italy before 1938? Very few indeed, he feared, a tiny minority, if even at Ferrara, as Alberto had told him many times, the number of those enrolled in the Fascist Party had always been extremely high. I myself had taken part in the *Littoriali della Cultura*. Wasn't I already reading 'the great' Croce's *History of Europe* just at that time? Or had I been waiting, before plunging into it, for the following year, the year of the *Anschluss* and the first warnings of Italian racism?

I submitted to him and smiled, occasionally rebelling, but more often not, overcome despite myself by his candour and sincerity, a bit crude and relentless without doubt, a bit too *goy*-ish – I'd tell myself – but in the end truly compassionate because essentially egalitarian and fraternal. However, when Malnate sometimes turned on Alberto, not entirely in jest, and accused him and his family of being 'at the end of the day' filthy landowners, evil proprietors of country estates and, on top of that, aristocrats clearly nostalgic for medieval feudalism, one reason why 'at the end of the day' it wasn't so unjust that now they should in some way pay the penalty for all the privileges they had hitherto enjoyed; and when Alberto, bent over double to protect himself from these hurricane blasts, would laugh till the tears came to his eyes, meanwhile nodding his head to show that yes, he, personally, was more than willing to pay the price, then I'd experience a surge of secret glee as I listened to him thundering against his friend. The child of the years before 1929, who walking beside his mother along the paths of the cemetery had always heard the Finzi-Continis' solitary monumental tomb defined as 'a total monstrosity', would suddenly re-emerge from the very depths of my being to applaud maliciously.

There were times when Malnate almost seemed to forget my presence. These generally occurred when he started recalling with Alberto the 'times' they had in Milan, the shared male and female friendships of that era, the restaurants they had been to together, the evenings at La Scala, the football matches at the Arena or at San Siro, the weekend trips to the mountains or to the Riviera. They had both belonged to a 'group' – one evening he honoured me with an explanation – whose demand on its members was a single one: intelligence. A truly wonderful time! he sighed. Characterized by scorn for every kind of provincialism and rhetoric, that time might be best defined, not only as that of their happy youth, but as the time of Gladys, a ballerina at the Lirico who had for some months been a friend of his – seriously, Gladys wasn't at all bad, a great laugh, 'good company', at heart utterly without designs on anyone, and blithely promiscuous . . . and then having lucklessly fallen for Alberto, she'd ended up breaking off all contact with both of them.

'Poor Gladys, I've never understood why Alberto always rejected her,' he added with a slight wink. Then he turned to Alberto:

'Come on. Spit it out. Three years have passed since then, and the scene of the crime is almost three hundred kilometres from here. Why don't we finally put our cards on the table?'

But in response Alberto only blushed, and warded off the question. And Gladys was never mentioned again.

He enjoyed the work that had brought him to our part of the world – he would often say – even Ferrara he liked, as a city, and it seemed absurd to him, to say the least, that Alberto and I looked on it as a kind of tomb or jail. Obviously our situation could be considered a rather special one. And yet we were wrong to believe ourselves the only minority group in Italy being persecuted. What were we thinking? The workers in the plant where his job was, what did we think they were – beasts without any feelings? He could name many of them who not only had never enrolled themselves in the Fascist Party but who were Socialists or Communists, and for this had often been beaten up or given the castor-oil 'treatment', and yet continued, uncowed, to stand by their principles. He had been at one of their meetings, and was delighted to find there not only the workers and farm labourers who'd come specially, on bikes perhaps, from as far away as Mésola and Goro, but also two or three of the most renowned lawyers in the city. Which went to prove that even here, in Ferrara, not all of the bourgeoisie were on the side of the Fascists, that not all of its ranks were filled with traitors. Had we ever heard Clelia Trotti spoken of? No? Well, she was an ex-primary school teacher, an old woman who when she was younger, they'd told him, had been the pillar of Ferrara's Socialist movement, and continued to be so – and what a force she was! Not a single meeting was held without her lively and vivid contributions. That was how he'd met her. Regarding her humanitarian kind of Socialism, the type of Andrea Costa, it might be better left without comment, and little could be expected of it. But what passion there was in her, what faith and hope! She reminded him, even physically, especially those blue eyes of hers, that hinted at the blonde she must once have been, of Signora Anna, Filippo Turati's companion, whom he'd got to know as a boy in Milan around 1922. His father, a lawyer, had served almost a year in prison with the Turati couple in 1898. A close friend of both of them, he was one of the few who, on Sunday afternoons, still dared to call on them in their small flat in the Galleria. And Malnate would often go along with him.

No, let's be honest, Ferrara was not at all the prison-house that someone overhearing us might think it was. It's true that seeing it from the industrial zone, shut up as it seemed to be within its old walls, especially on days of bad weather, the city might easily give the impression of solitude and isolation. Yet all round Ferrara was the countryside, rich, abundant, fertile, and beyond it, less than forty kilometres away, was the sea, with empty beaches bordered by lovely pine and ilex woods. And the sea is always a great resource. But this apart, the city itself, once you threw yourself into it as he'd decided to, once you considered it without prejudice, was like every other city, hiding treasures of human virtue, intelligence and goodness of heart, and even of courage, which only the deaf and blind, or rather the sterile, could ignore or misconstrue.

5

At first, Alberto kept on announcing his imminent departure for Milan. Then, bit by bit, he stopped mentioning it, and his graduation thesis ended up becoming a thorny question we had to skirt around with some caution. He made no further reference to it, and it was clear he wanted us to follow suit.

As I've already suggested, his interventions in our arguments were rare and almost always irrelevant. He was on Malnate's side, of this there was no doubt, happy if he should triumph, worried if, on the contrary, I seemed to be getting the upper hand. But mainly he kept silent. At the most, he would come out with some exclamation every now and then ('Ah, that's good, though! . . .', 'Yes, but, if looked at another way . . .', 'Hold on a second, let's be calm about this . . .'), following up with a short laugh or a little bit of embarrassed throat-clearing.

Even physically, he had the tendency of cringing back, of cancelling himself out, of disappearing. Malnate and I would generally sit facing each other, in the middle of the room, one on the sofa and the other on one of the two armchairs, with the table in the middle and both of us right under the light. We would only get up to go to the small bathroom next to the bedroom, or else to check what the weather was like through the big broad window which looked out over the park. By contrast, Alberto preferred to stay down there at the end of the room, protected by the double barricade of the desk and the draughtsman's table. Those times he bestirred himself, we would see him wander up and down the room on tiptoe, his elbows drawn into his sides. He would change the records on the radiogram, one after the other, careful that the volume did not drown out our voices, survey the ashtrays, and empty them in the bathroom when they were full, regulate the brightness of the side-lighting, ask in an undertone if we could do with a little more tea, straighten out and reposition certain objects. In short, he adopted the busy, discreet air of the master of the house concerned only about one thing: that the acute minds of his guests should be allowed to function properly within the best possible surroundings and conditions.

I'm convinced, though, that it was he, with his meticulous orderliness, with his stratagems, with his cautious unpredictable manoeuvres, who was responsible for diffusing the vague sense of oppression which shadowed the very air we breathed there. It was enough for him, in the pauses of the conversation, for instance, to start expatiating on the qualities of the armchair in which I was sitting, whose back 'guaranteed' the most correct and favourable 'anatomical' alignment for the spine; or, offering me the small, dark leather pouch for pipe tobacco, to catalogue the various kinds of cut according to him indispensable for our Dunhill or GBD to obtain the optimum flavour (such and such a quantity of sweet, of strong, of Maryland); or, for motives never quite made clear and known only to himself, to announce with a vague smile, lifting his chin towards the radiogram, the temporary exclusion of sound from one of the loudspeakers – in every case of such or similar kind, I would experience a bristling of nerves which was forever lying in wait, forever ready to burst forth.

One evening I didn't manage to suppress them. Certainly – I shouted out to Malnate – his dilettante-like behaviour, essentially that of a tourist, let him assume towards Ferrara a tone of tolerance and indulgence which I envied. But how would he, he who spoke so much about the treasures of human virtue, goodness, etc., how would he judge something that had happened to me, personally, only a few mornings ago?

I'd had the bright idea – I began to tell them – of taking myself, my papers and books, to the Reading Room of the Public Library in Via Scienze – a place I'd hung around since my school days and where I always felt at home. Everyone always treated me very courteously there, within those ancient walls. After I'd enrolled in the Faculty of Arts, the Director, Dr Ballola, had begun to consider me a scholar like himself. As soon as he spotted me, he'd sit down beside me to keep me abreast of the progress of some of his by now ten-year-old research material to do with a biography on Ariosto, filed away in his private study, research about which he declared himself confident 'of going some way beyond the renowned efforts of Catalano in the field'. So also with the various other staff members there, who acted towards me with such confidence and familiarity as not only to let me dispense with the boredom of filling out forms for the books, but even to let me smoke the occasional cigarette there.

Well, as I was saying, that morning I'd had the bright idea of spending some hours in the library. Except that I'd only just had time to sit myself down at a table in the Reading Room and get out all the stuff I needed, when one of the staff, a certain Poledrelli, a man in his sixties, fat, jovial, a famous eater of pasta and incapable of putting two words together which weren't in dialect, came up to me to suggest that I leave, and forthwith. All puffed up, trying to keep his belly in and even managing to speak in proper Italian, the good Poledrelli had explained in a loud official voice how the Director had given him very definite orders on this matter, and therefore – he repeated – would I be so kind as to get up and be gone. That morning the Reading Room was particularly full of boys from the middle school. The scene had been followed, in a sepulchral silence, by no less than fifty pairs of eyes and the same number of ears. As you can imagine, I went on, it was no joy to drag myself up, gather together all my things from the table, replace them in my briefcase and then to reach, one step at a time, the big glass entrance door. It's true – that poor wretch Poledrelli was only following orders. But he, Malnate, should take great care, in case he should get to meet him (who knows if Poledrelli himself didn't also belong to the schoolmistress Trotti's circle!), take great care not to be taken in by the deceptively amiable look of that big plebeian face. Inside that chest as huge as a wardrobe there lived a little heart no bigger than this. It might well pump good working-class blood, but it was no more dependable for that.

And then, and then! – I grew yet more heated – wasn't it at the very least out of place for him to come here preaching at, let's leave aside Alberto, whose family has always kept itself apart from the communal life of the city, but at me who, on the contrary, was born and brought up within a family that might even have been too inclined to be open, and to mix with others of every class? My father, a volunteer in the war, had joined the Fascist Party in 1919, and I myself until yesterday had belonged to the GUF. Then since we ourselves had always been very normal people, even banal in our normality, it would be absurd to expect us now, out of the blue, to start behaving abnormally. Called into the Federation to hear himself expelled from the party, then chased out of the Commercial Club as an undesirable person – it would be very odd for my father, poor fellow, to respond to such treatment with an expression any less anguished and bewildered than the one I saw on his face. And if my brother Ernesto wanted to go to university, should he apply to the Polytechnic in Grenoble? And should my sister Fanny, just thirteen, continue with her schooling at the Jewish College in Via Vigna-tagliata? From them too, abruptly torn away from their school friends, from the friends of their childhood, was it also fair to expect some especially appropriate behaviour? What nonsense! One of the most odious forms of anti-Semitism was precisely this: to complain that Jews aren't sufficiently *like* other people, and then, the opposite, once they've become almost totally assimilated with their surround-ings, to complain that they're just like everybody else, not even a fraction distinguished from the average.

I had got carried away by my anger, had moved somewhat outside the topic of our disagreement, and Malnate, who had carefully followed everything I'd been saying, did not fail to make a point of this. He an anti-Semite? – he stammered: it was frankly the first time he'd ever been referred to in that way! By now over-heated, I was about to return to the fray, to redouble my attack. Just at that moment, as he passed behind the back of my opponent with the ruffled speed of a frightened bird, Alberto cast a begging look towards me. 'Please stop!' that look was saying. That he, unbe-knownst to his bosom buddy, should this once make such an appeal to what was most secretly and exclusively shared between the two of us, struck me as extraordinary. I held back and said nothing more. Just at that moment, the first notes of a Beethoven quartet played by the Busch lifted into the smoky atmosphere of the room to seal my victory.

The evening was not only important because of this. Around eight o'clock it began to rain with such violence that Alberto, after a speedy telephone exchange perhaps with his mother, speaking in their usual jargon, asked us to stay for dinner.

Malnate said he'd be very glad to accept. He'd been dining nearly always at Giovanni's, he told us, 'lonely as a dog'. It seemed almost unbelievable to him to be able to spend an evening 'with a family'.

I also accepted, but asked if I could phone home first.

'Of course!' Alberto exclaimed.

I sat down where he usually sat, behind the desk, and dialled the number. As I waited, I looked to the side, through the windowpane striped with rain. Against the thick darkness, the dense trees hardly stood out at all. Beyond the black gulf of the park, hard to say where, a small light glimmered.

Finally my father was heard to reply in his usual complaining tones.

'Oh, it's you, is it?' he said. 'We were beginning to get worried. Where are you phoning from?'

'I'm staying out for supper,' I replied.

'In this rain!'

'Exactly. Because of it.'

'You're still at the Finzi-Continis'?'

'Yes.'

'Whenever you get back, stop in to see me, will you? Anyway, I can't get to sleep, as you know . . .'

I put down the receiver and lifted my eyes. Alberto was looking at me.

'Done?'

'Done.'

All three of us went out into the corridor, crossed through various large and small rooms, descended a big staircase at the foot of which, in a dinner jacket and white gloves, Perotti was waiting, and from there we passed directly into the dining room.

The rest of the family were already there. There was Professor Ermanno, Signora Olga, Signora Regina and one of the Venetian uncles, the phthisiology specialist, who, seeing Alberto come in, got up, went towards him and kissed him on both cheeks. After which, whilst distractedly tugging at his lower eyelid with a finger, he began to tell him what had brought him there. He'd had to go to Bologna for a consultation – he said – and then, on the way back, between trains, had thought it a good idea to stop for supper. When we came in, Professor Ermanno, his wife and brother-in-law were sitting in front of the lighted fire, with Jor stretched out at their feet in all his considerable length. Signora Regina was, however, seated at the table, exactly under the central light.

Inevitably, the memory of my first meal at the Finzi-Contini house (I think it was still January) tends to get confused with the memories of the many other dinners at the *magna domus* to which I was invited in the course of that winter. I do, however, recollect with unaccustomed clarity what we ate that evening: and that was a chicken liver and rice soup, minced turkey in jelly, corned tongue with black olives and spinach stalks in vinegar as side dishes, a chocolate cake, fresh and dried fruit, nuts, peanuts, grapes and pine kernels. I also remember clearly that almost at once, no sooner had we sat down at the table, Alberto decided to announce the story of my recent expulsion from the Public Library, and that I was once more struck by the lack of surprise with which this news was greeted by the four old people. The comments which followed on the current situation and on the Ballola–Poledrelli duo, brought up again every now and then throughout the meal, were not even, on their part, especially bitter, but, as usual, elegantly sardonic, almost light-hearted. And joyful, decidedly joyful and pleased, was the tone of voice with which, later, putting his arm round me, Professor Ermanno suggested from that time on I should make the most of the almost twenty thousand books in the house, a large number of which – he told me – concerned mid- and late-nineteenth-century literature.

But what struck me most, from that first evening on, was undoubtedly the dining room itself, with its floral-style furniture of dark red wood, its vast fireplace with a sinuous, arched, almost human mouth, its walls panelled with leather, except for one which was entirely of glass framing the dark, silent storm of the park like the *Nautilus*'s porthole – the whole thing so intimate, so sheltering, so – I was about to say – buried, and above all so well suited to who I was then – now I understand! – to shielding that kind of slow-burning ember which the hearts of the young so often are.

Crossing the threshold, both Malnate and I were received with great cordiality, and not only by Professor Ermanno, kind, jovial and lively as ever, but also by Signora Olga. It was she who showed us to our places at the table. Malnate was given the seat to her right, and I, at the other end of the table, to the right of her husband. The place on her left, between her, his sister, and their old mother, was reserved for Giulio. Even Signora Regina in the meantime, looking lovely with her rosy cheeks and her white silky hair thicker and shinier than ever, bestowed a friendly and amused gaze on all around.

The setting which faced me, complete with plates, glasses and cutlery, seemed to be waiting there prepared for a seventh guest. Whilst Perotti was already doing his rounds with the soup tureen with the *riso in brodo*, I asked Professor Ermanno in a low voice for whom the seat at his left had been prepared. He just as quietly replied that now the seat was 'presumably' waiting for no one – he checked the time on his big Omega wristwatch, shook his head and sighed – it being the seat which Micòl, or to be exact 'my Micòl', as he said, usually occupied.

6

Professor Ermanno was not exaggerating. Among the almost twenty thousand books in the house, many of them on scientific, historical, or a variety of scholarly topics (the latter mainly in German) there were many hundreds devoted to the literature of the New Italy. As for whatever had been published relating to Carducci's *fin-de-siècle* literary circle, from the decades in which he had taught in Bologna, there was practically nothing missing. There were volumes in verse and in prose not only by the Maestro himself, but also by Panzacchi, Severino Ferrari, Lorenzo Stecchetti, Ugo Brilli, Guido Mazzoni, by the young Pascoli, the young Panzini, the very young Valgimigli – generally first editions, nearly all of them bearing signed dedications to the Baroness Josette Artom di Susegana. Gathered in three separate glass bookcases which occupied a whole wall of a huge first-floor reception room next to Professor Ermanno's personal study, there was no doubt that these books together represented a collection of which any public library, including Bologna's Archiginnasio's, would be glad to boast. The collection even housed the little volumes, rare as hen's teeth, of the prose poems of Francesco Acri, the famous translator of Plato, till then only known to me as a translator: not such 'a saint', then, as Professor Meldolesi (who had also been a scholar of Acri's work) had, since the fifth form, insisted to us he was, as his dedications to Alberto and Micòl's grandmother were, out of the whole chorus of them, perhaps the most gallant and showed the most heightened masculine awareness of the proud beauty to which they alluded.

With an entire, specialized library at my disposal, and besides that, being oddly keen to be there every morning, in the great, warm, silent hall which received light from three big, high windows adorned with pelmets covered in red-striped white silk, and at the centre of which, clad in mouse-coloured felt, stretched the billiards table, I managed to complete my thesis on Panzacchi in the two and half months which followed. If I'd really wanted to, who knows, I might have been able to finish it earlier. But was that really what I wanted? Or rather hadn't I tried to eke out the time for as long as possible so as to have the right to visit the Finzi-Contini house in the mornings *as well*? What is certain is that around the middle of March (news having in the meantime been received of Micòl's graduation, with the marks of 110 out of 110), I still remained torpidly attached to the meagre privilege of these additional morning visits to the house from which she insisted on keeping such a distance. By this time only a few days separated us from the Catholic Easter, which fell that year almost at the same time as *Pesach*, the Jewish Passover. Although spring was almost at our doors, a week earlier it had snowed with extraordinary abundance, after which the cold had returned with a vengeance. It almost seemed as though the winter had no intention of ever ending. And I myself, my heart haunted by an obscure, shadowy lake of fear, held tight to the little desk which the previous January Professor Ermanno had had placed for me beneath the central window in the billiards room, as though, in so doing, I might be able to halt the inexorable progress of time. I would stand up, walk to the window and look down over the park. Buried under a mantle of snow half a metre deep, perfectly white, the Barchetto del Duca seemed turned into a landscape from a Norse saga. At times I surprised myself by hoping that the snow would never melt, would last for ever.

For two and a half months my days remained virtually unchanging. Punctual as a government clerk, I would leave home at half past eight in the cold, nearly always by bike, though occasionally on foot. After at most twenty minutes, there I would be ringing at the big gate at the end of Corso Ercole I d'Este, and from there I'd cross the park, which was infused, around the beginning of February, with the delicate scent of the yellow flowers of the calycanthus. By nine I was already in the billiards room where I'd remain until one o'clock, and where I'd return around three in the afternoon. Later, at about six, I would call in on Alberto, sure of also finding Malnate there. Finally, as I've already stated, both of us were often invited to stay for supper. In fact, very soon it had become so customary for me to stay to eat, that I no longer even phoned home to tell them. I might perhaps have told my mother as I left: 'I'll probably be staying out for supper there.' 'There' required no further clarifications.

I worked for hours and hours without seeing another soul, except Perotti who, around eleven o'clock, would come in bearing a small cup of coffee on a silver tray. This too, the eleven o'clock coffee, had almost immediately become a daily ritual, an acquired habit about which there was no point in either of us wasting any words. What Perotti would talk about, as he waited for me to finish sipping the coffee, was, if anything, the 'running' of the house, in his view seriously undermined by the over-extended absence of the 'Signorina', who, no doubt about it, had to become a teacher and everything, but . . . (and this 'but', accompanied by a grimace of doubt, might have alluded to a host of things: to the fact that his masters, fortunate creatures that they were, had really no need at all to earn their living, or perhaps to the Racial Laws which in any case would have turned *our* degree diplomas into mere bits of paper, without the slightest practical use) . . . even if a bit of a leave, seeing as without her the house was quickly going 'to the dogs', a bit of a leave, maybe a week away then a week back here, was something she could easily have sorted for herself. With me, Perotti always found some way to complain about his employers. As a sign of mistrust and disapproval, he tightened his lips, winked and shook his head. When he referred to Signora Olga, he even went as far as tapping his temple with his rough forefinger. Naturally I didn't encourage him, and stubbornly blanked his repeated attempts to have me join him in a servile complicity which, besides repelling me, were offensive to me personally. And so, in a short while, in the face of my silences, of my chill smiles, Perotti had no other option but to make off, leaving me once again alone.

One day his younger daughter, Dirce, arrived in his place. She too waited beside the desk for me to finish the coffee. I drank it and looked her up and down.

'What's your name again?' I asked her, giving her back the empty cup, as my heart began to beat rapidly.

'Dirce,' she smiled, and her face was suffused with a blush.

She was wearing her usual blue cotton blouse, its thick fabric strangely redolent of the nursery. She scurried off, ducking my gaze which had been seeking hers out. A moment later I'd already begun to feel ashamed of what had happened (but what after all *had* happened?) as the vilest and most squalid of betrayals.

The only family member who would occasionally appear was Professor Ermanno. With special caution he would open the study door at the far end of the room, and then, on tiptoe, he would make his way across the room, so that more often than not I only became aware of his presence when he was already at my side, leaning respectfully over the papers and books I'd laid out before me.

'How are things going?' he would ask in a contented voice. 'It seems like you are going ahead full steam!'

I would make as if to get up.

'No. No. Please keep on working,' he'd exclaim. 'I'll be leaving you straight away.'

Usually he stayed no more than five minutes, during which time he always found some way of showing me all the sympathy and respect he felt for the way I stuck to my work. He looked at me with fiery, shining eyes, as though from me, from my literary future, my future as a scholar, who knows what great things could be expected, as though he was counting on me to fulfil some secret design which transcended not only himself but me as well . . . And, *à propos*, I remember that this behaviour of his towards me, although flattering, also upset me a bit. Why did he have no such expectations about Alberto – I'd ask myself – who's actually his son? And why had he accepted without any protests or complaints Alberto having given up his degree? And what about Micòl? In Venice, Micòl was doing exactly the same thing as I was doing here – finishing her thesis. And yet he never had occasion to name her, Micòl, or, if he referred to her it was by way of a sigh. He seemed to be implying:

'She's only a girl, and it's better for women to be concerned with the home, rather than literature!' But should I really have believed him?

One morning he stayed to talk longer than usual. In a roundabout manner, he began to speak once again of Carducci's letters and his own 'little works' on the Venetian topic: all the stuff – he said, nodding towards his study behind me – which he kept 'back there'. He smiled mysteriously as he mentioned this, his face assuming a sly, inviting expression. It was obvious he wanted to lead me 'back there', and at the same time wanted it to be me who proposed I should be taken there.

I made haste to oblige him.

So we went to the study, which was a room hardly less grand than the billiards room, but reduced, rendered almost shrunken, by an incredible accumulation of disparate things.

To start with, there was an abundance of books. Those on literary subjects mixed up with the scientific (mathematics, physics, economics, agriculture, medicine, astronomy and so on); books on local history, Ferrarese or Venetian, with those on 'ancient Jewish history' – the volumes chaotically crowded the usual glass-fronted bookcases, and took up a good part of the big walnut table (behind which, if he were seated, Professor Ermanno would most likely show as little more than the top of his beret); they were heaped up in perilously unsteady piles on the chairs, stacked into towers even on the floor, and scattered around almost everywhere. An enormous map of the world, then a lectern, a microscope, half a dozen barometers, a steel safe painted dark red, a small white bed like you see in doctors' surgeries, several hourglasses of different sizes, a brass kettledrum, a little German upright piano topped by two metronomes shut in their pyramidical cases, and beyond, many other objects of uncertain use which I don't now recall, lent the surroundings the look of a Faustian laboratory, which Professor Ermanno himself was the first to make fun of and to excuse himself for as if it represented a personal, private weakness of his: almost as if it was all that remained of his childish fads. However, I was forgetting to mention the fact that as far as pictures went, in contrast to all the other rooms of the house, which were generally overladen with them, here there were none to be seen except one: a huge life-size portrait by Lenbach,[1] weighing on the wall behind the table like an altarpiece. The magnificent blond lady bodied forth in this, standing upright, her shoulders bared, a fan in her gloved hand and with the silken train of her white gown brought to the fore to emphasize her length of leg and fullness of form, was obviously no other than the Baroness Josette Artom di Susegana. What a marmoreal forehead, what eyes, what a scornful lip, what a bust! She truly looked like a queen. His mother's portrait was the only thing, among that host of objects in the study, which Professor Ermanno did not joke about – not that morning, not ever.

That very morning, though, I was at last presented with the two Venetian tracts. In one of them – the Professor explained to me – all the inscriptions of the Jewish cemetery at the Lido were assembled and translated. The second, on the other hand, was on a Jewish woman poet who had lived in Venice in the first half of the seventeenth century, and as renowned to her contemporaries as she was now, 'sadly', forgotten. She was called Sara Enriquez (or Enriques) Avigdòr. For some decades, at her house in the Old Ghetto, she had held an important literary salon, assiduously frequented not only by the extremely gifted Ferrarese-Venetian rabbi Leone da Modena but also by many first-rate literary figures of the age, foreign as well as Italian. She had composed a considerable number of the 'finest' sonnets, which still now awaited a scholar capable of reassessing and reasserting their beauty. She had undertaken a brilliant correspondence with the famous Ansaldo Cebà, a gentleman from Genoa, who had written an epic poem on Queen Esther, and had become fixated on the idea of converting her to Catholicism, but then, in the end, seeing how futile all his insistence had been, had had to renounce this plan. A great woman, all considered: the honour and boast of Italian Jewry at the height of the Counter-Reformation, and in some way a part of the 'family' – Professor Ermanno had added as he was writing a couple of lines as a book dedication for me – since it seemed certain that his wife, on her mother's side, was one of her descendants.

He got up, walked around the table, took me by the arm and led me into the window bay.

There was, however, something – he continued, lowering his voice as though he feared someone might overhear us – which he felt obliged to warn me about. If, in the future, I should ever happen to concern myself with this Sara Enriquez, or Enriques, Avigdòr (and the subject was such as to merit a far more deep and detailed study than he in his youth had been able to give to it), at a certain point, I would inevitably have to confront some contrary opinions . . . disagreements . . . in fact some writings by third-rate literary figures, most of them the poetess's contemporaries (libellous things that were glaringly envious and anti-Semitic), which insinuated that not all the sonnets signed by her in circulation, and not even all the letters written by her to Cebà were, let's say, written by her own hand. Well, he, if his memory served him well, had obviously been unable to ignore the existence of such slanders and had, in fact, as I'd see, properly documented them. In any case . . .

He broke off to look me in the eyes, uncertain of my reactions.

In any case – he continued – even if I should think 'some time in the future' . . . umm . . . if I should ever attempt a revaluation . . . a revision . . . he advised me, till then, not to give too much credit to these malicious rumours. They might well be intriguing, but in the end they were misplaced. What, finally, was it that made an excellent historian? He must set himself the ideal of arriving at the truth, without in the process losing a sense of what's right and appropriate. Didn't I think so?

I nodded my head to show I agreed, and he, relieved, patted me on the back with the palm of his hand.

This done, he moved away, hunched up, across the study and bent to tinker with the safe, which he opened. He then drew from it a small casket covered in blue velvet.

He turned round, once more all smiles, towards the window, and before opening up the small casket, he said that he could see that I'd already guessed its contents – within, indeed, was kept the famous Carducci correspondence. It amounted to fifteen letters: and not all of them – he added – would I perhaps judge to be of the most pressing interest, although at least five of the fifteen were concerned with a special '*salamo da sugo* from hereabouts' of which the poet, having received it as a gift, had been 'so greatly' appreciative. All the same, I would without doubt be struck by one of them. It was a letter of autumn 1875, written therefore at the time when the crisis of the Historic Right[2] was looming on the horizon. That autumn Carducci's political stance seemed to be that as a declared democrat, Republican and revolutionary, he was unable to join the ranks of Agostino Depretis's left. On the other hand, '*l'irto vinattier di Stradella*'[3] and the 'crowd' of his friends seemed to him common folk, 'little men'. People who would never be capable of restoring Italy to its calling, to make Italy a Great Nation, worthy of its ancient Forefathers . . .

We stayed there talking until dinnertime. The result, at the end of all this, was that from that morning on the communicating door between the billiards room and the next-door study, till then always shut, now often remained open. Most of the time, the two of us stayed in our respective rooms. Yet we saw each other a lot more than before, Professor Ermanno coming to seek me out, and I making my way to him. Through the door, when it was open, we even exchanged the odd word: 'What time is it?', 'How's the work going?' and such things. Some years later, during the spring of 1943, in jail, the phrases that I would exchange with an unknown neighbouring cellmate, shouting up towards the air-hole of the 'wolf's mouth', would be of this kind: spoken in just this way, above all from the need to hear your own voice, to sense that you are alive.

7

At home, that year, Passover was celebrated with a single dinner.

It was my father who wanted it this way. Also, given Ernesto's absence – he'd said – we'd best forget having a Passover like those of previous years. And then, apart from this, how could we have done otherwise? They, *my* Finzi-Continis, had once more managed things perfectly. With the excuse of the garden they had succeeded in keeping all their servants, from the first to the last, letting them pass as farm-workers adept in the cultivation of vegetable-garden produce. And ourselves? From the time we had been forced to give notice to Elisa and Mariuccia, and to assume in their place that dried fish of an old Cohen, in practice we had no one to call on. In such circumstances, even our mother would be unable to work a miracle.

'Isn't it true, my angel?'

My angel didn't nurse any warmer feelings for the sixty-year-old Signorina Ricca Cohen than my father did. Instead of being delighted, as always, to hear one of us speak ill of the poor old woman, Mamma had consented with heartfelt gratitude to the idea of a low-key Passover. All right then – she had agreed: just one dinner, and that's all, a meal for the first evening. So what do we need to make it? She and Fanny would take care of everything, almost unassisted, without 'that one' – here she tilted her chin towards Cohen, shut in the kitchen – getting into one of her usual strops. Plus, why not, so 'that one' wouldn't have to scramble to and fro with so many plates and pans, at the risk, among other things, weak in the legs as she was, of some disaster or other, why not arrange it in another way – rather than eat in the dining room, so far away from the kitchen, and this year, with the snow, chilly as

Siberia, rather than the dining room why not lay the table here in the breakfast room . . .

It was not a happy meal. At the table's centre, the hamper which apart from the ritual 'snacks' contained the tureen of *haroset*, the tufts of bitter herbs, the unleavened bread and the boiled egg reserved for me, the first-born, uselessly enthroned beneath the blue-and-white silk handkerchief which grandma Ester had embroidered with her own hands forty years ago. In spite of all the care taken, or rather because of it, the table had assumed a look closely resembling the one it wore those evenings of Yom Kippur, when it was set out only for Them, the family dead, whose mortal remains lay in the cemetery at the end of Via Montebello, and yet made their presence decidedly felt, here, in spirit or effigy. Here, that evening, in place of them, we, the living, sat to eat. But fewer of us compared to before, and no longer light-hearted, laughing, loud-voiced, but rather sad and wistful like the dead. I looked at my father and my mother, both of them much aged in those last months. I looked at Fanny, who was then already fifteen, but, as though some ancient fear had arrested her development, she seemed no more than twelve. I looked around, one by one, at uncles and aunts and cousins, a great number of whom, within a few years from then, would be swallowed up by German crematoria ovens, and no way would they have dreamt of ending up like that, nor would I myself have dreamt it, but all the same, then, that evening, already, even though I saw them looking so insignificant, their pitiful faces topped with dowdy bourgeois hats or framed by bourgeois perms, even if I was aware how obtuse their minds were, how utterly unable to grasp the realities of that present moment or to read anything of the future, already then they seemed to me swathed in the same aura of statue-like, mysterious fate that still, in memory, encircles them today. I looked at old Cohen, the few times she dared to peep out from behind the kitchen door: Ricca Cohen, the distinguished spinster in her sixties who had come from the old people's home at Via Vittoria to serve in the house of well-off co-religionists, but who wanted nothing other than to return there, to the home, and, before the times got any worse, to die. Finally I looked at myself, reflected within the dark waters of the mirror opposite, and even I was already a little grey-haired, even I was caught up in the same wheels, but reluctantly, still unresigned. I wasn't dead yet – I told myself – I was still bursting with life! And yet, if I was still alive, how come I was there with them, for what purpose? Why didn't I immediately leave that grotesque and desperate gathering of ghosts, or at least stop up my ears so as not to hear any more talk of 'discrimination', of 'patriotic awards of merit', of 'certificates of ancestry', of 'proportions of Jewish blood', so as not to have to listen to the narrow-minded keening, the grey, monotonous, futile dirge that relatives and kin were meekly intoning all around me? The meal would drag on like that, chewing over the same familiar sayings for who knows how long, with my father frequently bringing forth, in his bitter, relishing style, the various 'affronts' he'd had to submit to in the course of these last months, beginning with the time when in the Party Headquarters the Federal Secretary, Consul Bolognese, with a saddened, shifty look, had announced to him that he had been forced to 'cancel' him from the list of party members, and ending up with the time when the President of the Commercial Club, with an equally sorrowing look, had called him over to tell him that he should consider himself 'struck off'. Oh, he could tell us some stories! To keep us up till midnight, till one or two!

And then, what would follow? The final scene, the communal goodbyes. I could already see it. We would have gone down the dark stairs all together, like a besieged flock. Having reached the entrance hall, someone – perhaps me – would have gone on ahead to leave the street door ajar, and then, one final time, before separating, on everyone's part, and mine included, there would be a renewal of the goodnights, the best wishes, the hand-shakings, the embraces and the kisses on both cheeks. But then, suddenly, from the street door left half open, there, against the blackness of the night, a gust of wind would sweep through the entrance hall. A hurricane wind that came from the night. It would crash down the hallway, cross, then pass beyond it, whistling through the gates that divided the hall from the garden, and meanwhile disperse with its force any of the guests who might have wanted to delay, with its savage howl would suddenly quell and hush any who might still have wished to linger and talk. Thin voices, faint cries, immediately overwhelmed. All of them blown away – light as leaves, as bits of paper, as hairs from a head of hair turned grey with age and terror . . . Oh, in the end, Ernesto had been lucky not to have gone to university in Italy. He had written from Grenoble to say that he was suffering from hunger, and that, with the little French he knew, he could hardly understand anything of the lessons in the Polytechnic. But lucky him to be suffering from hunger and being scared he wouldn't pass his exams. I had stayed here, and for me who had stayed, and who'd once again chosen out of pride or sterility a solitude nourished by vague, nebulous, impotent hopes, for me there really was no hope at all.

But who can ever foretell the future?

Nearing eleven o'clock, as it happened, whilst my father, with the evident intent of dispelling the general low spirits, had begun singing the happy nonsense-verses of *Caprét ch'avea comperà il signor Padre*[1] (his favourite song, his 'battle-steed' as he would put it), it happened that at a certain point, by chance, lifting my eyes to the mirror opposite, I caught sight of the telephone cupboard's door very slowly opening a little, behind my back. Through the hatch cautiously jutted the face of old Cohen. She was looking right at me, and it seemed almost as though she was begging for my help.

I got up and went over.

'What's wrong?'

She nodded at the telephone receiver dangling on its wire, and disappeared through the doorway that gave onto the entrance hall.

Left alone, in utter darkness, before even lifting the receiver to my ear, I recognized the voice of Alberto.

'I can hear singing,' he was crying out in a strangely festive voice. 'At what point in the proceedings are you?'

'At the *Caprét ch'avea comperà il signor Padre* point.'

'That's good. We've already finished. Why don't you drop round?'

'Right now?' I exclaimed astonished.

'Why not? Here the conversation has begun to enter the doldrums and you, with your much acclaimed resources, would doubtless be able to lift it up again.'

He sniggered.

'And also . . .' he added, 'we've prepared a surprise for you.'

'A surprise? And what might that be?'

'Come and see.'

'Such mysteriousness.'

My heart was beating furiously.

'Put your cards on the table.'

'Go on, don't make me have to beg. I repeat: come and see.'

I immediately went to the entrance, took my overcoat, scarf and hat, stuck my head around the kitchen door, asking Cohen in a whisper to say, in case they asked where I was, that I'd had to go out for a moment, and two minutes later I was already on the street.

It was a magnificent moonlit night, frozen, clear as could be. There was no one, almost no one on the streets, and Corso Giovecca and Corso Ercole I d'Este, smooth, empty and of an almost salt-like whiteness, opened up in front of me like two huge ski-tracks. In the bright light, I swayed down the middle of the street, my ears numbed by the icy air. At supper I'd drunk a fair few glasses of wine, and not only could I not feel the cold, but I was actually sweating. My bike's front tyre barely rustled over the hardened snow, and the dry snow-dust it raised filled me with a sense of reckless joy, as though I was skiing. I raced on, without fear of skidding. Meanwhile I thought of the surprise, which, according to Alberto, would be awaiting me at the Finzi-Continis'. Had Micòl perhaps returned? Odd if she had. Why wouldn't she have come to the phone herself? And why, before supper, had no one seen her at the Temple? If she had been at the Temple, I would already have known of it. My father at the dinner table, making his usual survey of those present at the service – he'd done this especially for me: as an indirect reproach for my non-attendance – would certainly not have neglected to mention her. He had gone through the whole list, naming them one by one, of the Finzi-Continis and the Herreras, but not her. Was it possible she had come on her own at the last minute, on the direct, quarter-past-nine train?

In an even more intense brightness of moonlight and snow, I went on across the Barchetto del Duca. Halfway, a little before the bridge crosses the Panfilio canal, a gigantic shadow suddenly appeared before me. It was Jor. There was a moment's delay before I recognized him, just as I was about to cry out. But no sooner had I recognized him than the fear I felt was transformed into an almost equally paralysing sense of foreboding. So then it was true – I told myself – Micòl was back. Forewarned by the street bell, she must have got up from the table, gone downstairs and now, sending Jor out to meet me, was waiting for me at the threshold of the side door reserved exclusively for family and close friends. A few more pedallings, and there was Micòl herself, a small dark figure etched against an electric-light background of sheerest white, her back encircled by the protective breath of the central heating. Another moment or two and I would hear her voice, her 'Hi'.

'Hi,' Micòl said, motionless on the threshold. 'It's good of you to come.'

I had foreseen everything most exactly: everything except for the fact that I would kiss her. I had got off my bike, and replied, 'Hi. How long have you been here?' and she had just enough time to say, 'Since yesterday afternoon – I travelled down with my uncles', and then . . . then I kissed her on the mouth. It happened all of a sudden. But how? I was still there with my face hidden in her warm and scented neck – a strange mixed scent of a child's skin and talcum powder – and already I was asking myself how. How could it have happened? I had embraced her; she had managed a feeble effort to resist, and then let me carry on. Is that how it happened? Perhaps that was it. But what now?

I drew back slowly. Now she was there, her face a few inches from mine. I stared at her without speaking or moving, incredulous, that's it: incredulous. Her back against the door jamb, her shoulders covered with a black woollen shawl, she too stared at me in silence. She looked me in the eyes, and her steady, straight, hard look entered me with the shining ease of a sword.

I was the first to look away.

'I'm sorry,' I murmured.

'Why sorry? Perhaps it was my mistake coming down to meet you. It's my fault.'

She shook her head. Then tried to give a good-natured, affectionate smile.

'Such a lot of lovely snow!' she said, nodding towards the garden. 'Just imagine, in Venice not even a centimetre. If I'd only known so much had fallen here . . .'

She stopped, making a gesture of her hand, her right hand. She had drawn the shawl out from below, and I immediately noticed a ring.

I took her by the wrist.

'What's that?' I asked, touching the ring with my fingertip.

She grimaced, as though with distaste.

'I'm *engaged*. Didn't you know?'

She immediately burst out in a loud laugh.

'No, don't take it like that . . . can't you see I'm joking? It's just any old ring. Look.'

She took it off with an exaggerated movement of her elbows, handed it over, and it was indeed an insignificant ring: a little circle of gold with a small turquoise stone. Her grandmother Regina had given it to her many years ago – she explained – concealed inside an Easter egg.

Once she had the ring again, she replaced it on her finger, then took me by the hand.

'You'd better come along now,' she murmured, 'or else, upstairs, they might' – she laughed – 'start getting ideas.'

As we went, she kept hold of my hand, and never stopped talking for a moment. Only on the stairs she stopped, inspected my lips in the light, and concluded the examination with a detached 'Excellent!'

Yes – she was saying – the whole affair of the thesis had gone better than she'd dared hope. In the viva for graduation, she'd 'held forth' for a good hour, 'orating unstoppably'. In the end they'd sent her out, and happily ensconced behind the examination hall's frosted-glass door, she'd been easily able to hear everything the gaggle of professors had said about her work. The majority were opting for a *cum laude*, but there was one, the Professor of German (a dyed-in-the-wool Nazi!) who wouldn't hear of it. He'd made himself very clear, the 'worthy gentleman'. In his view, the *cum laude* could not be given her without provoking a serious scandal. What were they thinking! – he had shouted. The Signorina was Jewish, and not even excluded as she ought to have been, and now they were talking of awarding her this distinction. What a disgrace! She should be thankful they'd let her graduate at all . . . The chairman, who taught English, also supported by others, had energetically countered by saying the school was a school, intelligence and hard work (so kind of him!) had nothing whatsoever to do with blood relations, etc. etc. However, when the moment came to do their sums, obviously, the Nazi carried the day. And she'd had no other consolation, apart from the apologies which later, running after her down the stairs of Ca' Foscari, the Professor of English had given to her – poor thing, his chin was trembling, he had tears in his eyes . . . – she'd had no other consolation apart from greeting the verdict with the most impeccable Roman salute. In the very act of giving her the title of 'Doctor', the President of the Faculty had raised his arm. How was she supposed to have reacted? Limited herself to a charming little nod of the head? Not a chance.

She laughed joyfully, and I laughed too, drawn into her force field. In turn I recounted my eviction from the Public Library, dwelling on all the comic details. Yet when I asked her what had kept her in Venice for another month after her graduation (in Venice – I added – which, to listen to her, not only had she never found agreeable as a city but which was also a place in which she'd never found any real friends, male or female), she turned serious, withdrew her hand from mine, and her only reply was to cast a quick sideways glance.

We had a foretaste of the happy welcome we would receive in the dining room from Perotti, who was waiting in the vestibule. As soon as he saw us coming down the big staircase followed by Jor, he gave us an unusually joyous, almost conspiratorial smile. On a different occasion, his behaviour would have annoyed me; I would have been offended by it. But for some minutes I'd found myself in a most peculiar frame of mind. Suppressing within myself every reason for unease, I felt enriched by a strange lightness, as though borne up by invisible wings. At the end of the day Perotti's a good fellow – I thought. He too was happy that the 'Signorina' was back home. Why should one blame the poor old man? No doubt from then on he'd stop his grumbling.

Side by side, we made our appearance at the dining room doorway, and our presence was greeted, as I said, with the utmost rejoicing. All the diners' faces were rosy and lit up, expressing warmth and benevolence. And even the room itself, as all of a sudden it seemed to me that evening, was far more welcoming than usual – a rosy glow seemed to have spread over the furniture's polished wood, and the fire's tongue-like flames drew out subtle flesh tones from its grain. I had never seen it so filled with light. Apart from the glow unleashed from the burning logs, the great upturned corolla of the candelabra above the table (from which one could see the plates and cutlery had been cleared away) poured forth a veritable waterfall of light.

'Come on in!'

'Welcome!'

'We were beginning to think you'd decided not to come.'

It was Alberto who uttered this last sentence, but I could see that my arrival had filled him with sincere pleasure. Everyone was looking at me. Some, like Professor Ermanno, had turned right round in their seats, others were leaning over the table or pushing away from it with straightened arms, and others still, like Signora Olga, seated alone at the head of the table, with the fireplace behind her, was tilting her face forwards and half-closing her eyes. They watched me, they examined me, they looked me up and down, and they all seemed fully satisfied with me, and with the impression I made standing beside Micòl. Only Federico Herrera, the railway engineer, looking surprised, or worried, was slow to school himself to the general delight. But it was only a question of a moment. Having sought some explanation from his brother Giulio – I saw them quickly conferring behind their old mother's back, bringing their two bald heads together – he rapidly beamed his own share of warmth and approval towards me. Besides making a grimace which showed his outsized upper incisors, he even raised his arm in a gesture which, rather than greeting me, showed his solidarity, an almost sporting encouragement to me.

Professor Ermanno insisted I sit at his right. It was my usual place – he explained to Micòl who in the meantime had sat down at his left, facing me – where I 'normally' sat whenever I stayed for supper. Giampiero Malnate – he went on to say – Alberto's friend, would sit 'over there, on the other side', on Mamma's left. Micòl was listening to him with a strangely attentive air, part sardonic, part piqued – as though annoyed to discover how family life had proceeded in her absence, not exactly as she had foreseen, and yet pleased that things had, as it happened, gone in that direction.

I sat down, and only then, shocked to have been mistaken, did I notice that the table had not in fact been cleared. In the middle was a low, round, quite capacious silver tray, at the centre of which, surrounded at two hands' breadth away by a circle of small pieces of white card, each inscribed in red crayon with a letter of the alphabet, stood a solitary champagne flute.

'And what's that then?' I asked Alberto.

'That's the big surprise I was telling you about!' he exclaimed. 'It's absolutely wonderful. It just needs three or four people in a circle to put their fingers on the rim of the glass, and immediately it gives a reply, moving in every direction, one letter after another.'

'Gives a reply?!'

'It certainly does! At a fair pace it writes down all the replies. And it makes sense – you can't imagine how much!'

I hadn't seen Alberto so excited and euphoric for a long time.

'And this new wonder, where has it come from?' I asked.

'It's just a game,' Professor Ermanno broke in, placing a hand on my arm and shaking his head. 'Something Micòl brought back from Venice.'

'Ah, so you're the one responsible!' I said, turning to her. 'And can your glass also read the future?'

'You bet!' she exclaimed, laughing. 'I'd say that was its *real* speciality.'

Dirce came in at that moment, holding aloft and balancing on one hand a round tray of dark wood, overflowing with Passover sweets – her cheeks also were rosy, shining with health and good will.

As the guest, and the last arrived, I was served first. The sweets, called *zucarìn*, made of shortbread with raisins mixed in, looked almost the same as the ones I had just tasted at home, half an hour before. All the same those *zucarìn* at the Finzi-Contini house immediately seemed far better, much tastier, and I said as much, turning to Signora Olga who, busy as she was choosing from the plate that Dirce was offering her, seemed not to have noticed the compliment.

Next came Perotti, his big farm-labourer's hands clamped round the edge of a second tray (this time, pewter) which bore a flask of white wine and a number of glasses. And then, whilst we sat around the table, drinking Albana in little sips and nibbling at the *zucarìn*, Alberto went on explaining to me, in particular, the 'goblet's divinatory qualities'. It was true that for the moment it was keeping its counsel, but just a bit earlier it had been giving them replies of the most wonderful, extraordinary *acuteness*.

I wondered what they'd been asking it.

'Oh, a bit about everything.'

They had asked it, for instance – he went on – if he, some time or other, would ever get his degree in engineering; and the glass had, straight away, come back with the driest of 'No's. Then Micòl had wanted to know if she would get married, and if so, when; and the glass had become less peremptory – it seemed even a bit confused, giving a classic, oracular response, leaving open the most contradictory interpretations. They'd even interrogated it on the question of the tennis court – 'the poor old glass!' – trying to discover whether Papa would finally abandon his rigmarole of perpetually putting off, from year to year, starting the work of refurbishing it. And on this question, displaying considerable patience, the 'Delphic one' had reverted again to explicit mode, reassuring them that the longed-for improvements would be effected 'immediately', at least within the year.

But it was mainly in the matter of politics that the glass had worked miracles. Very soon, within a few months, it had predicted, war would break out: a long, bloody war, grievous for *everyone*, such as would turn the whole world upside down, but in the end, after many years of inconclusive battles, it would finish with complete victory for the forces of good. 'Of good?' Micòl, who always pounced on any *gaffe*, had asked at this point. 'And what, may I ask, would those forces of good be?' To which the glass, making everyone gawp with surprise, had replied with one word only: 'Stalin.'

'Can you imagine,' Alberto cried out among the general laughter, 'can you imagine how that would have pleased Giampi, had he been here? I must write to him about it.'

'Isn't he in Ferrara?'

'No. He left the other day. He's gone to spend Easter at home.'

Alberto kept on for quite some time about what the glass had said, until the game was begun once more. I too placed my index finger on the 'goblet'. I too asked questions and waited for the replies. But now, for some reason, nothing comprehensible emerged from the oracle. Alberto became most insistent, tenacious and stubborn as never before. But nothing.

For my part, at least, I wasn't greatly bothered. Rather than attending to him and to the business of the glass, most of the time I was looking at Micòl: Micòl who, every now and then, feeling my gaze on her, would smooth her forehead of the same frown she used to have when playing tennis, to reassure me with a quick, considerate smile.

I was staring at her lips, faintly coloured with lipstick. Just before, I had managed to kiss them. But had it happened too late? Why hadn't I done so six months earlier, when everything would still have been possible? Or at least during the previous winter? How much time we'd wasted, me here in Ferrara, and she in Venice! One Sunday I could easily have taken a train and gone to visit her. There was a fast train that left Ferrara at eight in the morning and arrived in Venice at half past ten. As soon as I'd got off the train, I could have phoned her, suggesting she took me to the Lido – so that, among other things, I could tell her, I'd finally get to see the famous

Jewish cemetery of San Niccolò. Towards one o'clock, we might have eaten something together somewhere nearby and, after, have made a phone call to her uncles' house to keep the *Fräulein* sweet (oh, I could just see Micòl's face as she phoned her, the pursed lips, the clownish grimaces!). After that, we could have gone for a long slow walk along the deserted beach. There would have been time for that too. Then, as far as my return went, I would have had the choice of two trains – one at five, the other at seven, both of them excellent so that not even my parents would have the first idea anything had happened. If only I'd done it then, when I *should* have, everything would have been easy. What a joke.

What time was it now? Half past one, maybe two. Soon I'd have to go, and most likely Micòl would accompany me down, as far as the garden gate.

Perhaps it was this that she was also thinking of, this that was worrying her. Room after room, corridor after corridor, we would have to walk side by side without having even the courage either to look at each other or to say a word. I could sense we were both fearing the same thing: the leave-taking, the ever nearer and ever less imaginable point of saying goodbye, the goodbye kiss. Otherwise, if Micòl should choose not to accompany me, offloading the job onto Alberto or even Perotti, in what state of mind would I have to bear the rest of the night? And the day after?

But perhaps not – I obstinately and desperately went back to dreaming – we wouldn't need to, we'd never have to get up from the table. The night would never have to end.

IV

I

Soon enough, the very next day, I began to realize how hard it would be for me to resume the rapport with Micòl that we had had before.

After much hesitation, getting on towards ten, I tried to telephone her. I was told (by Dirce) that the 'signorini' were still in bed, and would I be so kind as to call again 'at noon'. To while away the time, I threw myself on my bed. I picked up a book at random, *Le Rouge et le noir*, but however hard I tried I wasn't able to concentrate. And if I didn't call her at midday? In a short while, though, I changed my mind. All of a sudden it seemed to me that now I only wanted one thing from Micòl: her friendship. Rather than disappearing – I told myself – it would be far better if I behaved as though yesterday evening nothing had happened. She would understand. Impressed by my discretion, utterly reassured, she would quickly reward me with all her full confidence, the delightful confidence she had of old.

At midday on the dot I braced myself and dialled the number of the Finzi-Contini house.

I had to wait a long time, longer than usual.

'Ah, it's you.'

It was Micòl herself.

She yawned.

'What is it?'

Disconcerted, my mind a blank, I could think of nothing better to say than that I'd already called up once, two hours ago. Dirce had replied – I continued, stammering – suggesting I call again around midday.

Micòl heard me out. Then she began to complain about the day she had before her, all the many things she'd have to organize after being months and months away, suitcases to unpack, all kinds of papers to put in order, and so on, with the final prospect, not exactly enticing for her, of a second 'banquet'. That was the trouble with every trip away – that getting back to the usual dull routine cost even more effort than it had in the first place 'to take oneself off'.

I asked her if she meant to go along to the Temple later on.

She said she wasn't sure. Perhaps she would, but perhaps not . . . The way she felt at the moment she couldn't give me any guarantee it was at all likely.

She hung up without inviting me to come round again in the evening, and without arranging how or when we might see each other again.

That day I avoided ringing her up again. I didn't even go to the Temple. But around seven, passing by Via Mazzini, and noticing the Finzi-Continis' grey Dilambda parked behind the corner of the cobbled stretch of Via Scienze, with Perotti wearing his driver's beret and uniform seated at the wheel waiting, I couldn't resist the temptation of installing myself at the entrance of Via Vittoria to keep watch. I waited a long time, in the biting cold. It was the busiest time of the evening, the pre-prandial *passeggiata*. Along the two pavements of Via Mazzini, cluttered with dirty, already partly melted snow, the crowd was rushing in both directions. At last I had my reward. Suddenly, even though at a distance, I saw her emerge from the Temple's entrance and pause there on the threshold. She was wearing a short leopardskin coat, tied at the waist with a leather belt. Her blond hair shining with the light from the windows, she was looking around her as though searching for someone. Was I the one she was looking for? I was about to emerge from the shadows and come forward, when her relatives, who had evidently followed her down the stairs at a distance, arrived in a group behind her back. They were all there, including grandma Regina. Turning on my heels, I hastily made my way down Via Vittoria.

The next day and the days that followed I kept on with my phone calls, yet only occasionally did I manage to speak to her.

Nearly always, someone else came to the phone, either Alberto, Professor Ermanno, or Dirce, or even Perotti, all of whom, with the solitary exception of Dirce, who was curt and impassive as a telephone operator, and for that very reason daunting and disquieting, entangled me in long, futile conversations. At a certain point I would cut Perotti short. But with Alberto and the Professor things were harder for me. I let them talk away. I always hoped that it would be they who mentioned Micòl. But in vain. As though they had decided to avoid all reference to her, and had even discussed the matter with each other, both her brother and her father left it up to me to take the initiative. With the result that very often I hung up without having found the courage to ask for what had prompted me to call.

I then resumed my visits, both in the morning, with the excuse of the thesis, and in the afternoon, with my visits to Alberto. I did nothing to make Micòl aware of my presence in the house. I was sure she knew of it, and that one day or another she would appear.

Although my thesis was actually completed, I still had to copy it out. So I would bring my typewriter along with me, and its tap-tapping, as soon as it first broke the silence of the billiards room, immediately called forth Professor Ermanno to the doorway of his study.

'What are you up to? Are you already copying it out?' he called out merrily.

He came over to me, and wanted to have a look at the contraption. It was an Italian portable, a Littoria, which my father had given me a few years earlier, when I'd passed my final school exams. Its trade name did not, as I'd feared it might, provoke a smile from him. On the contrary. Claiming that 'even' in Italy now they made typewriters, like mine, which seemed to work perfectly, he appeared to be impressed with it. There at home – he told me – they had three of them, one for Alberto's use, one for Micòl and one for him – all three were American Underwoods. Those of his children were undoubtedly hardwearing portables, but not nearly as light as this one (at this point he weighed it on his hands). His own, on the other hand was the usual kind, an office typewriter. Yet . . .

Here he gave a little start.

Did I know, though, how many copies it let one make, if one wished? – he added, winking. As many as seven.

He led me to his study and showed it me, lifting, not without some effort, a black, funereal cover, probably made of metal, which till then I hadn't noticed. In front of such a museum item, evidently hardly ever used even when it was new, I shook my head. No thanks – I said. Using my Littoria I'd never be able to make more than three copies, and two of them on the thinnest paper. All the same I preferred to keep on with my own.

I typed out on its keys chapter after chapter, but my mind was elsewhere. And it wandered elsewhere also when, in the afternoons, I went upstairs to Alberto's studio. Malnate had returned from Milan a good week after Easter, full of indignation at what was happening at that time: the fall of Madrid – ah, but it wasn't over yet; the conquest of Albania – what a dreadful disgrace! what a total mess! As for this last event, he told us what certain Milanese friends of his and Alberto's had said to him. Rather than it being a scheme of il Duce the Albanian business had been a pet project of 'Ciano Galeazzo'. Obviously jealous of von Ribbentrop, that disgusting coward had wanted to show the world that he was a match for the German in matters of lightning-diplomacy. Could we believe it? It seems that even Cardinal Schuster had expressed himself on the subject in disparaging, warning terms, and though he had spoken in the utmost secrecy, the whole city soon knew of it. Giampi also told us other things about Milan: about a performance at La Scala of Mozart's *Don Giovanni*, which he had luckily been able to attend of an exhibition of paintings by a 'new group' in Via Bagutti, and of Gladys, herself, whom he'd met by chance in the Galleria all wrapped up in mink and arm in arm with a well-known industrialist who dealt in steel. Gladys, friendly as ever, had whilst passing him given him a tiny sign with her finger which meant without any doubt 'Phone me', or else 'I'll phone you'. What a shame that immediately after he'd had to return 'to the factory'! It would have been a joy to cuckold that famous steel magnate, soon-to-be war profiteer . . . he'd have done it most willingly . . . He talked on and on, as usual addressing me in particular, but, at least in the end, a bit less didactic and peremptory than in the previous months – as though after his trip to Milan, having enjoyed once more the affection of his family and friends, he had come by a new temperament, far more indulgent towards others and their opinions.

With Micòl, as I've already noted, I only had the odd brief talk on the telephone, during which both of us avoided reference to anything too intimate. But some days after I had waited for more than an hour in front of the Temple I was unable to resist complaining about her coldness.

'Did you know', I said, 'that the second evening of Passover I did see you?'

'Oh, is that right? Were you at the Temple too?'

'No. I was passing by Via Mazzini when I noticed your car, but I prefered to wait outside.'

'How odd of you.'

'You were most elegant. D'you want me to tell you what you were wearing?'

'No, really, I'll take your word for it. Where were you *lurking*?'

'On the pavement opposite, at the corner of Via Vittoria. At a certain moment you turned to look towards me. Tell me the truth – did you recognize me?'

'Don't be so silly. Why should I wish to deceive you? But as for you, I don't understand what you were thinking of . . . I'm sorry, but couldn't you have managed to put *a foot forward*?'

'I was about to. Then when I realized that you weren't alone, I abandoned the idea.'

'What a surprise that I wasn't alone! But you're a strange type. I reckon you could have come over to say hello all the same.'

'It's true when you think about it. The trouble is one can't always think clearly. And anyway, would you have been pleased if I had?

'Good Lord. What a fuss about nothing!' she sighed.

The next time I managed to speak to her, not less than twelve days later, she told me she was ill, suffering from a terrible cold and some signs of fever. What a bore! Why didn't I ever come to visit her? I'd quite forgotten her.

'Are you . . . are you in bed?' I stammered, disconcerted, feeling myself a victim of a huge injustice.

'I certainly am, and between the sheets to boot. Tell the truth – you're refusing to come for fear of catching the flu.'

'No, no, Micòl,' I replied bitterly. 'Don't make me out to be more pampered than I already am. I'm only astonished that you can accuse me of having forgotten you, when the truth is . . . I don't know if you remember,' and as I continued my voice came out stifled, 'but before you left for Venice phoning you was really easy, whilst now, I have to admit, it's become a complicated business. Didn't you know that I've come round to your house several times these last few days? Haven't they told you?'

'Yes.'

'Well then! If you'd wanted to see me, you knew quite well where to find me – in the billiards room in the mornings, and in the afternoons downstairs with your brother. The truth is you had no desire to see me.'

'What nonsense! I never liked going to Alberto's studio, especially when he has friends round. And as for looking in on you in the mornings, aren't you hard at work? If there's one thing I hate doing it's disturbing people when they're working. Still, if it's really what you want, tomorrow or the day after I'll call in for a moment to say hello.'

The morning of the day after, she didn't come, but in the afternoon, when I was with Alberto – it must have been seven o'clock – Malnate had brusquely taken leave of us a few minutes earlier – Perotti came in carrying a message from her. The 'Signorina' would be grateful if I should go upstairs for a moment – he announced, impassively but, it seemed to me, in a bad mood. She had sent her apologies. She was still in bed, otherwise she would have come down herself. Which did I prefer – to go up immediately, or stay for supper, and go up afterwards? The Signorina would prefer me to go on up straight away, since she had a bit of a headache and wanted to turn the light off very soon. But if I decided to stay . . .

'Heavens, no,' I said, and looked at Alberto. 'I'll go right now.'

I got up, preparing myself to follow Perotti.

'Please make yourself at home,' Alberto said, accompanying me considerately to the door. 'I think this evening at dinner Papa and I will be alone. Grandma is also in bed with the flu, and Mamma doesn't leave her room even for a minute. So, if it suits you to have something with us, and go up to see Micòl later . . . it would make Papa happy.'

I explained that I couldn't, that I had to meet 'someone' 'in the Piazza', and rushed out behind Perotti, who had already reached the end of the corridor.

Without exchanging a word we soon arrived at the foot of the long spiral staircase which led up and up to the little tower with the skylight. Micòl's rooms, as I knew, were those situated at the top of the house, only a half-flight below the topmost landing.

Not being aware of the lift, I began climbing the stairs.

'Just as well you're young,' Perotti said with a grin, 'but a hundred and twenty-three stairs are a fair number. Wouldn't you like us to take the lift? It does work, you know.'

He opened the black external cage, then the sliding door of the cabin, and only then stepped back to let me pass.

Getting into the lift, which was an antediluvian big tin box all ashine with wine-coloured wood and glittering slabs of glass adorned with the letters M, F and C elaborately interwoven; feeling my throat seized by the pungent, slightly suffocating smell, a cross between mould and turps, which impregnated the shut-in air of that narrow space, and being suddenly aware of a motiveless sense of calm, of resigned fatalism, even of ironic distance – these all collided and combined into a single sensation. But where had I smelled something like this before? – I asked myself – and when?

The lift cabin began to ascend quickly up through the stairwell. I sniffed the air, and at the same time looked at Perotti in front of me, at his back clad in pin-striped cotton. The old man had left the plush, velvet-covered seat entirely at my disposal. Standing, at a couple of hand's breadths away, self-absorbed, tense, with one hand grasping the brass handle of the sliding door and the other resting on the button panel – this too of glowing, well-polished brass – Perotti had closed himself once again in a silence open to all kinds of interpretation. But it was then I remembered and understood. Perotti was keeping silent not because he disapproved, as at a certain point I'd conjectured, that Micòl was receiving me in her room, but rather because the opportunity offered him to operate the lift (perhaps rare enough) filled him with a satisfaction as intense as it was private and intimate. The lift was no less dear to him than was the carriage, left down there in the coach-house. On such things, on such venerable witnesses to a past that was by then also his own, he could express his difficult love for the family he had served since he was a boy, the angry loyalty of an old domestic animal.

'It moves very well,' I exclaimed. 'Who are the makers?'

'It's American,' he replied, half-turning his face round, and twisting his mouth in that characteristic grimace of distaste behind which countrymen often conceal their admiration. 'She's been at it for more than forty years, but she could still haul up a regiment.'

'It must be a Westinghouse,' I guessed at random.

'Mah, sogio mi . . .'* he stammered. 'Some name like that.'

After this he started out telling me how and when the contraption had been 'put in'. But then – to his evident displeasure – the lift shuddered to a sudden halt and forced him to interrupt his story then and there.

---

* Ferrarese dialect with Veneto inflection: 'Don't ask me!'

2

In my frame of mind just then – a fragile serenity shorn of illusions – Micòl's welcome surprised me like an unexpected, undeserved gift. I'd been afraid she'd treat me badly, with the same cruel indifference as she had of late. And yet as soon as I entered her room (having introduced me Perotti had discreetly closed the door behind me) I saw she was smiling at me in a kind, friendly, open manner. More even than the explicit invitation to come on in, it was her luminous smile, full of forgiving warmth, which convinced me to move out from the dark end of the room and approach her.

So I came right up to the bed, laying both hands on the bed rail. With two cushions supporting her back, Micòl was sitting with the covers only up to her waist, wearing a long-sleeved, high-necked, dark-green pullover. Above her breasts the little gold medallion of the *shaddai* glinted over the wool . . . When I came in she had been reading – a French novel, as I'd quickly gathered, recognizing from a distance the familiar red and white covers, and it was probably reading rather than the cold which had made the skin under her eyes look tired. No, she was always beautiful – I told myself then, gazing at her – perhaps she'd never been quite so beautiful, so attractive. Beside the bed, at the height of the bolster, there was a walnut-wood trolley with two shelves, the upper one occupied by a lit articulated lamp, the telephone, a red earthenware teapot, a pair of white porcelain cups with gilded rims and a nickel silver thermos. Micòl stretched to place the book on the lower shelf, then turned in search of the hanging electric light switch on the opposite side of the headboard. Poor thing – she muttered at the same time between her teeth – it's not right I should be kept in a mortuary like this! The increase of light had hardly been effected when she greeted it with a long 'Aah!' of satisfaction.

She kept on talking: of the 'vicious' cold which had forced her to stay in bed for a good four days; of the aspirins with which, unbeknownst to Papa, and equally to her uncle Giulio, a sworn enemy of all sudorifics – in their opinion, they damaged the heart, but it wasn't true at all! – she'd tried in vain to bring her illness quickly to an end; of the boredom of endless hours of being stuck in bed without even the desire to read. Ah, reading! Once, at the time of the famous flu and fever she'd had when she was thirteen, she'd been capable of reading the whole of *War and Peace* in a few days or the complete cycle of Dumas's *Musketeers*, whilst now, in the course of a miserable cold, though it did affect her head too, she had to be thankful if she managed to put 'out of its misery' a little French novel, of the kind printed in big letters. Did I know Cocteau's *Les Enfants terribles*? – she asked, picking up the book again from the trolley and handing it to me. It wasn't bad, quite amusing and chic. But weighed beside *The Three Musketeers*, *Twenty Years After* and *The Viscount of Bragelonne*? Those were real novels! Let's be honest about it – even considered from the point of view of 'chic-ness' they worked 'much better'.

Suddenly she interrupted herself.

'But why are you standing there like a garden pole? Good heavens, you're worse than a baby! Take that little armchair' – as she pointed it out – 'and come and sit closer.'

I hurried to obey her, but that wasn't good enough. Now I *had* to drink something.

'Is there nothing I can offer you? Would you like some tea?'

'No thanks,' I replied, 'it's not good for me before supper – it swills about in my stomach and takes away my appetite.'

'Perhaps a little *Skiwasser*?'

'That has the same effect.'

'It's boiling hot, you know! If I'm not wrong, you've only tried the summertime version, the one with ice, an essentially heretical version of the *Himbeerwasser*.'

'Really, no thanks.'

'Good Lord,' she whined. 'D'you want me to ring the bell and have you brought an aperitif? We never take them, but I believe there's a bottle of Bitter Campari somewhere in the house. Perotti – *honi soit* – will undoubtedly know where to find it . . .'

I shook my head.

'So you really don't want anything!' she complained, disappointed. 'What a pain you are!'

'I prefer not to.'

I said 'I prefer not to' and she burst out laughing loudly.

'Why are you laughing?' I asked, a bit offended.

'You said "I prefer not to", just like Bartleby. With the same face.'

'Bartleby. And who would that gentleman be?'

'It just goes to show you've never read Melville's short stories.'

Of Melville – I said – I only knew *Moby Dick*, in Cesare Pavese's translation. Then she wanted me to get up, to go and fetch from the bookcase there in front of me, between the two windows, the volume of *Piazza Tales* and bring it to her. Whilst I was searching among the books, she told me the plot of the story. Bartleby was a clerk – she said – a scrivener employed by a New York lawyer – the latter a real professional, busy, capable, 'liberal', 'one of those nineteenth-century Americans that Spencer Tracy plays to perfection' – employed to copy out office work, legal documents and so on. Well, this Bartleby, so long as they got him to copy, would keep scribbling away conscientiously, bent over his desk. But if it crossed Spencer Tracy's mind to entrust him with some other small supplementary task, such as to collate a copy of the original text, or to nip down to the tobacco shop on the corner to buy a stamp, nothing doing – he would confine himself to an evasive smile and reply with stubborn politeness: '*I prefer not to.*'

'And why should he do that?' I asked, returning with the book in my hand.

'Because he wasn't prepared to be anything but a scrivener. A scrivener and nothing else.'

'I'm sorry, but', I objected, 'surely Spencer Tracy paid him a regular wage.'

'Of course,' Micòl relied. 'But why should that matter? The wage is paid for the work, not for the *person* who performs it.'

'I don't understand,' I insisted. 'Bartleby had been taken on in the office as a copyist by Spencer Tracy, but also, I suppose, so as to help things along in general. In the end what was he asking of him? A little *more* that may well have been *less*. For someone obliged to remain forever seated, nipping out to the tobacconist on the street corner might be seen as a pleasant change, a necessary break in the routine – whichever way you consider it, a perfect chance to stretch his legs a bit. No, I'm sorry. In my view, Spencer Tracy was quite right to protest that your Bartleby shouldn't hang about there playing the victim, and should immediately perform what had been asked of him.'

We went on for a long time arguing about poor Bartleby and Spencer Tracy. She reproached me for not understanding the whole point, for being unimaginative, the usual inveterate conformist. Conformist? She must be joking. The fact is that just before, with an air of commiserating, she'd compared me to Bartleby. And now, on the contrary, seeing I was on the side of the 'abject bosses' she had begun to laud in Bartleby 'the inalienable right of every human being not to collaborate', that is, to liberty. She just kept on criticizing me, but for contradictory reasons.

At a certain point the telephone rang. They were calling from the kitchen to ask if and when they should bring up the supper tray. Micòl declared that for now she wasn't hungry, and that she would ring them back later. Would some minestrone soup be all right? – she replied with a grimace to a detailed question that came to her through the ear-piece. Of course. But, please, they shouldn't start preparing it yet – she never liked food that 'had hung around'.

Having put down the receiver, she turned to me. She stared at me with eyes that were at once kind and serious, and for some moments said nothing.

'How are you?' she asked at last, in a low voice.

I swallowed.

'Just so-so.'

I smiled and turned up my eyes.

'It's strange,' I went on. 'Every detail of this room exactly matches how I'd imagined it. For instance, over there's the chaise longue. It's as though I'd already seen it. Well, actually I *have* seen it.'

I told her the dream I'd had six months ago, the night before she left for Venice. I pointed to the row of *làttimi*, glowing in the half-dark of their shelves: the only things here, I told her, which in my dream had seemed other than they really were. I explained how they'd appeared to me and she kept listening, serious, attentive, without once interrupting.

When I'd finished, she stroked the sleeve of my jacket with a light caress. I knelt by the side of the bed, embraced her, kissed her neck, her eyes, her lips. She let me do it, but always watching me and, with little manoeuvres of her head, always trying to stop me kissing her mouth.

'No ... no ...' she kept saying. 'Stop it now ... please ... Be good ... No, no ... someone might come in ... No.'

But all in vain. Gradually, first with one leg and then with the other, I got myself onto the bed. Then I was pressing down on her with my whole weight. I continued blindly kissing her face, but only rarely managing to meet her lips, and never succeeding in getting her to lower her eyelids. At last I buried my head in her neck. And whilst my body, as though almost independent of me, made convulsive movements over hers, immobile under the covers as a statue, suddenly, in a terrible pang deep within me, I had the precise impression that I was losing her, that I'd already lost her.

She was the first to speak.

'Please get up,' I heard her saying, very close to my ear. 'I can't breathe like this.'

I was literally annihilated. To get off that bed seemed to me an undertaking beyond my powers. Yet there was no other choice.

I dragged myself up. I took some steps around the room, hesitating. At length, I let myself fall once again on the little armchair beside the bed, and hid my face in my hands. My cheeks were burning.

'Why are you doing this?' Micól said. 'Can't you see it's useless?'

'Why is it useless?' I asked, quickly raising my eyes. 'May I ask why?'

She looked at me, the shadow of an impish smile playing round her lips.

'Won't you go in there for a moment?' she said, nodding towards the bathroom door. 'You're all red, *impizà** red. Go and wash your face.'

'Thanks, I will. Perhaps it's a good idea.'

I got up in a hurry and made towards the bathroom. Then, just at that moment, the door that gave onto the staircase was shaken by a vigorous blow. It seemed as though someone was trying to shoulder their way in.

'What is it?' I whispered.

'It's Jor,' Micòl replied calmly. 'Go and let him in.'

---

* Ferrarese dialect: flaming.

3

In the oval mirror above the sink I saw my face reflected.

I examined it carefully as though it wasn't mine, as though it belonged to someone else. Although I'd plunged it several times in cold water, it still looked completely red, *impizàda* red – as Micòl had said – with darker blotches between my nose and upper lip, above and around my cheekbones. I scrutinized with minute attention that large face lit up there in front of me, drawn first by the throbbing of the arteries under the skin of my forehead and temples, then by the dense mesh of tiny scarlet veins which, as I widened my eyes, seemed to lock the irises' blue discs down in a kind of siege, then by the hairs of my beard thickly bristling on my chin and along my jaw, then by a small spot that was barely visible . . . I was thinking of nothing. Through the thin dividing wall I could hear Micòl speaking on the phone. To whom? To the kitchen staff, probably, to stop them bringing up the supper. Good. The impending goodbye would then be less embarrassing. For both of us.

I came in as she was putting down the receiver, and once again, not without surprise, I realized she had nothing against me.

She leant from the bed to pour herself a cup of tea.

'Now please sit down,' she said 'and have something to drink.'

I obeyed in silence. I drank with slow deliberate sips, without raising my eyes. Sprawled out on the parquet behind me, Jor was asleep. His thick snoring, like a drunken tramp's, filled the room.

I put down the cup.

It was once again Micòl who started speaking. Without any reference to what had just happened, she began by saying how for a long time, for much longer than I might think, she'd meant to speak frankly about the situation which bit by bit had developed between us. Did I perhaps remember that time – she went on – last October when, so as not to get soaked, we'd ended up in the coach-house, and had gone to sit in the carriage? Well, it was exactly from that time on that she'd become aware of the way our relationship had taken a wrong turn. She'd understood immediately that something wrong, something false and dangerous had started up between us. And it was mainly her fault, she was only too ready to admit, if, since then, the landslide had gathered momentum and kept on rolling downhill. But what could she have done? The simple thing would have been to take me aside and be honest with me, at that point, without delay. But rather than that, like a real coward, she'd chosen the worst course – to escape. Oh yes. It's easy enough to cut the cord. But what comes of it? Especially where it's all become 'morbid'. Ninety-nine per cent of the time, the fire's still glowing under the cinders, with the wonderful result that later, when the two see each other again, for them to speak calmly, like good friends, has become hard as can be, almost impossible.

Even I could understand what she was saying – I put in at this point – and in the end I was very grateful to her for speaking so honestly.

But there was something I wanted her to explain. She'd suddenly rushed off without even saying goodbye to me, and after that, as soon as she'd arrived in Venice, she seemed concerned only with one thing: to be sure that I didn't stop seeing her brother Alberto.

'Why was that?' I asked. 'If, as you say, you really wanted me to forget you (forgive the cliché and don't start laughing in my face!), couldn't you have dropped me completely? I know it would have been hard on me. But not impossible that, for lack of fuel, to put it that way, all the cinders might go out, on their own.'

She looked at me without hiding a start of surprise, perhaps astonished that I could find in me the strength to move into a counter-attack, even if, all considered, with such small conviction behind it.

I wasn't wrong – she then agreed, with a troubled look, shaking her head – I wasn't wrong at all. But she begged me to believe that, acting as she had, there hadn't been the least intention on her part to stir up the water. She valued our friendship, that was all, valued it even in a slightly too possessive way. And then, seriously, she'd been thinking more about Alberto than about me – Alberto who'd been left here with no one, apart from Giampiero Malnate, he could have a chat with. Poor Alberto – she sighed. Hadn't I noticed, spending time with him these last few months, how much he needed company? For someone like him, used to spending the winter in Milan, with theatres, cinemas and everything else on tap, the prospect of being stuck here at Ferrara, shut up at home for months on end, and on top of that having nothing to do, was hardly a happy one, I had to agree. Poor Alberto! – she repeated. Compared to him, she was much stronger, much more independent – able to put up with, if need be, the most awful loneliness. And besides, it seemed to her she'd already told me, Venice was perhaps, as far as squalor goes, even worse in the winter than Ferrara, and her uncles' house no less sad and secluded than this one was.

'But this house isn't in the least bit sad,' I said, suddenly moved.

'D'you like it here?' she asked, brightening up. 'Then I have to confess something to you (but you mustn't get annoyed with me and accuse me of hypocrisy, or even of being two faced!) I very much wanted you to see it.'

'And why's that?'

'I don't know why. I can't explain to you why. I suppose it's for the same reason that, even as a child, at the Temple, I would happily have pulled you too under Papa's *tallit* . . . ah! If only I could have done! I can still see you there, under your father's *tallit*, on the bench in front of ours. What a pang I felt seeing you. It's stupid, I know, but I felt the same kind of sorrow as though you'd been an orphan, without a father and mother.'

She fell silent for some moments, her eyes fixed on the ceiling. Then, leaning her elbow on the bolster, she began to speak to me again – but this time seriously, almost solemnly.

She said she hated causing me pain, she really hated it. On the other hand she needed me to understand – it was absolutely unnecessary that we spoil, as we were risking doing, the lovely memories of a shared childhood. For us two to make love? Did it really seem feasible to me?

I asked her why she thought that so impossible.

For countless reasons – she replied – but mainly because the thought of making love to me disconcerted, embarrassed her: in the same way as if she were to imagine making love with a brother, with, say, Alberto. It was true that, as a child, she'd had 'a pash' on me, and, who knows, it was perhaps precisely this that was now blocking her so utterly with regard to me. I . . . I stood 'alongside' of her, didn't I see?, rather than 'in front' of her, whilst being in love (at least this was how she imagined it) was something for people who were determined to get the better of each other, a cruel, hard sport – far crueller and harder than tennis! – with no holds barred, with all kinds of low blows, and without any concern, just to palliate things, for the good of the soul or for notions of fairness.

> Maudit soit à jamais le rêveur inutile
> qui voulut le premier, dans sa stupidité,
> s'éprenant d'un problème insoluble et stérile,
> aux choses de l'amour mêler l'honnêteté![1]

– Baudelaire, who well understood, had warned. As for us? We were both stupidly honest, as alike as two drops of water ('and, you ought to believe me, people so alike should never fight each other'), so we'd never be able to try to get the better of each other, us two. Could I really see us wanting to 'wound' each other? No way! As the good Lord had made us like this, it meant the whole thing had neither prospects nor possibilities.

But even allowing for the unlikely hypothesis that we were made differently from the way we were, that between us there was in fact even the least possibility of a relationship of the kind that 'offered no hostages', how were we then supposed to behave? 'To get engaged', for instance, accompanied by an exchange of rings, parental visits, etc.? What an edifying image! If he were still alive, and got to hear of it, Israel Zangwill[2] himself might have had a juicy coda to add to his *Dreamers of the Ghetto*. And what a delight, what a 'pious' delight everyone would feel when we appeared together in the Italian synagogue for the next Yom Kippur: a bit wan in the face from fasting, but apart from that so good-looking, such a perfect couple! And seeing us, there'd certainly be someone there who'd give thanks to the Racial Laws, proclaiming that, faced with such a lovely union, the only thing to be said was: every cloud has a silver lining. Who knows if even the Secretary of the Fascist Party in Via Cavour might go a bit soft at the prospect! Even if in secret, wasn't that good fellow Consul Bolognesi really a lover of Jews? Pah!

Defeated, I kept silent.

She profited from this pause to lift the receiver and tell them in the kitchen to bring up the supper, but in a half-hour or so, not before, as – she repeated – that evening she wasn't 'in the least bit hungry'. Only the day after, going over it all, would I remember when, closed in the bathroom, I'd heard her talking on the telephone. So I was wrong – I told myself the next day. She might have been talking with anyone in the house (or even outside) but *not* with the kitchen.

But then I was immersed in a completely different train of thought. When Micòl put the receiver down I lifted my head.

'You said we were exactly alike,' I spoke again. 'In what way?'

But yes, yes we are – she exclaimed – in the way, like you, I've no access to that instinctive enjoyment of things that's typical of normal people. She could sense it very clearly: for me, no less than for her, the past counted far more than the present, remembering something far more than possessing it. Compared to memory, every possession can only ever seem disappointing, banal, inadequate . . . She understood me so well! My anxiety that the present 'immediately' turned into the past so that I could love it and dream about it at leisure was just like hers, was identical. It was 'our' vice, this: to go forwards with our heads forever turned back. Wasn't it true?

It was – I had to admit within myself – it was exactly so. When was it that I'd embraced her? At the most an hour before. And already everything had again become as unreal and mythical as ever: an event that was unbelievable, or a source of fear.

'Who knows,' I replied. 'Perhaps it's all much simpler. Perhaps you don't find me attractive. And that's all it is.'

'Don't talk nonsense,' she said in protest. 'What's that got to do with it?'

'It's got everything to do with it!'

'*You are fishing for compliments.*[3] And you know it. But I'm not going to give you the satisfaction, you don't deserve it. And anyway, even if I was now to try telling you once more all the praise I've lavished on your famous blue-green eyes (and not only on your eyes) what would I get from that? You'd be the first to judge me ill, as an utter hypocrite. You'd think, here we go, after the stick comes the carrot, the sweetener . . .'

'Unless . . .'

'Unless what?

I hesitated, and then finally decided.

'Unless', I went on, 'there's someone else involved.'

She shook her head to say no, looking me in the eyes.

'There's no one else in the least bit involved,' she replied. 'And who could there be?'

I believed her. But I was desperate and wanted to hurt her.

'You're asking me?' I said, pouting. 'It could be anyone. Who can assure me that this winter, in Venice, you haven't met someone else?'

She burst out laughing. Fresh, happy, crystalline laughter.

'What an idea!' she exclaimed. 'Given I've done nothing else but huddle over my thesis the whole time!'

'You don't mean to say that in these five years of university you've not been out with anyone. P-lease! There must have been someone there who was following you around!'

I was convinced she'd deny it. But I was wrong.

'Sure, I've had some admirers,' she admitted.

It was like a hand had grabbed hold of my stomach and twisted it.

'Many?' I managed to bring out.

Stretched out supine as she was, her eyes fixed on the ceiling, she slightly raised one arm.

'I wouldn't really know,' she replied. 'Let me think.'

'So you've had a lot, then?'

She gave me a sidelong look with a sly, decidedly lewd expression, which I didn't recognize in her and which completely floored me.

'Well . . . let's say three or four. Five to be precise . . . but all little flirtations, I should make it clear, quite innocuous things . . . and also fairly boring as it happens.'

'What kind of flirtations?'

'Oh, you know . . . long walks along the Lido . . . two or three routine trips to Torcello . . . every now and then a kiss . . . a great deal of holding hands . . . and going to the flicks. *Orgies* of cinema.'

'All with fellow students?'

'More or less.'

'And Catholics, I imagine.'

'Of course. Not as a point of principle, though. You understand: you have to make do with what's there.'

'But with . . .'

'No. With *Judim*, I have to say, not once. Not that there weren't any in the classes. But they were so serious and ugly.'

She turned once more to look at me.

'However, no one at all this winter,' she added, smiling. 'I could swear an oath on that. I've done nothing else but smoke and work, so much so that Signorina Blumenfeld herself had to prompt me to go out.'

She took out from under the pillows a packet of Lucky Strike, unopened.

'D'you want one? As you can see I've started off on the strong ones.'

I silently pointed to the pipe which I kept in my jacket pocket.

'You as well!' she laughed, highly amused. 'That Giampi of *yours* really is growing a crop of disciples!'

'And you, you keep on grumbling about having no friends in Venice!' I complained. 'What a lot of lies. It's clear you're just like the other girls.'

She shook her head, though I wasn't sure whether in sympathy with me or with herself.

'Flirtations, even insignificant ones, are not to be had with friends,' she said with sadness, 'and so, when I was speaking to you about friendship, you should see I was only being a bit dishonest. But you're right. I am just like other girls – a liar, a deceiver, *unfaithful* . . . in the end not much different from an Adriana Trentini.'

She had said 'un-faith-ful' separating each of the syllables in her usual fashion, but with an extra quality of bitter pride. She went on to say that if I had a fault it was that I'd always thought a bit too highly of her. In saying this she hadn't the least intention of excusing herself. And yet she'd always seen in my eyes so much 'idealism' that it had somehow forced her to appear better than she actually was.

Nothing much else was left to say. A little later, when Gina came in with the supper – it was already past nine o'clock – I stood up.

'I'm sorry, but I have to go now,' I said, holding out my hand.

'You know the way, don't you? Or would you like Gina to accompany you?'

'No, there's no need. I can manage it on my own.'

'Take the lift, it's a lot easier.'

'I shall.'

At the door I turned round. She was already bringing the spoon to her lips.

'Bye,' I said.

She smiled at me.

'Bye. I'll phone you tomorrow.'

4

But the worst part only began about three weeks later, when I returned from a trip to France I made in the last fortnight of April.

I'd gone to France, to Grenoble, for a very particular reason. The few hundred lire every month, legally permitted for us to send my brother Ernesto, were only enough, as he kept repeating in his letters, to pay for his rented room, at Place Vaucanson. So it was vital he received more money. For this reason, when I returned home later than usual one night, my father, who had been staying awake especially to speak to me, pressed me to take him the money in person. Why didn't I make the most of the opportunity? A chance to breathe some different air from 'this hereabouts', to see a bit of the world, to have a wander: that's what I ought to do! It would be good for my morale, and my body as well.

So I went. I stopped for two hours in Turin, four at Chambéry, and finally reached Grenoble. In the *pension* where Ernesto went to eat his meals I immediately got to know various Italian students, all in the same situation as my brother and all enrolled at the Polytechnic: a Levi from Turin, a Segre from Saluzzo, a Sorani from Trieste, a Mantuan Cantoni, a Florentine Castelnuovo, a Pincherle girl from Rome. I didn't hitch up with any of them. During the dozen days left to me, most of the time I spent in the Municipal Library, leafing through Stendhal's manuscripts. It was cold in Grenoble, and rainy. The peaks of the mountains at the back of the lodgings, hidden by mists and cloud, were only rarely visible, whilst in the evenings the blackout trials dampened any desire to go out. Ferrara seemed very far away to me, as though I'd never return. And Micòl? Since I'd left I had ceaselessly heard her voice in my ear, her voice the time she'd said to me: 'Why are you doing that? It's no use.' One day, however, something happened. As I was reading through one of Stendhal's notebooks and chanced upon these isolated words in English: *All lost, nothing lost*, as though by a miracle, I had a sudden feeling of being freed, healed. I got hold of a postcard, and wrote that line from Stendhal on it, just that, and then sent it off to her, Micòl, without adding a single word, not even a signature – she could make of it what she wanted. All lost, nothing lost. How true that was! I told myself. And felt I could breathe again.

I was fooling myself. Returning to Italy in the first days of May, I found the spring in full bloom, the meadows between Alessandria and Piacenza broadly swathed with yellow, the roads of the Emilian countryside thronged with girls on bikes revealing bare arms and legs, the big trees of the Ferrara walls laden with leaves. I'd arrived on a Sunday, towards midday. As soon as I got back home, I had a bath, took lunch with my family and answered a host of questions patiently enough. But the unexpected frenzy that gripped me the very moment when, from the train, I'd seen the towers and campaniles of Ferrara rise up from the horizon, made any further delays intolerable to me. At half past two I was already on my bike rushing along the Mura degli Angeli, my eyes fixed on the motionless green abundance of the Barchetto del Duca, which gradually drew closer on my left. Everything had turned back to how it was before, as though I'd spent the last fortnight asleep.

They were playing, down there on the tennis court – Micòl and a stout young man in long white socks who, it wasn't hard for me to make out, was Malnate. I too was quickly noticed and recognized, for the two of them stopped knocking up and began to wave their rackets in the air with extravagant gestures. They were not alone, however; Alberto was also there. Emerging from the leafy border, I saw him rush to the centre of the court, look out towards me and raise his hands to his mouth. He whistled two, three times. Might they be informed what it was I was doing on top of the Mura? – each of them, in their own way, seemed to be asking. And why on earth had I not come immediately into the garden, strange creature that I was? So then I steered towards the opening of Corso Ercole I d'Este, pedalling alongside the surrounding wall, and had come in sight of the gate when Alberto unleashed another of his 'oliphants'. 'Make sure you don't slink off!' his ever powerful whistles now seemed to be saying, though they had become in the meantime somehow good-natured, a shade less admonitory.

'Greetings!' I shouted as usual, when I emerged into the open from the gallery of climbing roses.

Micòl and Malnate had gone back to their game, and without stopping, replied together with another 'Greetings'. Alberto stood up and came to meet me.

'Would you tell us where you've been hiding all these days?' he asked. 'I phoned your house a fair few times, but you were never there.'

'He's been in France,' Micòl replied on my behalf from the court.

'In France!' Alberto exclaimed, his eyes full of an astonishment that seemed to me truly felt. 'Doing what?'

'I've been to see my brother Ernesto in Grenoble.'

'Oh, of course. It's true. Your brother's studying at Grenoble. And how is he? How is he coping?'

In the meantime we had parked ourselves on two deckchairs, placed one beside the other in front of the side-entrance to the court in an excellent position to follow the state of play. As distinct from last autumn, Micòl was not in shorts. She was wearing a pleated, white woollen dress, very old-fashioned, a shirt that was also white, with its sleeves rolled up, and curious long white cotton socks, almost like those of a Red Cross nurse. Covered in sweat, and red in the face, she was concentrating on striking the balls into the furthest corners of the court, powering her shots. Yet although he'd put on weight and was quite out of breath, Malnate was effortfully holding his own against her.

A tennis ball, rolling along, came to a stop within a short distance of us. Micòl approached to collect it, and for a moment our eyes met.

I saw her pull a face. Evidently annoyed, she brusquely turned back towards Malnate.

'Shall we play a set?' she shouted out.

'We could try,' he panted out. 'How many games handicap will you give me?'

'Not a single one,' Micòl replied, frowning. 'All I'll give you is the chance to serve first. Your service, then!'

She threw the ball over the net and got into position to receive her opponent's serve.

For some minutes Alberto and I watched them playing. I felt full of unease and misery. The '*tu*' form with which she addressed Malnate, her show of ignoring me, suddenly and fully revealed to me the length of time I'd been away. And as for Alberto, he as usual had eyes only for Giampi. But every now and then, I noticed, instead of admiring and praising him, he would start running him down.

There you see a type of person – he confided whisperingly to me, and so surprisingly that, however anguished I felt, I didn't miss a single syllable he said – there you see a type of person who, even if he took tennis lessons every blessed day from a Nüsslein or a Martin Plaa, would still never make a halfway decent player. What was it stopping him? His legs? Certainly not that, otherwise he'd never have become the accomplished mountaineer he undoubtedly was. Lungs? Nor them, for the same reason. Muscular power? He had enough of that to spare – you just have to shake his hand to feel it. What was it then? The truth is that tennis – he concluded with extraordinary emphasis – as well as being a sport is also an art, and since every art requires a particular talent, whoever's lacking in that will remain 'all elbows' their whole life.

'I ask you!' Malnate shouted out at a certain point. 'Will you two keep the noise down a bit?'

'Play on, play on,' Alberto retorted, 'and try not to let a woman get the better of you!'

I couldn't believe my ears. Was it possible? What had happened to all of Alberto's meekness, all his submissiveness to his friend? I looked at him carefully. His face seemed to me of a sudden wan, emaciated, as though wrinkled with the premature onset of old age. Was he ill?

I was tempted to ask him, but I lacked the courage. Instead, I asked him if this had been the first day they'd started playing tennis again, and why Bruno Lattes, Adriana Trentini and the rest of the zòzga* weren't there.

'Well, it's clear you know absolutely nothing!' he cried out, revealing his gums in a big laugh.

About a week ago – he immediately launched into the tale – having seen the good weather set in, Micòl and he had made ten or so phone calls, with the worthy intention of restarting last year's memorable tennis meets. They'd called Adriana Trentini, Bruno Lattes, that boy Sani, young Collevatti – and various splendid examples of both sexes selected from among the new generation who, last autumn, they hadn't even thought of. All of them, 'young and old' had accepted the invitation with commendable promptness, so that the day of the opening – Saturday, 1 May – looked well set to be a triumphal success to say the least. Not only had they played tennis, gossiped, flirted and so on, but they'd even danced, there, in the *Hütte*, to the accompaniment of the 'conveniently installed' Philips.

An even greater success – Alberto went on – had attended the second session, Sunday afternoon, 2 May. Except that as early as Monday morning things were already coming to a head. Heralded by a sibylline visiting card, towards eleven o'clock the lawyer Tabet arrived on his bicycle – yes, that big Fascist blockhead Geremia Tabet in person, who after being shut away in conference with Papa in his study, had passed on the mandatory order of the Party Secretary to cease forthwith the provocation of those scandalous daily gatherings that for some time had been held at the house, which apart from anything else were entirely lacking in any healthy sporting activity. It was really unacceptable, the Consul Bolognesi let it be known through his 'common' friend Tabet, it was really unacceptable, for obvious reasons, that the Finzi-Contini garden was gradually turning itself into a kind of rival tennis club to the Eleonora d'Este – the latter a much renowned institution of Ferrarese sporting life. So that was that. To avoid official sanctions, 'such as a forced stay for an undetermined period of time in Urbisaglia', from

* Ferrarese dialect: gang.

this time on no one who was a member of the Eleonora d'Este should be lured away from their natural habitat.

'And what did your father say in reply?' I asked.

'What could he say?' Alberto laughed. 'There was nothing left for him but to behave like Don Abbondio.[1] To bow and murmur "Your obedient servant". I think that's more or less how he expressed himself.'

'I hold Barbicinti responsible,' Micòl shouted out from the court, clearly not far enough away to have stopped her following our conversation closely. 'No one will change my mind that it was him who ran off crying to complain at Viale Cavour. I can just see it. But still, you have to sympathize with him, poor thing. When one's jealous, one becomes capable of anything . . .'

Although they were perhaps thrown off without any particular intent, these words of Micòl's stung me deeply. I was on the point of getting up and going away.

And who knows, maybe I would have done so, if I hadn't stopped at that very moment, as I turned towards Alberto, almost to invoke his witness and assistance, and again noticed how grey his face was, the afflicted scrawniness of his shoulders lost in a pullover now grown too big for him (he winked, as if telling me not to take it to heart, and began to hold forth on other things – the tennis court, the work to improve it 'from the foundations up' which, despite everything, would be starting within the week . . .) and if in that same instant I hadn't seen appearing, down there at the edge of the clearing, the black mournful little figures, close together, of Professor Ermanno and Signora Olga, coming from their afternoon stroll in the park and wending their way slowly towards us.

5

That whole long period which followed, up until the fateful last days of August 1939, until, that is, the eve of the Nazi invasion of Poland and the phoney war, I remember as a slow progressive descent into the Maelstrom. There were only four of us left in sole possession of the tennis court, which was soon to be covered with a fine coat of red shale from Imola – myself, Micòl, Alberto and Malnate. (Presumably lost in his pursuit of Adriana Trentini, Bruno Lattes was not to be numbered amongst us.) Swapping partners, we spent whole afternoons in long doubles matches, with Alberto, even though he was short of breath and easily tired, oddly driven, unwilling to give either us or himself any quarter.

What was it made me stubbornly return every day to a place where, as I well knew, I'd be rewarded with nothing but humiliation and bitterness? I couldn't say with any clarity. Perhaps I was hoping for a miracle, for a sudden change in the state of affairs, or perhaps I was actually going in search of humiliation and bitterness . . . We played tennis or else, stretched out on four deckchairs in front of the *Hütte*, we argued about the usual topics of art and politics. But when I asked Micòl, who, deep down, remained kindly towards me, sometimes even affectionate, for a turn in the park, it was very rarely that she accepted. If she did, she never followed me willingly, and every time her face would assume an expression poised between distaste and forbearance which made me regret having dragged her away from Alberto and Malnate.

All the same, I wasn't prepared to lay down my arms; I wouldn't give up. Caught between the impulse to break it all off, to disappear for ever, and its opposite: not to renounce being there, not to surrender at any cost, in the end I almost always turned up. Sometimes, it's true, a look from Micòl that was colder than usual, an impatient gesture of hers, one of her sarcastic, bored grimaces, would be enough for me to feel with utter sincerity that that was it, it was all over. But how long did I succeed in staying away? Three or four days at the most. On the fifth there I was again, parading my face with the good-humoured and detached expression of someone just returned from a most rewarding journey – I was always talking of having taken trips, comparing the journeys I'd made to Milan, to Florence, to Rome: it was just as well all three of them gave the impression of believing me! – but all the same I did so with a flayed heart and with eyes that once again began to seek out in those of Micòl some answer which was now impossible. That was the time, as she was to call it, of our 'marital rows'. During which, if ever the occasion permitted, I would try to kiss her. And she put up with it, never appearing to be uncivil.

One evening in June, however, things were to go differently.

We were seated beside each other on the steps outside the *Hütte*, and though it must have been about half past eight it was still not dark. I was watching Perotti, in the distance, busy taking down and rolling up the net on the tennis court, the surface of which, since the red shale had arrived from the Romagna, never seemed to him sufficiently well looked after. Malnate was taking a shower inside the hut – we could hear him panting noisily under the jet of hot water – and Alberto had taken his leave a little earlier with a melancholy 'bye-bye'. So the two of us, Micòl and I, had been left alone, and I'd immediately taken advantage of this to resume my eternal, boring, absurd campaign. As ever, I kept on trying to convince her she was wrong to believe a relationship between us would not work. As ever I accused her (in bad faith) of having lied to me when, less than a month before, she had assured me there was no third party involved. I put it to her that there was, or at least there had been, in Venice, during the winter.

'I'm telling you for the thousandth time you're wrong,' Micòl said in a low tone, 'but I know it's pointless. I know you'll want to return to the fray tomorrow with the same old story. What do you want me to say – that I'm plotting in secret, that I'm living a double life? If you really want that, I could certainly oblige you.'

'No, Micòl,' I replied in an equally low but far more agitated tone. 'I may be all kinds of things, but I'm not a masochist. If only you knew how normal, how terribly banal my hopes are – you'd laugh. If there's one thing I want, it's this – to hear you *swear* what you've said is true, and to believe you.'

'Well, I swear it. Now do you believe me?'

'No.'

'So much the worse for you then!'

'True, it's all the worse for me. And yet if I *could* really believe you . . .'

'Then what would you do? Let's hear.'

'Oh, just the most normal, banal stuff – that's the problem. This, for example.'

I grasped her hands, and began to cover them with kisses and tears.

For a while she let me. I hid my face in her knees, and the smell of her skin, smooth and soft, slightly salty, numbed me. I kissed her there, on the legs.

'Now, that's enough,' she said.

She withdrew her hands from mine, and stood up.

'Goodbye. I'm cold,' she went on, 'and you should go home. Dinner will be ready by now, and I have to wash and dress first. Get up, come on, and stop acting like a baby.'

'Goodbye,' she then shouted towards the *Hütte*. 'I'm going now.'

'Goodbye,' Malnate replied from inside, 'and thanks.'

'See you soon. Are you coming tomorrow?'

'I don't know about tomorrow. We'll see.'

Separated by the bicycle whose handlebars I was feverishly grasping, we made our way towards the *magna domus*, standing tall and dark in the summer dusk alive with bats and mosquitoes. We kept silent. A cart brimming with hay, drawn by a pair of yoked oxen, was going in the opposite direction to us. Seated on top of it was one of Perotti's sons who, coming level with us, doffed his beret and wished us good evening. Even though I'd accused Micòl without believing it, I'd still have liked to shout at her – telling her to stop play-acting with me. I wanted to insult her, even to slap her. And if I had? What would I have gained from it?

But I did something just as mistaken.

'It's pointless you denying it,' I said, 'and anyway I know who the *person* is.'

No sooner had these words escaped me than I regretted them.

Now aggrieved and in earnest, she looked at me.

'I see,' she said, 'and now, according to your calculations, I'll have to try to get you to spit out the name and surname you've hidden away, if you really have any name in mind at all. But I'm afraid that's it. I don't want to hear anything more. Only that, having arrived at this point, I'd be grateful if from now on you were a little less assiduous in your visits . . . I mean, if you were to come to our house less often. I'm telling you frankly: if I didn't fear being overwhelmed by gossip in the family – how come . . . why ever . . . etc., I'd beg you not to come at all, ever again.'

'Forgive me,' I murmured.

'No. That I can't do,' she replied, shaking her head. 'If I did, in a few days you'd only start again.'

She added that for a long time up till then my way of behaving had been undignified – both for her and for myself. She had told me and repeated it a thousand times that it was useless, that I shouldn't attempt to shift our relationship onto any other plane than that of friendship and affection. But what good was it? As soon as I could I did the opposite – I'd grab on to her, trying to kiss her and go further, as though I didn't know that in situations like ours there was nothing more disagreeable and ill-advised. Good heavens! Was it really possible I couldn't contain myself? If there'd been a physical relationship of a deeper kind between us than one based on the odd kiss, in that case she might have been able to understand how I . . . how she, so to speak, had got under my skin. But given the relations that had always been between us, my compulsion to embrace her, to rub myself up against her, was the sign of one thing only: my effective heartlessness, my constitutional inability to really care about another person. And what's more, what did my unexpected absences mean, and my sudden returns, the inquisitional or 'tragic' looks, the hangdog silences, the rudenesses, the irrational insinuations – the whole repertoire of rash and embarrassing behaviour which I tirelessly exhibited, without the least sense of shame? Perhaps she could have put up with it if these 'marital rows' had been reserved for her ears alone, apart from the others. But that her brother and Giampi Malnate should have to be witnesses, this no, and again no, she wouldn't put up with.

'Now it seems to me you're exaggerating,' I said. 'When have I ever made a scene in front of Malnate and Alberto?'

'Always. Continually!'

Every single time I'd come back after a week of being away – she went on – and declare I'd been to Rome or somewhere, and then I'd start laughing, laughing in nervous fits like a nutter, without the least reason, did I fool myself into thinking Alberto and Malnate would somehow not notice I was talking bullshit, that I'd never been anywhere near Rome, and that my fits of laughter 'straight out of *Cena delle beffe*'[1] weren't all directed towards her? And when in arguing, I'd jump up and start haranguing and screaming like a maniac, frequently taking everything personally – some day or other Giampi would get really annoyed, and he wouldn't be without some justification, poor thing that he was too! – did I think people would somehow not notice that she was the cause, albeit the innocent one, of all my crazy antics?

'I've understood,' I said, lowering my head. 'I've really understood you don't want to see me any more.'

'It's not my fault. It's you who, bit by bit, have become unbearable.'

'You said, though,' I stammered after a pause, 'you said that I could come round every so often, rather that I have to. Isn't that right?'

'Yes.'

'Well then . . . you must decide. How should I behave so as not to offend you further?'

'I don't know,' she replied, shrugging her shoulders. 'I'd say that, to start off with, you should leave a space of at least twenty days.

Then you can start visiting again, if you want to. But I beg you, *even after*, don't come round more than twice a week.'

'Tuesdays and Wednesdays, would that do? Like for piano lessons.'

'You idiot,' she muttered, smiling against her will. 'You really are an idiot.'

6

Although the effort, especially to begin with, was extremely hard, I
made it something of a point of honour to observe Micòl's prohib-
itions to the letter. Suffice it to say, having graduated on 29 June,
and having received a warm congratulatory note from Professor
Ermanno which contained, among other things, an invitation to
dinner, I thought it opportune to refuse, saying I was sorry but I
couldn't. I wrote that I'd been suffering from a bout of tonsilitis,
and that my father had stopped me going out in the evenings. My
refusal, however, was down to the fact that of the twenty days Micòl
had imposed on me, only sixteen had passed.

The effort was really hard. Though I was hoping that sooner or
later there'd be some recompense, my hopes remained somewhat
vague: I felt glad to be obeying Micòl and through this obedience I
thought I might once more have access to her and to the paradisal
regions I'd been shut out from. If before I'd always had something
to reproach her with, now I had nothing. I and I alone was the guilty
one. How many mistakes I'd made! – I told myself. I thought back
over all the times that, often by force, I'd kissed her on the lips, but
always and only to put her in the right, who, even in rejecting me,
had put up with me for so long, and to feel ashamed of my satyr-like
lustfulness, masked as sentimentality and idealism. The twenty days
having passed, I risked showing myself again, and, following that,
kept rigorously to the twice-weekly visits prescribed. But even this
didn't induce Micòl to descend from the pedestal of purity and moral
superiority on which, since being sent into exile, I'd placed her. She
continued to stay up there. And I felt myself lucky to keep on being
able to admire this distant image of her, no less beautiful inside

than she was on the outside. 'Like truth itself/like her, sad and beautiful . . .': these first two verses of a poem I never finished, though they were written much later, in Rome, soon after the war, refer back to that Micòl of August 1939, and the way I saw her then.

Chased out of Paradise, I waited in silence to be let back in. And yet I suffered – some days atrociously. It was with the intention somehow to alleviate the weight of an often intolerable distance and solitude that one week, soon after that final, disastrous conversation with Micòl, I had the notion of going to visit Malnate, to keep in contact at least with him.

I knew where to find him. As Professor Meldolesi once had, he also lived in the zone of small villas just outside Porta San Benedetto, between the Canile and the curve of the Doro. At that time, before the building speculation of these last fifteen years wrecked it, this area, even if a bit grey and modest, did not seem at all disagreeable. All on two floors, each one sporting its own little garden, these small villas generally belonged to magistrates, teachers, civil servants, state functionaries, etc., who, should you be passing by in summer after six in the evening, could be spotted beyond the bristling bars of their gates, sometimes in pyjamas, intent on busily watering and pruning their plants or hoeing the soil. Malnate's resident landlord was one of them, a tribunal judge. He was a Sicilian around fifty, thin as a rake, with long, thick grey hair. As soon as he noticed me, still not off my bike and holding on with both hands to the gate's pointed uprights as I peered into the garden, he set down the hosepipe with which he'd been watering the flower-beds.

'May I help you?' he asked, approaching.

'Is Dr Malnate here?'

'He lives here. Why?'

'Is he at home?'

'Who can say. Do you have an appointment?'

'I'm a friend of his. I was passing, and I thought I'd stop by for a moment to say hello to him.'

In the meantime, the judge had covered the ten or so metres which had separated us. And now I could only see the upper part of his bony, fanatical face, his black eyes, piercing as needles, looming above the edge of the metal plate linking the gate's uprights at the height of a man. He stared at me with suspicion. All the same, the examination must have ended up in my favour, because almost immediately the lock clicked open and I was let in.

'That way, please,' Judge Lalumìa finally said, lifting his skeletal arm. 'Just follow the paving that goes round the house. The little ground-floor door is the one to the doctor's apartment. Ring the bell. He may not be in. If he isn't, the door will be opened by my wife, who should be there at the moment, making up his bed.'

This said, he turned his back on me, and without taking any further notice of me attended once more to his hosepipe.

Instead of Malnate, a mature, blond, abundant woman in a dressing gown appeared in the small doorway I'd been directed to.

'Good evening,' I said. 'I was looking for Dr Malnate.'

'He hasn't come back yet,' Signora Lalumìa replied, all kindness, 'but he shouldn't be long. Almost every evening, soon as he gets out of the factory, he goes to play tennis round at the Finzi-Continis', you know, the house in Corso Ercole I . . . But he should, as I said, be back here any moment. Before supper,' she smiled, lowering her eyes in a rapt expression, 'before supper he always drops in at the house to see if there's any mail.'

I said that I'd come back later, and began to retrieve the bicycle I'd leant on the wall beside the door. But the Signora insisted I remain. She wanted me to come in and sit down on an armchair, and in the meantime, standing in front of me, she informed me that she herself was Ferrarese, 'a pure-blooded Ferrarese', that she knew my family very well, especially my mother, of whom 'something like forty years ago' (so saying she again smiled and bashfully lowered her eyes) she had been a class-mate at the Regina Elena elementary school, the one close by the church of San Giuseppe in Carlo Mayr. How was my mother? – she asked. I was, please, not to forget to send her greetings from Edvige, Edvige Santini, and my mother would then certainly know who she was. She made some remarks about the possibly imminent war and, sighing and shaking her head, referred to the Racial Laws, explaining that she had been deprived of 'home help' and so had had to organize everything on her own, including the kitchen, and then, having excused herself, she left me alone.

When the Signora had gone out, I looked around. The room was spacious but with a low ceiling and as well as being a place to sleep in served as a study and sitting room as well. The rays of the sunset, penetrating the big horizontal window, lit up the motes of dust in the air. I looked around at the furnishings: the bed-divan, half-bed, half-divan, as was confirmed by the wretched cotton coverlet patterned with red flowers which hid the mattress, the fat white pillow, uncovered and set on its own to one side, the small black table, in a vaguely oriental style, placed between the bed-divan and the single armchair, of imitation leather, on which I was sitting, the fake parchment lampshades scattered about the room, the cream-coloured telephone that stood out against the funereal black of an unsteady lawyer's desk, full of drawers, the crude oil-paintings hung on the walls. And although I told myself that Giampi had a nerve turning up his nose at Alberto's 'twentieth-century' furniture (how could that moral fervour which made him such a stern judge of others let him be so indulgent towards himself and his own things?), suddenly feeling my heart gripped by the thought of Micòl – and it was as though it was she in person gripping my heart, with her own hand – I renewed my solemn resolve to behave well with Malnate, not to quarrel or argue with him any more. When she found out, Micòl would have to take account of this as well.

Far off, the siren of one of the sugar factories of Pontelagoscuro sounded. Soon after, a heavy tread made the gravel grind on the garden path.

The judge's voice sounded very close by, on the other side of the wall.

'Ah, Doctor!' he was intoning in his distinctly nasal fashion, 'you've a friend waiting for you at home.'

'A friend?' Malnate said coldly. 'And who might that be?'

'Go on, go and see . . .' the other encouraged him. 'I said it was a friend.'

Tall and fat, taller and fatter than ever, perhaps from the effect of the low ceiling, Malnate appeared at the doorway.

'Who'd have thought it!' he exclaimed, his eyes wide with surprise as he adjusted his glasses on his nose.

He came forward, shook me energetically by the hand, and patted me several times on the back. Having always sensed some hostility in him towards me, since we'd first met, it was very odd to find him now so kind, considerate and communicative. What was happening? – I wondered, perplexed. Had he too come to a decision utterly to change his manner towards me? Perhaps. What was clear was that at this time, in his own house, there was nothing in him of the stubborn gainsayer who, under the watchful eyes of Alberto and Micòl, I'd so often done battle with. It was enough to see him, and I understood: between us, outside the Finzi-Continis' – and to think that in the last period we had quarrelled to the extent of offending each other, and almost actually came to blows! – every motive for conflict was destined to pass away, to melt like mist in the sun.

In the meantime Malnate was talking – in an astonishingly garrulous and cordial way. He asked me if I'd met his landlord whilst crossing the garden, and if so whether he'd been polite to me. I replied that I'd met him and, laughing, described the whole scene.

'Just as well.'

He proceeded to tell me about the judge and his wife, without leaving me time to say I'd already met them both: excellent people – he said – even if, all considered, their common resolve to protect him from the risks and snares of 'the big wide world' made them slightly interfering. Though decidedly anti-Fascist – being an ardent monarchist – the judge didn't want any problems, and so was continually on the alert, clearly anxious that Malnate, recognizable at a glance as a likely future client of the Special Tribunal – as he'd said on several occasions – shouldn't secretly bring home any dubious types: for instance any ex-political convict, anyone under surveillance, or some subversive. As regards Signora Edvige, she too was forever on the alert. She spent whole days perched behind the gaps in the blinds at the first-floor window or coming to his door even late at night, when she'd heard him returning. But her fears were of a completely different kind. Like the good Ferrarese she was – for she *was* Ferrarese, née Santini) she knew only too well, she told him, what the women of the city were like, both married and unmarried. In her view, a young man on his own, a graduate, from elsewhere, furnished with an apartment with its own door, was in great danger. In no time women would have reduced his spine to pulp. And he? He'd always done his very best to reassure her. But it was clear: only when she'd managed to transform him into a sad, beslippered codger in vest and pyjama bottoms, with his nose eternally parked above the kitchen pans, would 'Madame' Lalumìa find any peace.

'Well, in the end, what's so wrong with that?' I objected. 'I seem to remember you often running down restaurants and trattorias.'

'That's true,' he admitted with unusual compliance – a compliance that kept astonishing me. 'And besides there's no point in it. Freedom's undoubtedly a wonderful thing, but unless there's some limit set to it' (he winked at me as he said this) 'who knows where it'll all end?'

It was starting to get dark. Malnate got up from the divan-bed where he'd stretched out his considerable length, went to turn on the light, and then into the bathroom. He needed a shave – I heard from there. Would I give him the time to shave? Afterwards we could go out together.

We kept the conversation going in this way – he in the bathroom, I in the sitting room.

He mentioned that also that afternoon he'd been round at the Finzi-Continis', and had in fact just come back from there. They had played for more than two hours – first him and Micòl, then him and Alberto, and finally all three together. Did I like playing American doubles?

'Not much,' I replied.

'I can understand that,' he agreed. 'For someone like you who knows how to play, American doubles doesn't make much sense. But it can be fun.'

'So who won?'

'The American doubles?'

'Yes.'

'Micòl, naturally!' he said with a snigger. 'My respect to anyone who can contain her. Even on the court she's like a whirlwind . . .'

He then asked me why for some days I'd not shown my face. Had I been away somewhere?

Remembering what Micòl had told me, that no one believed me when, after each of my absences, I said that I'd been away on a trip, I replied that I'd got tired of going round and that, often, in the last period, I'd anyway had the impression my presence was irksome, above all to Micòl, and for this reason I'd decided to 'keep a bit of a distance'.

'What are you saying?' he asked in surprise. 'Far as I can see, Micòl has nothing at all against you. Are you sure you're not mistaken?'

'Sure as can be.'

He sighed, letting it pass. I too had nothing to add. Soon after, he came out of the bathroom, clean-shaven and smiling. He realized I was looking at the ugly pictures on the walls.

'So then,' he asked 'how does it strike you, this big mouse-trap of mine? You've yet to bestow your opinion.'

He grinned in his old manner, waiting in the doorway for my reply, but at the same time, I could see it in his eyes, determined not to take offence.

'I envy you,' I replied. 'If only I could have something similar at my disposal. I've always dreamt of something like this.'

He threw me a gladdened look. It was true – he consented: even he could clearly see the limits of the Lalumìa couple's sense of furnishings. And yet their taste, typical of the petit bourgeois ('and it's not for nothing' – he added parenthetically – 'they represent the very core and backbone of the nation'), always had something lively, vital, healthy about it – and this was probably directly related to its obviousness and vulgarity.

'After all, things are just things,' he concluded. 'Why become a slave to them?'

Should Alberto be considered in this light – he went on – it would be hard on him! With his determination to surround himself with exquisite, perfect, flawless things, one day or another he too will end up becoming . . .

He made towards the door without finishing his sentence.

'How is he?' I asked.

I too had got up, and had reached him at the doorway.

'Who, Alberto?' he said with a start.

I nodded.

'That's right,' I added. 'Of late he's seemed to me a bit tired and done in. Don't you think so? I have the feeling he's not well.'

He drew in his shoulders, then turned off the light. He went on out into the darkness in front of me and said nothing more till we reached the gate, except halfway there to return a 'Good evening' to Signora Lalumìa who had appeared at a window. Then at the gate he suggested I go with him to have supper at Giovanni's.

7

I had no illusions, however. I realized even then that Malnate was perfectly aware of all the reasons, without exception, which kept me away from the Finzi-Continis. Despite this, in the talks we had the topic never surfaced again. On the theme of the Finzi-Continis we both displayed an exceptional reserve and delicacy, and I was especially grateful that he pretended to believe all I'd said on the subject that first evening – grateful, in short, that he was prepared to play along with me and back me up.

We saw each other almost every evening. From the first days of June the heat had suddenly become stifling and emptied the city. Usually it was I who went round to his house, between seven and eight. When I found nobody there, I waited patiently for his return, sometimes entertained by the chatting of Signora Edvige. But most times, there he was, stretched out on his divan-bed in his vest, his hands joined behind his neck and his eyes fixed on the ceiling, or else sitting writing a letter to his mother, to whom he was attached with a deep, slightly exaggerated affection. As soon as he saw me, he'd rush to the bathroom to shave, and after this, we would go out, it being understood that we would also eat out together.

Usually we'd go to Giovanni's, sitting outside, in front of the Castello's towers which loomed above us like the walls of the Dolomites, and, like them, the tops of its towers were aglow with the last of the daylight. Or else we'd go to the Voltini, a trattoria outside Porta Reno. Sitting at its tables lined up under a graceful colonnade, exposed to the midday sun and, at that time, being open to the countryside, it was possible to look out as far as the huge fields of the airport. On hotter evenings, however, instead of heading towards the city, we made our way out along the lovely street of Pontelagoscuro, crossed the iron bridge over the Po, and pedalling side by side to the top of the embankment, with the river on our right and with the Veneto countryside on our left, after another fifteen minutes, halfway between Pontelagoscuro and Polesella, we reached the big, solitary Dogana Vecchia, famous for its fried eels. We always ate very slowly, and sat on at the table till late, drinking Lambrusco and vinello di Bosco and smoking our pipes. If we had dined in town, at a certain point we'd put down our napkins, each paying our own bills, and then, wheeling our bikes, we'd begin to stroll along the Giovecca, up and down from the Castello to the Prospettiva, or else along Viale Cavour, from the Castello as far as the station. Then it was he, usually around midnight, who would offer to accompany me back home. He would glance at his watch, announce that it was bedtime (he'd often solemnly remark, that even though the factory sirens only sounded at eight o'clock for them, the technicians, they always needed to be out of bed by quarter to seven 'at the latest'), and however much I would sometimes insist I accompany him, there was never an occasion when he let me. The last image I'd have of him was always the same: motionless in the middle of the street, astride his bike, he would be waiting there to check I'd properly closed the door on him.

On two or three evenings, after our meal, we ended up on the bastions of Porta Reno, where, that summer, an amusement park had been put up in the opening which lay between the Gazometro on one side and the Piazza Travaglio on the other. It was a cut-price affair, half a dozen huts with coconut shies huddled round the grey, patchworked canvas mushroom of a small equestrian circus. The place attracted me. I was drawn to and touched by the sad group of impoverished prostitutes, young thugs, soldiers, and a few wretched pederasts from the outskirts, who customarily frequented it. I quoted Apollinaire in an undertone, and Ungaretti. And though Malnate, somewhat with the air of being dragged along against his will, accused me of 'second-hand Crepuscularism', deep down it also pleased him, after we had dined at the Voltini, to go up there, into the big dusty square, to hang about eating slices of watermelon near the acetylene lamp of a coconut shy, or to try our luck for some twenty minutes shooting at the bull's-eye. Giampi was an excellent shot. Tall and corpulent, standing out in the well-pressed cream-coloured flannel jacket I'd seen him wearing since the beginning of the summer, calm as could be in taking his aim through his thick lenses rimmed with tortoiseshell, he'd obviously taken the fancy of the heavily made-up and foul-mouthed Tuscan girl – a kind of queen there – at whose stall, as soon as we could be seen on the stone staircase which led from Piazza Travaglio to the top of the bastion, we were imperiously invited to stop. Whilst Malnate took his aim, she, the girl, let loose a stream of sarcastic compliments with an undercurrent of obscenity, which he parried with great wit and with that calm detachment typical of someone who has spent many hours of their youth in a brothel.

One particularly airless August evening we happened, instead, to be in an open-air cinema where, I remember, they were showing a German film with Cristina Söderbaum. We had come in when the show had already begun, and without paying any attention to Malnate, who kept telling me to be careful, to stop making a racket, since it just wasn't worth it, I'd already begun whispering ironic comments before we'd even sat down. Malnate was only too right. In fact, suddenly getting to his feet against the milky background of the screen, a man in the row in front of me told me in a threatening manner to shut up. I replied with an insult, and he began to shout in dialect: 'Get out, you filthy Jew!' and jumped on me, grabbing me by the neck. Luckily for me, Malnate, without saying a word, was ready to shove my assailant back into his seat and drag me away.

'You're a complete idiot,' he shouted at me, after we'd both hurriedly collected the bicycles we'd left in the bike racks. 'And now, make yourself scarce, and you'd better pray to that God of yours that scumbag in there was only guessing.'

In this manner, one after another, we passed our evenings together, with the perpetual air of congratulating ourselves that now, in contrast to when Alberto was present, we managed to converse without coming to blows. It never seemed to cross our minds that with a simple phone call, Alberto might have come out too to stroll around with us.

We set aside all political topics. Both being sure that France and England, whose diplomatic missions had already reached Moscow some time ago, would end up in accord with the USSR – the agreement we believed inevitable would have saved Poland's independence as well as averting a war, provoking as a consequence not just the collapse of the Pact of Steel but also the fall at least of Mussolini – it was now of literature and art that we almost always spoke. Whilst his manner remained calm, without ever becoming polemical (besides – he affirmed – he could only understand art up to a certain point, it wasn't his thing), Malnate upheld a kind of rigid veto against everything I most loved: Eliot and Montale, García Lorca and Yesenin. He'd hear me out as I gave an impassioned recitation of 'Non chiederci la parola che squadri da ogni lato',[1] or passages from the 'Lament for Ignazio Sánchez Mejías'[2] and in vain I'd hope to have got through to him, to have converted him to my taste. Shaking his head, he'd declare that no, Montale's 'ciò che non siamo, ciò che non vogliamo' left him cold, indifferent; that true poetry shouldn't be founded on negation (don't bring in Leopardi, please! Leopardi's a different matter, and anyway he'd written his 'Ginestra', I oughtn't to forget . . .) but rather, on the contrary, it was founded on affirmation, on the Yes that the Poet in the final analysis had *no* choice but to raise up against the hostility of Nature and against Death. Even Morandi's paintings didn't convince him – he told me: so refined, undoubtedly delicate, but in his view too 'subjective' and 'unanchored'. A fear of reality, a fear of making mistakes: that was what Morandi's still lifes, his famous paintings of bottles and flower bouquets, expressed deep down. And fear, in art as well, had always been the worst adviser . . . Against all this, not without cursing him in secret, I never found any effective counter-argument. The thought that the next afternoon, he, the lucky one, would certainly be seeing Alberto and Micòl, perhaps talking to them about me, was enough to make me put aside any empty wish to rebel, and forced me to withdraw into my shell.

Despite this I would sometimes champ at the bit.

'Well, after all, you too,' I objected one evening, 'you too indulge in the same radical negation towards contemporary literature, the only living one, that you can't abide when it, our literature, shows the same towards life. Does this seem fair to you? Your ideal poets remain Victor Hugo and Carducci. Admit it.'

'And why shouldn't they be?' he replied. 'In my opinion Carducci's republican poetry, written before his political conversion, or rather, his infantile reversion to classicism and monarchism, still needs to be entirely rediscovered. Have you read those poems recently? Try them, and you'll see.'

I answered that I hadn't reread them, and had no desire to do so. For me they too were empty 'trumpetings', boringly stuffed full of patriotic rhetoric, and incomprehensible to boot. Though precisely because they were incomprehensible, there was something amusing – and in the end – 'surreal' about them.

On another evening, however, not so much because I wanted to cut a good figure, but rather driven by an undefined need to confess, to open myself up, which I'd been feeling the pressure of for some time, I gave in to the temptation to recite a poem of mine to him. I'd written it in the train, returning from Bologna after the graduation thesis viva, and although for some weeks I continued to believe that it faithfully reflected the deep desolation I felt at that time, the disgust I felt for myself, gradually as I recited it to Malnate, I clearly saw, with unease rather than dismay, all the falsity of emotion in it, how 'literary' it was. We were walking along the Giovecca, down towards the Prospettiva, beyond which the dark of the countryside was thickening into a kind of black wall. I declaimed the poem slowly, making myself stress the rhythm, overloading my voice with pathos in the attempt to pass off my damaged goods as the real thing, but ever more convinced, as I approached the ending, of the inevitable failure of my performance. And yet I was wrong. As soon as I finished, Malnate looked at me with remarkable seriousness, then, leaving me gaping, assured me that he had liked the poem very much indeed. He asked me to recite it a second time (and I immediately obliged him). After which he affirmed that in his modest opinion my 'lyric', on its own, was worth more than all 'the feeble efforts of Montale and Ungaretti combined'. He could feel real suffering within it, a 'moral commitment' absolutely new, and authentic. Was Malnate being sincere? At least on that occasion, I'm convinced he was. And from that evening on he started loudly repeating my verses, and kept on maintaining that in those few lines it was possible to see an 'opening' for a poetry such as that of contemporary Italian, stuck in the sad toils of Calligraphism and Hermeticism. As for me, I'm not ashamed to admit that it wasn't at all unpleasant listening to these views of his. Faced with his hyperbolic praises, I confined myself to launching the occasional feeble protest, my heart overflowing with gratitude and hope. Looking back now, I'm far more inclined to find this moving rather than contemptible.

In any case, on the subject of Malnate's taste in poetry, I feel obliged to add that neither Carducci nor Victor Hugo were really his favourite authors. He respected Carducci and Hugo, as an anti-Fascist, as a Marxist. But as a good citizen of Milan, his great passion was Porta, a poet to whom, before then, I'd always preferred Belli, but I was wrong, Malnate argued; how could I compare the funereal 'Counter-Reformation' monotony of Belli with the variety and human warmth of Porta?

He could quote hundreds of his verses from memory.

> Bravo el mè Baldissar! Bravo el mè nan!
> L'eva poeù vora de vegnì a trovamm:
> t'el seet mattascion porch che maneman
> l'è on mes che no te vegnet a ciollamm?
> Ah Cristo! Cristo! com'hin frecc sti man!*

he liked to declaim in his deep, slightly raucous Milanese accent, every night when, out strolling, we approached Via Sacca or Via

---

* Good on you, Baldissar! Well done at last, you midget!
  It was about time too you'd come to see me:
  d'you realize, you mad pig, it's nearly
  a month you've not been here to fuck me?
  Ah, Jesus! Jesus! How cold these hands have got!

Colomba, or dawdlingly made towards Via delle Volte, peeping through the half-closed doors at the lit-up interiors of brothels. He knew the whole of 'Ninetta del Verzee' by heart, and it was him who really taught me to appreciate it.

Threatening me with his finger, narrowing his eyes at me with a sly and suggestive expression – suggestive, I supposed, of some remote episode of his Milanese adolescence – he would often murmur:

> Nò Ghittin: no sont capazz
> de traditt: nò, stà pur franca.
> Mettem minga insemma a mazz
> coj gingitt e cont'i s'cianca . . .*

and so on. Or else in a heartfelt, bitter tone he would set about:

> Paracar, scappee de Lombardia . . .†

underscoring every verse of the sonnet with winks, directed naturally towards the Fascists rather than Napoleon's Frenchmen.

He quoted from the poetry of Ragazzoni and Delio Tessa with just as much enthusiasm and involvement, especially from Tessa, whose work (as I didn't fail to point out to him) seemed to me not to merit the epithet of 'classic' poet, overladen as it was with a 'Crepuscular', decadent sensibility. Yet the truth was that anything that had any connection whatsoever with Milan or its dialect always made him uncharacteristically indulgent. Concerning Milan, he was disposed to accept anything: everything to do with it induced in him a tolerant smile. In Milan even literary decadence, even Fascism itself, had some positive attribute.

---

* No, Ghittina: I'm incapable
   of betraying you: no, of that you can be sure.
   You oughtn't to lump me together
   with rascals and disreputables.
† Soldiers, fleeing from Lombardy . . .

He would declaim:

Pensa ed opra, varde e scolta,
tant se viv e tant se impara;
mi, quand nassi on'altra volta,
nassi on gatt de portinara!

Per esempi, in Rugabella,
nassi el gatt del sur Pinin . . .
. . . scartoseij de coradella,
polpa e fidegh, barretin

*del patron per dormigh sora . . .**

and laugh to himself, laugh aloud with tenderness and nostalgia.

Obviously I didn't understand everything in Milanese, and when I didn't I'd question him.

'Sorry, Giampi,' I asked him one evening 'but what's Rugabella? I've been to Milan though I can't claim to know the place. As you'd understand – of all the cities it's the one I'm most likely to get lost in – it's even worse than Venice.'

'How can you say that?' he replied with unexpected passion. 'You're referring to a city that's utterly straight and rational. I can't see how you dare compare it with Venice, that oppressive, overflowing shithouse!'

But he rapidly calmed down, explaining to me that Rugabella was

----

* Think and toil, watch and listen,
  the longer you live the more you learn;
  me, should I be born one more time,
  I'd be born a doorwoman's cat!

  For example, in Rugabella,
  if I were born as Signor Pinin's cat . . .
  . . . [there'd be] bags of heart scraps,
  mince and liver, the master's cap

  to sleep on top of . . .

a street, an old street near the Duomo, where he'd been born, where his parents still lived and where in a few months, perhaps before the year was out – that's if the Civic Authorities in Milan hadn't binned his request to be transferred! – he was once more hoping to live.

Because, let's be honest – he explained – Ferrara is a delightful, small city, lively, engaging in all sorts of ways, including its politics. He counted the two years' experience he'd gained here as important, not to say essential. But home was always home, there was no one like one's own mother, and as for the Lombard sky, 'so adorable when it was fine', there was no other sky in the world with which it could be compared.

8

Once the twentieth day of exile had passed, as I've already mentioned, I began once more to visit the Finzi-Contini house, every
Tuesday and Friday. But, at a loss as to how I should pass my Sundays
– even if I'd wanted to renew my contacts with old schoolfriends such
as Nino Bottecchiari or Otello Forti, for example, or with more
recent university friends made in the last years at Bologna, there
was no possibility since they'd already gone on holiday – after a
certain time had lapsed I started going there on Sundays as well.
Micòl let this go, and never held me to the letter of our agreement.

We were now most considerate to each other, perhaps over-
considerate. Both of us being aware just how precarious the equil-
brium we had achieved was, we took pains not to disturb it, to keep
ourselves in a safe zone which excluded not only the excessive
coldness between us but also any over-familiarity. If Alberto wanted
to play – and this happened ever more rarely – I willingly made up
the fourth. But most of the time I didn't even bother to get changed.
I preferred to umpire the long, hard singles matches fought out
between Micòl and Malnate, or else, seated under the big parasol at
the side of the court, to keep Alberto company.

Alberto's health was worrying me, deeply. I kept thinking about
it. I would stare at his face, which looked longer because of the
weight he'd lost. I would find myself checking his breathing as it
showed in his neck, which by contrast had become fatter and
swollen, and I'd feel my heart contract. I felt oppressed by a hidden
sense of remorse. There were moments when I would have given
anything to see him return to health.

'Why don't you go away for a while?' I once asked him.

He turned to look at me.

'D'you think I'm low?'

'Well, I wouldn't say low . . . You seem to me a bit thinner – that's all. Is the heat annoying you?'

'Certainly is.'

He raised his arms as he breathed in deeply.

'For some time, my dear fellow, breathing has been a real effort. Ah! To go away . . . but where, though?'

'Up in the mountains would do you good. What does your uncle say? Have you been to see him?'

'Of course. Uncle Giulio assures me it's nothing serious, which must be true, don't you think? Otherwise he would have prescribed some remedy or other . . . On the contrary, my uncle thinks I should play as much tennis as I want. What more could I ask? It must be the heat that's bringing me down. Actually I'm hardly eating any-thing . . . but it's really nothing.'

'So, given it's to do with the heat, why not spend a fortnight in the mountains?'

'In the mountains in August? I ask you. And then . . .' (here, he smiled) '. . . and then *Juden sind unerwünscht* everywhere. Had you forgotten?'

'That's nonsense. It's not true, for example, of San Martino di Castrozza. One can still go to San Martino, as you could, if you wanted, go the Venice Lido or to Alberoni . . . There was something about it in last week's *Corriere della Sera*.'

'What a bore. To spend the August bank holiday in a hotel, crammed in with sporty flocks of Levis and Cohens, I'm sorry I can't say that appeals. I'd prefer to stay where I am until September.'

The next evening, making the most of the new atmosphere of intimacy between me and Malnate, after I'd risked his judgement on my verses, I was determined to talk to him about Alberto's health. There was no doubt about it – I said: in my view Alberto had something. Hadn't he noticed the laboured way he was breath-ing? And didn't it seem strange at the very least that no one at his home, neither his uncle nor his father, had made the smallest effort to work out what was wrong? The medical uncle, the one from

Venice, had no faith in medicines, so that can be understood. But the rest of them, including his sister? They were all seraphically calm and smiling – not one of them was lifting a finger.

Malnate listened to me in silence.

'You shouldn't be so alarmed,' he finally replied, with a slight hint of embarrassment in his voice. 'Does he really seem to you so run down?'

'But, good God, can't you see!' I broke out. 'In two months he's lost ten kilos!'

'That's going a bit far. Ten kilos are an awful lot!'

'If not ten, it'll be seven or eight. At the least.'

He fell silent, lost in thought. He admitted that he too, for some time now, had realized that Alberto wasn't well. On the other hand – he added – were the two of us really sure we weren't getting worked up over nothing? If his own closest family weren't concerned, and if not even Professor Ermanno's face betrayed the least sign of worry, well then . . . That's the point – if Alberto really had been ill, it was fair to assume that Professor Ermanno wouldn't even have considered the possibility of bringing two lorry-loads of shale from Imola for the tennis court! And talking of the tennis court, did I know that in a few days the work to enlarge its famous surrounds was about to start?

So, taking our cue from Alberto and his presumed illness, we had unwittingly introduced into our night-time conversations the new theme, hitherto taboo, of the Finzi-Continis. Both of us were well aware we were walking over a minefield, and for this reason we always proceeded with great caution, very careful not to put a foot wrong. But it's worth saying that every time we spoke of them as a family, as an 'institution' – I'm not sure who first came up with this word but I remember that it gave us some satisfaction and made us laugh – Malnate made free with his criticisms, even the harshest. What impossible people they were! – he'd say. What a strange, absurd tangle of incurable contradictions they represented, 'socially'! At times, thinking about the thousands of hectares of land they possessed, and the thousands of labourers who worked it for them, the disciplined, submissive slaves of the Corporative Regime, at times he was tempted to prefer the grim 'regular' landlords, those who, in 1920, 1921 and 1922, had hardly paused a moment to fork out for the blackshirt squads with their strong-arm and castor-oil tactics. They 'at least' were Fascists. When the occasion presented itself, there wouldn't be any lingering doubts about how to treat *them*. But the Finzi-Continis?

And he would shake his head, with the expression of someone who, should they wish to, could even understand such subtleties and complications, but who is just not minded to. Such tiny fine discriminations, intriguing and engaging as they might be, at a certain point became irrelevant: they too would be swept away.

After the August bank holiday, late one night, we had stopped for a drink in a small bar in Via Gorgadello, alongside the Duomo, a few steps away from the place that had been the surgery of Dr Fadigati, the well-known ENT surgeon. Over several glasses of wine I'd told Malnate the story of the doctor, with whom, in the five months preceding his suicide 'for love', I had become close friends, the last and only friend he had left in town – when I said 'for love' Malnate couldn't resist a little sarcastic laugh of a typically undergraduate kind. From Fadigati to a more general discussion of homosexuality was just a few steps. On this topic Malnate had very uncomplicated views – like a true *goy*, I thought to myself. For him, pederasts were nothing but 'miserable wretches', poor 'obsessives', about whom there was no point bothering apart from a medical perspective or with a view to social prevention. By contrast, I maintained that love justified and sanctified everything, even pederasty. I went further, saying that love, when it was pure, by which I meant totally disinterested, is always abnormal, asocial and so on: exactly like art – I added – which when it's pure, and therefore useless, displeases the priests of every religion, including Socialism. Setting aside our good intentions to be moderate, just this once we went back to arguing almost in our ferocious, earlier style, until the moment when, both of us realizing we were slightly drunk, we simultaneously burst out laughing. After that, we had left the bar, crossed the half-deserted Listone, and gone back up San Romano to find ourselves wandering along Via delle Volte with no particular destination in mind.

Without any pavement, its cobbled surface full of holes, the street seemed even darker than usual. Whilst we all but groped our way forwards, guided only by the light that squeezed through the half-closed doors of the brothels, Malnate had set off again as usual declaiming some stanza of Porta's – this time, I remember, it wasn't from 'Ninetta', but from 'Marchionn di gamb avert'.

He recited the lines in a low voice, in the bitter, hurt tone he always assumed for the 'Lament':

> Finalment l'alba tance voeult spionada
> l'è comparsa anca lee di filidur . . .*

but at this point he suddenly stopped.

'What would you say', he asked me, pointing his chin towards a brothel door, 'to going in there to look around?'

The proposal was nothing out of the ordinary. And yet, coming from him, with whom I'd only ever had serious discussions, it surprised and embarrassed me.

'It's not one of the better ones,' I replied. 'I reckon it's one where you pay less than ten lire . . . but why not, if that's what you want.'

It was late, almost one o'clock, and the welcome that awaited us was far from warm. An old peasant-like woman, seated on a wickerwork chair behind the door, began to make a fuss about not wanting the bicycles brought in. And then the madam, a dry, raw, little woman with glasses, of an indefinable age, dressed in black like a nun, also started complaining about the bicycles and how late it was. Then a servant girl, who was already cleaning the small reception rooms with a worn-out, dusty brush, the handle of a dustpan under her arm, gave us a look full of scorn as we passed through the entrance hall. And even the girls, all gathered together and

---

* At last the dawn, so long looked out for,
  herself appears between the shutter's slats . . .

quietly talking with a small group of clients in a single room, didn't bother to say hello. None of them came forward to greet us. We waited not less than ten minutes, during which time Malnate and I sat facing each other in the small separate reception room that the madam had taken us away to, not bestowing on us a further word – through the walls the laughter of the girls and the drowsy voices of their client-friends reached us – until a small blonde with a refined air, and hair drawn back above the nape of her neck, soberly dressed like a schoolgirl from a good family, decided to appear in the doorway.

She at least didn't seem too fed up.

'Good evening,' she greeted us.

She calmly examined us, her blue eyes full of irony.

'And as for you, Little Blue-Eyes, what can we do for you?'

'What's your name?' I managed to stammer.

'Gisella.'

'Where are you from?'

'Bologna!' she boasted, widening her eyes as if vouchsafing who knows what pleasures.

But it wasn't true. Calm and in perfect control of himself, Malnate immediately saw through her claim.

'Bologna like hell!' he interjected. 'I'd say you were from Lombardy, but not even from Milan. You must be from somewhere around Como.'

'How did you guess that?' the girl asked, astonished.

The madam's ugly mug had meanwhile loomed behind her back.

'Uh-huh,' she grumbled. 'Here as well I can see all that's happening is a lot of blather.'

'Not at all,' the girl protested, smiling and pointing at me. 'Little Blue-Eyes over there has some serious intentions. So should we go?'

I turned towards Malnate. He too was looking at me in an encouraging, affectionate way.

'And you?' I asked.

He made a vague gesture with his hand, and let out a small laugh.

'Don't think about me. You go on up, and I'll wait for you.'

Everything happened very quickly. When we came back down,

Malnate was chatting with the madam. He'd brought out his pipe, and was talking and smoking. He was finding out about the 'financial status' of the prostitutes, their fortnightly 'rota' and their 'medical check-ups' etc., and the woman was responding with equal attention and care.

'*Bon*,' Malnate said at last, noticing my presence, and standing up.

We went back into the entrance waiting-room, making for the bicycles leant one on top of the other against the wall beside the street exit, whilst the madam, now become most considerate, rushed in front to open the door.

'Goodbye, then,' Malnate said to her.

He placed a coin in the doorwoman's outstretched palm, and went out first.

Gisella had remained in the background.

'Bye, darling,' she said in a sing-song voice. 'And come back again!'

She was yawning.

'Bye,' I replied as I went through the door.

'Goodnight, then, gentlemen,' the madam respectfully murmured behind our backs. As she closed the door I heard the bolt slide home.

Leaning on our bikes, we slowly went back up Via Scienze to the corner of Via Mazzini, and then took a right along the Saraceno. Now it was Malnate who mainly spoke. At Milan, some years back – he was telling me – he'd been a fairly regular visitor to the famous San Pietro all'Orto brothel, but it was only tonight that he'd had the idea of gathering precise information about the laws governing the 'system'. Christ, what a life whores have to live! And how abject the state was, the so-called 'ethical state', to set up such a market for human flesh!

Here he became aware of my silence.

'What's wrong?' he asked. 'Aren't you feeling well?'

'No. I'm fine.'

I heard him sigh.

'*Omne animal post coitum triste . . .*' he pronounced melan-cholically. 'Have a good sleep, and you'll see – tomorrow every-thing'll be as right as rain.'

'I know. I know.'

We turned left, down Via Borgo di Sotto, and Malnate nodded towards a modest little house on the right, in the direction of Via Fondo Banchetto.

'That's where the schoolmistress Trotti must live,' he said.

I didn't reply. He coughed.

'And so . . .' he went on, 'how are things going with Micòl?'

I was suddenly overwhelmed by a great need to confide in him, to open my heart to him.

'Badly. I have such a terrible crush on her.'

'Well, that we've been able to work out,' he said with a friendly laugh. 'For some time. But how is it going now. Is she still treating you badly?'

'No. As you'll have seen, of late we've reached a certain *modus vivendi*.'

'Sure. I've noticed you don't squabble like you used to. I'm glad you're becoming friends again. It was really absurd.'

My mouth twisted into a grimace, whilst tears misted over my sight.

Malnate immediately realized what was happening.

'Don't take it so badly,' he urged me, embarrassed. 'You mustn't let yourself go like this.'

I made an effort to swallow.

'I don't believe one bit that we'll be friends again,' I murmured. 'It's utterly futile.'

'Nonsense,' he replied. 'If you only knew how much she cares for you! When you're not there, and are being spoken of, woe betide anyone who dares say anything against you. She's like an adder ready to strike. And Alberto respects and really likes you too. I ought to tell you as well that a few days ago – perhaps it was indiscreet of me, I'm sorry – I even recited one of your poems to them. Good Lord! You've no idea how much he liked it, how much they both, yes, both of them liked it . . .'

'I'm not sure what use either their wishing me well or their high opinion is to me.'

We had come out into the little square in front of the Church of

Santa Maria in Vado. There wasn't a soul to be seen: neither there, nor the whole length of Via Scandiana up to Montagnone. We went along in silence towards the drinking-fountain beside the churchyard. Malnate leant down to drink, and after him I drank too, and washed my face.

'Listen,' Malnate continued as he kept on walking, 'in my opinion you're wrong. In times like these, nothing is more important than mutual affection and respect, friendship that is. Besides, it doesn't seem to me . . . It's quite possible that in time . . . What I mean is – why not come over and play tennis more often, as you did some months back? And anyway, who says absence is the best strategy? I've the feeling, my friend, that you don't know women very well.'

'But it was she herself who forced me to make my visits less frequent!' I blurted out. 'D'you think I can just take no notice? After all, it is her house!'

He remained silent for a few moments, deep in thought.

'It doesn't seem possible to me,' he said at last. 'Perhaps I could understand it, if something . . . really serious, irreparable, had come between you. But what, in the end, has happened?'

He scrutinized me, unsure.

'Forgive my not too . . . diplomatic question,' he went on, and smiled, 'but have you got so far at least as to kiss her?'

'I have indeed, many times,' I sighed desperately. 'Unfortunately for me.'

I then told him in minute detail the story of our relationship, going right back to the beginning and not concealing that episode of last May, in her room, an episode which I'd come to believe, I said, decisive in its negative impact, and irremediable. Amongst other things I wanted to describe to him how I kissed her, or at least how, time and again, and not only on that occasion in her bedroom, I'd tried to kiss her, as well as her various responses, sometimes more and sometimes less disgusted.

He let me get it all out, and I was so intent on, so lost in these bitter reconstructions that I paid little heed to his silence, which in the meanwhile had become hermetically sealed.

We'd been standing for almost half an hour outside my house.

I saw him give a start.

'Lord,' he murmured, checking his watch. 'It's a quarter past two. I really have to go. Otherwise how will I get myself up tomorrow?'

He leapt onto his saddle.

'Well, bye . . .' he said, leaving, 'and life goes on!'

I noticed his face had a strange grey look. Had my confidences annoyed or angered him?

I remained watching him as he quickly rode away. It was the first time that he'd left me standing like that, without waiting for me to shut the gate.

9

Although it was so late, my father had still not switched off his light.

Ever since the summer of 1937, when the newspapers took up the racial campaign, he had been afflicted by a severe kind of insomnia which reached its most acute phase in summertime, with the heat. He passed whole nights without shutting his eyes, reading for a while, then wandering around the house, listening for a while in the breakfast room to the radio's Italian-language foreign transmissions, chatting for a while with my mother in her room. If I got back after one o'clock, it was rare indeed for me to be able to reach the end of the corridor along which all the bedrooms were disposed (the first was my father's, the second my mother's, then came those of Ernesto and Fanny, and finally, at the very end, my own) without him hearing me. I would get a fair way down on tiptoe, having even taken off my shoes, for my father's very sharp ears would pick up the least creak or rustling.

'That you?'

On that night too, as might be expected, I failed to duck under his radar. Usually, in response to his 'That you?' I would immediately quicken my step, going straight on without replying, making as if I'd hadn't heard. But not that night. Though I could well imagine, and not without irritation, the kind of questions I'd have to answer, always the same for years on end ('How come you're so late?', 'D'you know what time it is?', 'Where've you been?' etc.), I chose to stop. As the door was shut, I put my head through the hatch.

'What are you doing there?' my father said at once, scanning me above his glasses. 'Come on in for a moment.'

He was not lying down, but seated in his nightshirt, leaning with his back and his nape against the headboard of blond carved wood, and covered no further than the base of his stomach with a single sheet. It struck me how everything about him and around him was white – his silver hair, his pallid, exhausted face, his white night-shirt, the pillow behind his kidneys, the sheet, the book open on his chest, and how that whiteness (a clinical whiteness, I thought at the time) was in keeping with the surprising and extraordinary serenity, the unexpectedly benign expression, full of wisdom, that lit up his bright eyes.

'How late you are!' he commented with a smile, giving a glance at the Rolex on his wrist, a waterproof affair he would never be parted from, not even in bed. 'D'you know what time it is? Two twenty-seven.'

For the first time, perhaps, since being given the front-door key at the age of eighteen, this recurrent phrase of his caused me no irritation.

'I've been wandering about,' I said quietly.

'With that friend of yours from Milan?'

'Yes.'

'What does he do? Is he still a student?'

'You must be joking. He's already twenty-six. He's employed . . . he works as a chemist in the industrial zone, in a Montecatini synthetic rubber factory.'

'Just goes to show. And I thought he was still at university. Why don't you ever ask him round to dinner?'

'I don't know . . . I thought it wasn't right to give Mamma more work than she already has.'

'Nonsense! It wouldn't be any trouble. It's just an extra bowl of soup after all. Bring him over, please do. And . . . where did you have dinner then? At Giovanni's?'

I nodded.

'So tell me what dainty dishes you had to eat?'

I complied with good grace, surprised at my own lack of contrari-ness, listing the various courses – those ordered by myself, and those by Malnate. In the meantime I'd sat down.

'I'm glad,' my father concluded, satisfied.

'And after,' my father went on after a pause, '*duv'èla mai ch'a si 'ndà a far dann, tutt du*?*' I bet' (here he raised a hand as though to forestall any denial of mine) 'I bet you've been running after women.'

On this subject, there had never been any exchange of confidences between us. A fierce modesty, a violent irrational need for freedom and independence, had always driven me to stifle at birth any of his timid attempts to broach this subject. But not that night. Whilst I looked at him, so white, so frail, so old, it was if something inside me, a kind of knot, an age-old secret tangle, was rapidly unravelling.

'It's true,' I said. 'You guessed right.'

'You'll have been to a brothel, I suppose.'

'Yes.'

'Excellent,' he gave his approval. 'At the age you two are, especially at your age, brothels are the best solution from every point of view, including that of health. But tell me – as regards money, how do you manage it? Does the weekly pocket money Mamma gives you suffice? If it's not enough, you can also ask me for some. Within the limits of possibility, I'd be happy to help.'

'Thanks.'

'Where have you been? Round at Maria Ludargnani's? In my time she was already holding the fort.'

'No. A place in Via delle Volte.'

'The only thing I'd advise you,' he continued, suddenly switching into the language of the medical profession he had only ever practised in his youth, having then, after my grandfather's death, devoted his energies exclusively to the administration of the land in Masi Torello and the two houses he owned in Via Vignatagliata, 'the only thing I'd advise you is to *never* neglect the necessary prophylactic measures. I know it's annoying. One would gladly do without. But it takes nothing to catch a nasty blennorrhagia, otherwise known as the clap, or worse. And above all: if you wake up in the morning and find something's not right, come immediately to the bathroom and let me see. In which case, I'll tell you what you should do.'

'I understand. Don't worry.'

---

* Ferrarese dialect: 'Where on earth have the two of you been out making trouble?'

I could feel he was searching for the right way to ask me more. Now that I'd graduated – I guessed he was about to ask – did I by chance have any ideas for the future, any plans? But instead he took a detour into politics. Before I'd come home – he said – between one o'clock and two, he'd managed to receive several foreign radio stations: Monteceneri, Paris, London, Beromünster. And now, on the basis of the latest news, he was convinced that the international situation was rapidly worsening. Unfortunately, there was no getting away from it – it was a real *'afàr negro'.** It seemed as though the Anglo-French diplomatic mission in Moscow was already on the point of breaking up (obviously without having achieved anything). Were they really prepared to leave Moscow just like that? There was reason to fear so. Which left nothing to be done but commend everyone's soul to God's care.

'What did you expect!' he exclaimed. 'Stalin's hardly the type to have many scruples. If he found it useful, I'm sure he wouldn't hesitate for a second to reach an agreement with Hitler!'

'An agreement between Germany and Russia?' I smiled weakly. 'No, I don't believe it. It doesn't seem feasible to me.'

'We'll see,' he replied, smiling in his turn. 'Let's hope God hears you!'

At this moment a moan was heard from the room next door. My mother had woken up.

'What did you say, Ghigo?' she asked. 'Is Hitler dead?!'

'If only!' my father sighed. 'Sleep, sleep, my angel, don't worry yourself.'

'What time is it?'

'Almost three.'

'Send that son of ours to bed!'

Mamma uttered a few more incomprehensible words, and then fell silent.

My father stared me in the eye for a long while. And then in a low voice, almost a whisper:

'Forgive me speaking to you about these things,' he said, 'but

---

* Ferrarese dialect: 'Black business.'

you'll understand . . . both your mother and I have been well aware, since last year, that you've fallen in love with . . . with Micòl Finzi-Contini. It's true, isn't it?'

'Yes.'

'And how is your relationship going? As badly as ever?'

'It couldn't get worse than it is now,' I murmured, suddenly realizing with absolute clarity that I was speaking the exact truth, that effectively our relationship really could not have got worse, and that never, despite Malnate's opinion to the contrary, would I be able to clamber back up from the bottom of that slope where I had been vainly groping for months.

My father let out a sigh.

'I know, these things are hard to bear . . . But in the end it's much better this way.'

I had lowered my head, and said nothing.

'It's the truth,' he continued, raising his voice a little. 'What were you really hoping to do? Get engaged?'

Micòl herself, that evening in her room, had also put the same question to me. She'd said: 'What was it you were hoping for? Did you really think we should get engaged?' It had taken my breath away. I could think of no reply. Just the same then, I thought, as now with my father.

'And why not?' I managed all the same, and looked at him.

He shook his head.

'D'you think I don't understand you?' he said. 'Even I can see how attractive she is. I've always liked her, since she was a baby . . . when she'd come down at the Temple, to receive her father's *berachah*. Attractive, no, beautiful – perhaps even (if that's possible) too beautiful! – intelligent, full of spirit . . . but to get en-gaged!' here he stressed both syllables, widening his eyes. 'To get engaged, my dear boy, means getting married. And in difficult times like these, without above all a reliable profession you can fall back on, tell me if you . . . I imagine you hadn't reckoned on me being able to support your family (and indeed I wouldn't have been able to lend you enough, I mean, to meet the need) nor that you'd planned to depend on *her*. The girl will certainly come with a magnificent dowry,' he added 'there's no doubt about that! But I don't imagine you'd . . .'

'Let's forget the dowry,' I said. 'If we loved each other, what would that matter?'

'You're right,' my father agreed. 'You're absolutely right. Me as well, when I got engaged to your mother, in 1911, I took no thought of such things. But the times were different then. We could look ahead, to the future, with a certain amount of tranquillity. And even if the future hasn't shown itself as happy and easy as the two of us imagined it would be (we got married in 1915, as you know, with the war having begun, and soon after I had to leave as a volunteer), the society we lived in was different, then, a society that guaranteed . . . Besides, I'd studied to be a doctor, whilst you . . .'

'Whilst I . . .'

'That's what I mean. Instead of medicine, you chose to study literature, and you know that since the moment came to decide I haven't ever tried to impede you in any way. That was your passion, and you and I, both, have done what we ought to – you choosing the route you felt you had to choose, and I doing nothing to stop you. But now? Even if, as a graduate, you'd aspired to a university career . . .'

I shook my head to say no.

'So much the worse!' he went on. 'Whilst it's quite true that nothing, even now, can stop you continuing your studies on your own account . . . to keep on developing so as one day to try, if it's possible, to become a writer, a most risky, difficult career, or a militant critic such as Edoardo Scarfoglio, Vincenzo Morello, Ugo Ojetti . . . or else, why not? a novelist, or . . .' – here he smiled – '. . . or a poet . . . But precisely for these reasons: how could you, at your age, being only twenty-three, with everything before you still to do . . . how could you think of taking a wife, of starting a family?'

He was speaking about my literary future – I told myself – as though it were a lovely seductive dream which could not be trans-lated into something tangible, real. He was speaking as though both he and I were already dead, and now, from a point outside space and time, together we were discussing life, everything which in the course of our respective lives might have, but actually didn't, happen. Had they reached an agreement, Hitler and Stalin? – I even asked myself. And why not? Most likely they had.

'But apart from this,' my father went on, 'and apart from a whole pile of other considerations, can I be frank with you, and give you the advice of a friend?'

'Go ahead.'

'I know that when someone, especially at your age, loses their head over a girl, he isn't going to enter into a whole set of calculations . . . and I also know that you have a rather special character . . . and don't think that two years ago when that poor wretch Dr Fadigati . . .'

In our house, since his death, Fadigati's name had never been spoken by any of us. So what had Fadigati to do with all this now?

I looked at his face.

'Please let me go on!' he said. 'Your temperament – I reckon you got it from your grandma Fanny – your temperament . . . you're too sensitive, that's what I mean, and so never satisfied . . . you're always in seach of . . .'

He didn't finish. A wave of his hand conjured up ideal worlds inhabited purely by chimeras.

'And forgive me,' he continued, 'but even as a family the Finzi-Continis were not suitable . . . they weren't people cut out for us . . . Marrying a girl of that kind, I'm sure that sooner or later you'd have found yourself in trouble . . . but yes, yes, it's the truth,' he insisted, perhaps fearing some word or gesture of mine in protest. 'You well know what my opinion has always been on that subject. They're different from us . . . they don't even seem to be *Judim* . . . Eh, I know: she, Micòl, perhaps for this reason was especially attractive to you . . . because she was superior to us . . . *socially*. But mark my words: it's better it's ended this way. The proverb says: "Choose oxen and women from your own country." And that girl, regardless of appearances, was certainly not from your own country. Not in the least.'

I had once again lowered my head, and was staring at my hands poised open on my knees.

'You'll get over it,' he continued, 'you'll get over it, and much sooner than you think. I am sorry: I can guess what you're feeling at this moment. But, do you know, I envy you a bit. In life, if you want to understand, seriously understand how things are in this world, at least once you *have to* die. And so, given that this is the law, it's better to die when you're young, when you still have so much time before you in which to pick yourself up and recover . . . To come to understand when you're old is unpleasant, much more unpleasant. It's hard to know how. There's no time left to start again from scratch, and our generation has made one blunder after another. In any case, you at least are still young enough to learn, God willing! In a few months, you'll see, all this that you've had to go through will no longer seem real. Perhaps you may even feel happy. You'll feel yourself enriched by this, feel yourself . . . I don't know . . . more mature . . .'

'Let's hope so,' I murmured.

'I'm glad to have been able to talk, to have got this lead weight off my chest . . . And now a final bit of advice, if you'll let me?'

I nodded.

'Don't go round to their house any more. Start studying again, busy yourself with something, maybe set about giving some private lessons – I've been hearing it said there's a great demand for them . . . And don't go round there any more. Apart from anything else, it's more manly not to.'

He was right. It was, apart from anything else, more manly.

'I'll try,' I said lifting up my eyes. 'I'll do all I can to keep to it.'

'That's the way!'

He looked at the time.

'And now go to sleep,' he added. 'That's what you need. And I myself'll try to shut my eyes for a second or two.'

I stood up, and leant down over him to kiss him, but the kiss we exchanged turned into a long embrace, silent and very tender.

10

And that was how I gave up Micòl.

The next evening, keeping faith with the promise I'd made my father, I abstained from going round to Malnate's, and the day after, which was a Friday, I didn't show up at the Finzi-Contini house. A week passed like this, the first, without me seeing anybody: neither Malnate, nor the others. Luckily, in all that time, I wasn't sought out by anyone, and this fact certainly helped me. Otherwise it's very probable I wouldn't have been able to resist. I would have let myself get caught up again.

Ten or so days after our last meeting, around the 25th of the month, Malnate called me. It had never happened before, and as it wasn't me that had answered the phone, I was tempted to have them say I wasn't home. But I immediately repented. I already felt strong enough: if not to see him again, at least to speak to him.

'Are you all right?' he began. 'You've really beached me high and dry.'

'I've been away.'

'Where to? Florence? Rome?' he asked, not without a flicker of irony.

'This time a bit further still,' I replied, already regretting the pathos of the phrase.

'*Bon*. I don't want to pry. So: are we going to meet?'

I said I couldn't that evening, but that tomorrow I'd almost certainly be passing by his house, at the usual time. But if he saw I was late – I added – he shouldn't wait for me. In that case, we'd meet directly round at Giovanni's. It was at Giovanni's he meant to eat?

'Most likely,' he confirmed, curtly. And then:

'Have you heard the news?'

'I've heard it.'

'What a mess! Do come, I'm relying on you, and we can talk about everything then.'

'Goodbye for now,' I replied gently.

'Goodbye.'

He hung up.

The next evening, straight after supper I went out on my bike, and having gone down the whole of the Giovecca, I went and stopped not more than a hundred metres from the restaurant. I wanted to check if Malnate was there, nothing more than that. And, in fact, as soon as I'd ascertained that he was – seated as usual at an open-air table, wearing his eternal flannel jacket – rather than go up to him I doubled back from there to lurk on top of one of the Castello's three drawbridges, the one facing Giovanni's. I worked out that this was the best way to observe him without running the risk that he'd notice me. And so it was. With my chest pressed against the stone edge of the parapet, for a long while I observed him as he ate. I watched him and the other clients down there in a line with the wall at their back, I watched the white-jacketed waiters bustling back and forth between the tables, and it seemed to me, in my suspended state, in the dark above the moat's glassy water, almost as though I was at the theatre, a hidden spectator of some pleasant but pointless performance. By now Malnate had started in on the fruit. He was reluctantly nibbling at a big bunch of grapes, one after the other, and every now and then, clearly expecting my arrival, he would turn his head to the left and the right. In doing so, the lenses of his 'fat glasses', as Micòl would call them, glinted: nervously, quiveringly . . . Having finished off the grapes, he called the waiter over with a sign, conferring with him for a moment. I thought he had asked for the bill, and I was already getting ready to leave, when I saw that the waiter was returning with an espresso cup. He drank it in a single swig. After this, from one of the two breast pockets of his flannel jacket, he took out something very small: a notebook, in which he immediately began to write with a pencil. What the hell was he writing? – I smiled to myself. Had he too taken to versifying? And there I left him, all bent and intent over that notebook of his from which, at rare intervals, he would lift his head to peer left and right, or else above, to the starry sky, as though searching for ideas or inspiration.

In the evenings that immediately followed, I kept on wandering haphazardly along the city streets, noticing everything, indiscriminately drawn by everything: by the headlines of newspapers that carpeted the newsagents' shops of the centre, headlines in big, block capitals, underlined in red ink; by the film photographs and announcement posters stuck up beside the cinema entrances; by the chatting clusters of drunks halted in the middle of the alleyways of the old city; by the number plates of the cars parked in a row in the Piazza del Duomo; by the various kinds of people leaving the brothels, or appearing in small groups out of the dark undergrowth of the Montagnone to consume ice creams, beers or fizzy drinks at the zinc counter of the kiosk that had recently been installed on the bastions of San Tomaso, at the end of the Scandiana . . .

One evening, around eleven, I found myself again in the vicinity of Piazza Travaglio, peeping into the half-dark interior of the renowned Caffè Scianghai, almost exclusively frequented by pavement prostitutes and workers from the nearby Borgo San Luca. From there, soon after, I went up onto the bastion above it to spectate a feeble shooting match between two unprepossessing youths competing under the hard eyes of that Tuscan girl who'd been so taken by Malnate.

I stayed there, at the side, without saying anything, or even dismounting from my bike, so that after a while the Tuscan girl addressed me in person.

'Hey, you there, young man,' she said. 'Why not step up and shoot a few yourself? Go on, take a risk, don't be scared. Show these two big sissies what you can do.'

'No thanks,' I replied.

'No thanks,' she repeated. 'God, what's happening to the young today! Where've you hidden that friend of yours? That one was a real man! Tell me, have you buried him somewhere?'

I kept silent, and she burst out laughing.

'Poor little thing!' she commiserated with me. 'Run along home now, or else your daddy'll take his belt to you. Go on, run along to your granny.'

The next evening, getting on towards midnight, without even knowing myself why, I was on the opposite side of the city, pedalling along the unpaved track which runs smoothly and sinuously within the circumference of the Mura degli Angeli. There was a magnificent full moon: so clear and bright in the perfectly serene sky as to render the front light unnecessary. I pedalled along briskly. I kept on passing new lovers stretched out on the grass. Some were half-naked, one moving on top of the other. Others, already disentangled, remained close, holding each other by the hand. Others still, embraced but motionless, seemed to be asleep. Along the way I counted more than thirty couples. And though I passed so close to some of them as almost to brush them with my wheels, no one ever gave any sign of noticing my silent presence. I felt like, and was, a kind of strange driven ghost, full both of life and death, of passion and compassion.

Having reached the heights of the Barchetto del Duca, I got off my bike, leant it against a tree trunk, and for some minutes, turned towards the silver unmoving stretch of the park, I stayed there to watch. I wasn't thinking of anything in particular. I was watching, and, listening to the paltry and immense outpourings of the crickets and frogs, surprised myself by the faint embarrassed smile that stretched my lips. 'Here it is,' I said slowly. I didn't know what to do, what I'd come there to do. I was suffused by a vague sense of the uselessness of any act of commemoration.

I began to walk along the edge of the grassy slope, my eyes fixed on the *magna domus*. All dark at the Finzi-Contini house. Although I couldn't see the windows of Micòl's room, which were south-facing, I was sure just the same that no light whatsoever would be issuing from them. Having at last come to that point exactly above the garden wall which was 'sacred', as Micòl would say, '*au vert paradis des amours enfantines*', I was seized by a sudden notion. What if I climbed over the wall and secretly entered the park? As a boy, in that far-off June afternoon, I hadn't dared do it. I'd been too afraid. But now?

Within a moment I was already down there, at the foot of the wall, encountering once again the same smell of nettles and dung. But the wall itself was different. Perhaps because it had aged ten years (as indeed I too had aged in the meantime, and grown in size and strength) it didn't seem either as unscalable or as high as I remembered it. After a first failed attempt I lit a match. The footholds were still there, perhaps even more of them. There was even that fat rusty nail still sticking out from the stones. I reached it on my second try, and, grabbing it, it was then easy enough for me to get to the top.

When I was seated up there, with my legs dangling on either side, it didn't take me long to notice a ladder leaning against the wall a little beneath my shoe. Rather than surprising me, this fact entertained me. 'I'll be damned,' I murmured with a smile, 'and there's the ladder as well.' However, before making use of it, I turned back round towards the Mura degli Angeli. There the tree was, and at its base the bike. It was an old crate, hardly a tempting prospect for anyone.

I made it down to the ground. After which, leaving the path that ran parallel to the garden wall, I cut down through the meadow scattered with fruit trees, with the intention of reaching the driveway somewhere almost equidistant between Perotti's farmhouse and the wooden bridge over the Panfilio. I trod the grass without making a sound: struck once in a while, it's true, by the glimmer of a misgiving, but every time it surfaced I shrugged my shoulders and shed it before it turned to worry and anxiety. How beautiful the Barchetto del Duca was by night – I thought – and how gently lit by the moon! In those milky shadows, in that silvery sea, what else could I want or look for? Even if I'd been surprised wandering about there, no one could have got that worked up about it. On the contrary. If everything was taken into account, I could even claim a certain right to be there.

I came out onto the drive, crossed the Panfilio bridge, and from there, turning left, reached the clearing of the tennis court. Professor

Ermanno had kept his promise: the playing area was already being enlarged. The metal wire surround was pulled down, and lay in a luminous tangled heap beside the court, on the opposite side to where the spectators usually sat. A zone of at least three metres beside the side lines and five behind the backcourt seemed to be all ploughed up . . . Alberto was ill. He hadn't long to live. It was necessary to conceal from him in some, even in *that* way, the seriousness of his illness. 'Good idea,' I agreed, and went on.

I went on out into the open, meaning to make a big circle round the clearing, nor was I surprised at a certain point to see, advancing towards me at a slow trot from the direction of the *Hütte*, the familiar shape of Jor. I waited stock still for him to arrive, and he too, as soon as he was about ten metres away, came to a halt. 'Jor!' I called in a stifled voice. Jor recognized me. After having conveyed to his tail a brief, mildly festive wag, he slowly turned back on his own steps.

Once in a while he would turn round to reassure himself I was following him. I wasn't following him, or rather, although progressively approaching the *Hütte*, I didn't detach myself from the far edge of the clearing. I was walking some twenty metres away from the curving row of huge dark trees that grew in that part of the park, my face continually turned to the left. I now had the moon at my back. The clearing, the tennis court, the big blind spur of the *magna domus*, and then, in the distance, lying above the leafy tops of the apple trees, the fig trees, the plum trees, the pear trees, there was the bastion of the Mura degli Angeli. Everything looked bright and clear-cut, as though in relief, even more so than by day.

Continuing like this, I suddenly found myself just a few steps away from the *Hütte* – not in front of it on the side facing the tennis court but behind among the trunks of the young larches and fir-trees it was close up against. Here I stopped. I stared at the black, rugged shape of the *Hütte* against the light. I suddenly felt uncertain, not knowing where to go, what direction to take.

'What should I do?' I was saying in a low voice. 'What should I do?'

I kept on staring at the *Hütte*. Then I began to think – without this thought even making my heart beat faster: accepting it with indifference as stilled water lets light pass through it – I began to think that yes, if after all it was here, at Micòl's, that Giampi Malnate would come every night after leaving me at the entrance of my house (why not? Wasn't it perhaps for this that before going out with me to supper he would shave himself with so much care?), well then, in that case the tennis changing-room would have undoubtedly provided them with the best, the most perfect refuge.

But of course – I calmly pursued this line of reasoning in a rapid internal whisper. It has to be. He would go wandering around with me only till it was late enough, and then, having so to speak tucked me up in bed, he would be on his way, pedalling at full speed round to her, already waiting for him in the garden. But of course. Now I understood that gesture of his at the brothel in Via delle Scienze. *You* go ahead. Making love every, or almost every night, it was hardly surprising that there comes a moment when you start missing your Mamma, the Lombard skies and so on. And the ladder against the garden wall? It could only have been Micòl who left it there, in *that* particular spot.

I was lucid, calm and clear. Everything added up. As in a jigsaw puzzle every piece fitted exactly.

Sure it was Micòl. With Giampi Malnate. The close friend of her sick brother. In secret from her brother and all the others in the house, parents, relatives, servants, and always at night. In the *Hütte* as a rule, but then perhaps even upstairs, in her bedroom, the room of the *làttimi*. Entirely in secret? Or rather had the others as ever pretended not to see, let it go on, even slyly approved of it, considering it only human and right that a twenty-three-year-old girl, if she didn't want to or wasn't able to marry, should all the same have everything that nature required. They, there at the house, even pretended not to notice. Alberto's illness. It was their system.

I listened out. Absolute silence.

And Jor? Where had he got to?

I took several steps on tiptoe towards the *Hütte*.

'Jor!' I called out, loudly.

And then, as if in reponse, from far away through the night air came a sound – feeble, heartbroken, almost human. I knew it immediately: it was the sound of the dear old voice of the piazza clock, striking the hours and the quarters. What was it telling? It was telling that once again I'd been out very late, that it was stupid and wicked of me to keep on in this way torturing my father, who, that night as well, worried because I hadn't returned home, would probably not have been able to get any sleep, and that now it was time that I gave him some peace. For good. For ever after.

'What a great novel,' I grinned, shaking my head as if at an incorrigible child.

And turning my back on the *Hütte*, I made my way off among the plants in the opposite direction.

Epilogue

The story of my relationship with Micòl Finzi-Contini ends here. And so it is right that this story also has an end, now, since anything I might add to it has nothing to do with her, but only, should it go on, with me.

I've already told at the beginning what was her fate, and her family's fate.

Alberto died before the others of a malign lymphogranuloma, in 1942, after a long agony in which, despite the deep chasm dug between its citizens by the Racial Laws, the whole of Ferrara was concerned at a distance. He suffocated. To help him breathe, oxygen was needed, in ever greater quantities. And since, in the city, because of the war, the canisters for oxygen had grown scarce, in the later stages the family had involved itself in a stockpiling operation across the whole region, sending people out to buy them, at whatever price, in Bologna, Ravenna, Rimini, Parma, Piacenza . . .

The others, in September 1942, were captured by the Republicans. After a brief stay in the jail at Via Piangipane, the following November they were sent to the concentration camp at Fòssoli, near Carpi, and from there, later on, to Germany. With regard to myself, however, I should say that in the four years between the summer of 1939 and the autumn of 1943 I never again saw any of them. Not even Micòl. At Alberto's funeral, from behind the windows of the old Dilambda, converted to running on methane, which followed the cortège at a walking pace, and which as soon as it crossed the entrance of the cemetery at the end of Via Montebello immediately turned back, it seemed to me, for a moment, that I could make out her ash-blond hair. Nothing more than that. Even in a city as small as Ferrara it's easy enough, if you should want, to disappear from each other for years and years, to live together as the dead do.

As for Malnate, who had been called back to Milan from November 1939 (he'd tried in vain to phone me in September, and had even gone so far as to write me a letter . . .), I never even saw him again after August of that year. Poor Giampi. He believed in the honest Lombard and Communist future which smiled down on him, then, in the dark days of the impending war: a distant future – he admitted – but one that was sure and infallible. But what does the heart really know? If I think of him, sent off to the Russian Front with the CSIR,[1] in 1941, never to return, I still have a vivid memory of how Micòl would react every time, between one tennis match and the next, he'd start off again 'catechizing' us. He would speak in that low, quiet, humming voice of his. But Micòl, in contrast to me, never took much heed of what he said. She'd never stop sniggering, goading, and making fun of him.

'But then, who's side *are* you on? The Fascists'?' I remember him asking her one day, shaking his big, sweaty head. He didn't understand.

So what had there been between the two of them? Nothing? Who knows.

It was really almost as if, with some presentiment of her own and her family's approaching end, Micòl would continually repeat even to Malnate that she didn't care a fig for *his* democratic and Socialist future, that for the future, in itself, she only harboured an abhorrence, far preferring to it *'le vierge, le vivace et le bel aujourd'hui'*[2] and preferring the past even more, 'the dear, the sweet, the sacred past'.

And since these, I know, were only words, the usual desperate, deceptive words that only a true kiss would have been able to stop her saying, with these words and just these, the little that the heart has been able to recall will here be sealed.

Notes

Part I
Chapter 1

1. *Cisalpine Republic*: In 1796 Napoleon created two states on either side of the River Po, which were merged together the next year with the province of Novara into the Cisalpine Republic (whose capital was Milan). This then adopted a new constitution based on that of the French Republic. It was dissolved after the French defeats in August 1799 but reformed at the Treaty of Lunéville in 1801. In 1802, with some territorial extensions, it became the Italian Republic and later, from 1805 to 1814, the Kingdom of Italy.

2. *Addizione Erculea*: A fortified extension of the city of Ferrara undertaken by Duke Ercole I d'Este. It was begun in 1484 after the war with Venice and more or less completed by 1510. Under the supervision of the court architect Biagio Rosetti, this was one of the greatest and most prestigious works of Renaissance urban planning, which almost doubled the size of the original city and surrounded the extended city with defensive walls and bastions.

Chapter 2

1. *infornata del Decennale*: Tenth anniversary of the Fascist Party's assumption of power, in which the membership was thrown open to all.

2. *Podestà*: Municipal Chief of Justice and Police during the Fascist era.

3. *the Albertine Statute*: This 'Statute', which King Carlo Alberto conceded to the Kingdom of Sardinia and most of north-west Italy in March 1848, was a kind of early constitution which was to have a

lasting impact on the future Italian state. Here the irony, most likely, resides in the fact that this reference by the rabbi would be entirely lost on his Fascist audience.

4. *Sansepolcrista*: One of those who were Fascists before the 1922 March on Rome.

5. *Opera Nazionale Ballila*: Fascist youth organization.

Chapter 3

1. *Liceo Ginnasio*: In the Italian school system, after attending *scuole elementari* (elementary schools) from roughly the ages of 6 to 11 and *scuole medie inferiori* (essentially middle schools) from 11 to 14, students then attend a choice of *licei* (upper schools). Of particular relevance to Bassani's novel is the *liceo classico*. This was, and still immutably is, divided in two: the *ginnasio* for the first two years (*primo* and *secondo superiore*), roughly from the ages of 14 to 16, and the *liceo* proper for three years (*terzo*, *quarto* and *quinto*), from the ages of 16 to 19.

2. *Giosuè Carducci*: (1835–1907), born in Valdicastello in the Maremma. He was one of the most renowned poets of his age and also Professor of Italian literature at Bologna until his retirement in 1904.

3. *O bionda . . . tramandarono*: 'O blond, O beautiful empress, O trusted one'; 'Where have you come from? Which past centuries / have bestowed you on us, you so mild and beautiful . . .'

Chapter 5

1. *fille aux cheveux de lin*: 'The girl with flaxen hair', a poem by Charles-Marie Leconte de Lisle (1818–94) from his *Chansons écossaises*, subsequently adapted for a lyrical piano piece by Claude Debussy.

Part II
Chapter 1

1. *fuori corso*: Students who have not finished their courses in time but who are at liberty to attend classes until they choose to take their exams.

2. *NH*: Nobil Huomo, a title.
3. *the Venice Littoriali*: Littoriali della Cultura: Fascist cultural competitions for students.
4. *Partner*: In English in the original.

Chapter 2

1. *Vittorio Alfieri*: (1749–1803), Piedmontese poet and tragedian. He is often considered a precursor of Romanticism: alienated from society, politically rebellious, emotionally charged.
2. *GUF*: Gruppo Universitario Fascista: Fascist university students' organization.
3. *Bombamano*: Hand-grenade. The 'old heavies' are a Fascist squad.
4. *Sciagura*: The word means disaster or misfortune.

Chapter 4

1. *'Era già l'ora che volge il disio . . .'*: Dante, *Purgatorio*, canto viii: 'It was already the hour when longing returns . . .'
2. *Giovanni Prati's Edmenegarda*: Prati (1814–84), Romantic poet born near Trento, perhaps best remembered for his sonnets and lyrics of the 1870s. *Edmenegarda* was a successful short prose fiction.
3. *Cecil Roth*: (1899–1970), born in London, Roth was Reader in Jewish Studies at the University of Oxford from 1939 to 1964 and a prolific writer on Jewish history. His *History of the Jews in Venice* was published in 1930, and *The History of the Jews of Italy* in 1946.

Chapter 5

1. *hermits of the Thebaid*: Hermits who lived in the desert in the Thebaid, a region in the southernmost part of Upper Egypt, between the second and the fifth century CE.
2. *But her sympathies . . . to exotic trees*: Up until the 1980 edition, this short paragraph was in a more ample form: 'Her sympathies, however, were by no means restricted to the exotic trees: they went out to the various species of palms; to the Manila tamarinds, which

produced small deformed pods full of honey-flavoured pulp; to the agaves that sprouted "in the manner of *menorah* candelabra", which – she explained to me – flower only once, after twenty, twenty-five years, and then die; to the eucalyptuses and the *Zelkoviae sinicae*, with their slender green trunks speckled with gold – regarding the eucalyptuses, she showed, without ever letting me know why, a peculiar diffidence: as if between her and "them", in the distant past, something not too pleasant had occurred, something best left undisturbed.'

3.   *'vert paradis des amours enfantines'*: From Charles Baudelaire's poem 'Moesta et errabunda'.

4.   *'Che fece . . . rifiuto'*: Dante, *Inferno*, canto iii: 'Who out of cowardice made the great refusal . . .', commonly interpreted as a reference to Pope Celestine V.

Part III
Chapter 1

1.   *Machatý's Nocturne*: Gustav Machatý (1901–63), born in Prague. One of his most acclaimed films is *Nocturno* (1934), known in English as *Nocturne*.

2.   *"Poems of an Avant-gardist"*: *Avanguardista* is ambiguous here, and most likely by intention. It may refer to a member of the Youth Fascist organization, the *Avanguardia giovanile fascista*, or to someone who belongs to an artistic vanguard.

3.   *"Non mi . . . sofferenza"*: 'Suffering, don't leave me yet.'

4.   *"tutti . . . a Dio"*: 'All/the females of all/the serene animals/closest to God' (Umberto Saba).

Chapter 2

1.   *shaddai*: One of the names of God, here inscribed on a pendant.

Chapter 4

1.   I died for Beauty – but was scarce
   Adjusted in the Tomb
   When One who died for Truth, was lain
   In an adjoining Room –

   He questioned softly 'Why I failed'?
   'For Beauty', I replied –
   'And I – for Truth – Themself are One –
   We Brethren, are', He said –

   And so, as Kinsmen, met at Night –
   We talked between the Rooms –
   Until the Moss had reached our lips –
   And covered up – our names –

2.   *the Invasion of the Hyksos*: The Hyksos (from an Egyptian phrase meaning 'rulers of foreign lands') are generally thought to be the Semitic or Asiatic Fifteenth Dynasty rulers of Lower and Middle Egypt (1674–1548 BCE), a succession of six kings. Their appearance has been described as an invasion by foreign barbarians with superior weapons.

Chapter 6

1.   *Lenbach*: Franz von Lenbach (1836–1904), Bavarian painter and portraitist who travelled and painted in Italy.
2.   *the Historic Right*: 'Destra storica', a moderate, liberal alliance which governed Italy between 1861 and 1876 and which created the basis of the new state.
3.   *'l'irto vinattier di Stradella'*: This phrase ('Stradella's bristly wine seller') is from Carducci's poem 'Roma' in his *Odi barbare*, (The Barbarian Odes, 1877, 1882 and 1889). Bassani has abbreviated the phrase which is actually: 'l'irto spettrale vinattier di Stradella'.

Chapter 7

1. *Caprèt . . . Padre*: 'The little goat the Father bought'.

Part IV
Chapter 3

1. *Maudit soit . . . l'honnêteté*: From the poem 'Femmes Damnés: Delphine et Hippolyte' by Charles Baudelaire:

    May that clueless dreamer be for ever cursed,
    who, stupidly obsessed with arid problems,
    first thought that anything to do with fairness
    might be involved with matters of the heart.

2. *Israel Zangwill*: (1864–1926), Jewish writer born in London whose most famous novel was *Children of the Ghetto* (1892). As well as being a successful novelist and dramatist, he was a pacifist, a supporter of women's suffrage and a political activist, strenuously involved in the Zionist aspiration to find a Jewish homeland.

3. *'You are fishing for compliments'*: In English in the original.

Chapter 4

1. *Don Abbondio*: One of the principal characters in Alessandro Manzoni's *I promessi sposi*.

Chapter 5

1. *Cena delle beffe*: The Feast of the Jesters play was written by Sem Benelli in 1909 and subsequently made into an opera and a film.

Chapter 7

1. *'Non chiederci . . . da ogni lato'*: The first line of a famous early poem by Eugenio Montale: 'Don't ask from us the word squared off on every side'. The next reference to the poem is its last line: (All that we can tell you today) 'is what we are *not*, what we *don't* want.'

2. *'Lament for . . . Mejías'*: 'Llanto por Ignacio Sánchez Mejías' by Federico García Lorca, an elegy for his friend, the bullfighter, fatally gored in the bullring at Manzanares.

Epilogue

1. *CSIR*: *Corpo di Spedizione Italiano in Russia*: Italian expeditionary troops sent to Russia in 1941.

2. *'le vierge, le vivace et le bel aujourd'hui'*: 'The virginal, evergreen, beautiful today': the opening line of the second of Stéphane Mallarmé's 'Plusieurs sonnets'.

PENGUIN MODERN CLASSICS

FORTY STORIES
DONALD BARTHELME

'A magical gift of deadpan incongruity' John Updike

In *Forty Stories*, Donald Barthelme invented a random universe in which time, reality, meaning and language are turned exuberantly upside-down. He describes a startling array of occurrences – a lumberjack falls in love with a tree nymph; the poet Goethe becomes a loveable buffoon, spouting such eccentric aphorisms as 'Music is the frozen tapioca in the ice chest of History'; St Anthony's reclusive behaviour causes consternation among his friends and neighbours; and a vast swarm of porcupines, about to descend upon a university to enrol, forces the Dean to turn wrangler to herd them away. Tangling with the ludicrous and challenging the familiar, these small masterpieces provide piercing and hilarious insights into human idiosyncrasies.

'Among the leading innovative writers of modern fiction' *The New York Times*

With an Introduction by Dave Eggers

PENGUIN MODERN CLASSICS

SIXTY STORIES
DONALD BARTHELME

'Reveals a rare exuberance, an unfailing joy in words and possibilities'
Anne Tyler

With these sixty audacious and blackly witty stories, Donald Barthelme depicts a rich miscellany of the absurdities of life. Surreal events abound – a thirty-five-year-old man finds himself back in sixth grade due to a baffling error; King Kong, now an adjunct professor of art history, climbs through a window to join a drinks party; the new owner of a little city becomes overwhelmed by the demands its citizens make on their proprietor; and the nonsense poet Edward Lear cheerfully invites his acquaintances to his bedside to witness his death. Constantly inventive and unsettling, Barthelme's stories create a dazzling world of language and thought, perception and memory, myths and dreams.

'These sixty stories show him inventing at full pitch' *Washington Post*

'The delight he offers to readers is beyond question, his originality is unmatched'
Los Angeles Times

With an Introduction by David Gates

PENGUIN MODERN CLASSICS

THE SHELTERING SKY
PAUL BOWLES

'A novel touched with genius ... a book of challenging power and penetration, a story of almost unbearable tensions' *Evening Standard*

After ten years of marriage, Kit and Port Moresby have drifted apart and are sexually estranged. Avoiding the chaos of Europe in the aftermath of the Second World War, they travel to the remote North African desert. Port hopes the journey will reunite them, but although they share similar emotions, they are divided by their conflicting outlooks on life. Kit fears the desert while Port is drawn to its beauty and remoteness. Oblivious to its dangers, he falls ill and they discover a hostile, violent world that threatens to destroy them both.

With an Introduction by Michael Hofmann

PENGUIN MODERN CLASSICS

THE GO-BETWEEN
L. P. HARTLEY

'Magical and disturbing' *Independent*

When one long, hot summer, young Leo is staying with a school-friend at Brandham Hall, he begins to act as a messenger between Ted, the farmer, and Marian, the beautiful young woman up at the hall. He becomes drawn deeper and deeper into their dangerous game of deceit and desire, until his role brings him to a shocking and premature revelation. The haunting story of a young boy's awakening into the secrets of the adult world, *The Go-Between* is also an unforgettable evocation of the boundaries of Edwardian society.

'On a first reading, it is a beautifully wrought description of a small boy's loss of innocence long ago. But, visited a second time, the knowledge of approaching, unavoidable tragedy makes it far more poignant and painful' *Express*

Edited with an Introduction and Notes by Douglas Brooks-Davies

PENGUIN MODERN CLASSICS

TENDER IS THE NIGHT
F. SCOTT FITZGERALD

'A tragedy backlit by beauty … captures the glittering hedonism of the South of France in the Twenties' *Express*

The French Riviera in the 1920s was 'discovered' by Dick and Nicole Diver who turned it into the playground of the rich and glamorous. Among their circle is Rosemary Hoyt, the beautiful starlet, who falls in love with Dick and is enraptured by Nicole, unaware of the corruption and dark secrets that haunt their marriage. When Dick becomes entangled with Rosemary, he fractures the delicate structure of his relationship with Nicole and the lustre of their life together begins to tarnish. *Tender is the Night* is an exquisite novel that reflects not only Fitzgerald's own personal tragedy, but also the shattered idealism of the society in which he lived.

Edited by Arnold Goldman

With an Introduction and Notes by Richard Godden

PENGUIN MODERN CLASSICS

DUBLINERS
JAMES JOYCE

'Joyce's early short stories remain undimmed in their brilliance' *Sunday Times*

Joyce's first major work, written when he was only twenty-five, brought his city to the world for the first time. His stories are rooted in the rich detail of Dublin life, portraying ordinary, often defeated lives with unflinching realism. He writes of social decline, sexual desire and exploitation, corruption and personal failure, yet creates a brilliantly compelling, unique vision of the world and of human experience.

'Joyce redeems his Dubliners, assures their identity, and makes their social existence appear permanent and immortal, like the streets they walk' Tom Paulin

With an Introduction and Notes by Terence Brown

PENGUIN MODERN CLASSICS

CHRIST STOPPED AT EBOLI
CARLO LEVI

'No message, human or divine, has reached this stubborn poverty ... to this shadowy land ... Christ did not come. Christ stopped at Eboli.'

Carlo Levi, one of the twentieth-century's most incisive commentators, was exiled to a remote and barren corner of southern Italy for his opposition to Mussolini. He entered a world cut off from history and the state, hedged in by custom and sorrow, without comfort or solace, where, eternally patient, the peasants lived in an age-old stillness and in the presence of death – for Christ did stop at Eboli.

'One of the most poetic and penetrating first-hand accounts of the confrontation between cultures' *The Times Literary Supplement*

Translated by Frances Frenaye

PENGUIN MODERN CLASSICS

MOMENTS OF REPRIEVE
PRIMO LEVI

'One of the most important and gifted writers of our time' Italo Calvino

Primo Levi was one of the most astonishing voices to emerge from the twentieth century: a man who survived one of the ugliest times in history, yet who was able to describe his own Auschwitz experience with an unaffected tenderness.

Levi was a master storyteller but he did not write fairytales. These stories are an elegy to the human figures who stood out against the tragic background of Auschwitz, 'the ones in whom I had recognised the will and capacity to react, and hence a rudiment of virtue'. Each centres on an individual who – whether it be through a juggling trick, a slice of apple or a letter – discovers one of the 'bizarre, marginal moments of reprieve'.

Translated by Ruth Feldman

With an Introduction by Michael Ignatieff

PENGUIN MODERN CLASSICS

THE SEARCH FOR ROOTS
PRIMO LEVI

'A dark, disturbing, bright and uplifting book' *The Times*

The Search for Roots is an anthology of writings that Primo Levi considered to be essential reading. Fiction, poetry, science, philosophy and travellers' tales are to be found among these thirty pieces, each with an introduction by Levi. He presents familiar voices – Swift, Conrad, T. S. Eliot and Arthur C. Clarke – and introduces us to less familiar ones: Lucretius, Giuseppe Belli, Fredric Brown and Hermann Langbein. All reflect Levi's deep passion for literature, his profound knowledge of science, and his survival of Auschwitz, making it a collection that is both universal and poignantly autobiographical.

'A book packed with pleasurable reading, value and, crucially, with profound insight into this most essential of writers' Robert S. C. Gordon, *Spectator*

'*The Search for Roots* … is Primo Levi's best autobiography'
Carole Angier, *New Statesman*

Translated with an Introduction by Peter Forbes

With an Afterword by Italo Calvino

PENGUIN MODERN CLASSICS

BRIDESHEAD REVISITED
EVELYN WAUGH

'Lush and evocative … the one Waugh which best expresses at once the profundity of change and the indomitable endurance of the human spirit'
The Times

The most nostalgic and reflective of Evelyn Waugh's novels, *Brideshead Revisited* looks back to the golden age before the Second World War. It tells the story of Charles Ryder's infatuation with the Marchmains and the rapidly disappearing world of privilege they inhabit. Enchanted first by Sebastian at Oxford, then by his doomed Catholic family, in particular his remote sister, Julia, Charles comes finally to recognize his spiritual and social distance from them.

PENGUIN MODERN CLASSICS

WINTER'S TALES
ISAK DINESEN (KAREN BLIXEN)

'Tales as delicate as Venetian glass' *The New York Times*

After the huge success of her autobiography *Out of Africa*, Isak Dinesen returned to a European setting in these exquisite, rapturous tales of rebirth and redemption.

Beginning with a sailor boy's bold progression into manhood, these stories are full of longing, a theme often mirrored in the desire to escape to sea, as in 'The Young Man with the Carnation' and 'Peter and Rosa'. This collection also includes 'Snow-Acre', a modern rendition of a folk-tale in which old ideals clash with the new order, and is considered by many to be one of her finest stories. Full of psychological insights, these luminous tales reveal the mystery and unexpectedness of human behaviour.

Contemporary ... Provocative ... Outrageous ...
Prophetic ... Groundbreaking ... Funny ... Disturbing ...
Different ... Moving ... Revolutionary ... Inspiring ...
Subversive ... Life-changing ...

What makes a modern classic?

At Penguin Classics our mission has always been to make the best
books ever written available to everyone. And that also means
constantly redefining and refreshing exactly what makes a 'classic'.
That's where Modern Classics come in. Since 1961 they have been an
organic, ever-growing and ever-evolving list of books from the last
hundred (or so) years that we believe will continue to be read over and
over again.

They could be books that have inspired political dissent, such as
Animal Farm. Some, like *Lolita* or *A Clockwork Orange*, may have
caused shock and outrage. Many have led to great films, from *In Cold
Blood* to *One Flew Over the Cuckoo's Nest*. They have broken down
barriers – whether social, sexual, or, in the case of *Ulysses*, the
boundaries of language itself. And they might – like *Goldfinger* or
Scoop – just be pure classic escapism. Whatever the reason, Penguin
Modern Classics continue to inspire, entertain and enlighten millions
of readers everywhere.

'No publisher has had more influence on reading habits than Penguin'
Independent

'Penguins provided a crash course in world literature'
Guardian

The best books ever written

P E N G U I N (🐧) C L A S S I C S

SINCE 1946

Find out more at www.penguinclassics.com